MW01200050

EMPIRE'S CURSE
DRAKKON

For Yusif, the love of my life. This book would not have been possible without your love and support– thank you, always.

NEWSLETTER & CONTENT WARNING

Join Maham Fatemi's newsletter to learn about new releases, sales, bonus content, and more! You can also find signed copies of her books on her website.
https://mahamfatemi.com

This book is an adult dark fantasy novel with violence, attempted assault, torture, captivity/kidnapping (not done by the male lead), and cursing/language. Reader discretion is advised.

1

DAIYU WAS IN LOVE WITH A DEAD MAN.

At least that's what she told herself as she collected wild jasmine and bright orchids from the colorful field before her. She placed the flowers in her overfilled, handwoven basket and continued through the thicket of bright blues and fuchsias. The early morning breeze sent a ripple across the bowing florae, carrying a sweet scent in its wake.

Lanfen, Daiyu's younger sister, smoothed down her worn, pale-yellow skirt with one hand and plucked an orange orchid with the other. "Don't you think that's enough?" she asked as she slipped the flower in Daiyu's basket. "I'm not sure if Heng will appreciate *all* these flowers."

Daiyu frowned at her brimming basket. "Heng loved flowers."

"No, he loved going here *with* you, not to see the flowers. He couldn't have cared less about"—Lanfen motioned toward the surrounding field—"all of this."

"Heng loved coming here with me, but he also loved the flowers."

"He's already ..." Her younger sister shrugged, letting the words hang. "I don't know. I don't think it matters too much."

"It matters." Daiyu tightened her hold on the bamboo basket. It mattered to her, at least.

"It's been four years already."

"I know." She had heard this a million times already, from Lanfen, her parents, and even her brothers. Everyone wanted her to move on, but how could she do that when Heng had been such a big part of her life for years? "You didn't have to come here."

Lanfen touched one of the long clusters of wild grass brushing her hips. "Do you really think he cares about any of this? I truly don't. But if it makes you feel better, all the more reason to do it."

Daiyu turned away from her, suddenly tired. Her younger sister had only been eleven when the war had ended and Heng never returned, so she probably didn't remember—or care—for him like Daiyu had.

They made their way to a familiar plum blossom tree with Heng's name etched into the ancient bark. Daiyu traced the inscription with the pads of her fingers, her chest growing heavy. Below his name, she could barely make out the characters of her own name. Neither of them knew how to read or write, but when a traveling merchant had passed through their village, Heng had begged him to teach him how to write his name and Daiyu's. He had then taught Daiyu her name. The memory tightened something in her chest as she ran her fingers over the rough bark.

When Heng had gone missing during the war, she had come here and torn off the bark until her fingers had bled. Because the promise on the tree—that they would be together forever—was a lie.

Swallowing down the thickness in her throat, Daiyu placed the flowers they had collected at the base of the tree. She closed her eyes and sent a silent prayer. That Heng was finally at peace, even as his body was likely buried beside hundreds of other unnamed soldiers. Even as he and his fellow brothers-in-arms had ultimately lost the war.

They stayed there for a little while longer until the breeze kicked up their offering and spread it back to the fields. Until the sadness ebbed away and Daiyu could finally breathe steadily again.

"Let's go back." Daiyu looped the now-empty basket in her arm.

They were silent as they headed back home. Lanfen fiddled with the cuff of her sleeve and kicked up pebbles on the dirt path toward the village. Along the way, they picked mushrooms with wide, flat caps and thick stems until their basket was filled once more. They walked past the terraced rice paddies with farmers tending to them, their shins sloshing through silty, watered soil. Daiyu waved to the familiar villagers and neighbors she had known her whole life.

Lanfen pushed a strand of hair behind her ear that had escaped from her bun. "I heard from Auntie Ju that farmer Bi Gan is looking for a bride for his son."

"Hm." Daiyu gave her sister a side-look. They slowed down the cobbled street with splashes of muddied water sprayed across the mismatched, discolored stones. "Is he now?"

"Yes, and you know how wealthy he is, right? Probably richer than people in the capital, don't you think?"

Bi Gan was the village's wealthiest man, but in terms of wealth throughout the empire, he didn't compare. Daiyu had seen the affluence of the capital when she had traveled there with Father to sell some of their rice. The wealth there had shocked her. Men and women dressed in vibrant silks, women sat in colorfully painted sedans as men carried them, and even the carriages looked so different from the wagons she was used to. Not to mention the sheer amount of jewelry and hairpins that glittered off everyone. Farmer Bi Gan's wealth seemed abysmal compared to everything she had seen.

"Where are you going with this?" Daiyu asked as they made their way through the forested area behind their home, away from the rice paddies and closer to their bamboo-fenced yard. "Are you looking to marry his son?"

"What? No!" Lanfen's expression soured. "You know I'm not interested in marriage so soon."

Daiyu gave her a pointed look as they approached their yard. "And neither am I."

"But ..." Lanfen lifted her shoulders, casting a wayward glance at the tall trees canopying the path. Tendrils of sunlight slipped through the covering of branches and leaves and made the browns of her eyes appear honey-gold. "You deserve to be happy. Don't you want that?"

"Lanfen," she said as gently as she could, "I'm happy—"

"He would want you to."

She cringed; the only man she was meant to marry was Heng, and he was dead, so she wasn't keen on the idea of romance anymore. Her family had pestered her over the years, and she hadn't relented, so she wasn't going to change her mind now.

"He would want the best for me, and the best for me right now is to take care of you all." Daiyu scrambled toward the gate leading to their garden. "Anyway, have you fed any of the chickens? Or checked for some eggs?"

"No, not yet."

"Can you do that for me then?" She unlatched the bamboo door and swung it open to reveal lush greenery and vegetation. The scent of earthy herbs and fragrant flowers greeted them as they went down the dirt path intersecting the garden beds. Daiyu kneeled in front of a cluster of cabbage heads and uprooted one of them, then added it to her basket of mushrooms.

"Grandmother hasn't been feeling too well since yesterday," Lanfen said, walking backward to the chicken coop. "Maybe we can make some cabbage broth or mung bean soup?"

"Sure. I'll also pick some mint and ginger for tea."

Daiyu picked the ingredients she needed and headed inside the house. Mother was huddled over the fire stove with the three-legged pot, simmering water. Upon seeing her, she smiled.

"Mother, what are you doing?" Daiyu placed the basket of wild mushrooms, vegetables, and herbs on the small countertop and led her mother to one of the wooden benches. "Here, sit. Has your back been hurting still?"

"Oh, you know how it is." Mother eased herself onto the cushioned seat and sighed against the backrest. "These days my back and hips are always hurting. I think it's years of working the rice fields that's getting to me."

"You need to rest more," she chided as she went to the stove. "Is everyone still asleep?"

"Yes, but they'll be starting their day soon. Where did you and Lanfen go?"

"We went to the flower fields." Daiyu went to work washing everything in the basket and chopping away at the cabbages, mushrooms, and herbs.

Mother was quiet for some time before she whispered, "Is that where you and Heng played together as children?"

She used to cry whenever she talked about Heng, but that sadness had faded with time. "Yes."

Lanfen soon joined them and helped Daiyu prepare breakfast. They made cabbage broth soup and gingered mint tea for their grandmother, fluffy rice, pan-fried mushrooms, eggs fried in scallion oil, and green tea for everyone else.

Father, Grandmother, and the twins Ran and Qianfan, woke soon after and crowded the table. Once all the food was laid out in the center, everyone ate. Daiyu sat cross-legged on the seating mat and served herself rice, fried eggs, and mushrooms smothered in garlicky sauce.

The twins, both thirteen, could barely keep their eyes open and kept nodding forward and snapping awake, and then repeating the behavior.

Mother clucked her tongue at them. "You both have a long day ahead of you and you're already falling asleep?!"

Ran rubbed the side of his face. "I'm awake!"

"I'm not." Qianfan yawned.

"Our food isn't delicious enough to wake you up?" Lanfen asked with mock offense.

5

"No," Qianfan said with a laugh, while Ran picked up a piece of mushroom from his bowl.

Daiyu smiled as Lanfen and Qianfan bickered about what was more important: food or sleep.

A series of banging against the front door interrupted their breakfast. Everyone froze, looking at one another. Daiyu swallowed down the apprehension climbing up her throat. Nobody in the village pounded on the door like that. Who could that be?

"I'll get it," Father said, rising from his seat. Right as he opened the door, three men dressed in dark leathers with a dragon stamped on their chests pushed their way through until they crowded their living room.

"E-Excuse me," Father started.

Daiyu jumped to her feet and joined her father's side as the men scanned the room.

"Who are you people and why are you barging into our home?" Daiyu demanded.

"We're looking for a young woman."

"Excuse me?" Daiyu asked sharply, looking between the terrified expressions on her family's faces to the guards in their living room. Lanfen grabbed Daiyu's arm and clung close to her. "Who are you people?"

"We are a part of the emperor's guard," the closest man said. His voice sounded old, gravelly, and through the slits of the black-scaled helmet he wore, Daiyu could make out the creases around his charcoal-colored eyes.

"And why are you here?" Daiyu stepped forward, even as Lanfen tried pulling her back. She stopped until she was in front of the man and peered up at him with narrowed eyes. "We have done nothing to warrant the emperor's men charging in here—"

"We are here on orders to bring one of you to the palace." His gaze flicked from Daiyu to Lanfen, and then to the rest of their family. "We heard a beautiful young woman lives here. Someone eligible for the royal selection."

Father came forward, his voice soft. "Please, we have nothing here for you. You must have mistaken us for someone else. Please leave."

One of the guards snorted. "We're not leaving without the woman." He jerked a thumb at Lanfen. "I think she's the one."

Lanfen gasped, and Daiyu shielded her with her body. "What do you mean?"

"The royal selection," the guard said with a huff, sounding annoyed. "We're to round up all the beautiful women in the nearby villages."

"No." Qianfan, her little brother, ran to stand between Daiyu and the guards. He balled his hands into fists. "I won't let you take her away!"

The older guard's eyes narrowed as he stared down at him. "Do you know what you're saying, boy?"

Qianfan's lower lip trembled. "I won't let you!"

The tension in the room thickened and one of the soldiers placed a hand on the pommel of his sword. "Are you saying you wish to go against the emperor's orders?"

Mother began sobbing, and Father looked as pale as snow. Her other brother, Ran, stilled as the implications seemed to set in. Going against the emperor meant death, even for a child. The emperor's words and his orders were absolute. Their entire family could be put to death for refusing.

Daiyu touched her brother's shoulder and pushed him behind her as well until the only thing standing between the guards and her siblings was her.

She squared her shoulders. "We aren't going against the emperor's orders. We will comply. However"—her voice trembled —"take me instead of my sister. She's too young—"

"Afraid we can't do that, miss." The guard stared down at her. "You're too old and not much to look at compared to your little sister right there."

Daiyu stilled; she had always been told she was beautiful, but it was true that Lanfen was much prettier than her. But to be told that she was too old? She was only twenty-four! Definitely not too old. These men didn't seem to like her, though. She could tell by the way they were looking around the room, likely irritated by her lack of compliance.

"Please," she whispered, stepping closer. "I'm still young and unmarried! I'm better suited than my sister. Please take me instead."

"No," the younger guard snapped. "The emperor doesn't want an old woman like you."

"But—"

The man reached forward and took a hold of Lanfen's shoulder and yanked her forward. Lanfen screamed, and Daiyu grabbed the guard's arm. "Please! Take me instead!"

"Back off!" One of the guards shoved her and she slammed to the floor.

Qianfan cried, holding on to Daiyu as two of the guards took Lanfen. The older of the guards stared down at Daiyu with contemptuous eyes.

"You should be grateful your sister is being taken to the royal selection. If she's chosen, you lot will live in luxury instead of"— he waved a hand at their home with a sneer—"this *hovel*."

Daiyu balled her hands together as the men dragged Lanfen, who screamed and kicked, out of their home.

Minutes passed and Mother continued to cry, while everyone remained frozen where they stood. Daiyu's mind was blank as she unsteadily rose to her feet.

This can't be happening.

Why was Lanfen chosen for the royal selection? Their village was close to the capital—a few days' ride away—but their village was poor. Why would the emperor want to round up women from such a small village anyway? Wouldn't it have made more sense for him to take concubines from noble families so he could form an alliance with them? What good would farm girls do him?

The pit in her stomach grew. Lanfen would be used as a bed warmer, nothing more, nothing less, if she was chosen by the accursed emperor.

Daiyu had heard tales of Emperor Drakkon Muyang. Of his injustices. His brutal strength. The strange magic he held—some said he was part dragon, part demon, part ... something sinister.

Heng had died fighting against that monster. Had died in Emperor Yan's army as Drakkon's forces usurped the throne four years ago. And now that monster wanted her sister.

Daiyu would never let him take Lanfen.

Never.

2

Daiyu trudged through the streets of the capital, her breath ragged and her feet aching from the travel. Normally, it took two days of horse-riding to reach it, three on a wagon with many breaks. On foot? Almost a week and a half for Daiyu. Tired was an understatement; she was exhausted, sweaty, and her feet were killing her.

Convincing her parents to let her go had been nearly impossible, and her brothers had said they would come with her too, but Daiyu couldn't let that happen. They were needed on their small farm, and anyone other than Daiyu going would mean less money and more financial burdens. It only made sense that Daiyu would be the one sneaking into the palace to rescue her sister.

How, though? She had absolutely no idea.

Now that she was here, in the dense streets of the capital, with people milling about around her, with the smell of woodsmoke, baked goods, and sweat pervading the sticky summer air, she was lost. She walked and walked, with only a handful of coins in her satchel, one outfit, and a few strips of dried fruit. She could see the looming palace, but the more she racked her mind on how to sneak in, the more she drew a blank.

The palace was heavily guarded, that much she could surmise.

And the guards were likely just as vicious as the emperor, so she had to have a solid excuse to slip inside—*if* she even got that far.

Maybe she could find employment inside the palace as an excuse to go inside? She doubted it would be easy sneaking in, and now that she was actually in the capital, her confidence waned.

What could she do?

Daiyu wove through the streets, keeping a watchful eye on the tall stone walls surrounding the palace that scraped toward the skies and the palace guards stationed near the ornate metal gates. She trudged to one side of the palace walls and continued along it. She made sure to keep her distance so no one would notice her inspecting it.

After twenty minutes of studying the walls, she came to three conclusions: there was more than one entrance, each were heavily guarded, and there was no way she could creep inside. The walls were too high to scale, and if she was caught, she'd be killed on suspicions of either being a spy, an assassin, or simply for breaching the palace.

Finally, when she couldn't think of anything to do, she straightened out her clothes, smoothed down her hair, and approached one of the guards.

"Excuse me—" She smiled politely at the young man.

He peered down at her with mistrusting, dark eyes. "Yes?"

"I've actually been recently hired as one of the kitchen helpers—"

"Your badge?"

"That's the thing"—her brows crinkled—"I ... don't know where I placed it."

"You *lost* it?" His eyes narrowed further. "So you're saying that anyone can enter the palace now with your lost badge? Is that correct?"

"Um, no," Daiyu quickly said. "How can anyone enter with you all guarding the palace? Surely, you've seen everyone's faces before, and you've seen me before too, haven't you?"

He tilted his head to better stare at her. "I've never seen you before."

"I've told you. I've recently been hired—"

"If you've got no badge or no other forms of identification, then leave."

"But—"

"*Leave.*" He glared at her, and the sunlight glinted off his steel helmet sinisterly as if the heavens were agreeing with him.

Daiyu pursed her lips together and scrambled away from the entrance. That didn't go well at all. If she had stayed and talked to him any longer, she wouldn't have been surprised if he decided to skewer her with his spear. Maybe she could try again later? Or maybe ...

Her mind became mush as she walked alongside the wall. She leaned her shoulder against it and wanted to slide down to the ground. Her feet were killing her and the constant walking back and forth, along with the tiring journey, made her bone-weary. Tears of frustration stung her eyes, but she refused to cry here, in the middle of the streets, in front of this insufferable palace.

Lanfen was trapped somewhere within these walls. There had to be *something* Daiyu could do.

"What are you doing?"

Daiyu spun around to find a man towering over her. He must've been at least a foot and a half taller than her. Satiny green and silver robes fluttered around the man, carrying the wind and the smell of cherry blossoms. A black and red dragon mask covered his face, and his long, midnight-colored hair trailed over his shoulders in silken streaks. He wore no weapons, and the royal insignia of a dragon was embroidered on the front of his long tunic.

The clothes gave him away—the green and silver robes meant he was one of the royal mages.

Daiyu's mouth dried up and she backed away, fear and panic engulfing her. A royal mage was said to be one of the strongest people in the empire. They wielded magic and could decimate cities in seconds, could warp to different locations with a snap of the finger, and could cause fire and water to erupt from their bodies at will—or so the rumors went. She had never met one before, nor seen their capabilities.

Until now.

Daiyu stared bug-eyed at the masked man. Words failed her, and she couldn't tell what he was thinking.

The man canted his head to the side. "Miss? Are you all right?"

"I-I—" A thousand deaths flashed before her eyes. Would this man kill her? Did he think she was suspicious? Why was he approaching her?

The man raised his hands and spoke slowly. "Are you all right? *Breathe.*"

"I'm fine, just passing along." Daiyu backed away and stumbled over her own feet.

The man reached out and steadied her by grabbing her elbow, but Daiyu shoved his hand away hastily as if his touch burned her. "Sorry, sorry." He raised his hands. "Didn't mean to spook you."

"I'm not spooked." She tried smiling, but it came out forced and she was sure it looked more like a grimace. "I was just passing by, sir. Please, let me go."

"I'm not holding you hostage." Another head tilt.

"Um." Daiyu licked her suddenly dry lips. The summer sun beat down on her and she wasn't sure what was making her sweat more: this mage or the sweltering heat. "That you aren't, sir. Um, so I suppose I'll get to"—she motioned to the streets of the capital —"where I need to go, yes?"

"You don't sound so sure of yourself."

"You're mistaken." She nodded and backed away. "Well, now, it's been a pleasure—"

"Miss, why have you been circling the royal palace five times?"

Daiyu's heart stopped. "What?"

"You've been circling the palace several times." He inched closer even as she continued to shrink away. "It's highly suspicious. Usually, people will only do that when ... say, they're trying to figure out how to break inside. Whether that be for spying, assassinating, or stealing. You don't *look* like a spy, or an assassin, or a thief ... So that makes me curious. What are you doing?"

Her back hit the wall and she was completely cornered by the masked mage, who now crossed his lean arms over his chest. A warm breeze settled between them, rustling his fine robes and her raggedy ones.

"Well, miss?" His voice was soft, velvety, and carried a hint of authority.

Daiyu scrambled for an answer, but her mind was blank. What could she say to him that wouldn't sound suspicious? Maybe that she was lost? That she was looking for something? That he was mistaken?

"I, um, I ..." Her small voice filled the void between them, and he waited, the red dragon eyes of his mask seeming to glow like the sun.

She stared down at her sandaled feet, at the fraying ends of her skirt, and at the cobbled streets they stood on. At the way that even his leather boots appeared sinister and powerful—a single kick could cave her skull in. She shivered, despite the summer heat.

Think, she told herself. *Think.*

"You must be mistaken," she finally squeaked.

Neither of them spoke. She stared up at him—at his dragon mask with its curling horns at the temples and mouth, and he continued to stare at her through the eye slits of the mask. Unimaginably black eyes peered at her.

"You ..." He slanted his head again, and if she weren't so panic-stricken, she might have asked him why he kept doing that. "You think I'm mistaken?"

"Yes." Daiyu couldn't think, not when she was in front of this powerful mage. It was a stupid, stupid lie that nobody would ever believe. She knew that, but it was better than stammering noth-ing, which was even more suspicious.

"Ah." He bobbed his head. "So I'm mistaken. You *weren't* suspiciously loitering around the palace, circumnavigating it, or appearing nervous when questioned about it."

"That ... that sounds about right." Daiyu's smile was wobbly as he stared at her unblinkingly.

"Hm." He placed a hand above her head against the wall, and she further sank to the ground, wanting to disappear altogether. "So you're *not* acting suspicious?"

"Correct, sir." Daiyu tried to wiggle away, but he placed another hand near her shoulder so she was caged in. He was so close she could smell the hints of lilacs and leather and earth clinging to him. "Now, I'll be going—" she began.

"Miss." He leaned closer until she was staring into the black depths of his eyes. "You—"

He was too close.

Daiyu pushed his chest, and it was like pushing against a solid wall of steel and muscle. "Get away from me," she started, trying again. This time, he let her, and he stepped away. The warmth of his body left immediately, and she could feel her face flushing with warmth. "Sir, please keep your distance. I'm an unmarried woman and I do *not* appreciate being pushed against a wall like this. It's improper and domineering. I'd appreciate if you'd take another step back and give me some space."

He blinked, and she blinked, and they both seemed to realize she was speaking to a royal *mage*. But instead of incinerating her on the spot, or calling the palace guards, he only lowered his head slightly. A show of respect.

"I apologize, miss. I didn't mean to disrespect you, nor push you out of your comfort zone."

She huffed, her heart hammering in her chest. "Thank you."

"But that doesn't change that you're acting suspicious and if I wanted to ..." He held his hand out and sparks of white lightning buzzed at his fingertips, the snapping and crackle making her gasp sharply.

She stared, transfixed, at the flickering light as it transformed

15

into an emerald shade, and then violet, before disappearing altogether. Burning smoke made her nose crinkle, but that wasn't enough to stop her amazement.

Magic.

She had never seen it before and certainly not so close and personal. And definitely not laced with a threat.

"I told you—" Daiyu began weakly, her gaze darting to the passing people in the distance, away from the palace walls. She wanted to disappear into the throngs of people, away from his knowing eyes.

"Miss, please don't insult my intelligence any further. What exactly are you doing here? You're trying to enter the palace, but I can't seem to understand *why*." He rubbed the curling, sharp tooth of the dragon mask. "I don't sense any hostility from you and you don't have any weapons on you either. So it's strange."

She swallowed. He could read her? Was this another magic spell? Or perhaps he could tell by looking at her?

"I would never dream of hurting anyone inside the palace," she whispered. "Trust me when I say that."

"Then what are you doing here?" He raised his hand before she could answer, and she noticed the calluses and scars crisscrossing over his pale skin. "And don't say any nonsense about how I'm mistaken. If it was anyone else in my position, you would already be in the palace dungeons for suspicious behavior. So speak cautiously and don't test my patience any further."

Daiyu clamped her mouth shut. She couldn't very well tell this man—one of the emperor's palace mages—that she wanted to steal one of the emperor's concubine candidates. But ... But if she didn't speak now, or come up with something believable, she would likely die.

The man waved his hand for her to speak when she continued stewing in her thoughts. "Well?"

"I ..." The lies she meant to speak died on her tongue and her eyes stung with tears. "I'm here to rescue my sister," she blurted out.

The man stilled. "Your sister? Did she commit a crime?"

"No, no." Daiyu shook her head and breathed out shakily, trying to keep the tears at bay, even though they threatened to fall. "My sister was chosen as one of the emperor's potential candidates for a concubine. You know, the royal selection. And ... And I told the guard that I would take her place, but they said I'm too old—" She sniffed, hating that she sounded so weak. She didn't want to cry in front of this stranger.

"Too old?" The man scoffed. "You don't look a day over thirty!"

She gasped. "Excuse me? I'm twenty-four!"

"Ah." He cleared his throat. "Continue."

"Well ... My sister—" She wiped her eyes furiously and cast him a sharp glare. "Do I really look that old?"

"No, no, *of course* not." His tone was light and she wasn't sure if he was joking or not. "So what happened to your sister then?"

"The guards took her for the selection," Daiyu breathed out. "I'm here to save her."

"How are you saving her? Becoming a concubine for the emperor is one of the greatest opportunities a woman can get. Imagine if she's chosen? She'll have unimaginable wealth. Your family would never need to worry about finances. And what if she gives birth to an heir? Her status will rise, as will your family's! I just don't see why you're treating it like a death sentence?"

Daiyu side-eyed the man, her attention lingering on the dragon insignia. *Of course* he would think that, being the emperor's mage and all. But for normal people, Drakkon Muyang was a terrifying ruler. He could kill Lanfen if he wanted to. Not to mention his court was cutthroat; if not him, someone else could kill her, and no one would care for a royal concubine. Especially not one who came from such humble roots.

Women were just pretty things to be used and tossed aside in court, especially for a concubine with no noble family.

"You wouldn't understand," Daiyu finally settled with. "Lanfen isn't meant for court life."

The man clucked his tongue. "Well, perhaps I wouldn't understand, but I must ask, how do you plan on doing such a thing? Sneaking inside the palace? Saving your sister? It all seems a bit ridiculous. And impossible, especially for a farm girl like yourself."

Daiyu frowned, not liking his tone. "I'm more than just a farm—*wait*. How do you know I'm a farm girl?"

"I can smell it on you. The manure. The pig shit." He shrugged. "I'm fairly certain everyone in the vicinity can smell—"

Daiyu gasped, a blush staining her cheeks. "You're joking! I do *not* smell."

"You're likely accustomed to the smell—"

"I am *not* smelly."

The man laughed softly. "Yes, I jest. I can tell you belong on a farm because your skin is tanned, your hands tell a life of hard work, and well, the most apparent indicator: I have magic, miss. The air around you tells me you work on a farm."

Daiyu gave him a strange look; was that truly the work of magic, or was he messing with her again?

"Anyway, miss, you're in luck." The man held his hand out to her. "If you'd like, I can take you inside the palace."

"Excuse me? Why would you help me?"

"I can't turn away from a woman in distress." Something twinkled in his black eyes. "I'm also very curious to see how you plan on rescuing your sister."

Daiyu eyed his hand suspiciously. His reasoning wasn't good enough for her to trust him so blindly, but he was the only sliver of hope she had of breaking into the place, so she nodded slowly. "I don't understand why you want to help me, but I can't say no to that."

She placed her hand in his, and all at once, their surroundings blurred and the colors seemed to stretch out and wane in a split second. Before Daiyu could open her mouth to scream or shout or say something, everything snapped into place. She blinked and the city's smells—briny fish, greasy food, and sweaty bodies—

disappeared altogether. In its place was the potent scent of incense and jasmine. And instead of the tall buildings and shops, wooden, paneled walls and jade-speckled pillars surrounded them.

Daiyu inhaled sharply—breathlessly—and turned to the room. Through the window, she could make out the capital streets she had just been on. She rushed to the windowsill and leaned over, her mouth dropping at the sprawling city and the guarded palace walls.

Sure enough, she was inside the palace.

3

"How?" Daiyu couldn't tear her eyes off the city beneath her. She had been standing on that street just a few seconds ago, and now she was ... She looked around the room once more, her mouth still gaping wide. How was any of this possible?

"Magic." The masked man watched her and she couldn't tell if he was grinning at her lack of knowledge and newness to magic, or if he was annoyed. Or *anything*, really. But the tone of his voice appeared ... neutral, perhaps?

"We were *just* there." She pointed to the street with wide eyes.

He came to stand beside her by the windowsill. He pointed to another street in a different direction. "Actually, we were closer to there."

Daiyu frowned. "You know what I mean. We were just—"

"I'm aware." He spread his hands out. "Magic, miss. That's the answer."

"It's just so fascinating." She turned to gawp at the streets once more. She had never warped before and hadn't even thought it was actually possible. Sure, she had heard rumors or stories of mages warping, but nobody she knew had actually seen it before. And not just seen it—been warped themselves.

"Don't you have a sister to save?"

Daiyu turned to the man sharply, her awe-filled moment shattering. "Of course I do."

"Then perhaps ...?" He waved to the doorway.

"You want me to get to it?" She sighed and placed a hand on her hip. "You can't fault a girl for being surprised and interested in magic, sir. Yes, I do have to save my sister, but she won't disappear if I don't go this *exact* second."

"But the *evil* emperor might snatch her away right as we speak."

Daiyu couldn't help but laugh, the tightness in her chest uncoiling. "Yes, yes, I can't forget about that." She headed toward the end of the room. "Thank you, sir, for allowing me inside."

"How do you plan on leaving?"

"I'll ..." She pursed her lips together. "I'll figure something out. The first thing is to find my sister."

He nodded slowly. "And then?"

"I just told you." Daiyu gave him a look. "I'll figure something out. Perhaps I'll sneak out in the gardens—"

"The guards will find you and execute you if you do that."

"Then the clothes bin—"

"And what of the laundresses?" He scoffed. "Once again, the guards will be alerted and you'll be executed."

"Then ..." She waved her hands. "Perhaps we'll escape through a window—"

"The guards would see you and"—he made a scythe-like motion over his neck—"you guessed it, execute you."

Her eyebrows pulled together and her voice rose in desperation. "Then perhaps we'll leave when the servants retire for the night!"

The masked mage chuckled. "The servants, dear, *live* here."

Daiyu chewed on her lower lip. Truthfully, she didn't think she'd even get this far. Her plan had many, many holes, and having him point out the obvious was frustrating, albeit embarrassing too. She paced the room, her thin sandals feeling cold against the polished floors.

"Then maybe I can bribe a guard?"

This time, he laughed loudly. "*Bribe* a guard? With what money? Miss, are you wealthy?"

"Well, no." She reached for the handful of coins in her pouch and held it up for him to see. "But I'm sure this will … help?"

She sighed, her hopes suddenly dashing away. She didn't have enough money to bribe the guards. She could see that. And there was nothing else she had that was worth anything.

"You came all this way to the palace *without* a plan?" The mage chuckled again, and this time it crawled under her flushed skin.

Daiyu shoved the coins back in her pouch under her sleeve and gave him a pointed look. "No need to be rude and laugh at me."

"Apologies." His chest shook even as he said that. "But what will you do, miss?"

An idea struck her as she stared at the man. "Well, there is one thing I can do."

"What is it?"

"You warped me in here, so …" She smiled hesitantly at him. "I'd forever be grateful if you could also warp us out."

The man crossed his arms over his chest. "Ah. There it is, but, miss, that doesn't sound like a request."

"Would you please warp me and my sister out of this palace?"

"What would I gain from this?" His tone shifted from playful mischievousness to tense and grim. He placed a gentle hand on the windowsill and peered at the sprawling city before turning to her, the wind tousling his long, inky hair. "I'm a powerful mage, a wealthy man, and a loyal subordinate to His Majesty. What could you possibly have that I would want?"

Words failed her and she suddenly felt small in that room. In her raggedy robes, with her near-empty purse of coins, standing in the perfumed room of the palace. What did she have that she could offer a mage?

It was true that coming here was naïve, but a part of her had believed that her hard work, that her stubbornness would somehow pay off—that she would figure something out. But now that she was here, it all felt ... utterly naïve.

Daiyu swallowed and lifted her gaze to meet the mage's. "What is it that you want?" she asked slowly.

"You tell me. What is it that you have?"

"I have a long life ahead of me." She placed a hand on her chest. "Take some years off my life. All mages want to live forever, don't they? Then surely—"

The man burst into laughter. For a moment, Daiyu only stared at him in shock and then embarrassment.

"Did I say something funny?"

"No, no—" The man slapped the windowsill and shook his head, his body trembling from the laughs. "Not at all, but, but you think I want your *life*? Miss, mages aren't like in the fairy tales. We don't chase after youthful maidens to steal their lifeforce and turn them into shriveled hags. Think of me as an ordinary man."

A blush crept up her face and ears. Well, how was she supposed to know that? She had never met a mage before, and she only had tales to go off on. "How about you tell me what you want from me? Since I clearly have no clue what an *ordinary* man like you would want."

Once his laughter subsided, he leaned against the wall beside the window and crossed his lean arms over his chest. "What about a favor?"

"What kind of favor?"

"You help me when I need you to, and in exchange, I'll warp you and your sister out of here."

Making a deal with a mage was a stupid, stupid idea. But she had nothing else to grasp onto, so she bobbed her head. "All right, then. That seems simple enough, so long as your favor doesn't entail me degrading myself in any way."

Another chuckle. "Miss, I'm a perfectly behaved gentleman, I'll have you know."

"Yes, I can see that."

"Then we have a deal." He nodded. "When you've found your sister, come to this room and call out my name. I'll warp you both out."

"All right."

"Good luck."

Daiyu headed toward the doorway but then realized she didn't know the man's name. "What's your—"

But when she turned, the room was empty and the man had disappeared.

~

Daiyu walked down the hallways with her head low. She carried a basket of dirty linens she had found outside one of the rooms and pretended like she was a servant. Maidservants brushed past her without stopping or giving her another look, and the guards were the same. So long as she looked like she was busy, they ignored her. They didn't seem to notice that her clothes were too plain, or that she stank of sweat and grime from her travels.

She peeked inside one of the sliding doors in the hallway, but it appeared to be an office. Another doorway led to a library, and another to an empty room. She hurried down to another corridor, sneaking around and taking a peek into the rooms she passed.

She needed to hurry.

Her luck would eventually run dry and somebody was bound to notice that she didn't look like a servant.

Right when she touched the handle to the door closest to her, a voice boomed from behind.

"What are you doing?"

Daiyu jumped around to find a young man in his twenties scowling at her a few feet away. He was dressed in long, red robes with fitted black pants and boots to match. Chainmail armor covered his chest and a long sword was strapped to his waist. His dark eyes narrowed at her, and Daiyu swallowed the bile clawing up her throat.

Beside the man was a young woman dressed in bright yellow and pink. Gold, ornate, dragon-shaped hairpins adorned her hair, showing her wealthy status.

Daiyu smiled, trying to ease the panic from her face. "I'm new here," she said, clutching the woven basket closer to her chest. "I'm a bit lost."

"That's my office." He pointed at the door she had just been about to open.

"I'm sorry." She lowered her head. "I meant no offense. I'm actually looking for the women for the royal selection. I'm supposed to gather their laundry." She held up the basket for emphasis. "Perhaps either of you can point me in the right direction? I would very much appreciate it."

The woman beside the man grinned. "The women for the royal selection are located upstairs in the Lotus wing. Would you like me to show you the way?"

"Jia." The man turned to the woman with furrowed brows. "A servant can help her."

"Nonsense! I'm not doing anything right now."

"But—"

"Come! I'll show the way!" Jia pointed to the end of the hallway and waved Daiyu forward. "Fang, I'll be back in a bit. You're probably just going to do some boring paperwork anyway, right?"

The man, Fang, frowned. "Hurry up."

Daiyu released a breath as Jia grabbed her by the arm and pulled her down the hall.

"I'm sorry about that. He can be a bit rude. Are you okay?"

"Ah, yes. I'm a bit ... overwhelmed. This palace is enormous."

Daiyu tried to smile, but it came out strained and unnatural. Her heart was still racing. "Who was that man?" When she peeked over her shoulder, the man was still standing there, his arms crossed over his chest and a disapproving scowl on his face. She quickly looked away. "Is he someone important?"

Jia blinked. "Oh, you mean Fang? Yes, he's, well, he's a general."

"A *general*?" Daiyu's eyes nearly bugged out. First, she had met a palace mage and now a *general*? Her luck was either unlimited, or it was running low because she had just survived two encounters with two powerful people and had left them unscathed.

"Yes, General Liang Fang." Jia smiled. "You didn't realize who he was?"

"No, I'm new here."

Jia nodded as they went up a flight of stairs. Chatters filled the next hallway they entered and they stopped outside a paper sliding door with pink and white cherry blossoms painted on them. She motioned to the door. "This is the place."

"Thank you, lady Jia." Daiyu smiled at her, relieved.

"No worries." Jia waved to her before leaving.

Daiyu breathed out deeply and touched the handle of the door. She prayed Lanfen was inside.

4

Daiyu flung the door open and stepped through. Almost instantly, a cloying floral smell hit her—an amalgamation of jasmine, rose, and cherries—so sweet she almost choked. Over three dozen women turned to her. For a moment, Daiyu froze, staring at their heavily painted faces, the silk dresses they wore, and the jewelry adorning their heads. They were all sprawled on couches with decorative, tasseled pillows.

Time slowed, and her heart sank as her gaze flitted over the women with white-powdered faces and red flowers etched onto their foreheads.

"Daiyu?" One of the women rose from her seat, her eyes wide.

The basket slipped from Daiyu's hand, forgotten as she pushed through the room. "Lanfen? Lanfen!"

Lanfen rushed to her and they both fell into a tight embrace. Daiyu's eyes burned with tears as she hugged her sister tightly. All the weariness from travel and the anxiety of getting to this point vanished in seconds. Her throat closed up and she breathed in the flowery and powdery scent from her sister.

"How are you here?" Lanfen asked, her voice barely a whisper.

"It's a long story." Daiyu closed her eyes. The other women in the room continued their chatter, ignoring them both. "I came to rescue you."

Lanfen pulled away from her. Her face was covered in white powder, but it didn't extend to her neck, which was still tanned from farm life. "How will we do that?"

"I've got my ways. Anyway, how are you? How have you been here?"

Daiyu eased onto one of the many couches along with her sister. Lanfen twiddled her hands together and ran her thumb over the silver embroidery on her sleeve. "I've been well. I haven't seen the emperor, if that's what you're asking. He hasn't come here even once, and some of the girls I talked to said they haven't seen him even though they've been here for months! It seems he has no interest in choosing one of us ..." Her gaze skated to the others in the room, and then back at Daiyu. "We might be stuck here for a while."

"No one has mistreated you, have they?"

She shook her head.

"Good." Daiyu placed a gentle hand on her sister's cheek. "You were very brave to come here, Lanfen."

Unshed tears shone in her eyes. "I want to go home."

Daiyu's chest tightened at the sight of her younger sister's anguished expression. She squeezed her hand tightly and gave her a reassuring smile. How lonely and terrifying must it have been to be thrust in the royal palace with no say of her future? Lanfen didn't want to be here; she would rather be home with her family. And yet she had no choice. Even if the emperor chose her, she wouldn't be able to say no.

"I'll take you back, I promise," Daiyu said.

Lanfen sniffled and wiped her eyes with the back of her hand, smudging the whitish makeup on her face. "But how will we do that?"

"I've got a connection here. He'll help us out."

She tilted her head to the side. "How do you know someone?"

"It's a long story. I'll explain when we're out of here."

Lanfen glanced at the door. "But we're not allowed to leave this wing."

"I didn't notice any guards, though."

"The guards are stationed at the bottom of the staircases on both sides of the hallway."

"But the hallway is unguarded?"

"Yes, since this wing holds all our bedrooms. Why?"

"So you have your own room?"

"Yes," Lanfen said. "Why?"

"Let's go to your room, then."

Lanfen led Daiyu out of the room and down the hallway. They entered a cramped room with a single bed in one corner, a small trunk of belongings, and a tiny, circular window with a geometric metal design. She hurried to the window and peered through the slats, her heart sinking. She had thought that maybe the window would be big enough for them to sneak through, or to climb out of, but this was impossible.

"Well?" Lanfen chewed on her lower lip.

"We can't jump through here." Her fingers trailed over the metal working of the window. They were also three stories high, so even if the window weren't so small, they probably wouldn't be able to climb down. Did the emperor do this on purpose? Lock up these women here with no hope of escape?

Lanfen kept her back pressed to the sliding door. "Daiyu, I don't think it's a good idea for you to be here. You look out of place with your clothes and I think it's too much trouble to try to sneak me out. You need to get out of here before anyone notices."

"I came here to save you. I'm not running away."

"But—"

"We'll come up with a plan! Don't worry." Even as she said that, her mind came to a stuttering halt. What could she do to sneak them both out? They had a way out—the masked man— but how could they get out of this hallway without garnering any attention?

"Maybe you can pretend to be one of us?" Lanfen pointed to

the wooden trunk. "They gave me two other dresses to wear. If you put one on, you'll blend in with everyone else."

Daiyu pursed her lips together. "But I'd like to leave as soon as possible—"

"I do too, but if any of those women tell the guards that you came here dressed like that, and you don't change, they'll realize you don't belong here." She swallowed. "I don't want to see you get dragged out here by the guards."

"Has that happened before?"

Lanfen averted her gaze, her face pale. "There was a girl who didn't want to be here. She kicked and screamed and cursed the emperor, so the guards took her away. I have no idea what happened to her."

Daiyu leaned against the wall of the room and closed her eyes. She had made it all the way up here pretending to be a servant, and that seemed to have worked. Maybe she could sneak out the same way? But that would require her finding some clothes for Lanfen that would make her blend in as a servant. Or she could pretend to be a part of the royal selection and try to run when there was a better opportunity.

"All right, I've got a plan." Daiyu gave her sister a level look. "I'm going to find some maidservant clothes for you, and then we'll both leave. The guards didn't bother me since I'm dressed like this." She waved to her worn-out dress. "So I'm sure they won't bother me again."

Lanfen shook her head. "What if they notice you? I've been in the palace for a week now, and one thing I've noticed is that the servants dress nice. Plain, but still nice! You're dressed too ..." Her gaze flicked down to her dried-grass sandals, the ragged hem of her dress, and the threadbare material.

"Too much like a farmer's daughter?" She smiled even as Lanfen cringed. "I know, Lanfen, but what else can I do?"

"You can pretend to be a part of the royal—"

"That'll be my last resort."

"Then maybe—" Lanfen shot forward and kneeled in front of

the trunk. She jerked the lid open and yanked out a shimmering pink dress with feathery soft sleeves and cranes embroidered on the skirts. "Take this with you. If someone stops you, tell them you're ..." She frowned. "I don't know, tell them something."

"That I'm ... on my way to a bath?" Daiyu offered, taking the pretty dress from her sister's hands. "This dress is beautiful," she whispered.

"It's not worth being in here for just that." She pointed to the dress and then gave Daiyu a sad look. "Please be safe."

She bundled the dress in her arms and nodded. "Of course."

THE PALACE WAS TOO LARGE, DAIYU DECIDED AS SHE stumbled through a random hallway. She had slipped out the women's wing with no problem. The guards at the ends of the staircases didn't give her a second glance and the other guards and servants milling about the palace mostly ignored her. Everyone was too focused on their own tasks to pay much attention to anyone else. That played in Daiyu's favor. But that also played against her because if she took the time to ask anyone anything, they grew suspicious. And so she clammed up and ventured through the winding halls by herself.

Her anxieties multiplied with every step. She couldn't find the servants' quarters, and the deeper into the palace she ventured, the less sure she became. If she couldn't even find clothes to fit her sister, how was she going to sneak out, find the mysterious masked man, and get out of here? She didn't even know the man's name, so how would she summon him?

She felt like she was wandering in circles. The hallways all looked the same: fancy, tiled floors; embellished, geometric designs on the walls; and heavy doors with intricate dragon embossing.

A man with light brown hair and eyes to match caught her attention in one of the halls. He was dressed in long, sapphire robes with a sword to his hip. They both made eye contact, and the man smiled from down the hall.

Crap. Why was he smiling at her?

Daiyu lowered her head and quickly glanced for an escape route. The only way out of this hallway was either behind her, or where he was—at the end of the hall.

If she turned around and left, would that be suspicious? But would he try to talk to her if she tried to make it to the end of the hallway?

Her mind swam with what to do. Her steps faltered, and right when she thought to turn around, it was too late. He was in front of her.

"Are you lost?"

She plastered a tight-lipped smile on her face that she hoped didn't look too strained. The man wasn't dressed like a soldier, but he had a sword—that probably meant he was in a high position, maybe?

"Uh, yes." Daiyu held the dress close to her chest.

"Maybe I can help you?" He eyed her and she wasn't sure if she saw mistrust in his gaze. But there was something there—something that told her this man was sharp. "You look like a maid? But you're not in the typical outfit of a maid. Why is that?"

Daiyu held the dress in her arms. "I just arrived here. I was chosen for the royal selection and was given this dress, along with the instruction to take a bath."

"Why didn't the lady in charge send you to the bath in the Lotus wing?"

"I'm a farmer's daughter," Daiyu quickly said, her mind scrambling with ideas as she shifted on her feet. "The others didn't take kindly to me using their bath, so they sent me off. Something about how I'll dirty their bath water with muck ..." She looked down at her grass sandals and wriggled her tanned toes for emphasis. "I think they were playing a mean joke on me because no matter where I go, I can't find a place to bathe."

The man nodded slowly, something akin to understanding flickering in his warm, brown eyes. "Women can be very cruel."

"Yes ..." Daiyu peered up at him. "I suppose I'll be off then—"

"Let me show you to the bath, yes?"

"Oh? Um, no need. I'm sure you're busy—"

"I can't turn away a lady in need." He smiled and there was something mischievous about it as he waved her forward.

Daiyu internally cursed herself for bumping into this man. He was probably being kind for leading her toward the bath, but she didn't need a bath—she needed to find some clothes.

They walked for a bit before finally stopping at a pair of doors guarded by two men. They straightened when they saw the man and lowered their heads.

The man motioned to the door. "The bath, my lady."

"Ah, thank you." Daiyu hesitated as the two guards gave her strange looks.

"But comm—" the guard began.

The man raised his hand. "It's fine. She's a woman for the royal selection. Once she's done with her bath, lead her to the Lotus wing."

"Understood," the guard said with a nod, but not before giving Daiyu another glance.

Daiyu paused at the door. She didn't want to take a bath right now, but if she left the bathroom without taking a bath, wouldn't that alert the guards that something was up? Would it be better to pretend to be a part of the selection and figure out another way to leave?

She pushed open the door and closed it behind her. The air was dense with steam and fog, but Daiyu could make out a pool in the center of the room with a statue of a dragon curling around the rim. She didn't give it much attention as she padded toward the stone bench. After dumping the fancy dress onto it, she began to untie her sash when she finally noticed that, through the steam, a man was sitting in the bath. She almost hadn't noticed him because he was so close to the dragon's gaping mouth of razored teeth and he blended in against the pale oranges and yellows of the statue.

The man had his midnight-like eyes set on her. Like an abyss waiting to yank someone to their demise.

Long, inky, silk-like hair fell over his lean shoulders. His powerful arms were braced against the rim casually, and she could make out a dragon tattoo on his forearm. His pale face was immaculate, not a single scar or imperfection. He pinned her with an amused look of someone powerful stepping into his den.

Daiyu's heart nearly stopped. *He has a dragon tattoo.*

"Who are you and what are you doing in my bathing chambers?" Even his voice was beautiful and powerful. Smooth and velvety. Perfect, if not for the power he radiated.

Daiyu slowly grabbed the dress from the bench. "I've made a mistake." Her voice came out as barely a whisper, like the wisps of steam fogging the room. "Apologies, sir. I'll be—"

"Leaving so soon? I think not." He pointed to the bench and the water rippled across the surface. "Sit."

Daiyu remained standing and turned her face away from the naked man. Her heart was pounding so loudly and hard in her chest, she felt like it would leap out. Her hands trembled and adrenaline coursed through her veins. She shouldn't be here—she didn't know who this strange man was, but she suddenly felt like prey in his presence.

"This is highly improper. I must leave." She tightened her hold on her dress, the silk creasing. "I'm an unmarried woman and you ... you are *naked*."

"That I am."

"And I ... I'm *unmarried*," she reiterated, choosing to stare at the metal lanterns hanging from the ceiling. "So, sir, I must leave. Now."

She could feel the man boring holes into her. There was something intoxicating about him, like if she stared for too long, she would unravel at the seams. And the more he stared, the more her body flushed with heat. She was becoming dizzy in the muggy room.

Daiyu's legs felt leaden as she stumbled toward the doorway. "Goodbye—"

"Do not run." There was a warning in his tone, and Daiyu almost face-planted hearing the grave timbre in his voice.

Daiyu's fingers dug into the doorframe. She didn't dare look back at the man.

"Your name?" he asked.

A fake name. She needed to give him a fake name.

Daiyu's mind was blank. "I-I have no name," she blurted.

A pause. "You ... have no name?"

He didn't sound convinced. And Daiyu cringed at her terrible quick thinking.

She finally looked over her shoulder at him. He hadn't moved and was still in the bath. His fingers skimmed the surface and he rubbed a petal between his fingers, his black gaze set on her. Warmth pooled in her chest at the same time an icy dread washed over her—something wasn't right.

"That's right. I have no name," she went with a strained smile. She barely choked the words out, unable to rip her gaze from those dark, dark eyes that seemed to consume her in swathes of shadows. "So, sir, I'll be leaving now. Good day to you and I apologize for disturbing your bath."

"Don't leave so soon—"

"No, no. You see, I'm in a hurry." She bobbed her head, swallowing down the dryness of her throat. "I have somewhere very important to go and seeing as how I'm unmarried and you ... you are likely unmarried too? Yes?" She sucked in a deep breath, the words tumbling out of her mouth too quickly for her to think straight past the haze of steam and the intoxicating smell of jasmine. "Yes. So seeing as how we both are in this improper situation, I think it's best I leave before anything escalates—"

"Escalates?" He raised a brow and she could tell that remark angered him by the tick in his jaw. "You think I would—"

"Yes, escalate! Because, you see, *I* would jump on you and I don't think you would want that. Right? Right. No one wants to be attacked. So as to preserve your chastity and mine, I will leave. Right now. Good day!" Without waiting for his response, she yanked the door open and scrambled out of the room. Slamming the door shut behind her, she slumped against it with a loud, shaky exhale.

One of the guards jumped and stared at her like she had grown two heads.

"Take me to the women's lotus, blossom—whatever it's called —wing, *please.*" Daiyu waved toward the hallway and the man blinked. "Now, please!"

"Err, yes."

The man led her down the hallway and Daiyu hurried after him. Her heart wouldn't stop racing wildly. She kept looking over her shoulder, expecting the man to chase her down.

He had a dragon tattoo.

Only royalty had that.

And she had just run away from him.

5

When Daiyu arrived in Lanfen's room, she couldn't stop trembling. Lanfen rubbed her back and had asked her several times what had happened, but Daiyu couldn't utter a word. She kept replaying the conversation she had with the man in the bathing chambers and couldn't shake her unease. If he truly was the emperor, she could easily be executed for speaking to him so rudely, so casually. Not to mention she had invaded his privacy.

"Daiyu—" Lanfen began for the dozenth time.

The door to Lanfen's room slid open with a loud crack. The woman barely looked at them as she glanced down the hallway, her expression panicked. "Come to the waiting room. *Now.*"

"Why?" Lanfen rose to her feet.

"Everyone is to report there!" The woman's eyebrows came together when she finally took notice of Daiyu. "Who are you?" A commotion in the hallway grabbed her attention and she waved at them. "Well, never mind that! Come now!"

Lanfen and Daiyu were ushered into the room with the couches. About fifty or so women were rounded up and filled the room. The smell of perfumes pervaded the air and Daiyu wanted to stick her head outside a window to just breathe properly.

"Ladies!" An older women waved the stragglers from the hall-

37

ways into the main room. "Come now! His Majesty is coming this way!"

All the color drained from Daiyu's face just as an excited murmur filled the room. It couldn't be, could it?

Was he coming all this way to drag her out of here and kill her?

Her gaze flicked over at the glass bead curtains sectioning off the interconnected room. No one seemed to be going there, so if she had to guess, the emperor would remain in the main room.

Daiyu gave Lanfen's hand a squeeze and leaned close to her ear. "I'll be in the next room, all right?"

"What, why?" Lanfen's eyes were wide as saucers and despite the heavy, mature makeup, she looked so young. "You're going to leave me alone here?"

"Come with me too, then." They both headed toward the glass beaded curtain with a swirling dragon design.

A hand grasped Daiyu's shoulder and a stern voice asked, "Where do you both think you're going?"

The older lady in charge gave them both a once-over, her mouth parting as she took in Daiyu's outfit—she never did get the chance to change out of her clothes.

"Who are you?" the woman demanded, tightening her hold on her shoulder.

"Sh-She's new!" Lanfen said, but the woman wasn't buying it.

The other women in the room giggled, lost in their own chatters about the emperor visiting, and their voices increased in volume. Daiyu shot a glance at the entrance. Was the emperor almost here?

"Well? The woman dug her fingernails so deep in her shoulder that Daiyu flinched.

"Please don't hold me like that." Daiyu wrenched her arm from the woman's grasp and rubbed where the woman had held her. "I'm not supposed to be here—"

"I can see that!" The woman's attention turned to the doorway and she quickly shooed Daiyu. "Go to that room! I'll deal with you after His Majesty leaves! And don't you dare show your face in front of him! I'll not have him think that I rounded up a"—she looked Daiyu up and down with distaste—"a dusty, country bumpkin as his potential concubine. Now go!"

Daiyu and Lanfen turned back to the curtains, but the woman pulled Lanfen back.

"Not you."

Daiyu reached forward to grab Lanfen, but the other woman was already dragging her toward the mass. For a moment, Daiyu was torn on whether she should take her sister back, or run behind to the next room. But the crowd hushed to silence and she chose the latter. She barely ducked through the curtains before she heard a chorus of, "Good afternoon, Your Majesty."

Daiyu's heart was pounding, adrenaline coursing through her flesh. She flicked one of the beaded threads of the curtain and peeked into the room. All the women were kneeling in front of a man dressed in heavily embroidered clothes and a gold threaded headdress. Three guards accompanied him, but Daiyu barely noticed them. Her entire attention was on the man. The air around him rippled, and even with her minimal experience with magic, she could feel the heaviness of it in the air. He demanded the attention of the room with a single glance.

Her throat dried up as she recognized the man from the bath.

Drakkon Muyang took a seat on one of the couches, his gaze drifting over the women, black eyes narrowed.

Daiyu swallowed. Had he really come here for her?

"Is this it?" Muyang frowned, looking at the women once more.

The woman in charge raised her head. "Your Majesty, these are all the women we've gathered from the nearby villages and cities."

Muyang leaned against the cushioned seat and propped his elbow on the armrest casually. "Is that so?" He waved a free hand at the crowd of kneeling women. "Raise your heads, all of you."

They all obliged. Daiyu couldn't see the expressions on the

women's faces from her position, but she could clearly see the dissatisfaction on the emperor's face.

One of the men by the emperor's side leaned down to whisper something in his ear, and Daiyu's mouth dropped open as she recognized the brown-haired man from earlier. He was the one who led her into the emperor's bathing chambers! If he knew the emperor well enough to be by his side, shouldn't he have known where the emperor's personal chambers were at? And so ... how could he have led Daiyu there? It was no mistake, she realized with mounting horror.

Muyang pointed to one of the women. "You. How old are you?"

"Fourteen, Your Majesty." She lowered her head.

The emperor made a face. "You are a child."

"I became a woman last year when my cycle began," she squeaked.

"A child pretending to be a woman," he said with a frown. He rested his chin on his fist and leaned into his seat casually. "These are truly *all* the women you've gathered?"

The woman in charge nodded. "Y-Yes, Your Majesty. Is something wrong?"

Daiyu felt bad for the woman, who seemed to be trembling in his presence. Everyone could probably tell that he was displeased, and she wondered how it must have felt to be in their shoes, bowing down in front of a man who barely looked at them and who was clearly unsatisfied with them. And they were all such beautiful women! Did he think he was better than them? Did he think they weren't good enough?

The emperor's attention turned to the curtains and Daiyu froze as his dark gaze landed on her. She didn't release the beaded thread—for that would give her away for sure—but her heart couldn't stop beating frantically. He shouldn't have been able to see her. Maybe he was just admiring the dragon design painted on these beads? That had to be it.

A slow smile curved over his soft mouth. A dark delight.

"Ah, I see." He turned to one of the women. "You, woman. Why do you wish to be my concubine?"

"Um, well," the woman stuttered. "It would be an honor."

"And how old are you?"

"Twenty-one."

"What is your father's occupation?"

"He is a government worker. He, um, collects taxes in our city."

"A respectable career." He drummed his fingers over the armrest and pointed to another woman. "And you? Why do you wish to be my concubine?"

The woman stammered a response while Daiyu remained petrified on her spot. Surely, the emperor couldn't have seen her? But then why did he smile like that? Like he had found something amusing?

Drakkon Muyang sat and listened for a bit as the women spoke about their reasoning to marry him, all the while he appeared disconnected from whatever they were saying. From time to time, his gaze flicked to the curtains. Daiyu was just about to step away when he pointed directly at her.

"You can come out now."

She froze.

"Yes, you." He flexed his finger forward. "Little rabbit, come out now."

Little rabbit? She made a face. She didn't like that nickname at all.

Daiyu stepped into the room slowly. Everyone turned to watch her. The woman in charge had her eyes so wide open that Daiyu was afraid they would pop out of her sockets.

"Y-Your Majesty! Please forgive me, but she isn't supposed to be here—" the woman began.

Muyang raised his hand, stopping the woman from speaking, and smiled. It sent a chill down Daiyu's back. He didn't look at the older woman. "Silence."

The woman clammed up while Daiyu stopped in front of

him. She dropped to a kneel, her hands trembling as they touched the polished floorboards.

"Greetings," Daiyu said. *Your Majesty* or *Your Highness*, which was more appropriate? Which was proper? She couldn't remember, so she decided on the latter. "Your High-jesty."

Her eyes widened at the mistake.

She wanted to bang her head on the floor.

What the hell, Daiyu?

A murmur of giggles filled the room and Daiyu wanted to sink into the wood fibers. When she peeked at the emperor, his lips were twisted into a smirk. She quickly looked away.

"Raise your head."

She obliged and peered up at him.

"Your name?" he asked. "And don't say you don't have one."

She cringed. "Yin Daiyu."

"Daiyu," he said with a nod. "Why do you wish to be my concubine?"

She didn't. Not at all. So the question threw her off because she hadn't thought in a million years that anyone would ask her such a thing. Her mind came to an abrupt halt as she stared at the man. The silence stretched, and she could feel the heat clawing up her neck as everyone stared at her, waiting, watching. Probably hoping she would fail in some way.

"Because—" She needed to come up with *something*. "Because I like"—her gaze skated to the room and then back at him—"the palace."

He blinked, opened his mouth, and closed it again.

Once more, she wanted to hit her head on the floors.

What was she even saying?

Was it her nerves that were making her blurt out unintelligent, clearly not well-thought-out answers? Or was she truly as stupid as she sounded?

She decided to just go with it. "The palace is beautiful," she continued, her face flushing with heat. "It's so large and, and ... *majestic*. I've been lost so many times and it's only my first day, so that truly is a testament to how large the place is. So yes, that is my reason."

The brown-haired man coughed, and it sounded all too much like a strangled laugh.

Muyang stared at her. "You wish to be my concubine because"—he gestured to one of the walls—"the palace is *large*?"

"Yes." She had never heard such a confident yes to such a stupid lie, but she nodded like she meant it.

It was better than telling him the truth. She could imagine that going down very well: *Actually, Your Highness, I don't want to be your concubine. In fact, I'm here to save my sister from you because I really, really don't want her to be your concubine either.*

She was sure if she told the truth, she'd be executed. Along with Lanfen.

The emperor covered his face with his hand and Daiyu noticed that his chest was shaking ever so slightly. Was he ... laughing?

Finally, he removed his hand to reveal a large grin. A grin that looked too sinister. Uneasiness washed over her.

"You," he said, leaning forward and bracing his elbows on his knees to better stare at her, "I want to make you my wife."

Gasps filled the air.

Muyang rose to his seat. "It's decided then. Yin Daiyu, you will be my wife."

6

Daiyu paced in circles around the room, her mind growing more tangled with every stride. Lanfen sat on the cushioned couch in the center of the room, her hands distractedly dancing over the intricate carvings of a slithering dragon on the armrest. She had been silent the entire time.

Wife. Wife? Wife!?

Daiyu must have heard wrong because there was no way *Drakkon Muyang* had said *she* was to be his wife.

She didn't even want to *be* here, much less be anything to the emperor.

But when she was whisked away into these fancy chambers with sprawling rooms divided by glass curtains, windows covered in aquamarine shaded paper screens—she came to the realization that the emperor did, in fact, choose her.

It was impossible. She didn't fit the beauty standard with the nobility—not with her tanned skin, which clearly showed her commoner status. Nor did she have any backing from an affluent and influential family.

Daiyu leaned against one of the jade-lacquered pillars in the room and ran a hand over the silk dress she wore. Lotuses were embroidered all along the dark green skirts, traveling up to the sapphire-colored sash, and even across the right lapel of her tunic. The one thing she truly couldn't complain about was the lavish dresses she had been given. She had never worn something so fancy.

She also couldn't complain about the food, or the constant scented baths, or the lack of work ... Truly, she couldn't complain about much. But it was only because she knew this was all temporary. There was no way she was going to go along with this absurd plan of being the emperor's concubine. Or wife. Or whatever the hell he wanted to do with her.

Her plan still hadn't changed: take Lanfen and get out.

But now there were complications, and she couldn't wrap her mind on how to solve them. For one, the emperor knew what she looked like. Two, he knew her name. Three, if she ran, wouldn't he come after her and potentially murder her and her entire family for rejecting him? Drakkon Muyang was known to be a vicious, cruel man, and going against him likely meant death for her and everyone related to her.

"Daiyu, what will we do now?" Lanfen folded her hands on her lap. Her anxiety was palpable, seeming to fill the room with waves and waves of tension. "Will you marry the emperor?"

The only good thing out of this arrangement was that Lanfen was saved from the emperor's eye, but even then, Daiyu couldn't say for certainty if that wouldn't change if they stayed here. Because if Drakkon Muyang *only* wanted Daiyu, why didn't he dismiss the rest of the ladies in the palace? Why was Lanfen still here? He must have been planning on taking *more* concubines after marrying Daiyu.

"Daiyu?" Lanfen was staring at her intently, and it took Daiyu a second to remember she had asked a question. She opened her mouth to reply, but another voice called from behind her.

"I'd love to know the answer to that too."

Startled, Daiyu screamed and whirled around, while Lanfen jolted upright from her seat. The masked mage was leaning against the other pillar in the room, his head tilted to the side. The mask he wore this time was a dazzling cerulean and emerald color, reminding her of a water dragon.

The mage pointed at Lanfen. "Are you planning on stabbing me with that?"

Daiyu followed his gaze to her sister, who had a hairpin in her hand, the sharp end of it aimed at him. "Lanfen—"

"Who are you?" Lanfen asked, wide-eyed and trembling.

"Lanfen! It's okay, I know him." Daiyu rushed to her side and placed a hand on her shoulder. "This is the man I was telling you about, the one who will help us."

She blinked, lowering the hairpin. "You know him?" She eyed his green robes. "He's ... He's a mage."

"Then you know how stupid it is to point a"—he stared at the hairpin, as if unsure what to call it—"weapon, at me."

Daiyu rolled her eyes and placed a hand on her hip. "A mighty mage like you, afraid of a hairpin? That's hardly a weapon! I'm sure you can just ..." She waved at the silver hairpin with a butterfly on one end of it, "make it disappear if you wanted to?"

Surely, if he could teleport from one location to the next, a measly hairpin must have been child's play against him?

"It's the insult that makes this all the more offensive." He lifted his shoulders, sounding mock hurt. "You didn't tell her *anything* about me? The heroic man who was going to rescue you both?"

Daiyu stifled a laugh, the tension in her knotted chest loosening. From the corner of her vision, Lanfen was watching her closely. "It slipped my mind."

"I can imagine. How did you manage that, by the way?" He pushed himself off the pillar and sauntered to the couch, where he unceremoniously plopped down on it. "You came here to rescue your sister and instead, you're going to marry the emperor now! If I weren't a mage, I would have suspected you of concocting some sort of spell to win the emperor's heart, with your sister as an excuse to weasel your way in here."

Heat flushed over Daiyu's face at the accusation. "That's not what happened. I truly did come here to rescue her."

"Yes, yes." He waved his hand dismissively and crossed his ankles together as he leaned deeper into the cushions of the couch. "That's why I prefaced it by saying that if I *weren't* a mage, I would have thought differently."

"How did you both meet?" Lanfen asked slowly, looking between the two of them in confusion.

"Long story." The man gestured to the empty couch across from him. "Anyhow, don't be shy. Have a seat."

Daiyu reluctantly sat on the couch, while Lanfen watched the mage uneasily. A budding tension headache throbbed in the back of her head. "Anyway," she said, lacing her hands together. "You never did tell me your name."

"I have no name to give." He shrugged. "And you never asked."

"No name?" Lanfen eased onto the spot beside Daiyu, her tone betraying her suspicion. "How do you have no name?"

Daiyu cringed as she thought of her first time meeting the emperor and how she had said the same thing: *I have no name.* Was this masked mage doing the same as her? Hiding his identity?

He waggled a finger in Lanfen's direction. "Well, little miss, I have no name because I must keep it a secret."

"Little miss?" Lanfen crinkled her nose. "Don't patronize me."

"I'm doing no such thing. But seeing as how I'm more than twenty years your senior, I think I can call you *little miss* since you are a literal *child* to me."

Daiyu blinked at him, unsure of how to proceed. Sure, she couldn't see the man's face, but she hadn't thought he was that much older than his early twenties. His voice certainly sounded young and lovely—

Lovely? Her mind came to a stuttering stop and she shook her head. She must be losing it.

The man drummed his fingers over the armrest. "I have a name, mind you, but I'm unable to say it."

"Why?" Daiyu asked.

"The same reason I wear this mask." He tapped the dragon's snarling mouth. "To hide my face. To hide who I am."

Lanfen frowned and leaned forward. "But *why*?"

"Because I'm the head mage in the entire empire, and the emperor has forced me to keep everything about myself a secret. This is to ensure ... well, I needn't say more."

Daiyu's eyes widened. "You're the head mage? Doesn't that mean you're the best mage in the entire empire?"

She couldn't see it, but she could imagine him grinning widely with the singsong way his voice came out. "Yes, yes, it does."

"We must name you *something*," Daiyu whispered. "Unless we should keep calling you mage?"

"You'll give me a name? I'm honored."

"Your name will be ..." Her gaze traveled to the jade necklace on her vanity and she snapped her fingers. "Bik!"

Lanfen burst into laughter while the masked mage canted his head. She couldn't see his expression, but she could tell he was befuddled.

"Bik?" he said slowly. "Is that ... truly the best you could come up with?"

Daiyu lifted her shoulder noncommittally but couldn't keep the grin off her face. "Do you have a problem with it?"

"Forgive me for saying this," he said dryly before waving a hand over his body, "but I am a man. Bik is a woman's name."

"You don't show us your face, so how do I know for sure that you aren't a woman?"

"You ..." His chest shook and it took her a second to realize he was laughing. He tipped his head back on the couch, and his voice came out dramatically. "You really have wounded me with that one, dear lady. Alas, I am a man. I thought you could tell—"

"We can't tell at all. Can you, Lanfen?" Daiyu asked innocently, while Lanfen shook her head. Daiyu nodded. "Yes, see? The only way to change your name is to perhaps unmask—"

"That name is taken by an occupant of the palace already, so I'm afraid we'll have to change the name," he interrupted.

Daiyu paused—someone else in this palace was named Bik? "Who?"

"The princess's cat."

The princess? She was confused for a moment because the emperor didn't have any children, but then she remembered the previous emperor, who Drakkon Muyang had slain, had daughters. Her smile faded. Those princesses were still in the palace? For some reason, she had expected them to be imprisoned somewhere else. Or dead.

"Anyway, I thought it would be interesting to see what nickname you could come up with for me. But I'm no longer amused. I do have a nickname I go by, which I think you both can call me." He placed his hands on his lap. "Feiyu."

They were all silent for a moment after that. Daiyu picked at the embroidered lotus by her knee and pressed her fingernail over the tight threads of it. All traces of jesting faded as her mind roved over her current predicament with the emperor and how messy everything had become. Finally, when she couldn't think straight anymore, she lifted her head to pin the mage with a curious look. "What are you doing here, anyway?"

"To see how *you're* doing." Feiyu folded his pale hands on his lap and the dragon face of his mask seemed to peer into her soul.

She shivered at the thought of it—could he see into her memories? Her thoughts? He was a mage, after all.

"And—" he added, straightening in his seat and readjusting his emerald robes, "to hear about your grand plans of escape. Which, I'm assuming, still require my assistance? *Unless*—"

Daiyu waited for him to finish, but he simply shrugged, and she pursed her lips together. "Unless? Unless what?" A thought

49

struck her and she gasped. "Unless you think my plans have changed because the emperor chose me?"

He shrugged again, and this time Daiyu couldn't help the mortification and embarrassment from flooding her face with fire. She wasn't naïve enough to think that being by the emperor's side meant she would live a lavish and full life.

She jumped to her feet, unable to hide her emotions any longer as she waved to the jade-veneered pillar, and then to the pretty blue window shades. "You think that these fancy things are enough to entice me?" She rushed to the dresser on the side of the room and picked up the jade necklaces and painted hairpins lining the top of it. She thrust them in his direction. "Or that these pieces of jewelry are enough for me to sell my soul to that wicked man?" She dropped the fine jewelry and they clunked against the surface of the dresser. Her breathing increased as she thought of Emperor Muyang with his beautiful dark eyes and the sinister smile on his cold face. "None of this is enough to sway me. I'm not so easy of a woman to be ... to be—" Her lower lip wobbled and she was all too aware that Lanfen was staring at her wide-eyed and that the mage was gravely silent. "To be put under a spell by the riches His Majesty has to offer. I don't need all of that! What I need is my family and my freedom, none of which he will ever offer me. I may be a simple farmer's girl, but I am not so blinded by the brightness of this palace to lose sight of what's important to me. So no, my original plan has *not* changed."

The back of her eyes stung with tears that threatened to spill, but she blinked rapidly to keep them at bay. She wasn't one to cry so easily—and especially not in front of a stranger and her younger sister—so she squared her shoulders and tried to appear as in control of the situation as possible.

Feiyu hadn't moved from his position and it maddened her that she couldn't see his face to determine what his expression was or what he was thinking, but he finally released a long breath and said, "I understand. So what will you do now? I can take you both away now, if you wish."

"Why would you help us?" Lanfen interjected, giving the strange man a once-over. "If you're working with the emperor, what do you gain from this?"

"Your sister and I already have a prior arrangement."

Daiyu had almost forgotten the favor she had promised him, and uneasiness spread over her chest at the thought of being indebted to this mysterious mage, but the bigger part of her reasoned that she needed him more than he needed her. If it wasn't for him, she wouldn't have gotten this far, so surely whatever favor he had in mind for her couldn't be that hard to fulfill? At least she hoped so.

She could feel Lanfen's sharp gaze on her as if asking her what exactly she had traded for his help, but Daiyu simply cleared her throat and said, "Well, although I would love for you to take both of us home, I'm afraid I'm in a bit of a bind now that the emperor knows my name and face. I don't think he would take too kindly for me to insult him by running away." She paced in the room, her rounded silk slippers padding softly against the intricately woven rugs and polished tiles. "Since he doesn't know about Lanfen, I think it would be best if you took her back home—"

"What?" Lanfen jumped to her feet, her dark eyes the size of saucers. She adamantly shook her head. "I'm not leaving you—"

"It's for your own safety." Daiyu crossed the distance between them and held her younger sister's hands gently. Unshed tears shone in Lanfen's eyes and Daiyu's chest tightened at the sight. So long as Lanfen could escape back home, it was worth coming here, even if it meant falling into a sticky trap. "This place is dangerous, and the longer you stay, the harder it'll be to remain safe. You need to go back home, or else all of this will be in vain." She brushed back the stray tear that rolled down her round cheek. "I know it's not easy, but I came here to rescue you, Lanfen, and I need to know you're safe back home. I can't have you attracting the emperor's attention."

Lanfen opened her mouth, clamped it shut, and then tried again. "I don't want to leave you here."

"I'll find a way to escape too, and then we'll be together again." She smiled, even as her throat closed up at the thought of them being apart again. Truthfully, she had no idea how she would escape from the emperor's clutches, but Lanfen didn't need to know that. "Just like how I made my way here, I'll make my way back out."

Lanfen pulled Daiyu into a tight embrace and buried her face into her shoulder. Her small body quivered and her voice was muffled as she spoke. "I wish we could leave together. It's not fair."

"I know, I know." She patted her back slowly. Suddenly, she was reminded back to when they were younger and Daiyu would hug her small body and rock her to sleep when their mother was too tired to console her after a long day of working in the rice paddies. The back of Daiyu's eyes burned and she squeezed her tightly as if that could make her stay longer.

"Do you wish for me to take her now?" Feiyu rose from his seat and brushed the nonexistent dust from his clothes.

"Yes." Daiyu pulled back from the embrace and gave an encouraging nod to Lanfen, who wiped her red eyes and nose on her sleeve. "Are you able to take her to our village?"

"Sadly, I can't. I must remain close to the palace grounds at all times," he said. "But I can warp her out of this palace and give her passage back to your home. Will that suffice?"

Daiyu didn't like the idea of trusting him so much like this. What if he instead kidnapped Lanfen? Or sent her somewhere else? Or ... Or sold her? But then again, keeping her here was a terrible fate in and of itself. Not only was the emperor her enemy here in the palace, but all the ladies and potential concubines would no doubt make her life harder.

"Is there any way you can do some sort of magic to keep your word?" Daiyu asked. "I find it hard to trust you so blindly."

Something flashed in his dark, glittering eyes, and all at once, Daiyu became aware that she was in the presence of a powerful mage. Her mouth dried up at the shift in the air. Had she offended him? But as soon as the change happened, it disappeared.

She blinked back, unsure if she had imagined it all.

"You'll just have to trust me," he said with a cheerful inflection in his velvety voice. "If I wanted to, I could turn you both into rabbits right now or electrify you on the spot, but I haven't done any such thing, now, have I? If I truly had ill intentions for either of you, I could very well do whatever I wish. So, Daiyu, you'll just have to trust me that I will send your sister safely on her way home."

Lanfen shivered beside Daiyu, and although what he was saying was true—that if he wanted to overpower them, he could very well do it with or without their cooperation—she couldn't help the unease that washed over her at those words. At the sheer power he held and how powerless she was.

Daiyu exhaled deeply. "I apologize if I've offended you, Great Mage. I would very much appreciate if you could send my sister on her way home."

"No need for such politeness." Feiyu held his hand out to Lanfen, who inched closer to Daiyu and didn't seem keen on going with him. "Come now, let's go."

"It's okay." Daiyu nudged Lanfen toward the mage. "You'll be fine."

Lanfen reluctantly stepped forward, gave Daiyu an uncertain glance, and placed her hand in Feiyu's.

For a moment, Daiyu wanted to step forward and call the whole thing off—surely, it would be better to have Lanfen on her side while she navigated the strange palace and her place here? And yet, she remained rooted in place, her tongue stuck to the roof of her mouth, and her eyes drinking in Lanfen's image like it would be the last time.

An electrifying charge shifted in the room and before Daiyu could say anything, Lanfen and Feiyu disappeared in a flash.

Daiyu blinked, and she was suddenly alone in the room. It had happened so fast that she couldn't do anything but stare at the spot they had just been at.

She prayed she had made the right decision in trusting the mage.

7

For the next three days, Daiyu didn't hear from Feiyu about Lanfen's whereabouts; in fact, she didn't see the mage at all. She had been locked inside her room, unable to leave, and her only interaction with people was the handful of maids who would bring in her food, help her change clothes, and who set up a bath for her. Anytime she tried to talk to any of them, they gave her the cold shoulder and didn't indulge her in any information about what would happen next.

It wasn't until one afternoon where Daiyu was lounging on one of the many couches in her suite that a series of knocks had her jumping to her feet.

"His Majesty has summoned you to his quarters," a booming male voice called through the set of double doors.

All the color drained from her face. Why would the emperor want her in his quarters? Was he going to sleep with her, abuse her, or had he heard of her plans of escape? Would he torture her? A million morbid ideas flitted through her mind and she wanted nothing more than to run as far away from this place as possible— but that was impossible.

So she squared her shoulders, brushed a shaky hand over the pale gold and sage dress she had on, fixed the honey-colored hairpins in her hair, and left her room, where a palace guard gave her a small nod and they walked her down the winding, polished halls. Her heart hammered in her chest to a wild tune. This was a good thing, she told herself. She'd be able to find a way to escape, surely? Perhaps the emperor was going to tell her that he had made a mistake in choosing her—a very obvious commoner—and was letting her go? Or, more logically, she could find a weakness of his to extort and exchange for her freedom? No, that would surely end in her death.

Her jumbled thoughts came to a stumbling halt when the guard stopped outside a grand set of gilded doors and rapped his knuckles gently on the embossed surface. "Your Majesty," he said. "She's here."

Daiyu's palms suddenly became slick and she wiped them on the sides of her dress, her gaze darting from the door to the end of the hallway. All she had to do was stay quiet, smile, and act docile, she told herself. So long as she didn't do anything outrightly rude, the emperor shouldn't find a problem with her ... Right?

And if she acted boring enough, there was a sure chance that he would toss her aside for someone more suited for him?

"Come in." She recognized the smooth, authoritative voice.

The guard yanked the door open and motioned her inside. Without wasting another breath, Daiyu sauntered inside, head low. It wasn't until the door shut behind her that she peeked inside the room. The emperor sat on the floor in front of a low table with an assortment of roasted meat, fried vegetables in hearty broth, and sticky white rice. A servant poured tea from a kettle into his cup, which he held in his palm loosely.

Drakkon Muyang's hair was undone, so unlike the polished version of him she had seen just days ago. Vibrant purple robes covered his body entirely, and gold flashed over his wrists and neck, and a jade-encrusted sword was laid in front of him next to his platter of food.

Upon seeing her, a small smile curved along the corners of his soft mouth, and it was only then that Daiyu remembered to drop to her knees in a bow. Her body went rigid and her insides felt like they were quivering.

"Greetings, Your Majesty," she whispered, her chest tightening with apprehension. This was the famed emperor said to have killed hundreds of thousands of innocent people. Who was rumored to have killed one of the princesses because she refused to bow to him. Who was said to be part demon.

And she was in his presence for the third time—she should've been considered lucky she was still alive at this point.

Muyang watched her for a moment, and Daiyu forced her face down, unable to meet his dark eyes. Her legs grew numb and a tingling sensation ran down her calves. A cold shiver ran over her body, and she wasn't sure if it was from being under his scrutiny or from nervousness of what was to come. She licked her chapped lips to moisten them. She was teetering on the edge of flight or fight—and both would sign her death.

He was too powerful, and evil, and *beautiful*, she reasoned. A combination that made her heart race like a prey caught in a spider's web.

"You may rise."

She jerked herself up, and her stiff legs complied. She placed her hands behind her back and tried to keep her gaze on anything but him—to the brilliant scarlet pillars erected throughout the room, to the hexagonal caisson ceiling with a dragon looping toward the center, the lush rugs with gold and emerald threads, and then to the table of food.

The servant in the room bowed low and drifted to one end of the room, where she kneeled, likely if the emperor needed anything from her. Meanwhile, Daiyu remained stuck in position by the door.

Muyang picked up his silver chopsticks and then a piece of roasted venison from his plate. He ate it quietly, and Daiyu could feel his cold gaze lingering on her, and it took all her strength to avoid his eyes.

Staring the emperor in the eyes could get her killed, after all.

"I called you here to have a meal together." His voice came out clipped and devoid of emotion, so unlike the amused tone he had used in their previous encounter. Gone was the curious man and in his place was someone cold—so very cold that she shook where she stood. "If I wanted you to stand in the corner, shivering like a fawn, I would have called forth another maid to decorate the wall. Come forward and *sit*."

Daiyu's legs moved on their own and she eased down onto the cushion across from him. Her stomach growled as the smells of garlicky meat, ginger, spices, and soy sauce pervaded the room, even as her appetite fled from her.

"Must I tell you to eat too?" he said, his voice growing more detached—more *bored*—and almost like he was losing patience with her.

This time, Daiyu lifted her head and she inhaled sharply as those black eyes were set on her. Something dark and sinister seemed to reflect off the obsidian void lying there, and she quickly averted herself to stare at her empty porcelain bowl.

She found her voice, though it came out in a squeak. "Thank you for the invitation, Your Majesty."

He didn't bother acknowledging her response and instead picked up a chicken drumstick and bit into it. His free hand thumbed the dark ruby cast inside the hilt of his jade sword. It reminded her of blood for some reason, and another tremor ran down her body. There was no reason to have a weapon at the table—especially not in front of someone like her.

Unless he doubted her.

The hairs on the back of her neck stood straight and she stiffly reached for the closest dish to her—stir-fried spinach doused in a brown sauce with diced garlic and red peppers—and filled her bowl. If she didn't eat, or annoyed him further, she was sure he would lop her head off right then and there. He must have been testing her, and by the way he was growing more bored of her—she feared she was failing.

She piled sticky white rice into her bowl and ate the food

silently. She barely tasted the rich sauces of the meal or the soft, chewy rice.

"How are you enjoying your stay at the palace?" He was watching her again, and this time she couldn't stop herself from meeting his gaze. Every pore in her body froze. There was a coldness about him that made him appear undead. A power that clung to him that made even the weight of his stare feel like cloying death. "You said you would love to become my concubine because of this *wonderful* palace, didn't you? Well, are you enjoying it?" His words came out in a sneer, and she realized she had offended him.

"I-I—" She couldn't formulate any words, and the room seemed to disappear altogether until it was just the two of them and his shiny sword sitting way too close to her. "Th-the palace is beautiful, but I've been confined to only my room. Um, I ... I hope I didn't offend you, Your Majesty?"

"Offend me?" He narrowed his eyes and then leaned back. "Of course not. Though it isn't every day that I'm met with a woman who's honest in her interest of my possessions rather than me."

She waited for him to reach for his sword and aim it at her—her body erect with anticipation—but he didn't. He continued to eat, his attention never straying from her.

Daiyu shoveled more food into her mouth. Maybe the faster she ate, the faster this entire ordeal would be over. She had hated the boring, monotonous stay in her palace room, but now she wanted nothing more than to run there and hide under the covers.

"Yin Daiyu, who are you?"

When she raised her head, she froze when the pointed edge of a dagger was inches from her face. Muyang's elbow was propped on the low table, and his chin rested on his closed fist, while he held the dagger precariously with his other hand. He appeared unbothered, uninterested, and wholly untrusting as he watched her with narrowed, obsidian-like eyes.

"I requested to find more information about you, little *rabbit*." There was a teasing quality in his voice, like he seemed to take delight in the fear that suddenly swamped her. "But then I came up blank. All the records we have of the women who were brought to my palace show that there is, in fact, *no* Yin Daiyu."

Daiyu couldn't rip her gaze from the dangerous glint of the dagger's blade. She felt like if she breathed, it would be her last.

"That either tells me that you're lying about who you are"— the cold tip of the dagger touched her throat, and he gently traced the column of her neck up—"or that you're a spy sent here to kill me. Which is it?"

The dagger dug into her throat and she gasped abruptly as sharp pain pricked her. She could feel the bead of warm blood running down her neck, and he followed the trail it created, his eyes growing impossibly dark.

"Th-There must be a mistake," she whispered, tears of fear filling her eyes suddenly. Her breathing became erratic as he moved the blade down further until it touched the lapel of her dress. "I—"

"A mistake?" Muyang chuckled, and a wave of wild, chaotic, and sinister energy seemed to reverberate from the small gesture. "That wasn't one of the options I gave you."

"Please! I know there's a mistake," she rushed, just as the edge of the blade touched her sternum between her breasts. She breathed in, her chest rising with the motion, and he stared down at her uninterestedly. "My sister was originally supposed to be taken, but I swapped places with her before she arrived at the palace. Believe me, I'm telling the truth," she said in a quick sentence. "You should have her information in the records. Yin Lanfen. Look her up, *please*."

He paused his tracing and scrutinized her coldly, and for a moment, she was afraid he wouldn't believe her small lie, but then his attention flickered to the servant on one side of the room— who Daiyu had completely forgotten was there. He gave her a nod, and the woman pulled out a scroll from her sleeve.

"If you're lying," he murmured, his beautiful voice lulling between seductive smoothness and a feral coldness, "your heart would make a beautiful adornment in my collection."

Daiyu's lower lip trembled. "I'm telling the truth."

The only noise between them was the unfurling of paper as the maidservant expanded the scroll further. Muyang kept the dagger on her chest, and he watched the rise and fall of her breasts with something akin to untamed desire—the first sign of interest he had shown her. She didn't even want to think about what he was thinking—about slicing her chest open and ripping her heart out.

Finally, the maidservant spoke. "I don't see a Yin Lanfen—"

Daiyu's blood ran cold.

"Ah? No Yin Lanfen?" Muyang's mouth curved up and the tip of the dagger pressed into the bony part of her sternum. "You—"

"Oh!" The maidservant squinted at the paper. "Forgive me, Your Majesty. I missed it in my haste, but yes, we do have a Yin Lanfen here."

Daiyu couldn't even breathe in relief because the emperor hadn't eased his blade from her. He blinked as if not expecting that answer, and then he retracted his blade ever so slowly. And even then, she didn't relax—she couldn't.

"Which village are you from?" he asked.

"H-Hanzi."

Again, he turned to the servant, who bobbed her head in confirmation as she read from the scroll.

Muyang sighed as if disappointed and slid his black dagger—with a curling dragon over the hilt—into its sheath. "Well then," he murmured, reaching forward for his cup of tea and taking a sip casually. "It appears you're truthful."

Daiyu's shoulders trembled and she bunched her hands together on her lap. No matter what she did, she couldn't stop herself from quivering. She had never felt such raw, primal pressure before. Such closeness to death that she could taste iron in her mouth.

"Eat." He motioned to her food and Daiyu stared at him dumbly, unable to make out what he meant. "Come now, we haven't finished our meal. So *eat*."

She picked up her chopsticks numbly, and the shaking grew so bad that she couldn't pick at any of her food. Muyang watched with mild amusement and continued his meal as if he hadn't tried to kill her seconds ago.

"It suits you," he said.

"H-Huh?" Daiyu looked at him and wished she hadn't. There was something cruel about his cold, vicious beauty. She had once heard her mother say that evil sometimes cloaked itself in beauty to entice its prey—and in this moment, she could see that he was the embodiment of that statement.

Muyang reached forward and she flinched when he touched her neck, but she didn't dare lean away from him. He dragged his finger along her throat and teased at the neckline—as if he would trace even lower—before pulling his hand away. A streak of her blood smeared his digit and he brought it to his mouth.

She watched with mounting horror as he licked her blood. "Red suits you."

The rest of the meal continued painstakingly slow, and Daiyu could barely choke down her food. It wasn't until the emperor dismissed her that she could finally breathe. When she nearly ran out of the room, she could feel his gaze lingering on her back, and she felt even more vulnerable.

But there was one thing that was sure in her mind—surer than anything she had ever felt in her life—she needed to escape from this palace and his clutches. Because if she remained here, she was certain she would not survive.

8

Early the next morning, Daiyu paced her room hastily, the rug muffling her steps. She was dressed in a beautiful powder blue dress with a pale-yellow sash that washed her out, and although the clothing was beautiful, she felt like an imposter. Like she didn't belong, and she truly didn't.

When she caught sight of herself in the mirror—of the gauze wrapped around her throat—she shuddered to think of Muyang and the cruelty he had displayed. Her hand touched the hollow of her throat and she suppressed another shiver.

She still hadn't seen Feiyu and these past few days—especially after yesterday's disastrous meal with the emperor—showed her that she badly needed an ally. But the masked mage hadn't made an appearance at all, and she felt utterly alone.

She needed to find an escape plan. Muyang knew which village she was from, so he could very easily find her family and murder them if she fled now. Which filled her with more anxiety and anger at herself. Yesterday had shown her that Muyang didn't know *exactly* who she was, and that meant if she had left with Lanfen a few days ago, he wouldn't have been able to track her. But she had fumbled her plan, and now she was stuck here.

What could she do to escape? Fake her death and flee? Make

the emperor grow bored with her? But the latter seemed dangerous—what if he killed her because she didn't interest him anymore?

Her mind grew more tangled and she kicked the corner of her couch's leg in frustration. A jolt of pain shot through her ankle and shin, and she hissed in pain. Flopping down on the cushions in frustration, she covered her face with a perfumed pillow, wanting to scream into it but holding herself back.

Tears burned the back of her eyes and she blinked them away quickly. She was just a simple farmer's daughter. How had she gotten caught up in all of this? She wasn't even the type to aspire for greatness, or to have ambitions like wooing the emperor, but here she was, plopped into a position that many women would kill for. And yet it appeared like she would die *because* of it.

For a while, she just lay on the couch, staring up at the square coffered ceiling of her room—each sunken indent containing a design of a dragon curling within itself. Everywhere she looked, something reminded her of the emperor's reign, whether it was the ceiling with his dragon symbol, the polished tiles beneath her feet that showed the luxury of the palace, or the platters of fruit with dragons etched around the rims.

Daiyu finally pushed herself into a sitting position. She couldn't remain here and feel sorry for herself. She didn't know when she would see Feiyu—or if she would ever see him again—so she needed to have a backup plan for when she would escape this place.

She jumped to her feet and hurried to the doorway. She placed her hands on the ornate doors but hesitated when she imagined Muyang's beautiful face twisted in suspicion at her. What if he thought it was strange for her to be loitering around the palace like a common thief? What if he still thought she was a spy? Would it be better to stay here?

No, she thought. If she remained, there was a good chance she would never leave this place. She needed a plan, and she needed to act, even if it meant drawing the emperor's suspicion.

Her mind made up, Daiyu pushed open the door and slipped into the hallway. The guard who was assigned to her door straightened and gave her a surprised look.

"My lady," he said, blinking at her like he hadn't seen her before. "You're not allowed—"

"Can't I wander the halls of the palace if I'm to be the emperor's wife?" Daiyu asked with a small smile, hoping she appeared innocent. When the guard frowned, she continued, "Surely, it won't hurt to walk for a bit so long as I have you by my side? I doubt His Majesty will care if I decide to cease my boredom by exploring this grand place. Don't you agree?"

The guard—a young man with a mop of black hair and round eyes—shifted on his feet uneasily. "I'm not sure ..." he said after another pause. "His Majesty didn't give me any direct orders ..."

"And so he didn't explicitly say to keep me locked in here, did he?" She jerked a thumb at her door and kept a cheery expression on her face. She prayed he allowed her to leave, even if it meant he was trailing behind her the whole time. "Come now, I'm bored and there's no one to talk to, so I'd love to wander the halls and the gardens. I'm sure His Majesty won't mind."

He swallowed, and finally, after another moment of awkward silence, he nodded. "I ... I suppose it wouldn't hurt."

"Excellent! How about you lead me to the royal gardens? I've heard wondrous stories of how magnificent they are." Daiyu ambled down the hall while the guard walked in front of her. He kept a tight grip on the shaft of his spear, his knuckles white with pressure. Daiyu briefly wondered if he was nervous to be with her, or if it was because he was straying from his usual duty of guarding her door.

As they continued through the halls, Daiyu kept track of where they were going and how many twists and turns they took. Her mind became jumbled with the many identical, polished corridors, but she tried to remember the intricate octagonal windows, tapestries, and different colors of each hall—something that made it stand out and would be easy to remember.

When they passed through a hallway with circular windows with delicate lattice work and, upon closer inspection, a snake and moon design around the circumference of it, Daiyu slowed in her steps. The snake and moon were the symbol of the previous MuRong dynasty, which Drakkon Muyang had overthrown. She would've thought that all signs of that dynasty would've been wiped from this palace when he took over four years ago.

The guard opened one of the doorways and more light flooded the passageway. He gave her a small nod. "This is the north entrance of the gardens. Unfortunately, you're only allowed in this part of the gardens, unless the emperor gives direct orders to allow you to the rest of the royal gardens."

She bobbed her head. "How many different sections of the gardens are there?"

"Four or five," he answered with a shrug as they stepped outside.

Birds tweeted above them and Daiyu breathed in the smell of jasmine, peonies, and sweet plum blossoms. Sprawling trees heavy with fruits and pink blossoms, beds of colorful orchids, and bushes of roses and lilacs surrounded them in thickets. From afar, she could see the stone benches, ponds full of colorful koi fish, animal statues, and stone pergolas embossed with designs she couldn't make out from the distance. For a moment, Daiyu could only pause and stare in awe. She hadn't expected to step into something straight from a fairy tale.

"My lady?" The guard turned to her with a curious, concerned expression. At seeing her stunned look, he glanced at the garden, clearly not as impressed as she was. "Shall we continue?"

"I ... Yes." Daiyu hurried after him as they strolled deeper. She almost forgot about her escape plan as she took in the sights of butterflies, dragonflies, birds, and flora.

Between gawping at colorful fish swimming in clear streams and searching for potential routes she could take, they went through the gardens slowly. She made a mental map and kept track of places she could potentially hide—like behind the benches, or the thickets of trees and bushes.

"Are there many guards here?" Daiyu asked as they passed two more guards, who barely gave them a side glance.

"Ah, yes. Since this is an open courtyard, we have to be careful that spies or intruders don't sneak in here."

"Oh? Is there a way to get inside here?"

He gave her a strange look, and Daiyu clamped her mouth shut. Was that too on the nose?

"Well, if they can climb up to the roofs." He shrugged and pointed to the curved roofs on one side. "The only other way is if they're already in the palace, but I don't see why they would want to enter here then."

A frown tugged at her lips. If this was a courtyard-style garden, then that meant she couldn't escape through the gardens.

"My lady, I think that's enough of a walk for today," the guard said, pausing as if to turn around.

She opened her mouth to protest, but something caught her attention at the edge of her vision. A trio of women were walking her way, and she recognized the woman in the middle. What was her name again? Jia?

The trio slowed when they noticed her, and the woman leading the pack tilted her head to the side at the sight of Daiyu. Her doe-like brown eyes widened and she snapped her fingers. "Oh!" the woman said. "I remember you!"

Daiyu smiled uncertainly. She was the woman who had helped lead her to the Lotus wing when she had been looking for Lanfen. "Ah, hello."

"Good morning, Lady Jia." The guard straightened and lowered his head in respect.

Jia nodded at him, then eyed the fine dress Daiyu was wearing, a crease forming between her painted eyebrows. "Weren't you ... a servant back then?"

Daiyu laced her hands together to keep them from fidgeting. "Actually, no. And I'm ... well, I'm in a strange position, to say the least." She laughed uncomfortably, and the other two women with Jia leaned forward to inspect her.

"A strange position?" one of the women asked.

The other woman raised her brows. "You ... You aren't possibly the woman His Majesty chose, are you?"

Jia gasped and gave Daiyu another once-over. "Oh, you are, aren't you?"

When Daiyu nodded, the three women exchanged surprised looks with one another. Jia stepped forward and took Daiyu's hands in her own, an excited jitter around her. "Oh, you must tell me *everything*! How did His Majesty choose you? *Why* did he choose you?" She giggled and turned to one of the women to her side. "You know he hasn't chosen anyone in years, so we're all so very curious about what you did!"

"Are you three ... here for the royal selection?" Daiyu asked.

Jia's eyes widened. "Oh, heavens, *no*. I'm already a married woman, and these two ladies here are my maidservants, Chun and Ying."

Chun and Ying bobbed their heads at the introduction.

"My husband is in a meeting with His Majesty, so I have a few hours to kill here. And anyway, what better way to spend the time than to hear about how you bewitched the emperor? You must tell us *everything*!" Jia looped her arm in Daiyu's and led her down one of the paths.

Daiyu could do nothing but be dragged by the giggling flock while her guard trailed behind them silently. She didn't particularly like the term *bewitched* and could only wonder what people had heard about her. Unease weighed on her chest, but it was probably better to converse with these people, especially since Jia seemed to be a noble lady, or someone of high importance if her husband was having a meeting with the emperor. Maybe she could get information out of her?

When they went inside a pergola by the lake, they all sat on the stone benches and began talking at once, asking her how and when she met Muyang.

Daiyu traced the crane carvings in the seat and picked at the debris indented in the lines. "W-Well," she said as the women leaned in closer to her. "It was nothing special, really. I came here —" She licked her lips, tasting the bitter cosmetic used to paint them red. It probably wasn't wise to tell them the truth, so she went with what she told the emperor. "I came here instead of my sister, and the emperor seemed to notice me and picked me. I didn't do anything special." She omitted the part about how she had accidentally bumped into him in his bathing chambers, as that didn't seem appropriate, and the last thing she wanted was rumors floating about how she had seduced the emperor.

A cool summer breeze wafted over them, carrying the sweet, floral scent of peonies and chrysanthemums. Daiyu noticed a small, spotted bird perched on one of the railings of the pergola and wondered briefly if there were eyes and ears everywhere. The emperor was known to have a plethora of mages under him— were even the birds listening in on her conversation? And were these women also the ears of the emperor?

She shivered, but not from the cold, and smiled stiffly at Jia, who was nearly bouncing on her seat with excitement.

"He must have fallen in love at first sight!" Jia said with a small squeal, while the other two girls tittered like chirping birds.

Daiyu momentarily touched the soft gauze on her neck and suppressed a shudder. She remembered Muyang's dark eyes and the pure enjoyment on his face as he drew her blood. There was no way a man like him could ever fall in love. And certainly not with her.

"I don't think it was *love* at first sight," she said with another nervous laugh. "I think he decided on a whim to choose me. I haven't the slightest idea why."

"There must be a reason." Jia smoothed down her soft pink dress with embroidered vines and flowers running along the sleeves and skirts. "From what I know of His Majesty, he isn't one to do something so random, and besides, he's had women in the palace for this selection for years, and he hasn't chosen anyone until now. There must be something you did to invoke his interest."

The last part came out as more of a question than a statement, and Jia watched her expectantly, but Daiyu didn't have an answer for her. She instead studied her silk shoes and pressed her lips together. Why did the emperor choose her? She truly didn't have an idea. Other than blubbering at him with flimsy lies in his bathing chambers, she hadn't done anything warranting a *marriage* between them.

"I wonder if this means the emperor will choose more women to be his concubines?" Chun mused. "If he's already chosen you, then he must be thinking of choosing others? I think it's about time. People were wondering why no one was good enough for him."

"I'm just surprised he chose *you.*" Ying gave her an apologetic look while Chun chuckled. "I mean no offense, but you're a commoner, aren't you? I can tell—" She gestured to Daiyu's hands, which were still tan from her work in the rice paddies, so unlike her face, which appeared pale due to all the white powders the maidservants had forced on her.

"I mean, we all thought Lady Yanlin would be chosen—" Chun began.

"Hush now, no need to talk about her," Jia said with a frown.

"But, my lady, it's true. Yanlin is beautiful, comes from a powerful and wealthy family, so of course it makes one wonder ..." Chun lifted her shoulders and stared at Daiyu strangely as if she truly did believe she had done something strange to entrap the emperor. "Not to mention all the other noble women who've come to the palace and have been either turned down or kept here for months and months. It's just so strange."

A blush of embarrassment warmed her cheeks and Daiyu clasped her hands together on her lap. "I ... I truly didn't do anything special."

Jia crossed her arms over her chest. "Well, I think you're just as beautiful as the rest, noble woman or not, so there really is no need to bring others into this." She frowned at Chun, who lowered her gaze. "None of us here know what the emperor is thinking, so we'll just have to chalk it up to love at first sight. At least that's what I believe. There's no other explanation."

An awkward silence filled the space between them, and Daiyu could only stare at the birds and colorful fish whirling in the pond. She didn't even know what to ask without sounding too suspicious. She doubted she could ask these three on how to leave this place, and with how much the two servants had been giggling, they seemed to be the gossiping type. She had to be careful with what she said.

"Have any of you interacted with the mages in the palace?" she asked, keeping her eyes wide, innocent, and simply curious. "I've heard they're highly dangerous. Is this true?"

Jia blinked rapidly as if not expecting that question. "Truthfully, I've never conversed with any of them, but they're mages. So naturally, they're powerful and mysterious."

"I try to avoid them." Ying shifted in her seat. "You never know what they know, and what they can do."

"I've seen a masked mage recently in the palace. Do you know anything about him?" Daiyu asked. It wasn't that she didn't trust Feiyu, but she wasn't completely sold on him and what he wanted from her. "He wears different masks from time to time—"

"Oh, you mean Feiyu?" Jia asked. "He's the head mage of the palace. I think he wears the mask to keep his identity a secret? Though I don't know why he needs to keep it a secret. He's powerful enough to end his enemies, right? Since he's a mage?" Jia seemed to be asking them, and yet she seemed lost in thought, her lower lip jutting out. "My husband doesn't really talk about him, even though they both serve directly under His Majesty."

"Why do you ask?" Chun tilted her head to watch her.

"No reason, just curiosity." Daiyu smiled. She hadn't gotten anything useful out of this conversation, other than confirming her suspicions that Feiyu was strange and that the emperor was even stranger. "Since I'll be in the palace more often, I thought it would be appropriate to familiarize myself with the people here."

"You're likely only going to remain in the inner palace, though," Chun continued with a frown. "In the Lotus wing, most likely, since that's where all the emperor's women are kept. And I'm sure His Majesty will now start choosing more women. It'll become more crowded in the coming weeks, I'm sure."

"That would be for the best," she muttered. She would rather Muyang's attention be on other women than her.

"Really? You don't feel jealous?" Ying asked. "I know I certainly would feel that way—"

"That's enough." Jia gave the two servants a stern look. "I really don't think you both need to be making her uneasy like that."

"Oh, I'm fine," Daiyu answered, raising her hands. "It's only natural the emperor will choose more women to become his concubines or his wives. I certainly won't be the last."

Or the first, she hoped.

Their conversation drifted to another topic, and soon, Daiyu found herself nodding and forcing a laugh at mundane things like the weather and court gossip about people she didn't know. And by the end of their chat, she was thoroughly exhausted and no closer to an escape plan than she had been an hour earlier.

9

DAIYU WAS GROWING MORE AND MORE BORED AT THE palace. She left her room any chance she got and explored as much of the hallways as she could while staving suspicion, but no matter how many paths she memorized, she was only allowed in the inner palace, which seemed to be deep in the palace and where most of the women were supposedly kept. Anytime she skirted the edges of the inner corridors, her guard would always lead her back inside, never allowing her to venture into the various other parts of the palace.

During the nights, her boredom worsened since she had nowhere to go, and the little activities she was allowed—poetry, books, and writing—were completely useless to her since she couldn't read or write.

The logs in her hearth in her chambers rumbled to life as a maidservant fed more fuel to them. Daiyu watched the woman with mild interest; she had tried befriending the servants, but they either ignored her or gave her snide looks. Nobody seemed happy to have her here. Which only made her wonder why the emperor was even interested in her.

"Thank you for that," Daiyu said when the servant backed

away from the roaring flames. "The nights grow chilly, so I appreciate it."

"Of course, my lady," the woman said quietly, stiffly.

She walked over to the tea table and poured a cup for her. "Would you like your tea now or after you undress, my lady?"

"Now would be fine," she said, since the lady had already poured the cup. She had already washed all the cosmetics off her face and undid the various hairpins from her hair, so she didn't need any more help. "What's your name?"

"My name is of no importance." The woman placed the tea in front of Daiyu on the table and stepped away, giving a small bow. "If that is all, I'd like to take my leave."

"Ah, yes, of course." Daiyu tried smiling at the woman, but she was already heading to the door. Her smile faded as the door clicked shut, and she leaned back into her couch, her shoulders slumping. She hadn't realized how lonely and dark her days and nights would be. She could understand why the servants were so rigid around her—most of the servants came from lesser important noble families—and they likely hated that they had to serve someone who was so beneath them in status. She was just a simple farmer's daughter. Nobody special, and yet the emperor was bent on propping her up and making her something she wasn't.

She rubbed her aching temples and reached for her tea. Her hands warmed instantly around the porcelain cup and she brought it to her mouth. It tasted sweet, earthy, and with hints of floral undertones. She sipped it quietly and stared off at the fire, which continued to flicker and bathe the room in an orange glow.

It had been two weeks since Lanfen had left the palace and Daiyu wasn't any closer to escaping. Thankfully, Muyang seemed to be busy with his own work to even ask for her, and she was eternally grateful for it. But she knew it wouldn't take long before he called for her again, and she dreaded how that meeting would go. She also hadn't heard from Feiyu either, which troubled her. Where was he? Why wasn't he informing her about anything?

Black dotted her vision and she blinked back, her eyebrows

coming together in confusion at the sudden surge of exhaustion coursing through her body.

Something ... wasn't right.

Just as she thought that, the back of her throat constricted and she brought a hand to her neck. Her airways tightened and she inhaled sharply, only to feel as though less air was coming through. The cup slipped from her hand and shattered on the floor, tiny shards splintering in every direction as she stumbled to her feet. She didn't even notice the sharp pain as she stepped over the broken pottery and tried to make it to the door.

Her vision continued to wane and she croaked, "H-Help—"

She could barely get the words out.

Her stomach tightened, and salty water filled her mouth. In seconds, she retched on the floor, nearly falling in the process. She held on to the decorative armrest of her couch and heaved in deep breaths, and yet she felt even more breathless.

Was it the tea? Did that servant poison her?

She staggered toward the door, her limbs heavy and her body moving like she was wading through thick syrup. More shadows swamped her vision and her throat closed up even further. Her knees slammed to the hard floor and she barely felt anything as her face cracked against the cold tiles. She clawed at her throat, savoring every tiny wisp of air.

"Help," she whispered weakly, staring at the door that seemed so far away. It seemed to stretch even farther from her as her vision tunneled.

Everything became blacker, like ink was spilling in her eyes and covering the entirety of her vision. Like a dark curtain was pulling in front of her. And she realized in that haunting moment that she would die right here. Alone, and weak, and unable to do anything.

"Feiyu," she managed to breathe out, her voice raspy and faint. "Feiyu—*help.*"

The seconds ticked by and her chest burned. She was like a fish flopping out of water, opening her mouth and trying to breathe. Tears streamed down her stinging eyes, further clouding her vision.

All of a sudden, something rustled in her room—clothing maybe—and she heard a hiss of a curse. She could barely open her eyes as someone rushed toward her, their boots clacking against the floor. Warmth touched her chest and then her mouth, then something cool slipped down her throat.

"*Shit*, what happened here?" a familiar voice said, but it came out muffled, like there was a screen covering her ears.

The coolness in her throat persisted, and she inhaled sharply as air filled her airways. She continued to breathe in large gulps of air, and it was only then that she took notice of the snarling black and red dragon staring down at her. She suppressed a scream, only to realize it was Feiyu's mask. He was cradling her in his arms, one hand gently placed on her stomach.

"What ... what are you doing here?" she barely managed to squawk, her throat feeling raw and scratchy.

"Saving your life," he said, his dark eyes boring into her through the sockets in the dragon mask. "You called for me."

Daiyu's stomach churned and she grimaced as waves of nausea rolled over her. "I think I was poisoned."

"It appears like it." He eyed the broken cup a few feet away from her. "Do you know who did it? Or why?"

She shook her head and her stomach clenched again. "I think —I think I'm going to—"

She didn't have time to warn him as she turned her head and emptied the contents of her stomach onto his lap. He stiffened and cursed again while she breathed out shakily, streams of bile and undigested food tracking down her mouth to his thigh.

"S-Sorry," she muttered.

Feiyu propped her into a sitting position, his gaze locked on the vomit staining his once-pristine emerald robes. "I suppose I should have expected that."

"I'm sorry," Daiyu said, her nose crinkling at the sour, fermented scent of her vomit.

He pulled her into his arms in one swoop and rose to his feet. Daiyu stifled a gasp as her hands flew to his broad chest. "Nothing a little water and soap won't fix," he grumbled, walking toward her couch.

A blush spread over her face immediately, and she averted his gaze as he carried her. She could feel the lean muscle of his arms and his chest, and there was a sweet scent that came off him that was mostly covered by the smell of her puke.

He gently laid her down on the couch and pulled away from her to inspect her feet, which had small cuts from the sharp slivers of the broken cup she had stepped on. "Who could have done this?" he asked, gently prodding her feet with curious fingers.

She almost retracted herself into a ball at the sudden touch, had she not noticed the green glow emitting from his hand. Almost at once, the imbedded shards pulled free from her feet and plinked to the floor.

"I don't know." Daiyu leaned her head into the plush pillows. A cooling and healing sensation covered her feet and she closed her eyes. "I didn't realize I had enemies here."

"You suspect the other women?"

"It's possible?" She remembered her conversation with Jia last week and shuddered. "The other women might be jealous that I was chosen, even though they've been here longer. And the emperor hasn't chosen anyone else yet, so I can only suspect it's one of them."

"Hm." The mage removed his hand from her and her eyes flew open at the now-empty feeling. She wanted to reach forward and ask him to continue his healing touch, but the thought sounded absurd to her ears, and her face flushed with warmth. What was wrong with her?

"W-Well." She cleared her sore throat. "I'd like to at least find the maid who gave me the tea. Is there any way you can track her? Like with magic?"

Feiyu nodded slowly, and through the holes of the mask, she could make out a scar on his eyelid. "I can try, but it might take me some time, since many people come and go into your room. What does she look like?"

"Tall." She tried remembering more of the maid, but the woman had kept her head low for most of their interaction. "She was very thin, and I think she had a mole above her eyebrow."

"Are you sure she didn't paint the mole on herself?"

"Why ... why would she do that?"

He shrugged. "The palace maids follow fashion trends, and that is a current trend among the noble ladies. Nonetheless, I will be on the lookout for the maid."

"Thank you," she said, and her throat closed up at the near-death experience. "For ... for also saving my life."

"I've neutralized the poison in your body, so you should be fine in a few hours."

"I said thank you," she said again.

This time, he chuckled, his broad chest rumbling with the motion. "Don't mention it. It makes me feel awkward."

"Why? Because you did something heroic?"

"Saving a damsel in distress? I *am* a hero, aren't I? I suppose I should bask in this feeling for longer. It appears you're indebted to me once again." There was a teasing quality in his voice and Daiyu wanted to laugh along with him, but she found she was bone-weary and unable to muster even a short giggle. So she only smiled, hoping he understood her sentiment.

Her limbs felt heavy and she could only lie there. "I don't like being indebted to a mage."

"I'm not going to steal your soul or anything." His gaze suddenly became serious and his voice dropped an octave. "You know that, right?"

She wondered briefly if he was frowning beneath his mask, but she found she didn't want to know. She didn't want to face whatever expression he wore because she was certain it was a tender one. Daiyu coughed and asked instead, "Did Lanfen make it back safe? I've been wanting to ask you for so long and if I had known it was this easy to summon you, I would have called for you much earlier."

"Always the caring sister," he tutted, taking a step away from her to inspect his ruined clothes. "She's safe and back home. I would have told you sooner, but I've been busy. There is an uprising, you know, so everyone here is swamped with work. And more so me, since I work directly under His Majesty."

There had been quite a few revolts since Muyang took over the empire four years ago, and although he had quelled them, they kept recurring, and some people were calling for the MuRong princes to take their rightful place on the throne.

In the midst of her boring palace stay, it was easy to forget that Feiyu had other things to do than to cater to her plans of escape. Deep down, she knew that, but considering how she had nothing else to focus on but herself, it was hard to realize that she was likely just a small smidge of a thought to him. And for some reason, she didn't like that.

Shaking her head from those thoughts, she rested a hand on her clammy forehead. "Do you think there's a way to make the emperor forget all about me?"

Feiyu tilted his head. "You wish to erase yourself from his memory?"

"It's the only way I can think of where he'll leave me alone," she said. "I've tried to think of how to escape, but even if I leave, it won't change that he knows where to find me and my family. Who's to say he won't murder us all for denying him? He's known to be bloodthirsty and insane—" Her lips curled into a sneer as she said those words, and the memory of Muyang's dark eyes on her as he placed the dagger on her throat surfaced. She shivered and held her arms closer to herself. "It's the only way I can leave without much of a trace."

"Unfortunately, I can't do that."

She jerked her head up. "What?"

"I can't do that." He shook his head and took another step back, creating more distance between them. "I can help you with many things, but treason isn't one of them. I think you've forgotten that I work *directly* under His Majesty. Tampering with his memories is one of the greatest acts of betrayal and I refuse to take part in it."

Daiyu's chest tightened with his words and even though what he was saying wasn't wrong, per se, it stung to hear his refusal. It was also another door shutting for her escape plan, and she felt even more confined than before. As if she were a small bird stuck in a gilded, beautiful cage.

"W-Well ... that's unfortunate." The tremor in her voice betrayed her hurt and disappointment, and she stared at the streaks of red on his dragon-mask that appeared too much like blood. Too much like Muyang's cursed reign. "Will you be reporting this to His Majesty?"

Feiyu clasped his hands behind his back and Daiyu held her breath as he paused to answer her. "Which part? The poisoning or the potential thoughts of treason?"

"Both." Her throat felt tight once more, and it wasn't because of the poison this time, but because she had foolishly thought to trust this man for a moment. She couldn't forget that he worked under His Majesty, and for all she knew, would conspire against her if she did anything out of line. Like even *thinking* of tinkering with the emperor's memories of her.

Feiyu was quiet for a moment too long. "I will inform him about your poisoning, as is my duty, but I won't mention anything else."

"And how will you explain how you came across me?" With how her last meeting with Muyang had gone, she was sure he still held some wariness toward her, and he would likely find it *very* suspicious that she was in contact with his head mage.

"I'll say I found you in the hallway outside your room nearly choking on your own vomit."

"A wonderful picture that paints," she grumbled. "Can't you just *not* tell him?"

He canted his head. "Why would you not want him to know?"

"I don't want him ..." Daiyu laughed at where her thoughts were carrying her. Was she stupid enough to think that Muyang would be worried about her if he heard she was poisoned? She doubted it, especially after he had turned a blade on her. "I don't want him to even *think* about me. I have no need for his attention and I'd rather be someone he quickly forgets."

"Unfortunately, since there was a threat to your life, I must tell him." He almost sounded apologetic.

Silence stretched between them until Daiyu motioned to the door. "I'd like to rest for a bit, if you don't mind, and I'm sure you'd like to clean up."

He placed a hand on his chest and lowered his head. "I understand. Good night, Daiyu."

She opened her mouth to tell him the same, but before she could even blink, he vanished.

10

Daiyu traced circles into the rough, moss-ridden bench she sat on beneath a giant plum blossom tree that rained pink petals on her and the pond a few feet from her feet. The late afternoon light warmed her skin and she longed to be back home with her family, where times were simpler and she never had to look over her shoulder. Previously, she had been slightly annoyed at having a guard shadow her whenever she went in the gardens, but after the attempt on her life two days ago, she was grateful for her guard's presence.

It was probably why when she heard footsteps approaching from behind, she didn't bother looking over her shoulder—the person was probably walking down one of the paths anyway. But when she heard a stuttered gasp from her guard, and a quick, "G-Greetings, Your Majesty!" she realized she had messed up.

Daiyu whirled in her seat and inhaled sharply at the sight of Muyang standing a few feet away from her. Her guard had lowered himself into a deep bow, but the emperor barely paid him any attention. His black eyes were hooked onto Daiyu, and every fiber of her being froze at the frosty look swirling beneath the surface. He was dressed in blue robes that were so dark they almost looked black, a gold crown that held his long hair in place, and gilded earrings that caught the sunlight every time he turned his head.

Even with the afternoon light glowing across his face, his eyes remained like cold chips of obsidian, never warming or shifting to a softer shade of brown. They remained bottomless pits of black. Empty. Like a void. Like evil itself.

Daiyu's heart thumped in her chest wildly, and she lurched off the bench and lowered herself like her guard was doing. "Your Majesty," she murmured, hating the tremble in her voice. "What a pleasant surprise."

"Leave us."

"Pardon?" She raised her head to find that he was talking to her guard, who promptly scurried away. It was then that she also noticed the emperor didn't have an entourage of guards or mages with him and was alone. She swallowed down the sudden fear clawing up her throat.

The corner of Muyang's lips curved into a sinister smirk, and he waved a pale hand toward the bench. "Don't let me scare you away from staring at the fish. Sit."

Daiyu stiffly and wordlessly sat down. She watched as he neared her and touched the back of the bench gently, his gaze flicking down at her and then at the pond with shimmering streaks of light bouncing across the rippling surface.

The silence felt even worse than if he was breathing down profanities or threats because she had no idea what he was thinking, and she didn't dare turn around and stare at him. She couldn't even meet his gaze, for fear that he might find that insulting.

"My head mage informed me you were poisoned a few days prior," he said, his voice coming out smooth and uncaring as if he were mentioning the weather rather than her life. "I see that you're doing well, so perhaps his worries were unfounded."

Heat spread over her face, but not from embarrassment. Anger suddenly spiked within herself. *It's only because of your head mage that I appear to be doing well, Your Majesty,* she wanted to quip. But she kept her lips pursed shut.

"You were lucky my mage found you." From her peripheral, she noted that his hand trailed over the bench before landing on her shoulder. Almost immediately, her body went rigid and she held her breath. His fingers were cool as he leaned forward and grasped her neck lightly. "Has it healed?"

She swallowed, and she was certain he could feel it by the way he was holding her throat. She didn't turn around to pin him with a glare, but the better part of her was terrified. She sat still as his nails grazed the delicate skin he had pierced over a week ago.

"It healed," Daiyu answered, suppressing a shiver as he leaned close enough that she could smell the jasmine and orange blossom clinging to his skin. She stared at the red and white fish dancing beneath the surface of the pond to keep herself from turning around, even though her reflexes told her to look at him.

"I'm glad to hear that." The warmth toward her back disappeared, but his hand instead traveled to her hair, and she gasped as he pulled one of her vermillion-colored hairpins out from her high bun. A strip of hair fell down her shoulder and she instinctively turned around.

"What are you—" The words died at her lips when she caught sight of him peering down at her with a look of boredom and *hunger.* She could see the desire on his face as clear as day, and her heart raced unexpectedly. Warmth rose up her neck and tingled her ears.

Muyang grabbed another hairpin and pulled it out effortlessly. More of her hair slipped from the bun her maid had done for her, but Daiyu couldn't stop him and couldn't rip her eyes from him. He watched her the entire time as he grasped another pin and tugged it free from the hairstyle. He dropped each hairpin, where they disappeared in the folds of grass.

Daiyu's cheeks flushed with warmth as he took the final pin from her hair. Her hair fell down her shoulders, finally free from the constraints, and Muyang stared at her wordlessly. His gaze raked over her face and neck, and she became increasingly aware that they were both alone here, and he was staring at her like a man who wanted to taste her.

He was evil, she told herself, trying to force herself to remember the moment he had pinned a blade to her neck. And yet, something seemed to awaken inside her to be scrutinized in such a way by a man so wickedly beautiful.

"There," he said, tossing the last hairpin to the ground. Finally, a smile lifted across his lips, and she didn't like the sudden heat pooling in her stomach. "Much better."

"I prefer my hair in a bun," she whispered.

"And I prefer you like this." He grasped a strand of her hair and positioned it over her shoulder. His finger dragged across her jaw until he grasped her chin. "If you are to wear hairpins, you should wear gold, silver, or jade. Not these gaudy, cheap wooden pins painted to appear opulent."

"And who will give me these gold, silver, and jade hairpins, Your Majesty? Will the maids bring them to me? The same maids who brought me poison just a few nights ago? Or will you give them to me, so that I may appear prettier in front of you and your nobles?" The words streamed out of her like a single breath, so quick she had to clamp her mouth shut to keep from spewing more.

Something flickered in his dark gaze, and it took all her power to keep from averting her eyes from him. He tilted her head up so she could see him better, and she hated the smirk pulling on his soft mouth. "In front of my nobles, you will appear with many luxuries. Many pieces of gold, silk, jade. But when you are solely in front of me, you will be free of *all* worldly constraints, little rabbit."

A blush stained her cheeks and she gasped quietly, so taken aback by his words. She finally turned her face away, ripping his touch from her. "T-That—" Her mouth was suddenly dry and she couldn't keep the embarrassment away. "That is highly inappropriate, Your Majesty. We aren't married yet, and so—"

Muyang smiled, and her blush deepened.

"Surely you've been with a man before?"

She whipped her head in his direction, her lips parting. "Certainly not! Why would you think that?"

His eyebrows lifted, and for a brief moment, she forgot that she was in the presence of a terrifying, bloodthirsty emperor. "You haven't? You appear old."

"O-Old?" She gasped and quickly turned away from him again. She didn't like the way their conversation was progressing, and she certainly didn't like the way her body reacted to him. She was only twenty-four! Sure, she wasn't young, but she certainly wasn't *old*. "I ... I didn't realize I appeared so ... well, I'm not—" She struggled to come up with the words. This was the third time a man had told her she was old. The first was when the soldiers had entered her family's home and rejected her for the royal selection because of her age, the second time was when Feiyu thought she was thirty, and now this man.

Did she really look that much older than the other women here? Were they simply just young, or did she age badly? Maybe her beauty regimen of fermented rice water on her face and hair wasn't as advanced as the noblewomen, but she didn't think she was *that* bad to look at compared to them.

"You chose me," she suddenly said. "And I doubt you would choose someone ancient and ugly, so if you have faults in my appearance—" She didn't finish the sentence, though it was clear what she wanted to say: *you brought it upon yourself.*

"I have no problems with your age," Muyang said with a low chuckle, and she wasn't sure if he was joking or not. "I prefer when my women are older. You're actually younger than what I prefer."

Daiyu blinked up at him. That was something she had never heard before.

She spun back around to stare at the pond, unable to shake the surge of conflicting emotions warring in her heart. She tried to remind herself that he was an evil, horrible man who had tried to kill her just a few days ago, and that this brief moment of conversation meant nothing. He was only lusting after her, as was his right as the emperor. This moment meant nothing. He would still murder her if she offended him.

"Don't clam up now." There was an authority in his voice that made her stiffen once more and reaffirmed her thoughts. He stepped around the bench and eased himself beside her. "Must I tell you to keep speaking?"

A shiver ran down her spine at their closeness and she braved a glance in his direction. He wasn't looking at her this time and was staring at the water with half-lidded, bored eyes. She could already see that he was growing tired of her again by the cold indifference of his expression.

Daiyu fidgeted with the pale pink sleeve of her dress. "If you order me to speak, then I will speak."

"And if I order you"—he pointed a lazy finger to the water and stared at her apathetically—"to walk into this pond and drown yourself, will you do it?"

Whatever warmth she had felt around him disappeared as those words sank in. She licked her lips and stared at the body of water, an uneasiness spreading over her like the undulating waves across the pond's surface.

He was joking, wasn't he?

"Well?" Muyang pinned her with a stare so cold and devoid of feeling it confirmed her darkest fears.

"Your command is ... is absolute, Your Majesty."

He smiled, and a shudder coursed through her body at the frostiness behind it. At the cruelty she could see just beneath the surface. "Then do it."

11

DAIYU MUST HAVE HEARD WRONG. DID HE WANT HER to ... go into the pond? She tried to smile to distill the growing discomfort in her chest and laughed nervously. "Your Majesty?"

"Walk." Muyang gestured her forward, and every instinct in her body told her to run far, far away from him. From the morbid curiosity on his face.

Daiyu pressed her heels into the grass beneath her feet and gripped the edge of the bench tightly. "Your Majesty, I don't think—"

"*Walk.*"

She flinched and knew that she couldn't talk her way out of it. He was serious, and he was watching her as if waiting for her to fail. And it was only then that she noticed the dagger strapped to his waist, with its dragon design and its beaded, ruby eye. Her shoulders trembled, and she looked between him and the pond, wanting for him to tell her he was jesting.

But he didn't.

Muyang didn't blink. "Yin Daiyu, are you refusing to obey me?"

She forced herself to her feet and a strong, cool wind ripped through her hair, sending more tremors over her body. Her gaze flicked to the rest of the garden, where the winding paths would lead to safety, but within these palace walls he owned, there was nowhere that was safe.

Daiyu took a step closer to the brink of the pond. She could make out the dark gray rocks beneath the surface, and now that she was even closer to it, it appeared deeper than it did earlier. Red, white, and orange fish slithered and wove through the smooth and jutted stones. Her only consolation when she slipped off her shoes and brought a foot into the water was that it was surprisingly warm, or warmer than she thought it would be.

She spared a glance over her shoulder at the emperor, but he was watching her coolly, not appearing at all like he would tell her to stop. Her lips pressed together in a firm line and she spun her head away from him. She hated this humiliation and being forced to do something like this.

Muyang didn't say anything when the water reached her hips. She shivered at the dropping temperature the deeper she went. The rocks were smooth and slippery, and she feared she would slide if she went any farther. She didn't actually want to drown, and she doubted he wanted her dead right then and there.

She turned back to him, her eyebrows pulled together. "Your Majesty, how much more?"

"Keep walking."

Daiyu bunched her fists together and wanted to shout at him, but when he raised his eyebrow, she twisted around and went forward. Never mind the fact that she knew how to swim—but *he* didn't know that. And most women in his court, she assumed, didn't know how to. So was he expecting her to actually drown herself for him? It was absurd, and he seemed to enjoy degrading her in such a manner.

Would she have to walk back to her room, dripping water everywhere, with servants snickering and gossiping behind her back? The thought made her cheeks warm and she decided she hated Drakkon Muyang, and she needed to escape from his clutches as soon as she could.

The pond grew colder the deeper she went, and at one moment, her foot slipped and she fully submerged into the water. The coldness sent a shock through her system and she bobbed up to the surface, inhaling sharply and kicking her legs and arms to keep herself afloat. Icy water streamed down her face and she blinked rapidly against the late afternoon sun. She shifted her attention to Muyang, who hadn't moved from his position on the bench and watched her with mild curiosity. She couldn't even bask in triumph at letting him realize she knew how to swim, for fear that he would force her to do something outrageous—like sink underwater, or hold her breath for as long as she could.

He didn't say anything and only stared at her, his expression neutral, and when the minutes ticked by without an order from him, Daiyu grew braver. "Your Majesty," she said, unable to keep the irritation from her voice, "do you wish for me to keep floating like this or to actually dive into the water and *drown*? If it's the latter, I hate to inform you that I have no plans of dying"—*even for you*, she omitted—"and I would very much appreciate being allowed to get out."

She waited for him to either lash out or laugh, but he did neither. He waved his hand forward as if uninterested by her response. "I'll grant it."

Before he could change her mind, she quickly swam to the bench and stepped out of the pond. A gust of wind blew over her and she quivered in the cold. Her dress clung to her every curve and she covered her breasts with her hands for fear that he could see too much. Her teeth chattered and she lowered her head. "Please allow me to go back to my room, Your Majesty."

"No."

She jerked her head up. No?

"Daiyu." Her name rolled off his tongue so easily, and she trembled. His gaze darkened as he stared up at her. "I have a few questions that have been bothering me about you. If you can answer them, I'll be satisfied."

She dug her elbows into her sides and hugged herself tighter, her lips quivering as another kind of cold overtook her body. This one more frigid than any body of water.

Did he realize she had been lying to him? Did Feiyu mention that she wanted to wipe her from his memories?

"Yes, Your Majesty?" she squeaked.

He propped his elbow on the armrest of the bench and tilted his head against his closed fist. There was a shift in his mood because the energy all around him seemed to dampen and darken. She couldn't explain it any other way than that it seemed like a darkness cloaked him.

It was then that she became aware that she was staring down at him, and she quickly dropped herself to her knees and pressed her hands onto the grass. She couldn't hide the tremor that wracked through her thin frame.

Muyang sighed, and she winced, waiting for him to snap.

"Daiyu, lift your head."

She did as she was told and peered up at him. He was only a foot away from her, and yet he appeared all too close. All too powerful, and much too indifferent.

"Why did you switch places with your sister?"

She licked her wet lips and tasted the briny, iron tang of the pond water. "My sister is too young and she—" She lowered her gaze, swallowing down the dryness of her throat. "She loved another, so I took her place so she could be with her true love."

It was a simple lie, one of many she had told him at this point. But it was the only thing she could think of without making herself out to be a sister-stepping, ambitious girl. Although it would probably do well for her to have him think negatively of her—and thus cast her aside—for some odd reason, she had a feeling that if she did that, he would kill her for a petty reason. Like tricking him into thinking she was something she wasn't.

"How noble," he said dryly.

"I didn't think I would be chosen," Daiyu murmured. "Especially since ... you haven't chosen anyone before."

Muyang's face seemed to be carved from stone as he looked

down at her, as unreadable as he was moments ago. "Li Jia told me that when she first saw you, you were holding a basket and told her you were doing laundry for the women in the Lotus wing. Why were you pretending to be a servant?"

"I was lost and needed help to get back to the Lotus wing." Her lips quivered and it took everything in her to hold his gaze, to tell him she was truthful when she wasn't.

"How did you leave the Lotus wing without anyone noticing? There are guards posted everywhere."

Her hands grew clammy and she tightened her hold on the grass. "I slipped out when they didn't notice."

"Why did you leave?"

"Because ..." Daiyu's voice lowered to a whisper. "Because I was hungry and wanted to eat something in the kitchens."

"But you have plenty of food in the Lotus wing. Calling a servant to bring you something to eat is easy to do." His eyes seemed to darken even further, and she squirmed beneath that oppressive stare. She felt like a butterfly whose flimsy wings were pinned down and who aggressively tried to break free but was unable to.

She wanted to vomit. This felt infinitely worse than when she had been poisoned and dying, because here, she was under the careful eye of an executioner.

She chose her next words carefully, the lies rolling off her tongue easily. "The other women don't like me much, so they don't ... they don't like when I call for things. Like food, or assistance, and the maids don't like me much either, since I come from a poor family. I'm much worse off than any of the other girls, so no one wanted to ... to tend to me."

His silence was deafeningly loud, and she wanted to sprint away from him, to lose herself in the palace halls, scream for Feiyu to warp her out, and to disappear from him forever. And yet she was still a bird trapped in a gilded cage, and if he chose to clip her wings or wring her neck and replace her, he could do just that.

"I see." Muyang continued to examine her coolly. "Is there anything else you'd like to tell me?"

Daiyu shook her head, the color draining from her face. "No, Your Majesty."

"Very well." He reached toward his waist and she jumped when he pulled out his dragon dagger—the same blade he had pinned to her neck—but instead of running her through, he held it out to her, hilt first.

Daiyu stared at the weapon dumbly.

"Take it."

She wordlessly took it from him, her fingers wrapping around the metal handle. She placed it on her lap tentatively and watched him carefully, expecting him to do something sinister. When he did nothing, she murmured, "Thank you?"

"Keep it for now until I come back for you. It's important to me, so don't lose it." Muyang drummed his fingers on the armrest of the bench. She still couldn't get a read on him, and even though his words seemed safe, she was on high alert. "I'll be gone to the north tomorrow and won't be back for a few weeks. Months, if this rebellion isn't quelled soon enough."

"You will fight in the war?"

Something gleamed in his eyes as he laughed, and she inched back at the crudeness of it. "I have enemies to kill, and I'd hate for someone else to do that favor. So yes, little rabbit, I plan on fighting."

Little rabbit.

She disliked the nickname and the way he said it—like she was a quivering, sniveling rabbit absolutely terrified out of her mind in his presence. And yet it seemed fitting, she thought bitterly as she lowered her gaze to the blade on her lap.

He grasped her chin and forced her to look up at him. His hands were cool to the touch and he didn't seem to mind the dampness of her skin. "I wanted to see you before I left."

It would've sounded romantic, if not for the humiliation he had caused her. If not for the fact that she was dripping wet, and that the winds were making her even colder, and that the dropping temperature as the sun dipped along the horizon made her teeth clatter together. If not for the fact that he could kill her and nobody would bat an eyelash.

Muyang studied her face like he was searching for something and released her promptly. She didn't know if he was satisfied with her or not, but she couldn't turn away from him. Not when he could still attack her. She needed to see his every move, even if she couldn't do anything about it.

"I ... I pray that you will be victorious," she said carefully.

"When I come back, we will marry," he said noncommittally. The waning sunlight glinted off the gold crown keeping his hair together and Daiyu squinted against the glare. "I'm hoping to arrive before the Autumn Festival."

Daiyu tried to hide the shudder that ran down her spine. He still wanted to marry her? She didn't understand *why*. Especially when he had so many other beautiful, willing women in the palace ready for him. And yet he chose *her*.

She hated him for it.

"I hope your campaign goes well and that you return promptly." The words left her mouth in a detached manner like someone else saying it and not her. "I pray that the Huo empire is successful in quelling these treasonous rebellions."

Muyang's eyes narrowed and another chill rattled her bones. Before she could surmise what he was thinking, he beckoned her forward with a single finger. "Come here."

Daiyu rose to her feet, dagger in hand, and shuffled closer to him. Her ruined, dripping clothes stuck to her uncomfortably and she hated the squelching feeling of her water-wrinkled toes plodding the grass. She stopped a foot away from him, and his fingers grazed her stomach gently. She nearly tripped backward, but he grabbed her elbow as if anticipating it.

"W-What—" Her face flushed with unexpected warmth and embarrassment, but before she could say anything else, he drew his hand away, and a trail of grimy water suspended into the air between them. Daiyu watched, transfixed, as the pond water was extracted from her dress in thin streams, culminating into a ball in his open palm. It took less than ten seconds for all the water to be pulled from her dress and even her hair. He flicked a hand and the ball of muddied water splatted against the ground.

Daiyu's mouth was still shaped like an O even after he finished. She shouldn't have been *that* shocked, considering how rumors said he was part demon or part dragon, but seeing it happen with her own eyes made the stories even more true.

"You seem surprised," Muyang said with a short chuckle. "Did you think I would be cruel enough to make you walk the palace halls looking like a drowned rat while the servants and nobles mocked you?"

Daiyu wouldn't have put it past him to do exactly that, but she shook her head. "I didn't think that low of you, Your Majesty."

"Good." He clambered to his feet, and Daiyu was once again taken aback by his impressive height. He towered over her and she felt even smaller to be so close to him.

"I will wait for your return." She took a step back, wanting to put as much distance between them as possible. She thumbed the dragon's face on the dagger distractedly. "I ... I do have a request before you leave, Your Majesty."

Muyang turned to leave but then paused and glanced down at her with raised eyebrows. "Oh?"

"I-I ... I hope it isn't too impudent of me to ask ... but ..." She lowered herself into a bow. Her heart wouldn't stop racing and she held her breath in case he did anything to her for even making a request. "But I was hoping you could dismiss the rest of the women in the palace and allow them to go back to their homes."

This time, she held her breath and didn't dare look up at him. After her poisoning, there was no way she could peacefully stay in the palace whilst her potential murderer was waiting in the Lotus wing. It was possible that the women would grow bolder in

Muyang's absence, and Daiyu couldn't risk another incident like before.

"Are you jealous of them?"

She jerked her face up to find him with his head angled to the side, his gold earrings catching in the light, and a curious smirk playing on his lips. Amusement seemed to dance in the depths of his richly black eyes. And once again she was struck at how painfully beautiful he was and how dangerous of a trap that was.

Daiyu couldn't tell him the truth—that she didn't trust the other women—but maybe it was better this way? For him to think she wanted him? Would that make him less suspicious of her? She wasn't entirely sure what the correct course to take was, but she nodded slowly.

He tipped his head back and laughed, and Daiyu froze. She wasn't sure if this was the foretelling of something cruel or something favorable for her. When he turned to look at her, there was a twinkle in his eyes that told her he wasn't furious, so she finally cracked a smile.

"Very well," he said in his velvety voice. "I'll have them dismissed tonight. Will that please you?"

"Yes, Your Majesty."

"Then consider it done."

Even though he grinned as he said it, a shudder ran through Daiyu's body. Whether he would follow through or not was the bigger question. She tightened her hold on his dagger and lowered her head for what felt like the hundredth time that day.

"Thank you, Your Majesty."

12

Daiyu walked through the now-empty halls of the Lotus wing, her footsteps padding against the polished wooden floors. She peeked into the rooms as she went by, her gaze glossing over the embroidered couches, the spacious sitting rooms, and the unoccupied beds. True to his word, Muyang had dismissed all the women in the wing—save for her, of course.

"My lady, where exactly are we going?" her guard, an older man with a gravelly voice and a long beard, said gruffly as he joined her in glancing into the perfume-infused quarters like he might find something.

"Nowhere in particular." Daiyu shrugged and continued down the corridor. She did feel *slightly* bad for forcing all the women to leave the opulent palace and all its luxurious wonders —like the soft beds, the fancy furniture, the maidservants who were at their beck and call, the arrays of food, and the expansive gardens—but anytime she remembered the horrible night of her poisoning, her resolve hardened and she knew this was the right choice to make. It was probably better for the women anyway, to not be tied down to a vicious monarch like Drakkon Muyang.

It had been a week since the emperor and all the women left the palace, but the palace still felt as ominous as it did with or without Muyang's presence. It was like power oozed from every wall and tile, regardless of whether the owner of the place was here or not. She had thought she would find some peace in his absence, but the halls felt emptier and creepier like they were watching her every move.

And maybe they were. Maybe Muyang had asked his mages to watch her with magic, or maybe there was something sinister within these walls. She had no way to figure it out, and she didn't plan to stay long enough to find out.

"Where do the mages stay?" she asked.

The guard gave her a strange look before staring straight ahead. "Wherever they please, I suppose."

"You don't know?" Daiyu laced her hands behind her back. "In my village, there are rumors that they live in towers."

"Maybe they do." He lifted his shoulders and shifted his spear into his other hand. "But I try to steer clear of the mages, and I suggest you do the same. Nothing good comes out of interfering with them."

She thought of Feiyu and a shiver ran down her spine. "I never ... I never said I would *interfere* with them. I'm just curious."

"It's best to keep yourself sparse around them," he said with another shrug. Another shudder crawled through her body when he spoke his next words, "You never know what they're thinking of or what they're capable of."

〜

When Daiyu arrived in her room after her lackluster walk through the gardens and the Lotus wing, she was surprised to find a maidservant waiting for her with a trunk with clusters of multicolored crystals along the base and lid, and another similarly bejeweled small box in the woman's hands.

"Good morning, my lady," the older woman said with a low bow. "His Majesty has sent these gifts to you and a note."

"Oh?" Daiyu couldn't hold back her surprise or her apprehension as she eyed the case. It had only been a week since the emperor left for war, and already he had war prizes that he wanted to gift her? Would he give her a severed head of his enemy? Or the decaying corpse of a traitor? She swallowed down the sudden nerves buzzing in the pit of her stomach.

"Here you go." The maidservant handed her a crisp, yellowed paper with swirling ink writing etched into it.

Daiyu stared at the elegant handwriting and turned the paper around. "I ..." Embarrassment flooded her and she tried to smile at the older woman, who was watching her expectantly. "I'm ... I'm actually unable to read. Would you mind reading it for me?"

Now it was the maid's turn to look surprised. She nodded quickly and took the note from Daiyu's hand. "I'm terribly sorry about that. I didn't realize." She blinked at the note and read, "To my dearest wife-to-be. I've noticed that you wear clothing that wash out your beautiful skin and make you look haggard. I've picked colors that I believe will suit you better. I believe they'll look better on you—and even better—" The maid gasped, her cheeks reddening as she looked between Daiyu and back at the note. "Do ... Do you wish for me to continue, my lady? This seems a little ... *private.*"

Daiyu's face flushed with color and although she hated that the maid was privy to the note, she had no other way of reading it, so she bobbed her head slowly. "Only if you can."

The older woman cleared her throat. "I believe they'll look better on you—and even better when I ... take them off you. I've also gifted a set of hairpins that, similarly, will look splendid on you. And even better when ... taken off. Yours, Muyang."

The maid nearly thrust the small box in her hand to her, like she didn't want any more part in this. Daiyu tentatively cracked open the box. There were six hairpins nestled inside velvet inserts. There were two gold hairpins embossed with swirling designs that, upon closer inspection, were tiny cranes. Two jade hairpins with dangling pearls on the ends. And two silver hairpins encrusted with sapphires. Her hands shook as she held the box; she had never received such a fancy gift before, and the idea of keeping something this luxurious made her heart nearly stop.

"Do you wish to look at the dresses, my lady?"

She set down the box of hairpins on her dresser and turned her attention on the trunk, her nerves getting the best of her as the maidservant unlatched the lid and threw it open. Daiyu was unprepared for the silk dresses inside. The shades of dresses ranged from fiery red to deep sapphires, lush emerald, creamy pearls, and rich golds. It was more than she could have imagined, and when she placed the clothes against her skin, they seemed to go well with her tan skin. All the pale dresses that were currently in her wardrobe seemed plain in comparison to these.

"These are stunning," she breathed, running her hands over the gold embroidered threads of a dark purple dress. In truth, these did seem to suit her more than the other clothes that had been assigned to her, and the thought of Muyang picking these out made her blush deepen. She *shouldn't* have been swayed by these expensive gifts, and yet ... she found her heart swelling with excitement.

"They *are* stunning," the maidservant remarked with a wide, toothy grin on her leathered face. She patted Daiyu's hand. "You'll be his bride and soon, all these gifts will seem so small compared to everything you'll have!"

Daiyu's smile faltered and she could only nod. The older woman had no clue she was planning on leaving, and the idea was like a slap of reality to her face.

She couldn't be too happy with these dresses, especially since she likely wouldn't wear them for long. She needed to go back home, where life was simpler. Where she wore worn-out clothes with too many patched up holes, where her grass-sandaled shoes were so thin she needed to make new ones, and where her family was patiently waiting for her.

"Would you like to try them on, my lady?" The maidservant

held up a dark green dress with swirling gold dragons dancing along the skirts.

"Maybe tomorrow," she replied weakly.

When the maidservant left and Daiyu was alone with all her gifts, guilt weighed heavily on her conscience. She shouldn't have been here. She was supposed to be home. She was supposed to tend to the family garden since Lanfen didn't have a green thumb, and make herbal tea for her grandmother to help with her aching body, and scrub the grime off her twin brother's clothes after they helped Father in the rice paddies. She was supposed to milk their family cow early in the morning since Mother liked to drink milk tea before setting to work. She was supposed to braid Lanfen's hair since she did her hair better than her. She was supposed to do more than sit here and be a pretty doll. Her hands were roughened with tough work, and they weren't meant to be idle.

She twiddled her fingers together to keep them from fussing over the dresses and to keep them from snatching one of the hairpins. She paced her room again, her mind growing more tangled with every step, every breath, and every thought. Her chance of escape seemed even slimmer than before. What could she do to leave this place?

Perhaps she could ask Feiyu to spirit her away and ask her family to move far, far away as well? But she shook that thought away the instant it formed. She couldn't burden her elderly parents like that, nor her siblings, who had friends and ambitions in the village. It would be too much for everyone to throw their lives away—everything they had worked for—and run because she had been naïve and unlucky enough to catch the wicked emperor's attention.

DAIYU TOSSED AND TURNED, HER GAZE FLICKING UP TO the roof of the bed and then to the carved wooden lattices along the four-poster frame. The only sound in the room was the flickering fire in the hearth, the howling of the wind outside her shut-tered windows, and the occasional booms of thunder. Even though she had lit a spiced incense stick an hour before bed, she couldn't sleep.

She pulled the silk sheets over her face and breathed in the sandalwood smell clinging to them from the incense. Nights were truly the hardest in the palace; it was also when she felt the most alone.

She turned her focus on the pitter-patter of rain hitting her shutters and tried to force herself to be lulled to sleep by it. Right when her eyelids began to feel heavy, the sound of wood creaking just outside her door and the jangle of her door handle snapped her awake. She sat upright in bed, and all of a sudden, the fire in her room died.

Everything became dark in an instant, and she knew that something was very, very wrong.

The door slowly swung open and if she wasn't awake, she might not have heard it clicking shut behind the intruder. Her heart hammered in her chest and she narrowed her eyes into the darkness of the room. Everything was too dark for her to make out anything.

Her heart hammered in her chest and she slowly reached for the emperor's dagger that she kept under her pillow. The smooth handle of the weapon seemed to fit perfectly in her hand as she brought it in front of her.

Footsteps padded through the room, and Daiyu carefully pulled the blankets off her now-clammy body. Her eyes slowly adjusted to the shadows in the room, and her stomach dropped to the floor at the sight of a figure approaching her, his arms spread out like he too couldn't see that well in the dark. But just as her eyesight was adjusting—his likely was too.

Daiyu eyed the doorway and then the man that was slowly creeping his way here. She couldn't easily run past him, but if she caught him off guard, then maybe ... maybe she had a chance.

Without wasting another second, she leaped off the bed and

sprinted to the door. The man grunted and lunged toward her. She was only a few feet away, but her vision blurred and a scream ripped through her throat as a body slammed into her. She crashed onto the floor and rolled with the man, who struggled to clasp his meaty hands around her throat. Daiyu waved the dagger in front of her body defensively and the blade was met with resistance. She yanked harder, and the man cursed loudly. Splotches of warm blood splattered her face and she continued flailing the weapon in front of her.

"Stop that!" the man growled, grasping her neck tightly.

Daiyu continued to thrash, her already-dark vision growing dimmer. She kicked him hard between the legs and he inhaled sharply, his hold on her loosening. It was all the time she needed to crawl out from under him.

"Feiyu!" she screamed, rushing to the door. "Feiyu—"

The intruder grabbed her ankle and yanked her backward. The room spun and she slammed to the floor once more, her chin cracking against the hard tile. She reached for her dagger, but it had skidded a foot away from her.

"Get off me! Help!" She clawed her way forward, her hands gripping the edge of her rug as the man continued to pull her. Her gaze was locked on the door, waiting for guards to bust through, or for Feiyu to teleport to her room like he had a few weeks ago. "Help!"

"You bitch." The intruder smothered a cloth over her face and she struggled against him, her limbs growing heavy. "Stop moving so much, or I'll accidentally cut that pretty neck of yours."

Something cold touched her throat, but she could barely keep her eyes open. He was saying something else too, but the words were muffled, like there was a barrier between them. In seconds, her world became a black void.

13

Daiyu groaned softly, her chin and elbow aching. Her eyes slowly fluttered open, and she was nearly blinded by the blaring sun. She inhaled sharply and looked around herself wildly. Where she expected to see the silhouettes of her four-poster bed or the familiar furniture of her room, she was instead met with hills, trees, and a cluster of men on horses surrounding her. Her body jostled forward, and she could barely sit up on the floor of the uncovered wagon she was on. Her hands were bound tightly with rope and bits of hay covered her night robes.

It took her a few minutes to realize the position she was in. Had she been ... kidnapped? Sold to a group of mercenaries? A band of thieves? Bandits? She couldn't tell, but by their gruff outfits and crude, chipped blades, they seemed like the latter.

"Hey! Look who's awake," one of the men closest to her wagon said with a loud laugh. He had a long scar running across his cheeks and nose, splitting his face in half and giving him an eerie expression.

Daiyu flinched as he flashed his yellowed teeth and blackened gums at her. "His Majesty's beautiful whore is awake!"

The other men turned their attention to her and Daiyu was

suddenly in the spotlight of their lustful leers and sneers. Her heart sped in pace and all the hairs on her body stood straight. She brought her bare feet closer to her body, curling herself into a defensive ball.

"I can't believe this pretty little thing caused you so much trouble, Bao," the scarred man said to one of the riders, who glared at her from his position a few feet away from the wagon. His hands were bound with gauze and he had a wad of bandages on his neck.

"Bugger off," the man grumbled.

Daiyu instantly recognized the man's voice from last night, and she gasped. "You're the man who attacked me yesterday!"

"Not *yesterday*." The scarred man continued to grin at her, and she found herself scooting farther back in the wagon, a cold sweat forming over her body. "It's been three days. You've been out cold thanks to the potion that bastard gave you." He jerked his chin in Bao's direction, and the man turned away, sniffing. "We were afraid you wouldn't wake up, and then this whole ordeal would have been for *nothing*."

"The ordeal of kidnapping me?" Daiyu tried to hide the tremble in her voice as she met the man's amused smirk. "Why would you steal me, of all people? I'm not important to anyone!"

The man tipped his head back and laughed loudly, and it boomed across the valley they were going through. Daiyu shivered, her gaze skating to the mountains in the distance and the woods on the horizon—how far had they been traveling? And where were they intending on taking her?

"You're precious to *His Majesty*," the man sneered, the mocking tilt in his voice coming off harsh. He touched the scar on his face and it somehow appeared angrier, redder, and uglier. But it must have been the light playing tricks on her eyes, or the twist of his lips that gave that impression. "Drakkon Muyang doesn't have many weaknesses, and so of course we had to take the one woman who seemed to matter to him."

Daiyu's mouth dropped open and she couldn't believe the words coming out of his mouth. "You ... You think I matter to him? He doesn't even know me!"

"He chose you for a reason." He narrowed his eyes at her. "We can use you in many ways to get to him, *my lady*." He hissed out the last part and gave a short laugh as if he found himself amusing.

All the color drained from Daiyu's face. These people actually thought they could anger Muyang by stealing her? It was the most absurd notion she had heard in weeks—besides the fact that Muyang had chosen her, for some apparent reason. How far would they go to get a reaction out of him? Would they torture her? Send bits and pieces of her body to him as presents? Wave her battered body on the battlefield as a warning? The more her mind traveled to morbid territory, the more lightheaded she became.

"Y-You've made a mistake," she heard herself breathe. "A terrible, terrible mistake."

"No, we haven't." One of the men chuckled, bringing his horse closer to the wagon so he could peer at her better. He tightened his hold on his reins and grinned. "I wonder what it'll be like to be with the emperor's whore—"

"Are you out of your mind?" Daiyu's eyes nearly bugged out from their sockets. "I'm not his ... his *whore*! I'm to be his wife, not—not—" Tears stung the back of her eyes when laughter filled the space around her. Everywhere she turned, a man was grinning at her salaciously. Like they wanted to strip her down and parade her in their little group. "You fiends! This isn't how you treat a woman—"

Another round of laughter, this time heartier than the last.

If she thought being stuck in the palace with Drakkon Muyang was bad, this was infinitely worse. This type of captivity, with obscene men who would do unimaginable things to her, appeared to be a different version of cruelty than Muyang offered. At least in the palace, she had a chance to escape. But here? She glanced at the fields of grass, at the weapons the men had, and then at the beaten path toward the mountainside. There were far too many variables to consider with escaping.

Her stomach twisted into a tight knot and she resisted the urge to vomit right then and there, even as waves of nausea rolled over her. First, she had to find a way out of these constraints. Then she could worry about outrunning these men.

Maybe it was better this way, she reasoned. If she managed to escape and run to her family, without notifying the emperor, then wouldn't that mean she successfully evaded him? He would assume she was either dead or still in the midst of the enemies, and he would eventually forget about her, and she could live her life without worry.

But even with the slim possibility of escaping from Muyang, the idea of fleeing from this group of bandits seemed more daunting and impossible. In the palace, she had Feiyu. But here there was no one to aid her.

Daiyu shimmied her wrists and cringed at the rawness of her skin and the rough material of the rope. "Is there any way you could remove these ropes from me?" she asked no one in particular. "There's no reason to keep me bound—"

"There's plenty of reason," Bao, the one who had snuck into her room and abducted her, snapped. He touched the bindings on his neck and glared at her darkly. "You're not as timid as you look. The next thing we'll know, you'll try to slit our throats."

The corner of the scarred man's mouth lifted. "That's a great point, Bao. We can't have her trying to kill us like she almost did with you."

Some of the men snorted, and Bao's face purpled. "She didn't manage to do anything."

"Doesn't look that way," one of them said with another cackle.

Daiyu frowned and tried pulling one of her hands from the constraints. "Where are you taking me?"

"None of your concerns." The scarred man pulled out a dagger from his belt and flipped it in the air before catching it quickly. It was only then that Daiyu noticed the dragon curled along the hilt and the ruby eyes.

She inhaled sharply. That was Muyang's dagger; he had told her to keep it safe, and yet a common bandit was whirling it around his fingers like it was a toy. She could only imagine what the emperor would do to her if he found out she lost his prized possession.

But that shouldn't have been her concern, she told herself. She had no plans of returning to Muyang, so he would never find out what happened here. He shouldn't have given his dagger to her in the first place if it was so important to him. He should've just kept it to himself. *He* was the naïve one for trusting her with it.

In fact, if it wasn't for Muyang, she wouldn't even *be* in this mess.

The scarred man pointed the end of the dagger at Daiyu, his eyes narrowing to slits. "This is *his* dagger, isn't it?"

"No." Daiyu leaned into the hay and stared at him levelly. She tried to keep a neutral expression, even as her heart nearly leaped from her chest. "A soldier gave me that dagger."

"That's not what your expression is saying." He waved the dagger closer to her and she turned her face away. "Your face is telling me that this is *really* important to you."

"Careful or you might fall off your horse," she said as calmly as she could muster, but her voice rose and there was a shrill quality to it, betraying her nervousness.

The man laughed and tucked the blade back into his belt, which carried two swords—one of which was rusted along the edge. "Do you know how I got this scar on my face?"

Daiyu tried not to look at the bumpy, raised scar tissue slicing his face in half. He shouldn't have even been alive after a wound like that.

"That bastard on the throne did this to me." His voice came out rough and gravelly, and his knuckles turned white as he held his reins tighter.

A chilling wind ripped through her hair and she shivered against the sudden cold. "His Majesty?"

"Yes, *that* bastard." He tapped the scar, his eyes glazing over and his mouth twitching into a scowl as if he was remembering something unpleasant. "I used to be a respectable soldier in the imperial army for Emperor Yan. And then, that bastard and his armies ... destroyed everything I had worked for my entire life. That *all* of us worked for." He waved to the group of men, most of whom were too focused on moving forward to look at them. "And now that he's the emperor, we're all enemies of the empire! Can you believe that? I've worked my whole life to protect this empire, and now ... now I'm *nothing*."

Daiyu eyed his worn weapons with renewed interest; that still didn't explain why he was now dressed like a bandit, with rusted weapons and a crude demeanor. Unless he had turned to thievery since he wasn't a soldier anymore. In that case, his intentions in the army were likely not honorable in the first place.

"My fiancé also served in the Emperor Yan's imperial army," she said slowly, hoping to draw some sympathy from him. "He died fighting against Drakkon Muyang, so I understand some of your frustrations."

He turned to her sharply. "Oh? But look at you now—cozying up to the same man who killed your fiancé."

"I don't have a choice." Daiyu pursed her lips together, sweat rolling down between her shoulder blades. "How can a lone woman defy the emperor after he's chosen her to be his? Women are no more than tools and pretty dolls in a man's world. I have no say in what I want. Capturing me will bring you nothing but—"

"And you'll be a tool for us too." A sinister grin curved his lips and caused the scar on his face to lift in a way that made her flinch back. "A symbol to prove to the world that we've taken from the emperor. He might not care for you as a person, but he chose you as his woman, and we've stolen from him. The act of taking what belongs to him is what will anger him, pretty lady."

"You ... you monster!" She wanted to scurry farther into the wagon, to be away from him and his ominous cackles, but the manure-smelling hay created a barrier between her and the railings of the wagon. There was no talking sense into this man or garnering sympathy. They would use her however they saw fit.

The man sniggered, and soon, the rest of the men joined him, their guffaws booming across the fields of swaying grass.

14

THE PARTY FINALLY STOPPED FOR A BREAK DURING THE evening. They tied their horses to the trees and made a campfire in the middle of the woods. Daiyu was still stuck in the wagon, her wrists bound but her ankles free. She watched the men as they ate dried meat from their sacks and drank water from sheep-skin cannisters. Nobody but Qian, the scarred man, seemed to be watching her.

Daiyu's stomach growled and she bit her bottom lip to keep from salivating. According to Qian and his goons, she had been unconscious for three days, so it was only natural that she felt like she hadn't eaten in years. She stared at the men who drank and ate happily, and her stomach continued to shrivel within itself, rumbling louder and louder.

Finally, when she couldn't take it anymore, she inched closer to the door of the wagon. "I'd like to eat and drink a little," she asked the closest man. "I'll starve at this rate."

The man glanced at her and then at Qian. "Well? I'm not giving my share to her."

"Let her starve," Bao said bitterly, glaring at her from his spot against a tree. "It'll teach her a lesson."

Some of the men snickered, and Daiyu's face flushed with

embarrassment. "That's not fair," she said, searching the scruffy faces for someone kind. "If you truly intend to use me as a symbol, then I hardly see why I have to be half-dead for your goal."

One of the horses stretched its legs and began to pee where it stood, and that caused Bao's face to twist into a grin as he jerked a thumb at it. "Why not give her some horse piss?"

"Excuse me?" Daiyu reeled back, her face paling.

Qian chuckled at Bao and chewed the end of his beef jerky. "You sure are bitter, huh?"

"I really don't feel that it's necessary or appropriate to let her starve," a cold voice broke through the sniggers and cruel laughs sent in her direction.

Qian turned to the young man who had spoken. He sharpened his sword against a smaller blade, his back pressed against a tree and an expressionless look on his face. He had a shock of dark gold hair that he cropped short, which was unlike the fashion in Huo, where everyone kept their hair long. His eyes were a vibrant green, and his skin was tanned to a deep honey-gold. Almost immediately, Daiyu recognized him as a foreigner—either Kadian or Sanguine. She was surprised she hadn't noticed him before, but it could have been because he seemed to keep himself distant from the others.

"If we're to sell her to General Keung, then it won't do to have her starved and dying," the young man continued. His small blade slid across the edge of his already sharpened sword, and the metal ground against the other with a screech. He met Qian's stare evenly. "It might lower her cost. Furthermore, how will he believe she's truly Drakkon's bride-to-be if she looks like a common, starved peasant?"

"Atreus," Qian said with a pointed look. "You're not the leader of this group. I will do as I see fit."

"I'm only advising you." The foreigner gave Daiyu a once-over and rose to his feet; it was then that she realized he was tall—maybe as tall as Muyang. He slid his swords into the baldric across his back and looked down at Qian with a distasteful sneer. "What you do with her is of no interest to me."

Daiyu watched as the young man spun around and walked over to his horse, which he began to brush with his palms. Qian spat in his direction, his own mouth twisted into a scowl. "Little bastard thinks he can order me around?"

"He did make a good point," one of the men murmured, his antsy gaze flicking from Daiyu and then to the scarred man. "What if we don't get a fair share because she's in bad condition?"

"I agree too ... to some extent," Bao grumbled, touching his bandages again. "It'll all be to waste if we don't get a good price."

Qian blew out air and waved to one of the men. "Fine. Give her the meat and some water."

Daiyu straightened where she sat. Her stomach continued to growl as one of the men approached her with slices of dried meat in his grimy hands. He crossed his forearms on the railing of the wagon and grinned at her.

"You sure are pretty." He held the meat a few inches from her face. "I want to see that mouth of yours work."

"E-Excuse me?" Daiyu pulled her legs in front of her to create more distance between herself and the man. The shadows of the night cast shadows across his gruff face, warping his leering expression into something more menacing. "Stop with your jokes and untie me." Her voice came out small and squeaky, and she hated the weakness in it.

"We can't untie you, so eat out of my hands, *my lady*." He said the last part with a mocking lilt in his voice.

Daiyu licked her lips and shot a glance at the other men, but they weren't paying her any attention, and by the way they all acted, she doubted they cared. She had no savior here. Not even the foreigner who had helped her case was stepping forward to aid her.

The man waved the meat and raised his eyebrows. "You don't want to eat?"

"You can place it on the floor of the wagon," she said uneasily.

"Where's the fun in that?" He held a water cannister in his other hand and held it up for her. "Or would you rather drink first?"

As if on cue, her stomach rumbled again. She pressed her lips together. Never in her life had she been so humiliated—even the pond incident with Muyang hadn't been *this* bad.

"Well?"

Daiyu leaned forward and took a slice of dried meat into her mouth. The man's lips curved into a grin. She barely tasted the salted food. The back of her eyes stung with mortification and she hated the way the man was staring down at her. Like he was imagining something much different.

After she ate the last of the food, he grabbed her mouth roughly and teased it open with his fingers. "The things I would —" he began.

She bit down—hard. Metallic blood filled her mouth and the man screamed, yanking his hand back, but not before she scraped a layer of his skin off with her bare teeth. He dropped the cannister of water on the floor of the wagon, so while he wailed and cursed, she spat out the blood, dropped forward and took the rim of the cannister with her mouth. She tried to drink from it and bit back a scream when the man grabbed a fistful of her hair and pulled her head back.

His face was purple with rage, and the veins on his throat and forehead bulged. "You *bitch*."

He slapped her and she slammed into the railing of the wagon, her head cracking against the uneven wood. Her vision darkened and she licked the inside of her cheek, where she could taste her own iron blood.

"Let her *go*," he growled.

Qian held the man's wrist, halting him from attacking her further. "I never said you could hit her. We need her in good condition."

"The bitch almost bit my finger off!"

"Then let this be a lesson not to get so damn close," the

scarred man snapped, releasing the other man. "If you want to hit her, hit her body, *not* the face."

The man cradled his wounded hand close to his chest and shot her a dirty look before scampering away. Qian watched him, his lips flattened into a firm line. When he turned to her, there was a warning on his face. "Don't attack my men. Next time you do, I'll have you strung naked in the back of this wagon. Do you understand?"

Daiyu swallowed, her mouth and throat dry.

He leaned against the railing, the wood groaning beneath his weight. "Do you understand?"

"Y-yes."

"Good."

He pushed away from the wagon and went back to the campfire. Daiyu lay back down on the foul-smelling hay, her shoulders aching from being forced behind her back for so long, and the skin on her wrists burning from the ropes.

The night sky was littered with tiny, sparkling stars, and she could only stare at them silently.

A week passed of simply traveling with the band of rugged bandits. During that time, Daiyu was mostly the center of jeers and ill intention. She was given enough food not to pass out, but not enough to be full every night. She hadn't made any attempts to leap off the wagon and make a run for it because when they started traveling through the mountains, she didn't want to risk dying by flinging herself into the sharp, uneven terrain below.

The more they traveled, the colder the climate became, and it was then that she noticed that all the men were dressed for winter in thick cloaks and furs, and that she was the only one in her flimsy, silk nightdress. They were likely going up north, where the weather was colder and wintery. It was also where Muyang was and likely where this General Keung person was.

It was only when they left the mountainside and were camped in a forest that Daiyu even considered running. The night air was cool against her skin, and Qian was more preoccupied with scolding one of his drunk bandits than he was with watching her. Daiyu inched closer to the edge of the wagon. The other men were either eating and tending to their weapons or talking amongst themselves in hushed voices. No one seemed to be paying her any attention.

Daiyu twisted her wrists against the ropes. She had been loosening her constraints against a snagged, splintered part of the wagon that she covered with hay for the past week. She had poked her wrist and fingers against the rough wood multiple times, and her flesh was sore and swollen from being pricked and prodded for so long. But her pain was worth it because when she shimmied her shoulders and yanked at her hand, the rope began slipping— just barely—down to her thumb. She tried to keep her face expressionless as she continued to slide her fingers free.

The skin of her wrists was raw and bleeding, but she barely glanced at them, her attention instead drawn to the rest of the men. Once again, they were ignoring her. They had become accustomed to her silence and her captivity—drunk on arrogance that she would never try anything against them.

Daiyu silently hauled herself over the railing of the wagon and landed on her feet by the wheels. Her breath came out strained, and her numb legs wobbled from not being used for over a week. The cold, damp earth felt rough against her bare feet, and she prayed it wouldn't slow her down. Her muscles screamed as she kept herself low and backed away from the men. Her heart raced and adrenaline rushed through her veins. It didn't matter where she ran—she needed to escape as far as possible from them.

She continued to creep backward and slipped behind a tree, her breaths coming out in small, raspy gasps that sounded too loud to her own blood-rushed ears. She froze when a twig snapped beneath her feet, but nobody moved—they continued conversing with one another.

Finally, she turned and hurried through the forest, trying as hard as she could not to barrel through the branches and bushes. Her breath puffed out in white streams as she jogged forward.

Someone shouted from behind her, and she dropped all her carefulness and sprinted. Branches ripped through her hair and cut her arms and legs, but she didn't let that slow her down. Her thighs and calves burned with exertion, and her lungs stung with every breath she took. She could hear grunts and shouts intensify behind her, and the snapping of branches and twigs. She didn't even register the pain of her feet—as fallen branches, bramble, and thorns cut through them.

She didn't dare turn around. She didn't dare lose focus on moving one foot in front of the other. She didn't dare—

Something—or someone—tackled her from behind and she shot forward, landing hard on her elbows and knees. She tried clawing the earth as the man grabbed a hold of her shoulder and neck. Tears blurred her vision and she kicked and screamed as he hauled her to her feet.

She had been so close.

So close to escaping from these rugged, evil men.

The man slapped her across the face, his breathing labored and his face twisted anger. She fell to the side, her face throbbing. He clamped a hand tightly on her bicep—tight enough to leave marks—and yanked her toward him. He was screaming something at her, but she couldn't hear him, not from the shrillness of her own shrieks.

He threw her over his shoulder and began heading back. She punched his back and flailed her legs, trying to hit any part of him. Tears of frustration and fear blurred her vision. Qian's threat boomed in her head, and she didn't want to imagine what he would do to her now that she tried to escape. Would he attack her? Torture her? Strip her naked as punishment?

When the men regrouped at their campsite, the man holding

her flung her to the ground. She crashed like a rag doll, the back of her head cracking against the cold earth, and a stab of pain shot up her back from an especially sharp rock she had landed on. She rolled over on her hands and knees, her entire body shivering.

"What do we do with her, boss?" one of the men said, spitting on the ground by her hands. "I say we take her as she is."

"Don't you dare touch me!" she spat, struggling to her feet. The world was spinning, and the group of men appeared to be doubling. When she blinked, her vision righted itself, but the darkness of the night made them look taller and more formidable. She had never felt so small and vulnerable in her life.

Qian stepped forward, his scarred face appearing more grotesque in the moonlight. His lips curled back. "I warned you."

"Stay away!" Daiyu backed away from him, but the men had created a ring around her. Each of their faces were carved with cruelty and salacious expectance. Her breaths heaved out of her body in quick succession. More adrenaline rushed through her body, and she curled her fists together to fight the first man who jumped on her.

Before any of them could inch closer, something moved quickly from behind Qian. One moment, the man was closing in on her, the next moment, something sharp poked out from his neck. Daiyu could barely blink back her confusion, time seeming to slow as Qian's face distorted in dazed confusion. Blood coated the tip of the blade sticking out from him. He reached forward to touch it, but the sword was yanked free before he could.

It all happened in a split second.

Just as Qian fell to his knees, the foreigner, wielding the now blood-stained sword, swung his weapon at the man beside him. The man barely saw it coming. The weapon bit into his neck and severed it easily. A spray of blood followed, raining down on Atreus, but he was already moving to the next bandit.

Daiyu watched in stunned silence as the men moved in slow motion to react, their hands fumbling over the hilts of their own weapons. He was too fast, though, and even when the others swarmed him, he disarmed them quickly. A stab here, a jab there —he lopped off limbs in seconds.

In the chaos and confusion, Daiyu backed away and scrambled to where the horses were tied. She wouldn't let this random act of infighting stop her from escaping. The horses were stamping and neighing, their ears shifting toward the screams and shouts. When she neared the first horse, she patted its neck and tried to calm it down.

"It's okay, it's okay," she said, her fingers dancing between the soft mane. "It's fine!"

When the horse calmed down enough where she didn't think it would stamp her to death, she began working on untying the ropes keeping it tied to a tree. Her hands shook violently, and she wasn't sure if it was from panic or fear.

Breathing out deeply, she undid the knot and tried reaching for the saddle. She had never ridden a horse before, and the creature loomed over her. She wondered briefly if it knew she was inexperienced, and a shiver ran down her spine at the thought of being flung off the horse or dragged by the reins.

"You don't," a ragged breath said from behind her, "need to do that."

Daiyu whirled on her feet to find Atreus a few feet away from her, his sword stuck to the ground and his chest heaving up and down. Blood drenched him completely, coating his face, his clothes, and his boots. She stared beyond him, to the corpses littering the campsite. Most of them were missing their hands and chunks of their faces, their blood fresh and appearing black in the dark of night.

Her blood ran cold and she looked back at the young man. She raised her hands slowly, her gaze never leaving his sword. "What do you want?"

She expected him to laugh at her and steal her away, or attack her with his weapon, but he did none of those things. He breathed out deeply, spat a glob of blood onto the ground, and lowered himself into a short bow.

"I'd like to escort you back to His Majesty, my lady."

Daiyu blinked back, waiting for him to spring forward and slice her neck. Her body was stiff in anticipation of an attack, but it didn't come. The only noise between them was the buzzing of insects, the chirr of crickets, and his heavy breathing.

"What did you say?" she finally breathed. "You want to take me back to ... His Majesty? Do you mean Drakkon Muyang or ... or whoever you serve?"

"I serve Drakkon Muyang." Atreus raised his head, and in the moonlight, his green eyes appeared softer. "I was sent on a mission to investigate a group of thugs working closely with the rebel cause. Never in a million years did I imagine they would try to kidnap one of His Majesty's women. I'm sorry I couldn't save you earlier. I was undecided on whether to continue with my mission or abort it. In the end, I couldn't allow them to harm you."

"Oh." All the fight seemed to drain from her body as relief took over. She wanted to sink to the ground and cry, but she instead steadied herself by grabbing onto a nearby tree. Her shoulder sagged against it, and she closed her eyes. "Oh. I see."

"His Majesty is located farther north, in Fort—"

"Wait." She held her hand up. "You want to take me to the emperor?"

He tilted his head to the side. "Well, yes. He is located a week's ride from here, and it would be faster to go to him than to go back to the palace."

"No." Daiyu was already shaking her head. She tried not to look at the dead bodies surrounding them or at the blood staining the grass and trees. "This is the perfect opportunity for me to run as far away as possible from His Majesty and all of his people. Don't you see? I wouldn't have been in this mess if I wasn't associated with him."

Atreus's golden brows drew together, a drop of blood sliding down between them. "You wish to ... flee? From His Majesty?"

"Tell him I died." She nodded to the dead, mangled bodies.

"That I was killed in the fray. That you—that you tried *desperately* to save me, but in the end, one of the men took me and killed me before you could do anything—"

"No."

"—and that you're—" She paused, taken aback as the young man stared at her levelly. "No? But, but it doesn't hurt you to say that you—"

"That I failed to protect His Majesty's woman?" he scoffed, his expression pinching together. "I can see no bigger failure than to have you die when you were so close to me. Furthermore, I will not lie to His Majesty."

Daiyu's chest constricted once more, and this time with apprehension. "Please, I can't—I can't go back to him! It's better this way; for him to believe that I'm dead. Please, you must tell him—"

"I will not lie to him." He straightened, and she inched back at the sight of his full height. This was still a warrior who had killed a dozen men single-handedly, and she had a feeling that it wasn't in her best interests to argue with him.

"Please," she begged, tears filling her eyes. "I can't go back to him."

"Why? Are you afraid of him?"

She thought of Muyang's dark eyes, of his wicked beauty, and the way his soft mouth would curve up into a cruel smile. He was terrifying. Not only because he was captivatingly beautiful, but he was too powerful. She could still remember the way he had held a blade to her neck, ready to kill her if she answered incorrectly. Yes, she *was* afraid of him.

She shivered to think about what he would do to her once he found out she had almost been used against him. Would he kill her so nobody else could shame him like that?

"He will not harm you," Atreus said, watching her carefully. He yanked a handkerchief from his pocket and cleaned his blade. Soon, the small cloth was stained with blood. "He will be happy to see that you are safe."

"Happy?" Her chest rose, and she couldn't imagine the emperor being *happy* over anything. Certainly not her well-being.

The young man sighed. "My lady, I do not wish to forcefully bring you back to His Majesty. I think that is cruel, especially after what you've been through. But it's my duty to return you to him, so you must comply."

She couldn't run from him, not only because he was strong enough to kill so many men, but because he knew she was alive, and she was certain he would tell Muyang even if she did manage to escape from him. She didn't have much of a choice, she realized with a sinking heart. Not if she wanted to keep her family safe.

More tears threatened to spill down her face, but she quickly pressed the heels of her hands to her eyes and inhaled sharply, trying to calm her erratic breathing. It would be fine, she told herself. She'd find another way.

"We'll have to take one of the men's cloaks," Atreus said, his attention skating to the corpses. "I'll have to see which one is in better condition—"

Daiyu began walking toward Qian, her stomach sinking further and further into the pits of her feet as she accepted her fate. She stopped by the scarred man. Blood was already crusting over the fatal wound on his neck, and he was holding his throat as if to stem the bleeding. But his eyes were glassy and pinned to the sky. She wondered, briefly, if he feared death before taking his last breath.

"My lady?"

She dropped down beside the corpse and tentatively peeled back his clothes, her hands skimming over his waist. Her fingers found what she was looking for and she yanked back the dragon dagger Muyang had entrusted her with. Blood spotted the hilt of the blade, and the edge of it was filmy with grease—Qian would sometimes use the dagger to eat with.

"I might as well take this with me," she said, holding the dagger up for Atreus to see.

"He gave that to you?"

"Yes—" She turned around to find Atreus reach down to his boot. Before she could ask him what he was doing, he pulled out an identical weapon.

A grin was spread on his face. "He must like you if he gave it to you."

"He didn't *give* it to me." She rose to her feet, her stomach twisting at the smell of iron pervading the air. "Anyway, we should head out."

"Of course, my lady."

They had a long journey ahead of them, Daiyu thought with a long sigh. She had been so close to freedom, and yet ... it always seemed to slip from her grasp.

15

Daiyu stretched her arms and legs out in the wagon as it rumbled forward. Atreus steered the two horses and was silent, like usual. She had lost count of how many days they had been traveling, but she knew they were close to Muyang. She tightened the grimy cloak closer to her body, her nose crinkling at the smell of sweat and blood. They had taken the cloak off one of the lesser mangled corpses, but it, unfortunately, was still stiff with blood and filth and who-knew-what. She wriggled her toes on the floor of the wagon and winced as pain shot through her cut and worn feet. She had bandaged herself up and yanked out the thorns and twigs that had been stuck to her feet during her run through the forest, but the pain remained even after all these days.

"How did you become His Majesty's spy?" Daiyu asked, sitting upright in the stack of hay to glance over at him. They were currently passing through empty valleys of grass. She had spotted villages in the distance, but Atreus had reassured her that they had enough resources to make it to Fort Xingia without stopping at "suspicious" villages that might be harboring rebel forces.

He didn't answer for a moment, and the only indication that

he had heard her was a slight tilt of his head. "I met him ten years ago in Sanguis."

"Oh, so you're from Sanguis?" That had been her guess—either that or Kadios, the other kingdom that neighbored them. "But why do you serve the emperor of the Huo empire and not your own country, then?"

"His Majesty saved me a decade ago when I was a boy, so I have a debt to repay him. Sanguis may be my home country, but I am not loyal to it. I am loyal to Muyang."

Her eyebrows rose. He had called him Muyang. *Simply* Muyang. Nobody was allowed to call the emperor by his name so casually, unless he allowed them to, and that was only if they had a close enough relationship.

She sat up straighter with renewed interest. The carriage bumped and rolled over stones, and her voice came out with a slight vibration. "You're close to him?"

"He helped me when no one else did."

"But ten years ago ... How old was he?" Daiyu picked at the frayed hem of the cloak as the blistering wind blew through her hair. Muyang appeared to be the same age as her, but he couldn't be that young, could he?

"I'm not sure. He looked the same as he does now."

"Oh?" That perked her interest even more. "So does he use magic to stay young?"

"Maybe you can ask him."

She slumped back into the hay, her lips twisting into a frown. She could already imagine how that conversation would go—and it wouldn't be pretty.

WHEN THEY APPROACHED A TALL, ENCLOSED FORTRESS with snowy mountains in the background and an ominous, formidable castle looming in the center behind the heavily guarded wall, Daiyu's nerves jittered and her stomach twisted into a pit of snakes. Muyang was within those walls; she knew it deep down in her bones. She could feel his heavy presence, could practically choke on the thickness of the foggy air.

She twiddled her hands together and fidgeted with the sleeve of her dress. It would be fine, she told herself. He wouldn't hurt her for getting kidnapped, right? And it wasn't like she had been taken advantage of, so there was no reason for him to kill her for sullying his reputation. In fact, she should have been safe when she entered those fortress walls. But still ... the image of Muyang's furious expression, the thought of a cold knife pressed to her neck, wouldn't leave her.

Atreus stopped the wagon a dozen feet away from the fortress. Daiyu spotted over ten guards on the wall, their arrows notched at them, and her heart thundered even louder.

"Who goes there?" one of the guards boomed. She couldn't see his expression behind his helmet, but the timbre of his voice made her shudder.

"It's me, Atreus," the young man called out, raising his hands defensively. "I've brought His Majesty his wife-to-be, who was kidnapped by a group of mercenaries. I wish for passage inside."

The guard gave a nod to the rest of the archers and they slowly lowered their weapons. "Very well," he called out. "I'll confirm it with the commander-in-chief."

He then disappeared along the bend of the wall, likely down a flight of stairs. Daiyu anxiously picked at the tattered end of her sleeve, her gaze darting between the back of Atreus's head and then to the archers, who were watching them suspiciously.

Finally, after what felt like forever, the giant door to the fort slowly grinded open. Atreus urged the horse forward and Daiyu clung to the edge of the wagon as they entered the fortress. Beyond the walls, dozens of soldiers were milling about the courtyard, busy with either sparring or sharpening their weapons. They watched the wagon roll to a stop, and Daiyu caught a few curious glances sent her way.

She must have looked like a bedraggled rat, she thought with flaming cheeks. Nothing like the esteemed fiancée of the emperor she *should* have looked like.

Atreus leaped off the wagon and came around the back to unlatch the back door for her. He held his hand out to her, but she shook her head and climbed down herself. A cold, mighty wind blew through her stringy, greasy hair and she pushed it behind her ears hastily. She didn't look appropriate at all. She didn't have any shoes, she was dressed in an oversized, dirty cloak, and her hair and face were grimy and caked with travel. What would the emperor say when he saw her? Would he be horrified?

"Atreus!" a loud, cheerful voice called out from the throngs of soldiers.

The crowds parted and a man with light brown hair and honey-colored eyes approached them. He was dressed in dark-red leathers and light armor, and there was something familiar about him that she couldn't quite put her finger on. Had she seen him at the palace?

"Bohai," Atreus said with a small, growing smile.

Bohai, who appeared to be in his late twenties, clapped the young man on the shoulder and grinned at him widely. "I didn't think I'd see you this early."

"My mission came to an unexpected halt," he explained, smoothing down the front of his heavy cloak.

Daiyu shifted on her feet uncomfortably. The cuts and scrapes on her flesh stung and she hated that she hadn't taken one of the dead bandit's shoes—Atreus had advised her to do so, but all the boots were more than double her size, and she had trouble walking in them, so she had opted out. Now, though, standing on the chilly pavement with nothing on but dirtied bandages, her feet felt too bare.

The light-haired man shifted his attention to Daiyu, and his eyebrows rose. "I'm shocked that you're here, Lady Daiyu."

She blinked at the man. "Oh. Yes. I'm surprised myself."

"Forgive the late introduction," the man said, placing a hand on his chest. "I'm the commander-in-chief, Yao Bohai."

"It's a pleasure to meet you, Lord Yao," she began, but then stopped as she registered his title. The commander-in-chief? *This* man? Her mouth nearly dropped open and she didn't know what to say as he spoke to Atreus. She hadn't expected him to be so young, nor to even know her name.

"His Majesty will be very shocked and very displeased," Bohai murmured to Atreus, shooting Daiyu a pitying look as he assessed her up and down. "Can you walk, Lady Daiyu? Or do you wish for one of us to carry you inside?"

The thought of Atreus or Commander Yao Bohai carrying her inside sent a new wave of embarrassment rolling over her. "I can walk," she said hurriedly, clasping her hands together to busy them. She could feel more and more eyes on her the longer she stood there, and she didn't know what to make of the stares.

"Very well." Bohai waved toward the castle, which appeared even taller up closer, with more than five levels that she could see. "When were you taken from the palace? I'm shocked that we haven't received any word from the palace, especially since our mages are usually top-notch in communicating with us."

Uneasiness grew in the hollow of her stomach as they entered the castle walls. The polished wood was icy beneath her feet, the cold seeping down into her bones. "Well, it happened ... maybe two weeks ago?"

"Hm, strange," he murmured, continuing down the hall. The passing soldiers lowered themselves to a bow as he passed them by. "I wonder if the mages didn't consider it important enough to inform His Majesty."

Daiyu flinched, unable to hide her surprise. Was she so insignificant that nobody cared to even *look* for her? More apprehension built in her chest and she struggled to keep up with the two men. She wanted to pause, sit down somewhere, and wallow in self-pity for *at least* an hour. Enough time for her to reflect on how meaningless and unimportant she would be if she became Drakkon Muyang's wife.

She could feel Atreus staring at her, but she ignored him and silently walked behind Bohai, who was already talking about something related to their next move in the north against General Keung—the major general for the rebel army. Daiyu stared at the geometric windows and the latticed metal screens covering them. She could make out the snow-encrusted mountains in the distance, and she longed to be far away from this place.

Finally, they stopped at a set of red painted doors with slithering dragons carved into the frame. Bohai knocked, and without waiting for an answer, strolled inside the room, beckoning Daiyu and Atreus forward.

Daiyu scrambled behind Atreus. They likely were going to wait to see Muyang, she decided, poking her head over Atreus's large body to peek inside the room. There was no way Muyang was inside here, especially since Bohai didn't even wait for him to answer—

Her breath caught in her throat.

Muyang was leaning his hip against a desk casually, a yellowed scroll in one hand and a cup of tea in the other as he scanned the parchment. Unlike at the palace, where he had been bedecked in royal regalia—in shimmering gold earrings, gold bracelets, and fancy hair crowns—he was clad entirely in menacing, black leathers. His hair was bound at the crown of his head, and his hair crown was blood-red and black, making him look all the more like a terrifying general than an emperor.

He lifted his head, and his black eyes flicked from Bohai, to Atreus, and then landed on her. For a moment, time froze, and Daiyu sucked in her cheeks as she took in his clean-shaven appearance, the hard planes of his wicked face, and his dark eyes that reminded her of a starless night sky.

He slowly lowered his steaming teacup on the desk behind him, his eyes never straying from hers. "What," he said, his voice cold and clipped, "are you doing here?"

That was all Daiyu needed to snap out of her trance. She lowered her head and dropped down to her knees in a low bow. Her hands trembled as she pressed them into the floor. "Greetings, Your Majesty. Forgive my insolence. I didn't expect to see you here."

Atreus shifted on his feet but didn't bow down like she was doing. He must've been closer to Muyang to forgo such a formality, she realized, keeping her head low.

"Atreus, explain what happened," Muyang snapped, and even from her peripheral vision, she could see the young man wince.

"I was on my mission like you told me to, but ... while I was there, Lady Daiyu was taken by the group, and so I decided to abandon my mission and rescue her instead." He said it all in one breath, like he was scared to take too many pauses. Like he wanted to get this conversation over with as soon as possible.

The air in the room seemed to shift, thicken, and turn colder. Daiyu spared a glance at Muyang and wished she hadn't—she had never seen such a look of cold fury on someone's face. He looked ready to murder someone, and she wasn't sure who his wrath was pointed to.

The scroll in his hand cracked, and he dropped it on his desk the next second. "Who did this to her? I want them all *dead*."

"Already done," Atreus said, his voice quiet. "I would never let them live."

Bohai didn't seem as petrified as Daiyu or as anxious as Atreus, and waved his hand dismissively. "Come on, Muyang. You know Atreus; he wouldn't let anyone who slighted you escape with their life," he said casually. "And besides, she got caught in the middle of this mess because she's *your* bride."

"They were planning on selling her to General Keung," Atreus continued.

"That bastard," Muyang growled, his black eyes flashing with something sinister. A promise of death, Daiyu surmised.

She remained on the floor, her legs growing numb and apprehension taking hold of her. A million thoughts raced through her mind—all of them ending in her demise. She felt nauseous, her mouth dry and sandy.

"Atreus, go get yourself cleaned up," Muyang finally said after a moment of silence. "You smell like blood and horseshit. And, Bohai, you're dismissed too."

The two men shuffled out of the room in the next second, neither of them seeming keen on lingering with Muyang's displeasure written all over his face. Daiyu wiped her sweaty palms on her dress, unable to meet Muyang's gaze—even as it remained on her.

He stepped closer, and she still couldn't look at him. It wasn't until he stopped in front of her, his black leather boots mere inches from her knees, that she dared to peer up at him. His beautiful face was carved from stone—callous and indifferent—as he kneeled in front of her.

"Did they hurt you?" Muyang's voice came out smooth and calm, but Daiyu flinched nonetheless and averted her gaze. He placed a gentle, cold hand on her cheek, and a shiver ran down her spine. "Look at me."

Daiyu complied, all the blood rushing to her ears and face as she met his obsidian-colored eyes. There was a coldness about him that put winter to shame, but the darkness that usually swamped his expression was nowhere to be seen. Instead, she found a tenderness she had never seen before.

"Did they hurt you?" he repeated, retracting his hand.

She wanted to lean into his touch and close her eyes; to breathe in the smell of jasmine and sandalwood. But then the imagery of a dagger pressed to her neck reemerged, and she couldn't forget that he was just as deadly as those bandits were.

"*Daiyu.*"

Her hands grew clammy again and she finally shook her head. "A little, but nothing I can't handle."

Muyang scrutinized her slowly, and she could have sworn she saw something dark flash over his face. "A little?"

"Your Majesty," she said, licking her dry lips, "I am well, if that is what you're asking. Nobody touched me and I'm unsullied."

She didn't want him to kill her because he thought she had been soiled by the men, and she certainly didn't want him to think of her as someone who would sully his reputation. She was supposed to be safe within these walls with Muyang, and yet she felt trapped once more. Like a cornered animal waiting to be slaughtered.

As if reading her mind, he slowly asked, "Did you think I would think less of you if those *fiends* attacked you?"

She raised her head to find his lips pursed together in anger. He leaned forward and suddenly took her face in his hands. She inhaled sharply, her eyes widening as he stared at her, searching for something. His eyes narrowed as he spoke, each word coming out rough. "Those bastards don't deserve to even look at you, much less breathe the same air that you breathe. Do you understand me, Daiyu?"

She didn't understand a thing. All she knew was that he was holding her gently, and warmth was pooling in her stomach. His touch was electrical, and she felt intoxicated by it.

"Your Majesty, unhand me," she whispered.

"Not until you tell me that you understand."

"I ..." She swallowed down the thickness in her throat. His face was only a few inches away from her, and his breath was fanning across her lips enticingly. She wanted to keep breathing in his warm scent of spices and jasmine. She wanted to lean closer and press her mouth against his, just to figure out what he tasted like. To understand what sweet, sweet, wicked beauty felt like. "What do you want me to understand?"

"That you are worth too much for those bastards. That you are above everyone else in this empire, and that anybody who dares look at what is mine without asking for permission should die where they stand." He inched closer to her, and her chest rose in anticipation. His black gaze seared into her. "Do you understand now?"

Daiyu's face flushed with warmth, and she hated the effect he had on her. "I understand, Your Majesty."

He released her and finally stepped away. The warmth of his presence felt like a cold slap, and she nearly fell forward, her sweaty hands cupping her knees like that was all that was holding her together. He was still peering down at her, and she didn't know what to make of his expression—it was a mixture of wild rage and barely contained desire, and something else. Something that was far more dangerous. Something that told her he cared, in some twisted way, about her.

Her pulse quickened, and she forced herself to remember that he was the evil emperor. That he would kill her if she stopped serving his purpose—whatever that purpose was—and that she was just a tool for him, a bride he could easily replace. She forced herself to remember how he had humiliated her at the pond, just to test his own power and how he had placed his dagger to her throat. *He* was the reason she had been kidnapped, and he didn't even have the gall to apologize to her for it.

"Your Majesty, if it isn't too much trouble," she said, dropping her head once more. "I would appreciate a bath, a change of clothes, and perhaps a meal."

"Certainly." He sidestepped around her and yanked the door open. He spoke to a few of the guards in the hallway and then came back inside. "Sit on the couch."

Daiyu clambered to her feet and finally took notice of the rest of the room—the desk with neat stacks of letters and scrolls, the box-style wooden couch at the end of the room with carved dragons forming the legs, the large map of Huo against the wall with colorful pins stuck at certain locations. She sat down on the cushioned couch and examined the green, tiger-embroidered pillows by the armrests.

"Can you explain to me everything that happened?" Muyang eased himself onto the matching couch across from her and propped his elbows on his knees in a casual but intimidating pose as he leaned forward. "At the palace and with the thugs."

Daiyu shifted in her seat, all too aware that she appeared much too dirty to be seated in front of the emperor. "Why do you ask?"

He blinked, as if not expecting that answer. "For many

reasons," he said slowly. "For one, it's interesting how you're always caught up in some sort of trouble. And secondly, I'm curious to know how you left the palace without anyone noticing."

Was he ... suspicious of her?

"Your Majesty," Daiyu said, barely controlling the rising anger in her tone. "I'm sure someone noticed I was missing, but since I'm simply a farmer's girl who's easily replaceable, they likely didn't think it was important enough to inform you of the matter."

Muyang reclined into the back cushions of the couch, his expression unchanging. "You're not easily replaceable."

"You don't even know me, Your Majesty." She rested her hands on her lap and resisted the itch to fidget with her sleeve. "And those servants in the palace don't care much for me. I'm just one of many women who will be in your palace."

The back of her eyes burned, and she didn't know why. She didn't want to be his wife—far from it—but she pitied the life of a noblewoman who would be tied to such a cruel man. A man who would never love her and who would replace her once she fulfilled his needs. A man who would take on dozens of dozens of women since she would never be enough. Daiyu didn't want to end up like that.

"I didn't realize you felt like no one cared in the palace," he said, watching her carefully. "I'll have to speak to the servants who serve you."

An awkward silence filled the space between them and Daiyu found that she couldn't meet his gaze—she didn't like the way he was examining her as if waiting for her to shatter like glass.

"Explain to me what happened the day you were kidnapped."

Before she could answer, a servant knocked on the door and promptly entered with a tray of tea and a plate of assorted nuts and diced fruit. He placed the drinks and the platter on the table, bowed, and left. Daiyu eyed the juicy, halved plums and her mouth instantly watered.

Muyang must've seen the hunger on her face because he waved to the food. "Take whatever you want. It's for you, anyway."

She picked up the silver chopsticks on the tray and picked up a piece of the plum, then plopped it into her mouth. The sweet fruit nearly melted into her mouth and she continued to pick at the rest of the food. Between eating and sipping tea, Daiyu recounted the entire incident since her kidnapping. Muyang listened attentively, his gaze never straying from hers. He didn't interrupt her or utter a word and only nodded from time to time.

Finally, when she finished snacking—and realized with horror that she ate everything on the platter—and her story was finished, she set the chopsticks on the tray and folded her hands together in sudden embarrassment. "Well, that's everything that happened," she said, clearing her throat. "Oh! And—"

She reached into the inner pocket of her cloak and pulled out the dragon dagger she had safely tucked in there. She held it out for him, her fingers wrapping around the cold dragon body of the hilt.

"Your dagger," she said. "I retrieved it from the men. Well, to be more specific, Atreus defeated the man and I took it back from him, but in the end, it's here."

Muyang's dark eyes flicked down to the silver blade and then back up at her. The corner of his mouth rose. "I didn't think I'd see the day when the little rabbit pointed a dagger at me."

Eyes widening, she hastily slapped the blade on the tea table. She hadn't even realized she had been rudely directing the edge at him. "I'm so sorry, Your Majesty—"

"No, no. You're fine." He picked up the dagger slowly, his soft mouth still curved into a smirk. "I would like to see it more. You, holding a blade to my throat. It would be quite riveting."

Daiyu could feel the blush clawing up her throat and singeing her cheeks. For some reason, it didn't sound dangerous at all, but sensual. And she didn't know what to make of that.

Muyang slipped the dagger onto his belt beside a short sword. "Take your cloak off."

"Excuse me?" She grabbed the front of the cloak and tightened her hold on it as if he would rip it off her in the next second. Although she had hated every second in the sweat-soaked, bloodied thing, she didn't want to take it off in front of him.

"Take it off." He gestured to the cloak as if she hadn't heard him correctly the first time. "You shouldn't be wearing something that belongs to a dead man."

"I'll ..." She swallowed, hating the tremble in her voice. But his calm demeanor seemed to bolster something in her because she found herself shaking her head. "I want to keep it on. At least until my bath."

Muyang canted his head to the side. "You refuse me?"

She continued staring at him, and he stared back, neither of them seeming to want to relent control. She didn't know why she was grasping onto this so tightly—it was just a stupid cloak that meant nothing to her—and yet she didn't want to lose what little power she had in front of him. Power that, she was well aware, he was allowing her to have.

Finally, he chuckled, low and soft and musical. "Fine, keep the cloak. But after your bath, I want you to burn it. Burn it and forget everything that transpired the past two weeks. Don't let any of those men haunt your dreams. From what I've learned in life is that the dead should stay dead, and the living should continue to live."

"Do you have experience with that, Your Majesty?"

"Oh, plenty." His eyes flashed. "Do you know how many men I've killed in my lifeline? Men on the battlefield, traitors in front of the throne who lick my boots, enemies who think they can take what's mine? If I let every single one of them linger in my thoughts for too long, I would not be able to continue walking with the weight of their dead hands on my shoulders. So every person I've killed, I quickly forgot. Because what's the point in continuing to think of a dead man? Let him stay dead."

Whatever little moment was conspiring between them seemed to crack and splinter at the edges as reality sank in—when he was in front of her talking so casually and calmly, it was easy to forget that he was a powerful emperor who had killed countless people. She almost forgot how much blood stained his legacy. How many people had to die for him to take the throne. Including her dead fiancé, Heng.

Daiyu pushed back a strand of hair behind her ear and Qian's words wouldn't stop bouncing in her mind.

Look at you now—cozying up to the same man who killed your fiancé.

An uncomfortable, heavy, and stifling feeling took hold of her chest, seeming to choke what little energy she had. Was she actually enjoying conversing with Muyang? That couldn't be true. She was terrified of him and was planning on leaving him and everything he stood for, after all. And yet, uneasiness rooted within her, like a seed growing too rapidly to fit inside its pot. She didn't like the effect Muyang was having on her and how guilty her conscience felt in his presence. She needed to find a way to end this faster, before things became more complicated.

Daiyu coughed and rubbed the nape of her neck to busy her fidgeting hands. "Your Majesty, is my bath ready?"

"It should be." Muyang stood up and motioned to the door. "Come with me."

16

DAIYU TRAILED BEHIND MUYANG AS THEY WALKED through the winding, busy halls of the castle. Soldiers dropped down to low bows when Muyang passed, but he only gave them a short nod of acknowledgment before breezing past them. It felt strange to see the waves of people lower themselves in front of him, and it almost felt like they were bowing to *her*, since she was walking so close to him.

It wasn't a feeling she could ever get used to, or want to get used to. It made her uncomfortable more than anything else.

When they reached a hallway that was less hectic than the rest, on one of the top levels, Muyang swung open the door and marched inside without a backward glance at her. She scrambled after him, taking in the spacious room with two couches across from one another, a large metal-braced window showcasing the fortress courtyard below, and the sliding doors sectioning the other chambers of the room. In the center, a giant wooden bathtub was placed upon a multicolored rug with tigers and dragons and snakes dancing over it. A large hearth warmed the room and painted it in hues of orange.

Steam from the bathwater fogged the window panes beyond the latticed metal design, and the smell of jasmine and herbs and sandalwood pervaded the air densely. She approached the tub tentatively, feeling all the more dirt-stained and mucky standing in such an opulent, spotless, fragranced room.

Muyang strolled deeper into the room and unceremoniously dropped on one of the couches. When Daiyu didn't move and only stared at him with bug eyes, he waved to the bathtub with a lazy hand.

"A bath, like you requested."

She blinked at the steam curling above the bathwater and then back at Muyang, who made no plans to get up and leave. "Your Majesty," she said slowly. "I did indeed request a bath, but ... I plan to bathe alone." When his amusement deepened, she reiterated, "With no company. Certainly not a man whom I'm not married to."

And, she wanted to add, *certainly not you.*

A touch of mischief played on his face for a split second—so quickly that if she blinked, she would have missed the slight glitter in his eyes. "I'm not just any man, Daiyu. I'm to be your husband."

"But you're not my husband." She shifted on her feet and dug her bandaged toes into the cool hardwood floor. Technically, the emperor could have whatever he wanted. Whether that was to watch her bathe or to take her right then and there; nobody would stop him, and nobody would fault him for taking what he desired.

"But I am the emperor." His ebony eyes appeared more sinister against the dark evening sky in the background and the orange-red fire glowing in the hearth a few feet from him.

"You *are* the emperor." Daiyu licked her dry, chapped lips nervously. "You can have whatever you desire, but I ask that you respect my wishes. I am unmarried, and I don't want to bathe in front of anyone."

"I remember you telling me that you would jump on me if you continued to remain in my bathing chambers with me. And that, to preserve both of our chastity, you would leave to stop

139

yourself. Do you remember, little rabbit?" He tapped his fingernails against the wooden armrest of the couch and she couldn't read the expression carved into his stony face. But there was a teasing quality to his tone that didn't ring any alarm bells, so she didn't think to back away.

"I—" She lowered her face so he couldn't see the flush that was spreading. She hated how she was always blushing and being embarrassed around him and how she had made such a fool of herself during their first meeting. "I remember."

"Unlike you, I have a bit more control," he said with a small, growing smile. "I won't jump you."

"But it's still improper." She gripped the rim of the bathtub, tendrils of steam rising over her face and warming her cheeks. "I don't think it's appropriate for a man to watch a woman bathe if she isn't his wife, and for a man to touch a woman who isn't his wife."

"You don't want me to watch you, nor touch you?"

"Correct." Her fingers turned white from holding the bathtub so tightly, and she hoped he didn't see her shaking legs. Standing up to the emperor and refusing him was an act punishable by death, but she hoped that whatever was budding between them was enough for him to forgo that route.

Muyang studied her, face expressionless, and seemed to mull over her words. She waited with bated breath, and he finally climbed to his feet.

"Very well. But I'll hold you to that when we're married," he said, walking to the door. "Oh, and before I forget, dinner will be served in an hour downstairs in the dining hall."

With that, the door clicked shut and Daiyu was all alone. She slumped over the bathtub, the energy seeming to leave her shaking legs, and exhaled deeply. She had somehow survived another interaction with him, and this time it didn't end with a dagger pressed to her throat or a dunk in the garden pond.

She hastily undid the clasp of the cloak and let it drop to the floor. She peeled back her soiled night robes, the dirtied bandages around her feet, and folded them next to the cloak. It didn't take her long to slip into the bath and begin to scrub the weeks of dirt and grime from her body and hair.

For the longest time, she simply lay in the tub and stared up at the ceiling, her eyelids growing heavy and the water turning cold.

If she had been told a few months ago that she would be one of the women chosen to be the emperor's wife, that she would be living in the royal palace, that she would be poisoned, kidnapped, and escape from a band of thieves—she would have thought someone had accidentally told the storyline of a convoluted poem rather than that of her life.

But alas, here she was. Soaking in a bath filled with rosebuds and fermented rice water. With the emperor somewhere in the fortress. And with hundreds of soldiers packed inside this fortress.

Daiyu rose to her feet, the bathwater sloshing over the rim and sopping into the rug below. She cringed as she stepped out, her toes squelching against the now-wet rug.

Spotting a towel on the couch—along with a folded set of deep-blue clothes, a pair of matching shoes, and two black hairpins—Daiyu wrung the water from her body and quickly donned the silk dress. Her hands skimmed over the dark material; it was a blend of dark purple and sapphire, with gold dragons embroidered on the sleeves and golden lotuses etched throughout the skirt. She hadn't realized how accustomed she had become to the fancy clothes from the upper class, so different than the rough, over-washed, and patchy cotton or linen she had worn for most of her life.

She dried her hair with the towel as best as she could and styled it into a low bun with the two hairpins. Finally, she appeared somewhat like a normal human being and not like a bedraggled, wet rat.

Once she was ready, she left the room and set out for the dining hall. She hoped the rest of her stay here would go smoothly and that she'd find a loophole to escape from Muyang.

~

THE DINING HALL WAS ARRANGED WITH ROWS OF LONG, low tables, where soldiers sat on cushioned mats on the floor. At the end of the room, on a dais, there was a shorter table where the emperor sat with his closest people. When Daiyu entered the room, she spotted Muyang immediately. He was picking at his food and listening to something Bohai, who sat beside him, was saying. There was another man beside him that she vaguely recognized but couldn't put her finger on where she had seen him. Along the table with the emperor sat a dozen more people, all of them seeming to vie for his attention. At the very end of the table sat Atreus and a young man who couldn't have been older than fifteen.

Almost immediately, everyone's attention drew to her and she hesitated by the doorway, unsure if she should spin on her heels and run back to her room. But then her gaze locked with Muyang, and all at once, everyone seemed to blur away until there was only him. She hated him, she told herself, and yet there was something oddly beautiful about him. The way he sat among his men, the way his black fitted outfit seemed to accentuate his wickedness. The way his handsome face was void of any emotion. Those oppressive, dark eyes seemed to trap her in place, and it was only when he beckoned her forward that her trance was broken.

Heat clawed up her throat and she hoped nobody had noticed her gawking. She walked between the rows slowly, the men's conversations seeming to hush as she hurried toward the emperor's table.

"Daiyu, have a seat." Muyang motioned to the end of his table, beside Atreus and the young man.

She gingerly took the vacant seat between the young man and Atreus. All at once, everyone began their conversations again as if she hadn't entered the room. The young man gave her a curious look, and she smiled at him. He had long hair that was pulled back at the crown of his head and held in place with various gold pins slotted into his silver dragon hair crown. Jade beaded necklaces adorned his neck and just above his collar, she spotted the undeniable royal tattoo of a snake slithering around a moon—the symbol of the MuRong dynasty.

"Oh." She blinked at the young man. She racked through her mind of the MuRong princes who were still alive but couldn't remember their names. "You must be ... a prince?"

"Yes, I'm Prince Yat-sen," he said with a small nod. "And you must be Lady Daiyu."

"Ah, yes." She couldn't believe she was in the presence of what many called the *rightful* heir to the throne. She would have thought someone like Muyang would keep the prince locked away in the palace to rot, but maybe he wanted to keep his enemies close.

Atreus picked a slice of roasted beef off the many platters of food arranged in front of them and placed it atop his bowl of rice and vegetables. "No need to speak to him too much, Lady Daiyu," he said coldly, shooting the young man a sharp glare. "It's better not to involve yourself."

Yat-sen flinched and tightened his hold on his chopsticks. Daiyu could feel the tension in the air between the two and she picked up her own utensils tentatively. "What do you mean?" she asked, piling sautéed vegetables, sticky rice, and savory meat into her own empty bowl.

"It's better not to speak to a cursed heir with questionable loyalties."

Yat-sen seemed to shrink within himself, his gaze locked onto his food.

"Oh. Thank you, Atreus." She looked between the two young men, unsure of what to say. It appeared like Yat-sen was similar to her—an outsider here. "But I think I'll speak to whoever I see fit." She pointed to the soy-glazed mushrooms in Yat-sen's bowl. "Are those good? Not too sweet?"

He blinked rapidly, turning to her and then to the food in front of him as if seeing it for the first time. "Err, it tastes good," he answered after a moment. "It's not sweet at all, mostly salty. I think … you should give it a try. It's good."

"I'll have to take your word for it, then." Daiyu smiled warmly at him as she loaded the mushrooms into her bowl and then took a bite of it. "You're right; it tastes pretty salty!"

"I prefer the saltiness," he said with a small grin.

She could feel Atreus's disapproving look on them, but she ignored it and continued to eat her food. Her gaze wandered to Muyang, who was several feet away from them at the other side of the table. He was speaking with Bohai and the other familiar-looking man. They seemed to be deep in conversation because he didn't even look her way, nor did his stony expression change.

"Who's the man beside His Majesty?" Daiyu asked in a low voice. "I think I've seen him before."

Yat-sen followed her gaze, but it was Atreus who spoke. "That's General Liang Fang. You might have seen him in the palace."

"Hm." She stared at him for a moment longer. He was dressed in the usual Huo military attire and had an icy expression on his face. She felt like she had seen him before, but … where? Finally, a mental image formed in her mind. The first day she had entered the palace, she had run into Jia and him, and he had seemed suspicious of her.

"He appears mean, but he's not that bad," Atreus said between mouthfuls of juicy chicken and savory noodles. "He doesn't spend nearly as much time in the palace as Bohai does, so you might have seen Bohai more often than him. But then again … I don't think either of them ever step foot in the Lotus wing."

Daiyu lowered her chopstick and turned her attention on Bohai—truth be told, something about him was bugging her. She had definitely seen him in the palace—not the Lotus wing, she was sure—but she couldn't pinpoint what it was about him that bothered her.

"Is he …?" She frowned. She had definitely seen him before.

"Commander Yao is half Kadian," Yat-sen said.

She shook her head. "No, that's not what I meant—"

"He may be half-Kadian, but he has more loyalty than your supposedly *pure*-blooded Huo self," Atreus quipped at the prince, shooting the youth another scowl. "It would be better for you not to comment on others."

"I didn't mean it in an offensive way—"

"I doubt it."

Daiyu looked between the two of them uneasily. She didn't like *literally* being in between the tension, and she felt like she had no choice but to be a part of it. "That's not really fair, Atreus," she said carefully, picking at her own food with a frown. She was all too aware that Atreus had saved her, and she should have been more grateful, but she couldn't sit idly while he snapped at the prince. Not when she was caught in the middle. "I don't believe he meant it maliciously."

"You don't know him, Lady Daiyu." Atreus narrowed his flinty, emerald eyes and pointed his chopstick at Yat-sen. "He's the son of the dead Emperor Yan. We can't trust anything that comes out of his mouth."

"Atreus, that's rude." She waved the eating utensil away from her and gave him a stern scowl.

The rest of the meal went awkwardly, with neither Yat-sen nor Atreus speaking. Daiyu ate in silence, occasionally glancing between the two youths and then at the emperor, who wasn't paying much attention to her.

It was a good thing, she told herself, even as a pang shot through her chest. She didn't need his attention and she was planning on leaving sometime in the future anyway. She needed to discard any ties she had with him, and she definitely needed to get rid of the strange attraction that seemed to be budding between them—or more accurately, *her* attraction toward him.

Muyang abruptly rose from his seat, and all movement froze. Everyone's utensils stopped midair as they watched the emperor slowly descend from the dais, his dark eyes flicking from person to person. The energy in the air seemed to ripple with ominous force, and Daiyu lowered her chopsticks onto her plate with trembling fingers.

"Continue your meals," he said, raising a hand as he walked through the rows of seats. Even from the distance, Daiyu could feel the magic stemming from his every step. It sent her heart racing—in anticipation of something cruel to happen—and every hair on her body rose. But Muyang didn't begin torturing anyone or blasting his magic through the room. He only said, "I'll be retiring for the night. Eat well."

"Yes, Your Majesty." The chorus of voices blended together and Daiyu flinched in surprise at the loudness.

And like that, he left the room. Everyone resumed their meals and Daiyu felt like the odd one out who didn't know what to do. She stared down at her meal, her chest still tight with apprehension. What was that about? Why had she been so terrified of him? Was it magic? Or was he truly just that powerful that she feared for the worst?

"I too will be retiring for the night. It's been a long day and a long journey," Atreus said, placing his chopsticks neatly on the table beside his empty bowl. He gave her a small nod, ignoring Yat-sen completely, and clambered to his feet.

"Ah, good evening then," she said.

"You should sleep too." He eyed her swiftly before turning his attention to the open doorway. "You must be exhausted."

"As soon as I'm done with my meal."

"Good night then, Lady Daiyu." He bowed and hastily left.

With Atreus gone, Yat-sen visibly relaxed, his shoulders slumping and a long sigh escaping from his lips. Daiyu watched him from the corner of her eye and plopped a sliver of beef in her mouth. The savory, tender meat nearly melted as she chewed.

"It seems we both are alike," she said.

"Hm?" He tilted his head to the side and the bright lights flaring in the sconces throughout the room seemed to catch onto the silver hair crown he wore. "You think we're similar?"

Daiyu nodded, stirring the remaining broccoli and mushrooms left in her bowl. "Yes. We both seem to be ..." *Outsiders,* she wanted to say, but she didn't want to offend him, so she instead said, "Alone here."

Yat-sen's eyebrows came together and he looked at the people at the table, all of whom were ignoring them both. "I suppose you're correct, Lady Daiyu. Nobody seems to wish to speak to a cursed prince, nor to you, His Majesty's favored. I believe they fear that talking to us will bring treason."

"You're not cursed—"

"*I am.*" He turned to her sharply, seriousness overcoming his dark eyes. He lowered his voice. "It's best you think so too."

He was the son of the previous emperor, so of course he would be hated, but would admitting that he wasn't cursed be enough for Muyang to punish her? A shiver ran down her spine as she remembered the energy that rippled from Muyang as he left the room. That hadn't been an accident; that had been a show of power.

"Atreus isn't the only one unkind to me," Yat-sen continued, picking up his cup of water. His fingers tightened around the metal. "The rest of the *Peccata* treat me poorly as well."

"*Peccata?*" Daiyu had never heard the word before, and it clearly seemed to be foreign. "What is that?"

"Oh. The *Peccata* is a group of His Majesty's personal ... soldiers? I don't even know what to call them because they're really just a group of young men and women whom His Majesty has helped raise. They do various things for him: assassinations, spying, and other sorts of missions." Yat-sen sipped his water. "Atreus is one of them. There are six in total and you'll likely meet them all throughout your stay in the palace, or even here. I believe Nikator is planning on arriving at this base in a few days."

Nikator was a foreign name she had never heard of, and seeing as how Atreus was also foreign, she wondered if the rest of the *Peccata* were foreign. It wasn't strange for an emperor to help raise a group of people in hopes that they would become his trusted special soldiers, but she found it hard to believe that Muyang, who appeared so young, would be able to help raise anyone to adulthood.

"By raise, you mean like he acted as their patron, right?"

"I'm not sure on the details." Yat-sen slurped the rest of his drink and placed it beside his empty bowl. Streaks of brown sauce were still left over on the sides of the white ceramic, and he stared at them intently, his thoughts seemingly elsewhere. "I don't know Emperor Drakkon much, and I don't know anything about his life prior to ... his ascension to the throne."

The ascension to the throne—meaning, after he brutally murdered more than half of Yat-sen's family.

"Has he always been so powerful?" Her voice dropped to a whisper, and she glanced over at Commander Yao Bohai and General Liang Fang, who were in their own world speaking to one another. She looked at the other people at the table, but none seemed to be paying attention to her. "He seems to have powerful magic, but I've never heard of a commoner having—"

Yat-sen grabbed her forearm tightly, his eyes wide with alarm as he scanned the table. "Do not," he said under his breath, so quietly that it was almost lost in the sea of conversations around them, "*ever* call him a commoner."

A shudder ran through her body and she found herself bobbing her head quickly. She was too scared to speak, even when he released her. That simple sentence—an accident, really—could sentence her to death, and she knew it. The emperor was a divine being, and saying otherwise was treason.

He cleared his throat and fiddled with the sleeve of his vermillion silk robes. "Anyone can become powerful with magic, commoner or not," he said, his voice still quiet. "It has to do with how much yin and yang energy you are born with. The more balanced the two are within you, the more powerful you are."

Once again, she felt like he was speaking in tongues she had no idea about. The very concept was foreign to her, but the vast majority of the population was ignorant when it came to magic, so she couldn't feel too down on herself.

"So you're saying that the emperor has a very balanced energy?"

He nodded. "Correct."

"And everyone is born with these two energies?"

"Yes."

"You seem to know a lot about magic," she said, folding her hands on her lap. She had finished her meal already, as did he, but she didn't want to leave just yet. She wanted to learn more about magic, even though her bones were heavy with fatigue and her eyes burned with sleepiness. "Can you tell how much yin and yang I have?"

An apologetic smile graced his thin lips. "I'm sorry, but I'm not good at reading people. You can ask His Majesty or any of the mages in the palace—"

"Oh, no, thank you." She was already shaking her head, an awkward laugh bubbling from her. "I'd rather not."

She didn't want Muyang to become even more suspicious of her. But she supposed she could ask Feiyu when she went back to the palace. She was sure he would know how to read her—

She stopped those thoughts. There was no reason for her to know any of this. She was planning on leaving, not staying to learn magic.

"I understand." He chuckled, and his dark brown eyes softened, his guard seeming to slip. "His Majesty is very ... intimidating, as are the mages."

"Oh, so you understand me!" She laughed too, and the tension in her shoulders seemed to ease. He was easy to talk to, and she didn't feel like she needed to put air around him. "It's difficult to be in his presence when he's so powerful and his reputation ... well, you know. Anyway, how do you know so much about magic?"

"I had to learn all about it since I was a child. The royal family—err, I mean, the *previous* royal family—" Yat-sen cleared his throat. "The MuRong family has been blessed to have equal amounts of both yin and yang energy, which makes us very powerful magically. But that doesn't mean that nobody else is like that—there are thousands of commoners born with the same type as us."

Daiyu bobbed her head, but a realization struck her in that moment. Didn't that make him even more of a threat to Muyang? If Yat-sen, and presumably the rest of his living siblings, were able to learn powerful magic, wouldn't that make them extremely threatening to Muyang's reign? She could hardly see why the youth was even alive if that was the case.

"I've always been interested in magic," he said. "I find it all so intriguing ..."

"I think it's fascinating too." She thought of all the times Feiyu had warped in and out of places, and how jarring and intriguing that had been to see. A stabbing of guilt tightened her chest. She was sure her brothers would have loved to see magic up close, or even her elderly parents. Or her grandmother. Her smile soon turned sad, and she sighed. "I wish I could use magic. At least then I'd be able to see my family."

Concern washed over the youth's face. "Oh. I ... I'm sorry."

"It's been weeks since I've seen them." Her words barely squeezed out of her constricted throat and she tried to banish the guilt, sadness, and anxiety that came with thoughts of her family. "I wonder if they're doing well without me."

"I can ... I can probably help?" He twisted the gold ring on his finger and cast a quick look around the room to see if anyone was looking, and then whispered, "I can let you see if they're all right, at least."

Daiyu's eyes widened and she held her breath, unable to think properly as he smiled hesitantly at her. He was ... able to help? As soon as those words registered, she grasped his hands tightly and excitedly. "Can you really?"

"Y-Yes." He eased her hands off him and she quickly pulled back.

"Ah, I'm so sorry—"

"No, it's fine—"

"I'm just ..." Tears stung her eyes and she couldn't hold back her smile. "I would be extremely grateful if you can help."

"I can but ..." He nodded at the door, and then back at the others at the table. "We have to keep it a secret."

"I can do that." Daiyu bobbed her head rapidly. "Of course."

"Please don't tell His Majesty."

It was just another secret she would have to keep from Muyang, but considering how she already had a plethora of lies she had told him, she doubted keeping another would harm her at all.

17

DAIYU AND THE PRINCE LEFT THE DINING HALL AND when there were no guards or soldiers present, snuck into the cellar beneath the fortress kitchen that housed most of the wine, rice, barley, and potatoes. It was apparently one of the only rooms that wasn't frequented after dinner, and they found a hiding place between two large shelves stuffed with barrels of wheat.

They both kneeled in the small space. It was dark in the cellar, and the only light came from sconces attached to the cold, gray walls. Their breaths came out in white streams, and even though they were mostly alone—save for the occasional servant who came down to retrieve bottles of wine—she felt like there were eyes and ears everywhere.

"Lady Daiyu." He held his hand out to her. "I can basically open a portal for us to see how your family is doing, but since I know nothing about where they're located, I need you to create a mental image of your home, or a certain person you want me to locate."

She slipped her hand into his clammy one. "I can do that, but ..." Her blood ran cold and she swallowed down the apprehension climbing up her throat. She glanced at the cracks between the barrels of wheat, half-expecting someone to be staring back at them. "Does this mean that anyone with magic can peek into what we're doing?" She didn't like the idea of Muyang, or someone else, watching her whenever he felt like it. Or even Feiyu. All at once, it felt like her privacy was stripped from her and she wondered if that skin-crawling feeling she had felt in the palace— of eyes and ears everywhere—was because there truly *were* people spying on her like this.

"People who are proficient with this kind of magic are able to spy on other people, yes," he said. "But don't worry, anyone who knows how to use even basic magic can put up a barrier. I have a barrier on me at all times that protects me from it. So no one is able to peek into what we're doing right now."

Her relief was short-lived because it wasn't like *she* had a barrier on her at all times like Yat-sen did. Muyang, Feiyu, and other mages could spy on her whenever they wanted to. Whether she was eating, sleeping, or ... even *bathing*.

The thought sent a smoldering blush over her cheeks, and she was glad Yat-sen wasn't able to see her in this darkness. "Well ... that's reassuring."

"You can also buy a trinket or magicked jewelry item that has protection barriers on it," he explained, tightening his hold on her fingers. "Anyway, let's try to hurry before anyone comes in here."

"Ah, yes, or course." She couldn't forget the task at hand: seeing how her family was faring. She came up with a mental image of her family home. With the tall bamboo fences around their garden, the leveled rice paddies surrounding their stone house, the smell of warm earth and grains and soft summer winds.

Yat-sen closed his eyes, his forehead creasing with concentration. A tingle of electrifying magic warmed their joined hands and Daiyu watched in amazement as a swirl of bluish-green energy buzzed a foot away from them. The tendrils of blue-green grew larger until there was a circular window in front of them, the edges hazy and glimmering purple. An image formed in the portal, and Daiyu gasped as she noticed her familiar home.

"That's it!" she said, excitement leaking into her voice. "That's—"

But something was wrong. Even in the darkness of night, with the clouded moon barely shining onto the property, the leveled fields looked ... wrong. There were no swaying tall rice stalks. The fence around the home was destroyed. The walls of the house appeared scorched and damaged. The shingles on one side of the roof were completely broken and marred black.

A dizzying panic took hold of her. Maybe it wasn't her home —but that hopeful thought was quickly dashed when she recognized their smashed chicken coop with its distinctive green shade and swirling designs she had painted when she was a young girl. Even in the night, she could make out the childish whorls she had drawn to mimic clouds.

"It's ... everything's destroyed." The walls of the cellar seemed to close in on her and she couldn't breathe, her chest contracting like someone was twisting a cork. Tighter and tighter, until she couldn't think straight. Until her breaths came in small gasps. "My family—"

The image shifted to the inside of her home, and she spotted her family sleeping in the living room. She counted the bundled figures, recognizing the twins by their pretzeled sleeping position across the floor, and sighed in relief once everyone was accounted for. No one was dead at least.

"Who could have done that?" Yat-sen asked quietly. "Your home ... the rice paddies, the gardens ..."

She shook her head, finding it hard to speak without breaking down in tears. Everyone was alive and she was grateful for that, but their livelihood—their rice paddies—were completely destroyed. She couldn't even imagine how they would live without this year's harvest. Her only consolation was that most of their home garden seemed to be intact, so they could definitely survive the rest of the summer with their vegetables and whatever was in their storage ... But that would run out quickly, especially with six mouths to feed.

Why would anyone demolish it all?

"Did His Majesty ...?" The question hung in the air and she didn't want to voice it. Didn't want to think about what it meant to make the emperor her enemy. And yet ...

"No." Yat-sen stared at the images of her sleeping family—of Lanfen with the covers up to her chin, of Grandmother lying on the extra cushioned bedroll, of her parents sleeping near one another, and her twin brothers sprawled closely together. "His Majesty gains nothing from harming your family. And trust me when I say that if His Majesty wanted to destroy their home ... there would be nothing left. It appears like someone used magic to blight the fields? At least that's what I think, since it seems too precise. Do you have any enemies?"

"No, of course not—" But then she remembered how someone had tried to poison her a few weeks ago, and she wasn't so sure anymore. "Maybe."

Was someone trying to dissuade her from marrying Muyang? But even the thought was laughable—she didn't have a *choice* in the matter.

Was it Feiyu? She found it hard to believe that he would want to hurt her family—after all, he gained nothing from doing that—but he hadn't helped her when she was kidnapped. He was a powerful mage, so it was possible. But why would he even want to do that?

Her thoughts became cloudy and beside the guilt, horror, and angst swirling in the pits of her stomach, another raw, surprising emotion surfaced: *rage*.

Rage at the fact that before Muyang chose her, she had no enemies.

Rage at the fact that, even though she wanted to help her family, she seemed to be making life more complicated and difficult.

Rage at the fact that she couldn't control her destiny and was forced to be a pawn in this game.

And worst of all, an overwhelming anger over her own uselessness.

"I'm sorry I couldn't help ..." Yat-sen winced at their clasped hands, and she quickly released him, realizing a moment too late that she had been squeezing the life out of him. The portal of magic disrupted once their connection was broken and disappeared the next second. He rubbed his fingers with another cringe and looked over his shoulder. "We should probably leave soon."

Daiyu could only nod, her legs numb from crouching for so long and her heart heavy. "Thank you for your help," she said with a strained smile. The corners of her eyes burned with unshed tears and she quickly blinked them away, not wanting to weep in front of a stranger. She instead looked between him and the wooden barrels of wheat surrounding them. "I wish I could repay you, but ... I don't really have anything to offer."

Yat-sen dusted his pants. "No worries. I didn't expect this to be a transaction." Even in the dim lighting, she could make out his small smile. "You were kind to me in this place full of vipers. I appreciate it. I just wish I could have helped more—"

"You've done enough. Thank you."

Because now, with this new information hanging over her head, she needed to come up with a plan faster. Her family needed her more than ever, and she had to find a way to leave here as soon as possible.

DAIYU BARELY REMEMBERED THE WALK UP TO HER room. She didn't know exactly where she was going, but she knew that the room she had bathed in—supposedly, her room—was on one of the top levels, so she kept walking up the flights of stairs. Her body and mind were numb, and the images of her destroyed home kept replaying in her mind like a horrible nightmare.

She rubbed her eyes when she reached a somewhat familiar-looking hallway. There were no guards on this level, but she could

156

feel a denseness in the air that reminded her too much of Muyang. This was likely the floor he was on, she realized with a shudder.

"My lady?"

She jumped and whirled on her feet to find Commander Yao Bohai a few feet away from her, an amused expression on his face. She touched her chest, breathing out deeply. "You scared me," she breathed.

"My apologies." He chuckled and glanced at the hallway behind her. "Are you lost?"

"Ah, yes. A little." She followed his gaze to the darkening corridor, with its waning firelight and the creepy, sinister aura encompassing it. "I can't seem to remember which room is mine."

"You're on the right floor. It's the fifth door to your right." He pointed in the distance. "If you need help—"

Daiyu gasped, the overwhelming feeling of déjà vu washing over her. "I remember you now!" How could she have forgotten the face of the man who had told her on her first day of the palace where the bathing chambers were? *He* was the reason she had that first awkward interaction with Muyang. "You misled me!"

Bohai's warm, brown eyes reminded her of tree bark on sunny summer days as he chuckled softly. "Oh, *that*."

"You ..." She wanted to shout a string of profanities at him and scold him for placing her in such a compromising position, but seeing as how he was the commander-in-chief of the military, she didn't think it was wise to make an enemy out of him. "Well, I suppose I have to thank you for helping me catch the emperor's attention," she said, trying to mask the bitter undertones in her voice.

"That's one way to look at it." He laughed again, and she wanted to wring his neck. He could have gotten her killed for that! "Anyhow, if that's all, I'll be off then. Good night, Lady Daiyu."

"And the same to you, Commander Yao." She could only give him a tight-lipped smile as he disappeared down the end of the corridor. If he hadn't pointed her to the emperor's bathing chambers that fateful day, was it possible that Muyang wouldn't have chosen her to be his bride? If it wasn't for that ... She didn't want to think about too many what-ifs, and her brain was mush after all that transpired that day, so she shoved her intrusive thoughts aside and dragged herself to her door.

Cracking the door open, she peeked inside. The last thing she needed was for him to point her to another wrong room and cause *another* strange interaction. But she breathed in relief as she recognized the two couches, the metal covered window, and the ornate hearth. The only thing missing was the bathtub, which someone must have hauled off after her bath.

Slipping inside, she rubbed her stiff shoulders and headed to the sliding door partitioning the room off. This probably led to the sleeping chambers, she thought with a yawn. She would love to crash onto a soft bed and forget about today. So much had happened—her tumultuous journey from the palace to this fortress, seeing Muyang again, and now her family's misfortune.

She slid the door to the chambers open, her eyes adjusting to the darkness, and shut it behind her when she entered. The only light came from the intricately interlaced windows, which showered slivers of moonlight onto the massive four-poster bed in the center of the room with silk curtains enclosing it.

She walked over to one of the dressers on the side of the room and took her hairpins out. Her hair tumbled down her shoulders and she sighed in relief as she massaged her sore scalp. Then she slowly took off her outer robes until she was wearing her simple underdress.

Finally. She headed to the bed and unfurled one flap of the curtain. She could collapse onto the mattress and sleep—

She inhaled sharply; all thoughts of slumber fled from her mind as she took in the sight in front of her: sleeping on the bed, with the gold-threaded blankets barely covering his chest, lay the emperor.

Daiyu couldn't breathe as a mounting horror overwhelmed her thoughts. She was in His Majesty's bedchambers.

18

From what she could see, Muyang wore a simple white, cross-collared tunic to bed, but the lapels of his shirt were undone—likely from tossing and turning—and revealed the smooth, hard planes of his toned chest. In the moonlight, his skin appeared silver, and Daiyu could only gawk at him, her gaze trailing over his exposed flesh, and then to his peaceful, sleeping face. Even asleep, he appeared like a beautiful, carved piece of work.

Her grip on the curtain tightened and her first instinct was to run out of this room, but something kept her rooted in place. For the first time since she had met him, she didn't fear him—not when he appeared so peacefully at sleep, unaware of her presence.

"Muyang," she whispered, tasting the forbidden name on her tongue. She could never call him that when he was awake and she could never look at him so unashamedly like she was now—or else she'd be killed for daring such a thing—but there was nobody around, and nobody would know.

He was so utterly ... beautiful, and she hated that. Hated how his wicked beauty caused something to stir in her stomach. How he was so evil, but was somehow blessed with such a beautiful, beautiful face.

She stared at his chest and warmth flooded her cheeks—she shouldn't have been here, and she especially shouldn't be staring. It was too improper. Too inappropriate—

"Are you here to seduce me?"

She bit back a stifled scream and released the curtain like it was made of fire. But even then, she could see Muyang gazing at her through the gaps. He sat upright, the blanket falling down to his hips, and pushed the curtain open further with the back of his hand. His long, silk-like hair fell over his shoulders, and she inhaled again at how wrong this was—for both of them to be in their undergarments, in the middle of the night, in his bedchambers.

"Hm, *Daiyu*?"

Her legs trembled and she suddenly felt weak in the knees. It was probably the effects of the night, with how indecent this was, that she felt something warm in the pit of her stomach. Or maybe it was the way he drawled her name.

She hated the effect it had on her.

Her mouth was dry, and she blinked at him like a gawping fish out of water. "I ... I didn't mean—"

"You didn't mean to *what*?" His hand reached out and before she could say something, he snatched her wrist and yanked her forward. She yelped, her knees hitting the edge of the mattress as she tumbled forward. Her face smacked into his chest and she braced her hand on his thigh instinctively. Their faces were inches apart, and she could feel every pore in her body erupt in flames. He didn't let go of her wrist and smiled down at her. "You didn't mean to come into my bedchambers in the deep of night? It's not often that women frequent a man's bed with *pure* intentions."

Her breath hitched, and she moved her hand away from his powerful, sturdy thigh, instead choosing to press the mattress. She wanted to pull away from him, but she couldn't move, not with those tantalizing eyes grazing her face and body.

"Your Majesty, I didn't come here—" She swallowed the

thickness in her throat, her pulse fluttering in her neck. "I didn't realize you would be sleeping here. I thought this was my room."

Muyang's breath warmed the delicate skin of her collarbones and bare throat. He was so close she could smell the sandalwood and jasmine on his skin.

"This is—"

"Inappropriate?" he finished for her.

"Yes."

He chuckled and finally released her wrist. She nearly fell over him but quickly scooted over to the edge of the mattress. He watched her with mounting amusement, his eyes seeming to meld into the darkness. She hugged her wrist to her chest, unsure of what to do. She felt cold without his touch, and she hated that she wanted to lean into him. But they weren't married, and she didn't want anything to do with him, she told herself.

Muyang eased onto the many pillows surrounding his bed and she could feel his gaze tracking over her body—at her soft curves that were usually hidden under her dresses. "You don't have a room here," he said. "You'll be sharing these chambers with me."

Her eyebrows came together, her face further flushing. "Excuse me?"

"All the bedchambers in this fortress are occupied by my men. You will be here in my room."

"I ... I am an unmarried woman," she finally breathed. She hugged herself tightly, for fear that if she touched anything else, she'd be drawn to him. "I would like my own room, or my own bedchamber. Or ... Or even a couch."

"We'll marry soon." He lifted a shoulder but watched her carefully.

"And yet we are not married right *now*." She curled her legs underneath her. He could do whatever he wanted with her and just her speaking her mind like this was punishable by death. If the emperor wanted her, he could have her. With or without marrying her. She knew that, and yet ... she wanted him to respect her wishes. A part of her hoped he would do that.

But he was the ruthless emperor with innocent blood staining his reign.

Muyang touched her chin and lifted her face. She found herself complying, staring deep into those dark, mesmerizing eyes that seemed to see right through her.

"You do not need to be so terrified in my presence. I would never force myself on a woman." He searched her face as if asking her to believe him, and she nodded slowly. Something akin to relief momentarily flickered over his face and he let go of her.

Daiyu licked her suddenly chapped lips. Even though his words should have reassured her, the tightening anxiety in her chest didn't loosen. The shadows of the night seemed darker here, and everything was too quiet. His gaze was too inquisitive, too oppressive, too mysterious. She wasn't sure if she could even believe him. Not when they were alone in his bedchambers.

She wanted to leave, but her legs were leaden, weighing more than the discomfort flitting in her twisted stomach.

Muyang watched her and she wished she could read his blank expression—she wished she could figure out what he was thinking, what he was feeling—but he was a monochrome canvas. No matter how much she tried to stare into his dark eyes, they were shuttered.

"I can imagine your ordeal with those ruffians was quite terrifying." His voice came out smoothly, lowly, and with a hint of anger.

She blinked, taken aback by this new turn of conversation. "It ..." Without warning, her throat tightened and her voice thickened. "It was horrifying."

Daiyu hadn't wanted to linger on the overwhelming fear she had felt while captive. Of the terrifying thoughts of torture, murder, and assault she had thought she would go through. Any time her kidnappers laughed or inched too close to her, she was stricken with unimaginable anxiety—fearing that her worst nightmare would occur right then and there. And that continued for days. Not sleeping well, not eating well, not being able to relieve herself without someone sneering and leering at her.

She had tried to bury those thoughts away the instant Atreus had saved her. She had thought she had numbed herself to it all. But right here, with Muyang examining her so closely, with the secrecy of night surrounding them in lush darkness, her heart trembled.

"The worst thing I've gone through, by far," she whispered, squeezing her eyes shut as she thought of Qian, Bao, and the rest of the grim-faced bandits. "I thought ... I thought so many horrible things would happen to me."

"I apologize if I'm reminding you of them."

"You—You're nothing like them, Your Majesty," she said quickly and what surprised her the most—she actually meant it. He was many things, but she couldn't imagine him being like those rough bandits. She couldn't imagine him sniggering at her and ogling her like those men had done, and the truth of that shocked her.

But you don't know him, a small voice whispered. *He could very well be just as terrible as those men.*

Tenseness grew between them and Muyang shifted on the bed until he was sitting cross-legged—and farther away from her. He tilted his head to the side, his long hair falling over his shoulder. "If Atreus hadn't killed them, I would have brought each of them to your feet so you could cut their throats with your own hands," he said quietly, a low rumble in his voice.

Daiyu cringed. She had already seen them die horribly by Atreus's sword—well, truthfully, she had been more concerned with fleeing than watching them die, but she had seen the gruesome outcome. "I don't think I can handle killing someone."

"Everyone starts somewhere." He reached forward as if to touch a strand of her hair but stopped short and let his hand drop on his thigh. "You'll learn."

Was that what it meant to be his wife? To be just like him? To kill like him? To *enjoy* killing? She shivered but not from the cold. "They're already dead, so I ..." She remembered his earlier words that day and lifted her chin to stare at him squarely. "I'll let them stay dead."

The corner of his mouth curled. "If you don't wish to kill those who wrong you, that is fine. I won't let blood dirty your hands."

"Your Majesty?"

"Until you wish it, I'll be the one driving a dagger through the hearts of your enemies." His smile grew, and something fluttered in her chest at the dark promise. "I'll be your villain for as long as you need me to be."

Daiyu suddenly couldn't meet his gaze and stared down at her hands, which couldn't stop fidgeting over the fur blankets and silk sheets—anything to keep them busy and as far away from him as possible. Heat traveled up her neck and warmed her cheeks. She couldn't think straight, her tongue tied together and her thought even more tangled.

"At the palace, I'll have one of my trusted soldiers as your personal guard. Her name is Vita. I think you'll feel more at ease having another woman keep close to you."

"Oh." She didn't know if she should feel relieved or more tense at the idea of someone watching over her. It could be that he was assigning a spy to watch her every move, or it was simply for her own protection. "Vita ... I've never heard that name before."

"She's from Sanguis."

"The same as Atreus?" A thought struck her. Was Vita also a member of the *Peccata*, like Yat-sen had mentioned?

"Yes. She's Atreus's ... sister, in a sense." He lifted his shoulders. "Not by blood, though."

"Oh. Well, thank you, Your Majesty ... I'll feel more at ease knowing someone will protect me." Maybe this way she wouldn't get poisoned again. Or kidnapped. Or worse.

But it also made it harder for her to slip away—and now with the pressing issue of her family badly needing her, she had to speed up her process.

"I'll let you sleep, now." Muyang swung his legs over the bed and rose to his feet. He pulled open the drapes of the bed further to step out but stopped to stare down at her. "Good night, my little rabbit."

Little rabbit.

She hated that she was prey.

But she couldn't hate him completely for calling her that—not when he promised her such a strange, strange thing.

"Good night, Your Majesty."

Muyang let the curtains fall, and she could hear his light footsteps head to the door. It slid open and then clicked shut. It was only then that she felt truly alone in the cold, dark room. She flopped down on the thick fur blankets and inhaled the scent of jasmine and sandalwood still fresh against the sheets. Her face was a patchwork of blotchy, blushing skin, and she slid between the covers to better stave off the chill. But that only made everything worse because with his scent enveloping her in a sweet embrace, and knowing that she was in his bed, she couldn't stop the warring, confusing emotions in her chest.

What in the world was happening with her? She truly couldn't be interested in him in any way. She reminded herself of his cruelty and how many terrible things he had done. How many lives he had ruined.

But as her eyelids grew heavier, the last thing she could remember was the softness of his voice as he apologized to her. And her heart felt lighter as she replayed their conversation until sleep lulled her away.

19

DAIYU WAS RUNNING THROUGH A FIELD OF BLURRING chrysanthemums and swaying grass, her hands outstretched toward a shadowed figure. The distance between them grew wider with every sluggish step she took forward.

"Heng! Heng!" she shouted, pushing her way through to reach her dead fiancé. She felt like she was running in slow motion. The fields of flowers were hazy and indistinct as she shoved her way headfirst. Her breath came in gasps. And yet Heng was even farther away now. Her legs moved like they were stuck in sticky, thick syrup. "Heng! Wait, *please!*"

Tears of frustration stung her eyes. He was going to leave her, again, but ... but she needed to explain herself to him. To tell him that she still loved him, even though—

She didn't want to think of Muyang.

"Heng!"

Her cries fell on deaf ears and she dropped down to her knees. More tears streamed down her face and she couldn't stop the torrent of guilt and sadness washing over her. If the war hadn't taken Heng away, would they be happily married at this point?

"I seem to have dropped by at an unexpectedly emotional moment," a smooth voice said from behind her.

A shiver ran down her spine and she spun around to find a giant tree a few feet away from her. Underneath the heavy branches full of lustrous reddish-yellow leaves, Feiyu sat cross-legged, his head tilted to the side, and a black and gold dragon mask covering his face. His green robes fluttered against the wind, and his long hair joined it as well.

All thoughts of sadness and grief seemed to dull in that moment.

Daiyu's eyebrows pulled together. "Feiyu? What are *you* doing here?"

He chuckled softly. "To see you, of course. I needed to confirm that you aren't dead."

"What?" It was at that exact instant that she realized she was dreaming. She looked around herself at the changing scenery— she was now in the woods, with the sun falling over them and trees canopying the sky. She could hear a river rippling in the distance and birds tweeting atop the branches.

"I needed to make sure—" he started again.

"You're a few weeks too late," Daiyu finally said with a long sigh. She pushed herself to her feet and wiped her damp cheeks. She turned her anger onto Feiyu, who hadn't moved from his position. "I've been through hell and back! I can't believe you didn't even help me!"

It was all a dream, so she didn't need to worry about what he thought or how she shouldn't anger a high mage.

"Who was that?" Feiyu's voice came out softer. "A former lover?"

Her chest tightened and she turned to glance over her shoulder as if she might catch a glimpse of Heng farther away. "My fiancé."

"Is he ...?"

"Dead? Very much so." It had been four years since he had passed and she hated how she couldn't even remember his face that well anymore. She couldn't remember the tiny details that had made him so loveable. So charming. So ... like Heng.

"What was he like?"

"He was my best friend." A warm breeze pushed past them, and she breathed in the scent of summer and grass. "He was ... kind, caring, and a bit naïve about the world. He thought he could become a hero."

"I'm sorry to hear it."

Daiyu shook her head, the guilt still heavy in her chest. "You didn't answer my question. Why didn't you help me?"

"You didn't ask a question." He laughed this time, and she wanted to reach forward and yank his mask off. But something seemed to be keeping them apart—like an invisible barrier. "But, well, I was busy, unfortunately. Because of the impending war with the rebels led by General Keung, I've been doing some tasks for His Majesty. I didn't notice you went missing until it was too late."

"Even in a dream, you're ..." She struggled to come up with the words as she stepped closer, but the distance between them remained the same.

"Handsome? Charming? Mysterious?" he offered.

"Annoying."

He threw his head back and laughed, and it grated on her nerves that he was so carefree while she had gone through so many horrors. From the kidnapping, to traveling with bandits, to now being stuck in a military fortress with the emperor and his men. The last one wasn't *that* bad, she had to admit, but with the new information that her family's livelihood had been burned down, she felt like she was trapped in a prison.

"Is this ... really a dream?" Daiyu asked slowly, looking between him and the swinging trees. "Or is this some sort of magic?"

"Huh. You're smarter than I gave you credit for."

She could have sworn he was grinning behind his mask by the playful quality in his tone.

"Most people—especially those inexperienced with magic—

are unable to tell if someone magically visits them in their dreams."

She wasn't sure if she should feel flattered or frustrated. She frowned. "Well, thanks. I guess. But when it comes to you, I know things are never simple, which is why I asked. And besides, this doesn't *feel* like a dream anymore." She held her hand out to feel the warmth of the wind. "Like I can smell and feel things."

"It's all magic." He clambered up to his feet and brushed a hand over his clothes to dispel dust that wasn't there. When he caught her staring, he laughed again. "A habit, if you will."

"Anyway, I'm sure you've come here to tell me something important then, yes?" She quirked an eyebrow and shifted on her feet. "Like how I can leave this place?"

"You still wish to leave?"

"My plans are the same," she said stiffly. "I haven't become enamored by the glitter and glam of the royal palace, if that's what you're insinuating. The only good that's come out of this whole ordeal is nothing! I've been poisoned, on the brink of death, kidnapped, and tossed around like a piece in a game! And to make matters worse—" Daiyu's throat closed up and she found it hard to speak without bursting into tears.

Feiyu's jovial temperament sobered up and the winds grew fiercer, like a storm approaching. "What happened?"

"My family—" She choked back the tears and breathed out shakily. Blinking away the tears, she continued in an unsteady voice, "My family's rice fields have been scorched and ruined by someone. I don't know who, but someone is out for us. I think it's related to me being chosen by the emperor. Someone must be jealous and wants to ... I don't know ... scare me?"

Feiyu canted his head, and the gold eyes of his dragon mask seemed to glow unnaturally. "Is that so?"

"I need to find a way to help them."

"You could marry the emperor."

Daiyu made a choking sound, completely taken aback by his words. "What? That's what I'm trying to avoid!"

"Well, yes, but who's better to protect you than the emperor himself? If you marry him, your family will likely be gifted a new home, new job positions if they wish it, and prestige. You'll be guaranteeing their future."

"That ... that's not true."

"Why?" He tapped his feet beside a cluster of bobbing dandelions. "Historically, all the families of the wives and concubines of the emperor were given great liberties, great treasures, and were held in high esteem. Just because Drakkon Muyang hasn't married or chosen a concubine, doesn't mean he wouldn't do the same."

"But ... but he's ..." *Wicked, cruel, terrible.* She had so many words to describe Muyang and everything she had heard about him. His reign was soaked in blood. He was part demon, part dragon. All evil. "He wouldn't—"

And yet, he had apologized to her. He hadn't forced himself upon her. He had seemed like he actually *cared.*

But that was too low of a bar, she told herself. She forced herself to remember how he had humiliated her in the gardens. How he had pressed a knife to her neck. How all of her problems originated from him.

"Who's to say more enemies won't crop up and do worse to me and my family?" she found herself saying at last. "The more involved I remain with His Majesty, the more troubled my life will become. I want to go back to my normal life. Back when my biggest worry was about harvesting our carrots on time, or making sure our ginger plant yielded enough for the winter. Or ... or, making sure I feed the chickens in the morning, or that I don't oversleep and forget to make breakfast, or ... or ..." Her eyes misted over, and a heavier guilt rooted itself in her chest. If she hadn't become entangled with the emperor, her family's livelihood wouldn't have gotten to this state. How worried were Mother and Father? Were they growing sick because they had lost a daughter for a few months, along with losing their rice fields? How much more worry was she going to cause them?

"It's something to consider," Feiyu said softly.

She wanted to refute his statement—tell him that he was wrong for even *considering* such an option—but she couldn't. Her voice wouldn't come out, no matter how much she wanted it to. There was a truth in what he was saying, but she didn't want to admit it. She didn't want to be the wife of a cold-blooded emperor, who would replace her in a few weeks once he grew bored with her. She didn't want to live the life of one of the many wives of His Majesty, who would likely be cast away once she was older and uglier. Whose children would fight and curse and hate their half-siblings over the throne. Who would constantly be looking for the emperor's favor.

Before her mind could become more entrenched with the horrors of becoming Muyang's wife, Feiyu spoke, "There seems to be a commotion happening around you."

"Huh?" She looked around herself, but the scenery was the same as it was minutes ago. That could only mean he was talking about the real world. But she was sleeping alone in Muyang's room. "Are you talking about in the fortress?"

"Yes. I'll try to keep my message short." He held his hand out, where a beaded bracelet appeared from thin air. It glowed gold for a few seconds before flickering off into a light green shade. "I'll teleport this magic item to you. This will offer you some protection. If you're really in a bind, try pouring your energy into it and it might help you."

"That sounds awfully vague. Can't you just teleport here and help me instead?"

"I'm unable to leave the royal palace grounds, unless His Majesty allows it."

"But—" She stared at the jade bracelet; how was it going to help her? Would it make it so no one could spy on her? Like Yatsen was saying the other day? "But what does it do, exactly?"

"It will protect you," he said simply. "I don't have much time—"

"When can I see you again? What if I need your help?"

"I can't help you when I'm so far away," he said, and there was a touch of sadness in his tone. "We'll meet again in the palace. Until then, stay alive and stay safe."

"Feiyu—"

Before she could ask any more of him, something jolted her. A loud blaring sound.

~

DAIYU'S EYES FLEW OPEN AND SHE INSTANTLY COVERED her ears as a horn blasted in the fortress. She threw the thick covers off her body, but the motion caused something to skid across the hardwood floors. Hurling the curtains of the bed aside, she spotted a jade bracelet on the floor a few feet from the bed. She blinked at it in astonishment. So it really wasn't just a dream.

She didn't have much time to think about everything Feiyu had told her—not with the constant horn sounding all around her—so she scooped up the piece of jewelry, slipped it on her wrist, and quickly began to dress herself from the discarded pile of clothes she had left last night by the dresser. She combed her hair with her fingers and created a simple, low bun with her two hairpins.

Daiyu peeked out the latticed window for signs of an invading army or a fight ensuing down below, but the courtyard was completely empty. The blood drained from her face and she jammed her feet into her silk slippers. What in the world was happening? Were they going into battle?

When she scrambled out of the emperor's chambers and into the hallway, it was hauntingly empty, mimicking the courtyard. She hurried down the flight of stairs to the level below it, but it was the same—no soldiers in sight. She kept continuing down until she reached the first floor. There, she spotted dozens of soldiers rushing down the hallway, all of them chattering with one another. Their faces were grim, and she swallowed down her burgeoning anxiety.

"What's going on?" she asked the closest soldier as she followed the mob down the broad corridor.

The soldier didn't even glance her way. "His Majesty is calling everyone to the main hall."

"Why? What does the horn mean?"

He finally looked over at her and his eyes widened as if realizing she wasn't a soldier. He cleared his throat, turning away. "It usually means he has an announcement to make, or we'll be attacking soon."

"No," another soldier from behind them said, his voice mingling with the chatter of the crowd. "I heard a spy was caught."

"A spy?" Daiyu breathed, her eyebrows coming together. This was a turn of events she hadn't expected and it wasn't her place to be involved in any of it, but curiosity kept her following the groups of soldiers.

They entered what she had thought was the banquet hall, but all the tables were gone and there was nothing inside the room except for the sea of soldiers who stood in front of a dais at the end of the hall. All conversations ceased the instant they entered the room, and as if she were entering a different dimension, a shudder ran through her when she stepped through the double-doored threshold. Her breath caught in her throat at the denseness of the air, like something was trying to suffocate her. She wasn't the only one who noticed—everyone markedly stiffened.

Drakkon Muyang sat on what looked like a makeshift throne, but what Daiyu realized with mounting horror was a pile of corpses dressed in military attire. He was leaning back, his fingers drumming over the leather hilt of the gleaming, blood-stained sword sitting on his lap. At his feet, blood pooled around the bodies and dripped off the dais in a macabre fashion.

Daiyu reeled back and nearly bumped into the soldier behind her. She had never seen such a horrifying image. Something within her—an instinct that made every hair on her body stand straight—told her to run as fast as possible. And yet a morbid curiosity compelled her to remain rooted in place.

Raw power radiated from Muyang, so thick and bone-rattling that Daiyu wasn't sure if it was his magic causing such a reaction, or simply because *he* was that powerful.

Off to the side of the dais stood Prince Yat-sen, Atreus, General Liang Fang, and a handful of men Daiyu recognized from Muyang's dinner table from the night before. They all wore stoic expressions as if used to such a horrifying display.

"Bring in the traitor," Muyang spoke calmly and quietly, and yet his voice seemed to echo off the walls.

All at once, the soldiers parted ways and Bohai entered the room. He held a long chain in his hand, which rattled off the polished floors. A few feet behind him, a bruised, battered, and bloodied man limped forward. The man's face was a map work of purple and blue, and fresh blood dribbled down his chin. One of his eyes was swollen shut and even from the distance, Daiyu could see that his fingers were missing. His hands were covered in dirty, maroon-colored gauze that oozed with blood and pus.

Daiyu's stomach churned and she swallowed down the bile clawing up her throat. Bohai bowed in front of Muyang, straightened, and yanked the chain until the man collapsed toward the dais.

"The traitor, Your Majesty," Bohai said with a wave at the prisoner. He wore a pleasant smile as if he wasn't carting around a half-dead man. "We caught him conspiring with those soldiers." He nodded at the dead bodies Muyang sat upon so brazenly. "They were planning on storming this fortress."

Muyang peered down at the prisoner with barely veiled disgust. "So I'm to assume there are more of these soldiers waiting close by to attack us?"

"Correct, Your Majesty."

"Hm." The shadows of the room seemed to warp and grow darker, and Daiyu watched with bated breath as he tapped his finger over his sword's hilt.

Tap. Tap. Tap.

Time slowed, and everyone seemed to hold their breath.

Finally, he spoke again. "What do you have to say for yourself? Will you beg for your life, or cry about how wrong you were, or will you hurl insults and die on that treasonous hill of yours?"

The prisoner turned to look at the crowded room, licked the crusted blood on his chapped lips, and shifted his attention back to Muyang. "Y-You—" he rasped, then cleared his throat. "You're a monster who sits upon someone else's throne! You don't deserve to have all these people worship and follow you!"

Silence filled the hall.

Daiyu gasped, the hairs on her arms rising expectantly. The soldiers around her didn't dare rip their attention away from the scene, some of them appearing just as horrified as she felt, and others looking thrilled—as if *excited* to smell the blood that would undoubtedly spill.

Muyang's neutral expression didn't change. "Ah, so you're the latter type."

"Th-the rightful heir will bring this empire back to its glory!" the man continued to shout, spinning around to face the soldiers. "You all will die gruesomely for your treason against the MuRong blood! The rightful heir will win! The heavens favor the MuRong dynasty!"

A laugh escaped from Muyang's lips—both velvety and rich —and a shiver ran down Daiyu's spine. The room seemed to darken as amusement flashed over his face, and he reclined into his throne of corpses. "You're quite the jester." He lightly stroked the blood coagulating against the flat of his blade. "The rightful heir will never sit upon any throne and he will condemn you for your actions. Isn't that right, Prince Yat-sen?"

Prince Yat-sen stiffened as the emperor gestured toward him. His youthful face was smoothed down to neutrality, but Daiyu could see that he was clutching his hands together too tightly. He swallowed, his Adam's apple bobbing. "You're correct, Your Majesty."

"You *will* sit on the throne! One of these days!" The prisoner lurched forward, but Bohai wrenched the chain back and the man collapsed on the floor. He clawed at the wood with his stubbed hands and tried to stand, blood seeping through his bandages, and a frantic, crazed look in his eyes when he looked back at the crowd. "We will bring this empire back to its former glory and eradicate the Drakkon dynasty! If not you, Prince Yat-sen, then your younger brother, Prince Daewon!"

"Yat-sen will never sit on the throne," Muyang said slowly. "And neither will his brother. Nor his sisters. Nor his sisters' children. Or their children. Or their children's children. Do you understand me, treasonous rat? No MuRong will sit here so long as I breathe, and I intend to breathe for a long, long time." Shadows twirled around his hand, and red lightning zapped from his fingers, smelling like burning flesh. The room dimmed, the shadows in every crevice seeming to have eyes as they blackened further. Muyang rose to his impressive height and more shadowy wisps gathered at his feet, pulling across the thickening blood coating the dais. "Since you love the MuRong bastards so much, maybe you should meet them in the hereafter? I'll grant you that mercy, filth."

The man climbed to his feet unsteadily. "You will never defeat—"

Muyang swung his sword and sliced the man's neck in one go. Daiyu inhaled sharply and covered her mouth. Blood gushed from the wound and the man's severed head rolled on the floor. She could see the bone and sinew of the man's stump of a neck as his body buckled. The chain that had been around the man's throat fell beside his body with a loud, rattling clank. Muyang swung his sword again, the air slashing loudly, and blood danced off the blade and speckled against the dais.

"Spike his head and display it on the fortress gates so all can see what happens to traitors and cowards," Muyang said, thrusting the sword into the dais where it stuck out ominously.

He fell back onto his chair of dead bodies and waved to Bohai. "And if you catch any more traitors, do the same."

"Yes, Your Majesty." Bohai bowed low.

Daiyu was grateful she couldn't see the detached head or where it had rolled off to, but she was becoming more uneasy in the throne room. Hopefully, this would be the end of this morbid scene and she could crawl back into her room where she could forget all of this happened.

But right when she thought the emperor would dismiss everyone, he said, "Prince Yat-sen, step forward."

Daiyu's breath caught in her throat as she shifted her attention to the pallid prince, who blinked in surprise, clearly not expecting this either. The others in the room were deathly silent, but the shifting in their feet told her that they didn't know what would happen either.

Yat-sen swallowed, looking at the people beside him, and then turned back to Muyang, who watched him expressionlessly.

"Y-Your Majesty?"

His black eyes narrowed, and a flash of annoyance flitted over his face. "Don't make me repeat myself."

Yat-sen scrambled forward and fell to his knees on the dais, his pants soaking up the thickening blood on the floor from the corpses. "Forgive me, Your Majesty. I'm ..." His shoulders trembled. "I'm just a bit surprised, is all."

"Why are you surprised?" Muyang nodded to someone in the crowd and in seconds, a servant rushed forward, nearly slipping on the spilled blood, and held a silver platter with a metal bowl on it. He took the drink wordlessly, swirled it, and drank from it. All the while, the servant disappeared back into the folds of the crowd and Yat-sen remained still as a stone on the floor. "You should know why I'm displeased with you." He took another sip, his gaze never straying from the prince. "Why don't you tell me what you did?"

Daiyu's stomach clenched together tightly, more so than when Muyang had interrogated and killed the prisoner, because this was Yat-sen, someone she knew. Someone who was kind to her. Someone who had helped her.

She didn't want to see the emperor's wrath on the poor prince.

Yat-sen shivered and lowered his head further until he was touching the floor, no doubt smearing blood on his forehead and face. "I don't know what you mean, Your Majesty. Please forgive me."

Muyang drank from his bowl nonchalantly, and that made him appear all the more terrifying. The fact that this was routine for him. Even as Yat-sen shook like a leaf.

"You don't know?" The words came out slowly as he rested the bowl on his lap. His eyes narrowed.

"I don't, Your Majesty," Yat-sen whispered.

Muyang tossed his drink to the side and it clattered off the dais and into the formation of soldiers. His lips curled back in disgust as he spat, "You used magic last night, princeling. Did you think I wouldn't smell it on you?"

All the color drained from Daiyu's face and her knees weakened. Yat-sen stammered something, but no clear words came out from him. Indeed, he had used magic. To help *her*. To make it so she could see what had happened to her family. And now ... the emperor was suspicious of him.

"I ... I ..." Yat-sen shook harder. "I didn't mean to, Your Maj—"

"Are you a traitor just like the rat before your feet? Did you conspire with that lowlife to throw me off my throne?" Muyang rose to his feet again and this time, fire roared in the sconces around the room, illuminating the space in ominous shades of fiery reds and orange. "What did you use your magic for, Prince?"

Yat-sen raised his head, and Daiyu could hear the tears from his voice. "P-Please! I didn't do anything bad! It was a mistake!"

Daiyu's head spun and she felt the urge to vomit right then and there. The flashing fire all around them made her clothes feel sticky against her skin, and it was suddenly hard to breathe.

"A mistake? You know you're to *never* use magic." Muyang stopped a foot away from the prince and stared down at him with merciless, cold eyes. The gaze of a man who had done this many times before. "You dare defy me?"

"No, Your Majesty! I don't—"

"*Silence.*" A strangled sob escaped from Yat-sen as Muyang grabbed him by the collar of his tunic and yanked him to his feet in one swoop. He leaned closer, his words echoing throughout the room. "You know what happens to those who disappoint me, Yat-sen."

Daiyu gasped when Muyang flung Yat-sen off the dais, where he slammed onto the floor beside the dead body of the prisoner. Yat-sen cried as he tried to sit up, his hands slipping on the blood and his expression horrified as he stared up at the emperor. Dark magic radiated from Muyang's hands and a blustering sound came from the writhing shadowy whips swarming around his arm. It was like it had a life of its own, the shadows snapping and screaming like loud winds. Muyang pointed at Yat-sen and all at once, the magic show moved forward and consumed him. The youth screamed, twisting on the floor as the tendrils attacked him like a hound of dogs.

"S-stop," Daiyu whispered, the words barely audible over Yat-sen's terrified and painful shrieks.

Guilt and nausea weighed heavily on her chest and the room began to spin. The flickering fire seemed to mature and brighten, nearly blinding her while the shadowy magic sent wafts of chilly air. She wanted to puke. She wanted to faint. And she wanted to flee from everything.

But she couldn't. Not when the youth was suffering. *Because of her.*

"Stop!" she finally shouted.

The soldiers next to her turned to her slowly, and even Muyang, who had been watching Yat-sen expressionlessly, lifted his black, void-like eyes to search the crowds. Daiyu was unsteady on her feet and her breathing hitched in her throat as more soldiers turned to her. The ones nearby inched away as if they didn't want any association with her.

Finally, Muyang's gaze found hers and whatever determination she had seemed to wither at the wrathful sight of his anger. She swallowed down the nausea building within her and pushed her way through the swarm of soldiers until she was in the clearing leading to the dais. She gripped the sides of her dress tightly and avoided the emperor's eyes.

Yat-sen continued to thrash on the floor, his limbs flailing to fight off the onslaught of shadowy magic. Daiyu stared at the floor and spotted the severed head of the prisoner a few feet away from her. Her stomach heaved and she bit her bottom lip to keep from gagging at the sight of its unseeing eyes, the gaping mouth, and the bones poking through the bottom.

"Please stop this, Your Majesty," Daiyu said, her voice wavering as she approached the dais. She lowered herself into a bow, and the prisoner's blood stained her dark purple and blue skirts. "Prince Yat-sen used his magic to help me."

"What do *you* think you're doing here?" Muyang breathed, and she flinched, unable to look at him.

"Your Majesty, please spare him!" She placed her hands on the floor, her fingers brushing over the drying blood caking the polished wood, and she lowered her head. "Please! He was only trying to help me!"

Time slowed, and Daiyu squeezed her eyes shut to erase the image of the detached head mere feet away from her and Yat-sen's pained cries. Muyang didn't speak, but she could feel his dark gaze boring holes into her. Contemplating on whether or not he should punish her. Or maybe he would kill her right then and there? Chop her head off just like the traitor?

Before she knew it, he was in front of her. He grasped her shoulders and yanked her up to her feet. She barely had time to gasp as she peered up at him. There was something dark and ferocious lingering on his face, and she wanted to squirm inwardly at his expression.

"Your—"

Their surroundings shifted in a split second. One moment they were standing in the hall, and the next she was inside the bedroom she had come from. She blinked back rapidly as Muyang released her. She reeled backward, her stomach heaving and her eyes adjusting to the new sights—the framed bed, the paneled walls, the caisson ceiling. Her nose crinkled, almost confused at the rush of new smells—of jasmine and incense, replacing the metallic blood and sweat scent that had lingered in the hall. She had warped before with Feiyu, but this felt more unnatural than before. Like she had been ripped from one place and shoved into another—and that's exactly what had happened.

"What—" she began, but she could barely get the word out before her mouth filled with salty water and her stomach heaved. She leaned forward and violently vomited on the floor a foot away from the emperor. A bitter, bile taste filled her mouth and she gasped sharply, her stomach continuing to empty itself. She hadn't felt this discombobulated when Feiyu had warped her.

Wiping her mouth with her sleeve, she raised her head to meet Muyang's glare.

"What have you done?" There was a deep warning in his tone, and Daiyu wondered for a moment if this was when she would die—alone, covered in blood and vomit, and at the hands of the terrifying, wicked emperor.

20

Daiyu's mouth dried up and she gaped like a fish, unable to come up with anything. Muyang was breathing heavy and labored, like he had run all the way here instead of warping, and he staggered forward and grabbed the wooden frame of the bed for support. She instinctively moved toward him. "A-are you okay?"

"*Daiyu.*" His black eyes were on her again, and this time, they were harder than before, flashing with anger. She shrank back, biting her tongue for even suggesting that he needed help. "What have you done?"

"I—" She swallowed down the fear that made her shiver like a newborn fawn. "I went to see what the ringing bells were about, and that's when I came upon the room and—"

"I'm not talking about that." The dark look was back on his face, seeming more intense than before. "I'm asking what you've done with the princeling. Have you conspired with him against me?"

"What? No!" She shook her head and wiped her clammy, trembling hands on her thighs. "I'm not conspiring against you! Please, you have to believe me!"

"Then why were you with him?!" he roared, pushing away

from the bed frame. "Why did you need to use magic with him? And on the same day that the traitor was caught? Are you behind all of this?"

"No! No, I'm not! You have to believe me!" Tears of panic stung her eyes and she didn't care about anything other than saving her neck as she strode over her puddle of vomit laced with bile, and grabbed the front of his black, military-style robes. "Please, Your Majesty. I would never try to conspire against you! I just wanted to see how my family was doing! Please, you have to—"

Muyang wrenched her hands away from him and drew away from her. "I don't believe anything you say," he sneered. Heavy magic seemed to fill the dense air and Daiyu suppressed a sob as he continued to glare at her. "What did you need his magic for?"

If the emperor didn't believe her, she'd die. Her family would die. Everyone she cared for would die. Maybe even her whole village would be burned down. The morbid thoughts made her whole body feel like it was turning inside out. She couldn't see anything beyond Muyang and his furious expression.

"I'm telling you!" Her hands quivered and she could barely breathe through the thickening fog between them. "You can use magic to see if I'm lying, or—or something to see if I'm being truthful! Please, I would never do anything against you—"

Muyang grabbed her face and turned it so she was staring up at him. He didn't grip her tightly, and yet she shuddered in fear. His breath was warm against her face, like a gentle caress, so unlike the violence he seemed to be teetering toward. "Little rabbit, you've displeased me. You should have never used him for whatever you needed. If you're lying to me—"

"I'm not," she interrupted, tears filling up her eyes and spilling down her cheeks.

He searched her for answers and she couldn't stop from crumpling her face in terror. He would kill her, wouldn't he? There was no reason for him to keep her alive. She was disposable and worthless, and he could find hundreds of women to replace her with.

Finally, Muyang released her. "What did you need his magic for?"

"My family—" She struggled to come up with something coherent, her mind racing. "I wanted to see how they were doing. I haven't seen them in weeks. My sister—I wanted to see ... And, and, and my brothers—"

"Why did you need his magic for that?"

"I ... I don't know." Daiyu stared at the jade bracelet wound around her wrist and remembered what Feiyu had told her—that this bracelet would protect her somehow. She wished so badly in that moment for Feiyu to be here, to save her from the emperor's wrath. "I thought he could help me, so I asked for his help. I didn't mean to get him in trouble, nor did I intend to invoke your anger. I just wanted to see if my family was doing well; that's all."

Muyang continued to stare at her mistrustingly. Daiyu wrung her hands together and breathed through her nose. She didn't trust herself not to burst into sobs and beg at his feet—something she thought he would take great disgust in.

He exhaled loudly and ran a hand over his face. "I'll believe you, for *now*. But"—he turned to her sharply and she couldn't even breathe a sigh of relief as his eyes narrowed—"do *not* use Yatsen, or anyone, for their magic. I will not have my woman entertaining different men, asking *them* for help when you can come to *me*."

Daiyu tightened her hold on the bracelet on her wrist and didn't dare mention how Feiyu had helped her countless times. She mutely bobbed her head.

He looked from her to the vomit on the floor, and then to her stained skirts. His lips curled back in thinly veiled revulsion. "Clean yourself up and don't irritate me again."

Muyang turned to leave and Daiyu laced her hands in front of her tightly. He would be leaving in a matter of seconds, and she would be free from his anger. She had somehow survived. She had lived through his anger, even when he suspected her.

But she was about to toss it all away.

She squeaked, "Y-Your Majesty?"

Muyang paused in front of the door and glanced over his shoulder at her. She had been so close to leaving this unscathed, but something continued to bother her and she couldn't hold herself back.

"I—" She cleared her throat, willing her voice to be stronger as she raised her chin and stared at him levelly. Her heart pounded loudly in her chest and she could feel the sweat collecting at the nape of her neck. "I would appreciate it if you didn't punish Yatsen for helping me. He was only doing what I asked him to do, and it's not his fault. Please."

In seconds, his expression darkened. The entire room seemed to have stilled, and a loud, whistling wind banged against the shuttered windows. "You beg for me to save that child from punishment?"

"Yes." Her voice didn't waver, even as her whole body quivered.

"He knew what the punishment for his crime was when he helped you," Muyang snarled. He grasped the doorframe of the sliding door and it cracked under pressure, his fingers leaving indents in the now-splintered wood. "I will not spare him. Not even for you."

"But—"

"Silence!" He treaded toward her and she scrambled back until she slammed into the wall. He was inches away from her and she couldn't stop from staring up at him with wide, saucer-like eyes. She had never seen him look so infuriated; she was accustomed to seeing a neutral, sometimes maniacal air to him. But not this—not pure fury and animosity that seemed directed at her. "I don't want you defending worthless scum like him."

"But he didn't do anything wrong!"

Muyang's face morphed into something darker and Daiyu bit

her tongue. He slammed his fist above her head, closing her in with his body, but not touching her. She was cornered, unable to turn away—and even if she could, she wasn't sure she'd be able to escape his ire. "He defied me by using his magic. I will not tolerate *anyone* defying me in any way."

Daiyu's mouth dried up and she wanted to disappear into the wall, away from him and away from this fortress. She wanted to shout at him for being unreasonable, for being a tyrant, and for terrifying her. But she still had some sanity left, so she sealed her lips together and tried not to cry in frustration or fear.

For a moment, they both just stared at each other. The sharp planes of his face appeared unforgiving and harsh, but something in those black, starless eyes seemed to soften. Just for a split second, enough for her to cling onto hope.

"Your Majesty, you aren't a kind ruler, I know that." The words spilled from her so quietly that the flickering flames in the sconces almost drowned her away. "You're powerful and you hate those who oppose you. I don't want to upset or anger you, but I urge you to forgive him. For my sake, at least."

Muyang's eyebrows came together and a soft, musical, and chilling laugh escaped from him. He threw his head back and laughed harder, running a hand over his face. A shiver darted down Daiyu's spine. Finally, his nasty laugh subsided enough for him to pin her with a brutal, withering stare. "For *your* sake?" He stepped closer and grasped a tendril of her hair. His knuckles grazed her jaw and she forgot to breathe. He inched closer until they were a hair's breadth apart. She breathed in deeply, her breasts rising and brushing against his chest. They were too close, and yet there was no intimacy between them. No desire. Nothing but cruelty and fear and hatred.

"Who the hell do you think you are?" Muyang tilted his head as he continued to scrutinize her like she was nothing. The darkness in his eyes seemed to encapsulate a wickedness she had never witnessed before, had never dreamed of seeing. "You have no sway over me, Yin Daiyu."

She should have just remained silent. Should have balked at his intimidation and silently cried at the uselessness she felt at being in his presence. At the fact that, in front of him, she was unable to change her fate. That she was forced to listen to everything he said.

But something inside her cracked. It splintered at the edges of her heart—at her sanity—and she couldn't hold back her own irritation, frustration, and anger. So much *anger*.

He was the reason she was even here in the first place. Kidnapped, almost ransomed, with her family's farm burned to crisps. And he was the one who was cornering her here, making it so she was unable to leave him. He was the bane of her existence, and now *he* was saying that she didn't matter?

"Then why keep me here?" Daiyu whispered fiercely, her hands clenching together into tight fists. She stared up at him unabashedly; if she was in court right now, with his trusted advisors surrounding him and the nobles who loved to gossip and sneer so much, she was sure she would be beheaded on the spot for even daring to stare at the emperor in such a hateful way. She didn't even try to disguise her anger as she spat, "Then why choose me from all those other women? If I really don't matter to you, if I hold no sway to you, then why keep me here? Why *burden* me in such a way?"

A muscle in his jaw ticked and his eyes widened a fraction of an inch, but she wasn't sure if it was from surprise or anger or insult. "Do not speak to me in such a manner, *woman*." His lips curled back, and she could smell the jasmine and incense on his clothes, mingling with the rusted, iron scent of blood that clung to him like a second skin. A reminder of what he was capable of. That his beauty was only a façade for the violence he carried out. "You are replaceable among the many, many women in my palace. In my *empire*."

Daiyu placed her palms on his chest and shoved him, but he didn't budge. It was like pushing against an impenetrable fortress wall. "Then replace me!" She couldn't hold back her own rage.

Her own hurt ego that felt worthless in front of him. If she was nothing, then why was she even going through this? All this pain and suffering? "Then replace me! Why won't you discard me if I mean nothing to you?" She tried sliding out from under him, but he grabbed her wrist and pulled her back, slamming her into his hard body.

"Don't you dare run from me."

"Unhand me!" She tried yanking away from him, but he held her tighter. "You're a ruthless monster! I hate you and I hate everything you stand for!"

"*Don't* call me that," Muyang snarled the words like a snapping dragon and she could feel the warmth of his skin, of his flesh pressed against hers, and the intoxicating denseness of the dark magic that surrounded him.

"Toss me aside and let me go!" Daiyu shouted at him, her voice growing shriller as she tried to twist free from his grasp. She hated the feel of his strong body flush against hers, the feel of his strong, lean arms holding her in place, and the way her body reacted. The way warmth pooled in her stomach. The way she wanted to pretend that this was a lovers' embrace, and not one of mutual distaste. "You hideous, grotesque demon! Free me and let me live my life!"

"I could have you killed for saying that to me." He breathed into her neck and a shiver tickled her spine—and she wasn't sure if it was from fear or thrill. His arm tightened around her waist, but not painfully, and he slowly placed his other hand atop her left breast. Heat coursed through her veins, staining her cheeks. "I could rip your heart out for even *thinking* those words."

Her chest rose and fell in an erratic rhythm. "You would love to do that, wouldn't you?" Her own lips curled in hatred, and she couldn't stop from sneering. "You only love violence, Your Majesty, and I'm sure you'd love to break me."

"There are many things I would love to do with you, little *fiend*." He breathed against her hair, and another shudder ran down her body. "But breaking you is not one of them."

He finally released her and she staggered forward, her legs weak and her knees wobbling against the other. She whirled around to face him, her balance nearly making her collapse. "Why are you doing this to me? Why can't you let me go—"

"Because you're *mine.*" Muyang was in front of her again, but this time, he didn't touch her. He only stared at her, his fiery rage seeming to have been stoked into a steady ember. Something dark and thrilling and possessive reflected back against his void-like eyes, and for a moment she wondered about how she could get lost in the blackness of his gaze—at the wickedness that showed the window to his soullessness. "What I decide to do with you is up to me. Whether that is to keep you forever locked within my walls or discard you onto the streets like a pauper. You are mine, and mine alone, Yin Daiyu."

"I am not an item to be kept or tossed!" She raised her hand to slap him, but he must have known what she was up to because he grabbed her wrist before she could strike. She screamed something incoherent and raised her other hand, but he took hold of that too. "You can't keep me here forever! I will *never* be yours!"

"You already are."

"You—you—*you monster!*"

He let her go again and this time he strode to the door, seemingly done with this conversation. A frustrated sob ripped from her throat and she wanted to punch something—or someone— and scream loudly for the world to hear. She hated him with all her being, and yet there was something about him that broke something within her. The thought that she was worthless and replaceable stung more than it should have.

"I hate you!" Daiyu shouted through her tears as he slammed the sliding door open. The bamboo panels of the door shook with the force, and when Muyang glared at her from over his shoulder, she was sure he would run forward and do his worst. But he simply left the room, leaving her with nothing but tears and shame and animosity.

21

DAIYU HATED DRAKKON MUYANG MORE THAN ANYONE else, she decided as she paced her bedroom—*his* bedroom—for the hundredth time that day. She had been given a change of clothes soon after Muyang had left the room—no doubt his doing—and had eaten breakfast—also likely his doing. But all of that did nothing to stave the burning rage she felt toward the insufferable monarch.

He didn't return to the room any time that day, and that gave her more time to think about her next options. There was no way —absolutely *no way*—she was going to stay here any longer. She didn't want to forever be under his thumb, and now that her family had already lost their livelihood, it was probably better to just sneak out of here and run as far away as possible with her family. They would have to start a new life somewhere—maybe even change their family name just in case—but it would save them in the long run.

She didn't have an escape plan, but later in the evening, after she had stuffed herself with a heavy dinner, she slipped into one of the storage rooms on the same floor as Muyang's room, and waited by a glass window for the perfect chance to escape. The room was surprisingly clean, had crates of black and scarlet military style cloaks and uniforms, and had a large banner of the Drakkon dynasty pinned to the wall like a trophy. The dragon symbol seemed to stare at her, knowing her intentions of fleeing, and she couldn't help the fear that gripped her tightly.

Soon, she told herself, pressing her forehead against the windowpane, she would escape this place. Her plan was simple: when it became night, she would break this window—the only glass window that wasn't barricaded with intricate metal designs —and climb down the five stories with the rope she made from the cloaks stuffed in the boxes. It was an incredibly stupid plan —she knew that—but she was desperate. There was no other way she could leave this guarded fortress without alerting Muyang. Once she was away from the fortress, she would run to the nearest village—a day's walk away. She could do it. She *had* to.

As night descended, her eyelids grew heavy and before she knew it, she dozed against the window. It was only when a door clicked shut that her eyes flew open. She sat upright, her heart racing. *He found out. He found out that I'm trying to escape and now everything is doomed—*

But Muyang wasn't in the room, and nobody was tossing her into the dungeons, and she was still alone in the room. She rubbed the side of her face and noticed the blanket that had been draped over her shoulders. It was heavily embroidered with golden dragons and seemed to be stuffed with feathers with how light it was. Her hands skimmed over the deep purple shade. She recognized it from Muyang's bedrooms, and all at once, guilt riddled her.

No.

She tossed the blanket on the floor. She wasn't so weak as to be swayed by a freaking *blanket*. Was she so morally starved from affection that this small, small act was enough to keep her here?

No, she told herself as she stretched her legs and stood. She remembered all the times he had humiliated her and made her feel terrible. And then she recalled their conversation earlier that day.

About how replaceable she was, and the fires of her wrath were stoked once more.

Judging by the black skyline, it was well into midnight, and her plan was still in motion. Daiyu wasted no time running to one of the crates, shoving the lid off, and retrieving the cloaks she had tied together. She opened five more crates to unveil the rest of the makeshift rope and tied the sections together tightly before securing them onto the biggest crate—which held the metal armor. She tugged at the crude rope and prayed it was enough to hold her weight.

If she ended up falling to her doom, at least she had *tried* to escape, she thought grimly. At least she didn't weep and wallow in self-pity. At least she had tried to change her bleak fate.

It must have taken an hour to get all the cloak sections tied together and secure, and the only thing left was breaking the window. She had to break it in such a way that she wouldn't cut herself on the way through it, but she also didn't want to cut up her hands in the process. After much deliberation, she went back to the lid of one of the crates and chucked it as hard as she could at the window.

The glass shattered immediately on impact. Daiyu gasped sharply and stumbled back as pieces of it sprayed the room. The blood rushed to her ears and she couldn't hear beyond the pounding of her own heart. She waited for the guards to swarm the room, her gaze glued to the jagged window, at the shiny, sharp shards of glass glistening silver in the moonlight. She continued to wait, but nobody charged into the room. Nobody shouted from down below—from outside the fortress walls. And it was only then that she realized she had to move to the next phase of her plan: actually getting out.

Daiyu licked her lips as she approached the window gingerly. She wadded her hands with Muyang's blanket and carefully punched the serrated edge of the window until it was smoother. She winced as a shard of glass cut through the padding and sliced open her knuckle. Hissing, she dropped the blanket on the floor and grabbed her hand tightly. Blood welled instantly, slipping from the wound and spotting against the shimmery glass shavings below.

Tears blurred her vision and she breathed out shakily. She willed herself not to break down in sobs, even as her throat constricted. This was a stupid, *stupid* plan. She was going to end up killing herself at this rate. But what other choice did she have? She couldn't stay here with Muyang—that was another death sentence, albeit a slow and torturous one.

It took a full fifteen minutes of crying, applying pressure to her cut knuckle, until she was ready to move along. She tossed the end of her cloak rope through the window and watched with bated breath as it fell down the fortress wall. She couldn't tell if it reached all the way down to the ground, but she was almost certain that it did—it had to, after all. Or else ...

Daiyu didn't let herself think too hard about what it meant if she failed.

Flexing her hands and carefully brushing down the bits of broken glass on the windowsill with the blanket, she hauled herself onto it. A chilly night breeze ripped through her hair and she inhaled sharply against the cold, her breaths puffing out in front of her. She stared down at the ground, which seemed to loom farther and farther away, and swallowed down the fear gripping her.

You can do this. You don't have a choice.

Breathing out shakily, she held on to the rope tighter. Her cut knuckle stung and protested, but she ignored it. She had to do this, she told herself. Muyang had driven her to a corner, and this was the only way she could attain freedom. The only way—

Before she could change her mind, she jumped.

A scream almost escaped her lips as her hands slipped down the rope. Air whooshed over her face, ripping through her hair and freeing all the hairpins that had kept her hair in a low bun. She slid down the rope, the skin of her hands chafing raw and her legs dangling as she tried to get a grip. She was falling—*fast.*

The rough material of the cloaks shredded through her hands and a blind panic rushed over her as she continued to descend the rope—but not out of her own will. She tried to stop the breakneck speed in which she was falling, but she had no upper body strength that could hold her in place. Anytime she tried to flail her legs against the wall, her body slammed into it instead, and the wall scraped down her side painfully. She suppressed her own screams of panic and pain, and it wasn't until she was a few feet from the end of the rope that she finally slowed.

She held on to the rope so tightly that she was sure her hands would detach from her body and the rest of her would spiral and splat on the ground. Her legs dangled and she finally dared to peek down below. She was at the end of the rope and was maybe five feet from the ground.

It was only then that her body gave out.

Daiyu screamed as she crashed down below. Her shoulder slammed into the hardened, packed earth and she rolled a few times, the rough terrain ripping through her clothes and scraping her skin. She finally rotated onto her back until she was staring at the star-speckled night sky. A tremor ran over her and she couldn't stop from breathing heavily. Somehow, she was alive.

It took her several minutes to calm her breathing before she even attempted to sit up and assess her injuries. The adrenaline and shock kept the pain at bay, but she was in terrible condition. Her shoulder throbbed, the skin on her hands was completely ripped off and raw, and she had several cuts and gashes along her legs and torso.

But she was alive, and that was all that mattered.

She pushed herself to her feet and tightened the cloak around herself with numb, shaking hands. She headed straight for the woods—the same woods she had traversed with Atreus. The wind howled above her and her skin turned frigid against the wintry weather of Geru, but there was something exhilarating about it. She was free. Finally *free*.

~

DAIYU WALKED FOR HOURS, HER LEGS THROBBING WITH every step and the rest of her injuries aching excruciatingly. Now that the adrenaline and rush of escaping had left her, she was sore, in pain, exhausted, and *freezing*.

Her hair whipped around her with the wind and she turned her numb and frozen face away from the worst of it. She kept walking and walking until she wasn't even sure where she was headed anymore. The sun rose and continued to dance along the skyline for hours. Hunger and thirst took hold of her, and every little noise—the rustling of leaves and barren branches, the scurry of wild animals—had her on edge and thinking that Muyang's men had caught up to her.

It wasn't until the afternoon that she finally stumbled upon a village. She wanted to burst in tears at the first sight of smoke streaming out of a chimney. When she reached the streets, she almost keeled over and collapsed from exhaustion. But she pushed herself forward.

People ignored her—with how bedraggled and torn her clothing had turned out during her escape, she couldn't fault them. At best, she probably looked like a weary traveler, and at worst ... she didn't want to think about it. Did she look like a runaway, abused wife? Or a beggar? But one thing was clear: nobody wanted to involve themselves with her.

Daiyu approached an inn and pushed open the rickety, worn door. Warm air breathed against her instantly and she sighed in relief as she staggered inside. Her stomach growled, and she scanned the bustling room quickly. The inn was jampacked with men, all of them wearing thick fur cloaks and their voices bouncing off the walls. The smell of chicken stew and savory broth made her mouth water and she stumbled toward the back counter with stiff legs.

"We don't have any empty tables, miss," one of the men, who balanced a metal serving platter with six steaming tea cups, said as he passed her by to the crowded table to her left. He handed the drinks to the men and gave her a once-over. "You'll have to share with others. Is that okay?"

Daiyu's tongue felt heavy in her dry mouth and she bobbed her head quickly. She didn't care, so long as she was able to drink water and fill her empty belly. "That's fine," she rasped, then coughed and rubbed her rigid fingers together.

He jerked his chin to one of the tables at the center of the room. "There's an empty seat there. All we've got for today is hot chicken noodles. We're out of beef or any other kind of meat."

"That sounds delicious." She licked her chapped lips. "Thank you."

"I'll bring it over in a minute."

Daiyu nearly crumpled onto the empty chair the man had pointed out to her. The other men at the table barely paid her any heed, and she tipped her head back to stare up at the ceiling. She was beyond bone-weary. Every muscle in her body ached; not to mention the cuts and injuries littering her body like a patchwork quilt.

But the prospect of a warm meal and a warm bed to sleep in washed all her worries away. She would pay for a way out of here tomorrow morning, she decided as she thumbed the few silver coins in her pocket she had pilfered from Muyang's bedroom earlier that day. Tonight, she'd sleep in her own room, without worrying about Muyang jumping into her bedroom. She wouldn't have to deal with his dark, alluring gaze ever again.

When the innkeeper arrived with a cup of water and a steaming bowl of chicken, noodles, and wilted vegetables, Daiyu nearly melted in her seat. She downed the water and slurped the noodles like it would be her last meal. It was savory, salty, and garlicky, and even though she had grown accustomed to the decadent food in the royal palace for the past few weeks, this was the best meal she'd had in months.

It wasn't until she was at the very ends of her bowl, with only a few tendrils of chewy, delicate noodles left and three soggy pieces of broccoli that she *really* noticed the men in the room. She slowed down on chewing and lowered her chopsticks, suddenly aware that all of these men seemed to be a bit *too* bulky. She had seen hundreds of men at the fortress bundled in fur cloaks with armor underneath, and that was the same kind of cumbersomeness these men seemed to have. Like they were prepared for a battle.

It's not a big deal, Daiyu. She swallowed down a mushy broccoli. *They're probably just men from His Majesty's army.*

But even as she thought that, it didn't make sense. Wouldn't they be in the fortress if that was the case? And why were they wearing cloaks that didn't have the royal colors or insignia on them?

She reached for her cup of water, almost forgetting that she had drunk it already. Her hands shook and she tightened her hold on it. She could remember Atreus's warning that there were many villages that were harboring rebel soldiers.

It wasn't her problem.

Daiyu finished her food silently, a nervous sheen of sweat coating her hands and body. She didn't want to be involved in whatever trouble these men were looking for. And if they found out who she was, they would do the same thing the bandits Atreus had saved her from had done—kidnap her and sell her to General Keung, one of the leaders of the rebel army.

She hadn't noticed it before, probably because she was starved and scarfing down her food without a thought or care in the world, but some of the men were staring at her from time to time. Particularly the ones at her table.

Were they staring because she was a woman, or because they suspected who she was?

Uneasiness crept under her skin. Had she unknowingly fled from one prison just to end up in another? She folded her raw, peeling, and damaged hands on her lap and tried thinking of a plan. She could stay here for the night and leave in the morning like she had planned, and forget everything she had noticed today.

Or she could leave now and not take the risk of being found out. It was still mid-afternoon, so she could probably find a ride to a different village.

"What happened to your hands?" one of the men, a thin, lanky middle-aged man with a wispy beard and beady, narrowed eyes said as he nodded at her.

Daiyu jumped in her seat and laced her fingers together tighter. "Excuse me?"

"Your hands." The man pointed a chopstick at her lap and then speared a hunk of chicken in his bowl and chewed it right off the end of it. All the while, he didn't take his eyes off her. The other five men at the table were now staring at her too, and she stiffened at the attention.

The hairs on Daiyu's arms rose and she forced a smile. She could tell by his lack of table manners that he was rude and brutish—not the type of person she wanted to converse with—and she hoped he hadn't noticed anything strange about her. "I scraped them earlier. Not a big deal."

"Huh." He took a swig of his rice wine and belched loudly. "How'd that happen?"

"It's a long story." She rose to her feet and bobbed her head at the other men. "Good day to you all."

It was better that she got out of this place as fast as possible. Whatever plans she had for a warm bed were instantly scratched off her priority list. She needed to find a ride out of here *now*.

She turned to leave, but the man suddenly grasped her wrist tightly. He smelled like sour wine and sweat, and Daiyu tried tugging away from him, but he held her firmly. His dark eyes narrowed. "Where'd you get that cloak?"

"Let go." She snatched her hand away, her heart racing. The other men at the table were still staring, but now there seemed to be a renewed interest in her clothing, which they eyed wordlessly. Daiyu's throat constricted and she looked between the lanky man, the others, and then down at her cloak. It wasn't anything special —just a plain dark cloak with a deep-scarlet undercoat.

But all the color drained from her face as she noticed the metal dragon-shaped clasp that held the cloak together. Surely, they hadn't noticed it? *She* barely noticed it until now.

"I found it." Daiyu stepped back, glancing toward the exit and then at the room again. Nobody else was noticing the interaction, save for the people at her table. She fished for a coin in her pocket and placed it beside her empty bowl and cup. "Good day to you all."

She spun around and made a beeline to the door. She wove between the seats, dodged a few drunk, swaying men, and exited the densely packed building. The frigid, wintry air slapped her the instant she stepped out, and she breathed in the frost clinging to the wind. This time, she welcomed the icy weather. It was less suffocating than inside.

Daiyu hurried down the streets, her gaze skating to the buildings and the sparse people in the streets. She needed to find the stables and someone who could take her out of here.

Glancing over her shoulder, her heart stopped. The six men at her table had left the inn and were now standing by the entrance. They looked around themselves as if looking for something—or *someone*—before one of them spotted her. He nudged to his companions and said something, and all of a sudden, they all turned to her.

Daiyu ripped her gaze away and rushed down the street, no longer caring about the horses or the stables or finding a way out.

They knew who she was.

22

OR AT THE VERY LEAST, ACCORDING TO DAIYU'S CLOAK, they thought she sided with the emperor. And if anything, they probably wanted to get rid of her because she had seen them—the rebels.

She heard a few shouts behind her, but none of that mattered anymore. She shoved through the streets, her shoulders and elbows colliding with others, but she barely paid attention to that. She sprinted to the edge of the village and entered the woods she had come from. Her worn-out feet, covered in thinned silk shoes, pounded the uneven, twig-ridden ground. Her breath streamed out behind her in streaks of white and the scenery blurred to trees and snow. Branches tugged through her hair and ripped through her clothes, but she kept running.

She didn't dare turn around. Not even when she heard the curses and grunts of the men. Nor the familiar, metallic clang of a sword unsheathing from its scabbard.

Adrenaline pumped through her veins and all her exhaustion disappeared, overridden by the primal instinct to survive.

They had been drinking, so she had an advantage over them, right? They were likely clumsy right now and not expecting for her to run. She had a head start—

An arrow whizzed past her face and buried itself into the trunk of a hollowed, dying tree. Daiyu suppressed a shriek and pushed herself faster.

"Get back here!"

Her thighs felt like they would split open and her eyes burned from the stinging, cold wind. She didn't even know where she was headed. All she knew was that she had to outrun them somehow.

How had she gotten into this mess?

Why was this happening to her?

She was just a simple farm girl.

Daiyu kept running and running, her legs feeling like they would give out at any moment. Her lungs filled with fire and every breath seemed to be her last. More arrows missed her and struck the ground. That only pushed her harder, faster, until she felt like she would collapse. Until her vision was nothing but browns, whites, and blurs of arrows.

The men continued shouting, their voices growing closer with every passing minute.

One second, she was upright, sprinting with all her might, and the next, she crashed. She didn't even realize what happened until she slammed into the ground, the air knocking out of her as she rolled against the packed earth. Excruciating pain radiated from her leg and when she shakily pushed herself to her elbows and looked down, her stomach twisted into knots. An arrow was jammed into her thigh, the arrowhead poking out to the front of her thigh. Blood seeped from the wound, staining her dress and dripping against the fresh snow beneath her.

The men were closer now, maybe a minute away. Daiyu hauled herself to her feet, her injured leg refusing to move. She bit her bottom lip to keep from groaning. Her thighs quivered, and she couldn't think outside the white-hot throbbing of her leg. She limped forward, but the pain was too much and her body collapsed onto the blood-stained snow.

A strangled sob escaped from her as she dragged herself toward a tree. Right then, she noticed the glittering jade bracelet adorned to her wrist. She had almost forgotten about it and its supposed magical properties. What had Feiyu told her about it?

If you're really in a bind, try pouring your energy into it and it might help you.

She didn't know what else to do, so she grabbed the beaded ornament and tried forcing her energy into it.

"Please, please, *please!*" Tears of frustration, panic, and pain ran down her cheeks and she squeezed her fingers over the beads until her hands were white and bloodless. Nothing happened, and she could hear the men approaching now, the snow crunching beneath their boots. "*Please!*"

It wasn't working; the bracelet wasn't helping, and it appeared like she would die here. Releasing a frustrated sob, she tried pulling herself upright again. Did Feiyu really give her a useless piece of jewelry? Or maybe she didn't know how to use it properly? He shouldn't have given her something she didn't know how to use, she thought bitterly as she clawed the earth to yank herself forward.

The men were only a dozen feet away. All of their hurried impatience seemed to dissolve at the sight of her writhing on the ground, pinned with an arrow. She could even hear them chuckling and talking amongst themselves, but their words didn't register to her. Not with the blood rushing to her ears and her tunneling vision toward the horizon.

She shouldn't have run away. She should have stayed put in the fortress. She should have waited for a better opportunity to escape. She should have—

Daiyu cradled her wrist to her chest, another sob ripping from her scratchy throat. "Please help! Please!" she whisper-cried. And for some reason, instead of thinking of Feiyu coming to rescue her, she thought of Muyang. If he were here, he wouldn't have allowed anyone to injure her. He would have destroyed everyone in his path. He would have tortured these men for even daring to look at her.

In her moment of desperation, the person she wanted to save

her was a villainous, powerful man who would make these rebels suffer for putting her through this. The thought alone shattered something within her. Because Drakkon Muyang was many things, and she found that she preferred his darkness in that moment. She preferred the twisted, shadowy power he held. She wished more than anything in that moment for him to be here, to *protect* her.

"Muyang, please," she whispered through tears, "please save me."

All at once, the jade bracelet began to glow and grow hot, nearly scalding her wrist. A white light shone in front of her and a powerful gust blew around her. She watched with squinting eyes as a figure flashed before her, the winds dying off as the light dimmed and flickered.

Clad in black, leathery-scaled armor that hugged his impressively tall and lean figure, and with a glinting gold hair crown, Muyang appeared like a dark general ready for battle. His inky hair feathered across his pale, beautiful face, and his black eyes went straight to her. He held her stunned gaze, his expression just as shocked as hers, before shifting his attention to her blood sprayed across the snow. Darkness and rage immediately flashed in his eyes and the winds howled louder.

"Daiyu?" he spoke slowly as he kneeled beside her, his hand hovering inches away from her shoulder. "What happened to you? Who did this?"

She couldn't speak as she blinked up at him in shock. Was she hallucinating? How was it possible that he was standing right in front of her?

His eyebrows pulled together and a look of concern washed over his face, cracking his unreadable mask. He opened his mouth to say something, but an arrow shot toward him. Without even blinking, a tendril of smoke whipped out from the ground and caught the arrow midair. Muyang stonily turned to the six men standing a few feet from them. Daiyu followed his gaze at the men —all of whom had their weapons drawn.

"Are you six responsible for harming her?" he practically snarled, rising to his feet. A powerful, electrifying wind emitted from him, sending a shiver down Daiyu's spine. She could practically taste the magic in the air—it was so thick and suffocating.

She pushed herself into a sitting position and winced as her thigh throbbed painfully. Her attention drew to the jade bracelet, which was still warm against her skin, and she blinked down at it in dazed silence. Had she ... *summoned* Muyang? It was the only explanation.

The confusion, adrenaline, and shock seemed to dull the pain in her thigh. She looked between Muyang and the group of men, who were now circling them like a pack of wolves. The lanky man raised his sword higher, his eyes narrowing.

"Th-they're rebels," Daiyu managed to whisper, her voice hoarse and her throat dry. Her arms trembled from holding herself up and she wanted nothing more than to collapse into the snow. Now that Muyang was here, she was *safe*.

"Kill the bitch first," one of the men said to the archer in the group, who was already nocking an arrow.

Muyang unsheathed his sword in one fell swoop, the sharp silver blade glittering in the sunlight. In seconds, shadows warped around the blade, swallowing the sharp edge and rising off it like steam. He didn't look at Daiyu as he stepped in front of her protectively.

One of the men charged at Muyang from the side with his sword raised. Daiyu barely had time to blink before Muyang was in front of that man. He swung his own weapon and the man parried with his sword, but Muyang was stronger—much stronger. Daiyu watched wide-eyed as the shadow-drenched sword sliced through the other man's sword like it was butter, and then cut the man in half. It happened so fast that Daiyu didn't even see the blood spray against the snow until Muyang had already moved on to the next assailant.

She blinked, her breath coming in ragged gasps as she stared at the body carved in half. The man's mouth was still opening and closing, his fingers twitching and his gaze locked onto the sky. An expression of pure confusion colored his pale face and Daiyu watched as the life drained out of him—quiet literally as he bled out in seconds.

An arrow shot through the confusion, missing Muyang by a hair's breadth. The other men were swarming him, seeming to have forgotten all about her. They stood no chance against Muyang's monstrous strength. He cut through their weapons with ease, lopping off hands and limbs like they were made of air instead of flesh and bone. Blood splattered against his pale face, marring his immaculate beauty with death and horror. He looked more like a demon general than anything else.

Daiyu didn't know what to pay attention to—Muyang's quick moves as he fought through the men, or the bodies collapsing with grotesque, fatal wounds. Her stomach twisted at the sights and she inhaled sharply whenever a hacked body part splatted on the ground.

When everyone was either dead or their bodies were twitching—and close to death—Muyang released a shuddered breath and stuck his sword into the partially frozen earth. He was breathing harder than usual, which was expected, but for some reason, she thought he didn't have a *need* for anything— not water, nor food, and certainly not to catch his breath. He seemed too powerful in that moment, and yet mortal at the same time.

Daiyu opened her mouth to speak, but something out of the corner of her eye caught her attention. Time seemed to move in slow motion as the lanky rebel, whose legs were twisted beneath him in unnatural directions raised his dagger and, with the last of his strength, shot it at her.

Before she could even breathe—*even think*—Muyang dove forward. The dagger buried itself into his shoulder as he rolled on the ground and grunted upon impact. He raised his hand and a blast of black-blue light beamed out of it and smote the man on the spot until he was only a hunk of charcoal. The smell of burning flesh and iron filled the air, and smoke rose from the charred, blackened corpse.

Muyang shoved himself into a sitting position, his soft mouth curled into a scowl as he gripped the leathered handle of the dagger and yanked it from his wound.

"Y-Your Majesty?" Daiyu inhaled sharply, the heat entering her lungs and her nose crinkling as the scent cleared her sinuses. She looked between him and the burned corpse, and then at the rest of the grisly scene. He had taken the hit for her, she realized with swelling horror. His uniform was already darkening at the shoulder. If he hadn't done that ... she would be dead. Or close to death.

His glittering black eyes flicked to her and she flinched back at the amount of blood bespattered across his face. He was breathing heavily still, his face appearing more pallid than it had minutes ago. "Did they hurt you?"

The words didn't register to her until he dropped down to his knees in front of her, his gaze never leaving her.

"Daiyu?"

"No, no ..." She reached forward to touch his shoulder but stopped herself short, her hands hovering over the seeping wound. Her shock kept her from speaking politely, formally, or correctly. She blurted, "Why didn't you use your magic? Why ... *why*?"

"Why are you worrying about me when you're the one bleeding out?" Muyang arched an eyebrow and her cheeks flushed with unexpected warmth. He laughed softly, and it surprised her more than anything else—to see him chuckling while covered in blood with the corpses of his enemies at his feet. The corners of his eyes crinkled and for a moment, she couldn't breathe as she took in his wickedly beautiful face. He looked so carefree in that moment, so *alive*.

Daiyu swallowed down the dryness of her throat and shifted into a more comfortable sitting position, only to be shot with excruciating, white-hot pain. A stifled gasp fell from her lips and she steadied her hands onto the cold, wintry snow to keep herself from flopping on the ground. Her thigh throbbed painfully, and she could feel the blood dripping from the wound and the arrow digging into her flesh with every slight movement.

Muyang grabbed her by the shoulders and tried to hold her upright, but that only made the pain worse. Daiyu slapped his hand away, her vision blotting with black spots.

"Stop, stop—just let me breathe—" She squeezed her eyes shut and tried to calm her breathing, even as her thigh ached more and more. Now that the adrenaline and shock from the fight was wearing off, her pain shot through the roof, tingling every single one of her senses. In the back of her mind, she couldn't believe she had slapped the emperor's hand away, but all her other senses were screaming at her to handle the pain.

Muyang scooped her into his arms without a warning. Daiyu bit back a scream and her vision darkened. She tried smacking him to keep him away—to keep the pain away—but she couldn't do anything but writhe in his arms.

"Shh." He pushed back the errant strands of hair obscuring her clammy face. "Breathe, Daiyu."

"It hurts—it hurts so bad," she whispered, pursing her lips together to keep from screaming in agony. Tears burned the back of her eyes. "Why does it hurt so much now?"

"It's because you're not panicking as much anymore, because you're safe now." He continued to brush back her hair and cradle her in his arms. "You know that everything will be fine now, so your body is reacting to the pain."

"It hurts," she repeated through the tears. She didn't even care that he was holding her so tenderly, or that he was brushing back her hair like a lover would. None of that mattered, not when she looked into his black, black eyes and saw nothing but her own pained reflection.

"I know, I know." He held her tighter and winced when she took hold of his injured shoulder. "It will only last a few more minutes."

She held on to him tighter, her fingers slick with her blood—and his. "Make it stop."

"*Shh.*" Muyang's hand hovered over the arrow.

"Wait—" Before she could tell him to stop, he yanked the arrow out from her wound. Her vision doubled and blackened, and she screamed piercingly. The wound, which had begun clotting just a bit, felt as though he ripped through the flesh all over again. Her dress quickly became drenched in fresh, warm blood, and she convulsed in his arms, her limbs flailing as she cried in torment. He held her the whole time, whispering soothing words she couldn't understand.

Finally, when she thought she would break, tranquility fell upon her that was unmatched for the circumstance. Her hazy, blotchy vision righted itself and the pain abated until her thigh only stung. Her erratic breathing calmed and she opened her eyes to stare up at the misty, gloomy, gray sky. Tiny snowflakes cascaded on her and every inhale filled her lungs with a wintry frost.

Muyang's breath streamed out of his mouth in white clouds. His skin was paler than before, and sweat dotted his creased forehead. It took her a second to realize his palm was covering her wound and that a golden light was emitting from his hands directly onto her.

"What are you doing?" Daiyu said, blinking up at him like she was seeing him for the first time.

"What does it feel like, little rabbit?"

She closed her eyes and groaned as the pain lessened further. "I hate that—" she mumbled.

"You hate that I'm healing you?"

"No, no, not *that.*" She stared up at him and for the first time in a long time, she didn't feel absolutely terrified to be looking at him so unabashedly. Maybe it was the shock or the effects of his magic that made her feel loopy, but she felt ... safe here. "I hate being called a *little* rabbit. It feels so ... condescending? Like you're the monster and I'm the prey? I just hate it. I hate being a weak little *thing*."

"And what do you think would be more appropriate?" Muyang's fingers caressed her thigh slowly, and pulses of tingling magic seeped into her flesh, pulling the fibers together. "From what I remember, I truly am a monster, aren't I? And you, the innocent maiden who fell into my wicked trap."

Warmth pooled in her stomach and she tried to stop the blush from spreading up her face. "That's not ... I didn't mean to call you a monster."

"You didn't mean to? I recall you accusing me at *least* three times."

"It was at *most* three times," she said with a cough.

"Well then, little fiend, what should I call you instead?"

She didn't have a nickname to tell him, or even something elegant. Truthfully, she didn't know what alternative to little rabbit there was, but surely it was better than to be called that. "I don't know," she managed, resting her head against his chest. The smell of irony blood, jasmine, and musk mingled together in the leather clothes he wore, and her cheek felt cold against him. "Something fiercer, maybe."

Muyang exhaled deeply, his breaths short. "Maybe *little dragon* is more fitting."

"*Little* anything doesn't inspire much fear or courage," she whispered, peering up at him. "Little bird, little mouse, little rabbit, little dragon, little wolf ... it's all—" She finally noticed that he had his eyes closed and was breathing more raggedly than before. His skin matched the graying clouds above and there was a bone-weariness about him that made her shiver in anxiety. He was still holding her thigh gently, the magic spilling from his hands in thick streams like honey.

"Your Majesty?" She hesitated to touch his face, but when her hand finally pressed against his cheek, his eyes flew open. Ubiquitous black reflected back at her, so dark and rich and void-like that she almost lost herself in them.

"You wish to be feared?" he asked, blinking as if trying to re-immerse himself in their conversation.

"Well, it certainly wouldn't hurt," Daiyu found herself saying, but her attention was honed in on him. The way he appeared exhausted, how he too was injured, and yet was healing her. She eyed his bloodied shoulder but couldn't tell if he had healed himself already or not. "Are you well?"

"I should be asking you that." Muyang pulled his hand back, now stained scarlet, and inspected the wound over her thigh. He peeled back the shredded, blood-soaked sections of her skirt to reveal the smooth, pink scar beneath. It was still muddied with blood, some fresh and some crusted, but it was undeniably healed.

Daiyu gasped. "You healed me?"

He didn't bother answering her question and instead furrowed his eyebrows. A flash of something sinister crossed his face. "Forgive me, I was unable to hide the damage. You'll be left with a scar for the rest of your life." There was something sorrowful and furious about the way he said it—the two emotions seeming to war for domi-nance. When he met her gaze, there was only sympathy in them. "I'm not as skilled in the art of healing as I am with destruction."

She understood the weight of what he was saying—and what he wasn't saying—but her mind stuttered over the fact that the *emperor* was apologizing to her. Scars on her body meant she was marred, no longer desirable for many men. Some would even turn their noses at her if they knew. Others would pity her.

Would Muyang discard her because of this hideous, large imperfection on her body? For a moment, her mind wandered to that thought—and she realized with growing horror how terrible that idea made her—but she became aware of another, less bewil-dering, thought: didn't she *want* that? Wasn't the whole reason she was caught up in this mess *because* she was trying to flee from him and her tumultuous fate with him?

She didn't want him. And yet, why did her chest ache at the mere idea of him casting her aside?

"Your hands ..." Muyang gently took her raw, peeling, and damaged hands in his. His forehead creased even more. His gaze flicked up from her aching hands to her face, and he studied her for a moment as if knowing what she had done to escape from him. "You're injured all over, little fiend. What have you done?"

Her throat dried up, and a blustering wind blew over her face in that exact second, obscuring her expression with her hair. All the injuries on her body—her hands, her feet, her thigh—were a testament of her desire to flee. To escape from her impending doom. She should have remained resolute in that—she had staked her life on it. But here, in his presence, her mind was scrambled and she couldn't form coherent thoughts.

"It doesn't matter, does it?" Daiyu tried wrenching her hands away, but he held her wrists tighter.

"It matters to me." He stared at her levelly, and she couldn't look past the blood speckled on his face or the darkness of his eyes. "It matters to me, Daiyu."

"Why?" She remembered his earlier words—about how replaceable she was to him—and her throat constricted together. She didn't like the way her stomach twisted together like a pit of writhing snakes.

Muyang didn't answer. He held her hands lightly, a golden glow returning from his fingertips. Her skin warmed as the magic touched her and she watched as the flesh repaired itself. He healed every part of her that was injured, whether it was a scratch on her arm or the gashes on her feet. He was silent the entire time, moving on to each wound methodically. It wasn't until she was completely healed that he spoke again.

"You will have some scars. It angers me to think that these scum"—he spat in the direction of the corpses, his voice riddled with vitriol—"dared to touch and wound you so, but I can't do more than kill them. And seeing as how they're already dead, I can't torture them for the wrong they have committed against you. I should have let them breathe their last breaths at your feet, begging for forgiveness, but my fury took the better part of my decisions and I dashed that hope prematurely."

Daiyu stared down at her healed hands and stretched her cold, stiff fingers. Her hands weren't scarred, but even healed, they were rough with all the work she had done throughout her life—all the farming, cooking, cleaning, and manual labor made her hands different than that of a noble woman's. She didn't have delicate, pink hands that were unused to work. She had roughened, dry, and patchy hands. Embarrassment flooded her at the sight. He probably thought her hands were like this because she had injured them recently. Little did he know.

The textured, pink scar on her thigh was just another imperfection on her already imperfect body. He didn't seem to realize just how flawed she was. Or how this new scar made her *lesser* than all those other women who already had an advantage over her.

"It really doesn't matter, Your Majesty." Daiyu's breath fogged in front of her and she rubbed circles over her shoulders. Her cloak was torn in several areas, but she barely felt the cold. Not when she was so close to him and practically sitting on his lap. She shifted her body away from his warmth. "These unfortunate men are already dead, and whether they begged at my feet or not wouldn't change my fate ... or theirs."

"What do you mean it doesn't matter?" A hint of anger leaked into his voice and he reached forward to grab her chin, but she shook her head away before he could. "They *hurt* you, Daiyu. Of course it matters—"

"If that was enough reason for it to matter, then it matters not."

"What are you saying?"

"You've wounded me, and it doesn't matter now, does it?" Her lower lip wobbled and she hated the vulnerability in her voice, or the way his eyes widened a fraction of an inch in surprise.

Muyang blinked slowly. "I've wounded you? When?"

"When you told me I'm replaceable." Her throat closed up

and her eyes misted with unshed tears. It was the painful truth she didn't want to face—the fact that his words affected her more than they should have. Her voice thickened as she continued, "And now my worth is even less than all those women in the empire who are already better than me. I'm already old, and rough, and now *scarred* to top it all off! Who will ever want to marry me now? Who will ever *want* me?"

She didn't know why she was saying all of that—she had resigned herself to a fate of never marrying, but now ... now, her heart felt empty. Lonely. *Afraid.*

"It doesn't matter what happened, or what will happen, or how all of this came to be. All I know is that I'm miserable, hurt, and cold, and my body is scarred, and I ... I ..." More tears streamed down her face and she had a million different threads of thoughts running through her mind, each of them intersecting with one another and confusing her. "I don't know what to feel anymore."

"*Daiyu.*" Muyang stared at her squarely, his voice barely above a fierce whisper. His black hair swayed with the motion of the wintry wind, and something dark passed over his features. "Do you think I want you less because you're *scarred*? There is not a single thing in this empire—in this *world*—that can mar your beauty or your worth. Never think that you are worth less than anyone else." He reached forward and grasped a tendril of her hair. Something possessive seemed to take ahold of him as he narrowed his eyes at her. "And you speak as if someone else would dare to marry you when you are *mine.*"

The last of her tears fell onto her lap and she could only stare at him, dumbfounded. He wanted her, despite ... despite everything? Her confusing emotions entangled further and she swiped at her damp cheeks with the palms of her hands. It shouldn't matter, she told herself, and yet she found that it *did.*

"But I ..." She swallowed down the heaviness in her throat. She wanted to *leave* him. That was why she was even in this mess. There was no reason for her to fling herself on him when he had done nothing for her but put her in this situation. She should hate him, not desire him, and she should particularly hate the twisted, possessive attention he gave her.

She shoved her messy, confusing thoughts away when Muyang suddenly rested his head against her shoulder. Daiyu nearly squeaked at the contact, her face flushing with unexpected warmth.

"Y-your Majesty?"

"Let me ... just ... rest my head for a second," he breathed.

A blush spread over her cheeks as he wrapped his arms around her waist and enveloped her in a loose embrace. "Your Majesty? This isn't appropriate—"

And before she could question him further, his body went limp against hers.

23

Daiyu fell back in the snow with the weight of Muyang's body pinning her to the ground. She blinked up at the gray sky. The back of her clothes slowly seeped with dampness from the snow. She tried nudging Muyang, but he remained unmoving and *heavy.*

"Your Majesty?" Daiyu wriggled beneath him. He was like an anchor sitting on her chest, making it harder to breathe, but even as she pushed him, he didn't budge. "Are you seriously ..." *Unconscious?*

She didn't say the word out loud in case she came across as rude, but when he didn't answer, she intensified her efforts to free herself from under him. After much struggling, cursing, and grunting, Daiyu somehow managed to pry herself free and squirm out from beneath his weight. Once free, she pushed and pulled him until he was lying on his back.

"You truly are a giant of a man," she said through exasperated gasps, falling back onto her bottom. In the afternoon sunlight—mostly overcast by the crepuscular sky—he appeared as pallid and colorless as his surroundings. The only dash of color on him, except for his inky hair and clothes, and the drying blood of his enemies on his face, was the stain of vermillion on the snow where his shoulder had been.

He had healed her, but by the looks of his own injuries, he hadn't bothered to extend the same magic to himself. He was puzzling in many ways, and she didn't know if she wanted to delve deeper into what that meant for her and her changing perception of him. Sometimes she felt like he wasn't so bad—like now—but other times ...

Daiyu shoved those thoughts aside and crawled over to him. She would have to think about her messy feelings later. Right now, he needed her.

"Are you able to hear me?" She touched his injured shoulder and cringed at the sticky residue left behind on her fingers. Why had he pulled the dagger out of his shoulder? Wasn't that risky since the blade would stave the bleeding? Or was she naïve in thinking that? Had the blade been poisoned?

Daiyu looked around herself for something to clot the bleeding, but other than the corpses littering the woods, she didn't find anything useful. Stifling a curse of her own, she went to one of the less disturbing, twisted bodies and pried the man's sword from his cold, dead fingers. She sawed off sections of the rebel soldier's cloak and went back to Muyang. It didn't take her long to pad his injury with the cloth. She would have been able to do a better job if she could strip his clothes, disinfect the injury, and then bandage him, but seeing as how he was still the emperor, she figured undressing him might have been pushing her luck.

She sat beside him, unsure of what to do. Her mind was a maelstrom of wildness. Was he dying? Was he poisoned? She couldn't rush back to the village for a healer because the place was already chock-full of rebel soldiers who would happily kill Muyang the instant they saw him. Could she make it back to the fortress while lugging him around? What would happen once the sun set? Surely, imperial soldiers would come looking for Muyang once they realized he wasn't at the fortress—should she wait for them?

Daiyu tinkered with the now-colorless beaded bracelet on her wrist. The jade color had vanished soon after she had used the magicked item, and now it appeared like a cheap, glass beaded trinket.

"Feiyu, can you hear me?" she whispered into the piece of jewelry. She gave a quick side glance to Muyang, who hadn't moved in the past hour. "I could really use your help right about now."

She waited for a response, but nothing came.

"Feiyu?"

Still nothing.

Daiyu cursed and almost flung the bracelet across the woods, but thought better of it at the last second. She rubbed the smooth beads absentmindedly and looked between Muyang's unconscious state, the gloomy sky that foretold either snow or rain, and then the corpses. She wanted nothing more than to leave this place in the woods—where so much death and chaos had occurred—but she wasn't too fond of the idea of dragging Muyang through snow, branches, and who-knew-what.

"Wake up. *Please.*" She patted Muyang's cold cheek. Under normal circumstances, she could be executed for touching the emperor without permission. She could imagine Muyang's court, and all the gossipy women in the Lotus wing, gasping at how inappropriate all of this was. She wondered what they would think of her behavior thus far. It was scandalous, for sure, and she deliberated if a noblewoman would have acted the same way.

She stared down at the harsh planes of Muyang's sculpted jaw, his long lashes, and his soft mouth. For a moment, she wanted to run her fingers through his silken hair—*just because*—and she wanted to touch those lips with her fingers. A blush spread over her face the more she studied him, and she finally had to rip her gaze away to stop her creeping. He truly was too beautiful to be an evil emperor.

"You've caused me a lot of trouble, but I reckon I'd be dead without you so ... I suppose I should thank you?" Daiyu murmured, pulling her legs to her chest and hugging herself tightly. A light flurry of snow danced from the sky and powdered his leathered, scaly armor. "Well, to be fair, if you hadn't chosen me to be your bride, I wouldn't be in this mess, so I suppose I don't *have* to thank you."

She sighed and peered up at the sky. She would probably have to make a decision soon: leave him behind to search for help, or drag him all the way to the fortress? Surely, the rebel soldiers would come here looking for their missing brethren, so she doubted they could stay here for too long.

"Aren't you supposed to be all powerful? I remember you doing all sorts of magic back at the fortress, so why are you unconscious now?" She nudged his uninjured shoulder with the tip of her worn-out shoes. Still, he didn't budge. "Makes me wonder if you really are just human like me. I thought you were part demon ... and part dragon."

Daiyu dusted off the flecks of snow on her cloak and exhaled deeply, her breath misty. The temperature was continuing to drop, and it would probably only get colder once the sun set.

A groan piqued her attention and she whipped her head in his direction. Muyang's lips twitched and he winced, his eyes still closed. She sucked in her breath and inched closer to him. Grabbing a hold of his shoulder, she shook it slightly.

"Your Majesty! Are you awake?"

He mumbled something incoherent, and Daiyu shook him harder. She needed him awake so he could warp them out of this mess. Or if he couldn't manage that, at least walk himself back to the fortress.

"Your Majesty?"

Muyang grumbled louder, his eyes flying open. Even injured and half-conscious, he had a scowl on his face. Upon seeing her, he sighed, his displeasure rumbling over his chest. "What happened?"

"You fell unconscious." Daiyu retracted her hand and wrung them together. "I didn't know what to do, so I was just waiting for you to either wake up, or for your soldiers to come here and save us. Looking back, I probably should have just dragged us farther away from this place, right? Maybe so the rebel soldiers don't follow us here? But I didn't think I'd be able to drag your body since you're so heavy—" She realized she was rambling and clamped her mouth shut.

He watched her neutrally and pushed himself into a sitting position. He hissed back a curse and nearly fell back onto the ground. Daiyu rushed forward and grabbed his shoulders, helping him sit up.

"Are you well?" she asked, aware that she was too close to him —his face was inches away from hers. If she leaned any closer, she'd be pressed up against him. But the thought alone made her face flush with color—why was she thinking of that when he was injured? That should have been the last thing on her mind. "You should have healed your shoulder."

"I wouldn't have been able to heal you if I did that." He ran one hand over his face and cringed again. "How long have I been out?"

"Maybe an hour?"

"An hour ..." Muyang pursed his lips together and stared off at the six bodies, and then up at the skyline. "We should head back to the fort."

"Like ... walk?"

"Yes." He turned to her sharply, the blacks of his eyes appearing all the more starless and glittering against the backdrop of barren trees and crystalizing snow.

She canted her head. "But that will take us forever."

"You've only been gone for half the day. If you've made it this far by yourself, I'm sure we can make it back in one piece," he said dryly. "Unless you disappeared during the night, in which case, we will likely have to walk quite the distance."

Daiyu licked her lips nervously, not wanting to tell him that was exactly what she had done. "Why can't you just use your magic to teleport us to the fortress?"

He grimaced as he pushed himself up to his feet, but she wasn't sure if it was from the pain. "I can't."

"Why not?"

"It requires too much magic. I don't have enough to warp both of us."

"You don't have enough?" Another head tilt. Wasn't he supposed to be all-powerful? Completely unmatched? It was plausible to think that she was completely out of touch with how magic really worked and how much energy it required, but she would have thought after seeing him display his deadly magic on several occasions that he was powerful enough to do *more*.

But perhaps that was her inexperience talking.

"Let's go." Muyang turned his head as if sniffing the air and stared off at the distance with narrowed eyes. Finally, he jerked his chin to the side. "The fortress is this way."

"How do you know?"

"I can feel it."

"How?"

"The magic of the fortress." He shifted his weighted gaze to her, and a flash of mild irritation passed over his face, quickly overshadowed by his frown. "Come on, let's go."

Daiyu followed him as they headed off in the direction he had pointed to. His breaths came labored as he trudged forward, his normally neutral mask slipping to reveal pain every few seconds. Daiyu subconsciously reached forward to help him, but he waved her off.

"I can handle myself."

"Are you sure? You don't ..." She let the sentence hang, not wanting to say what she was thinking. Was it treasonous to tell him he appeared weakened and likely needed help? He hadn't liked it the last time she had mentioned it to him.

"I'm certain," he said in a clipped voice.

They both walked in silence for a few minutes. With him plodding through the snow like his legs were leaden, and her trailing behind him slowly. After the fourth time of Muyang almost tripping and falling to his knees, Daiyu touched his lower back and came to stand beside him.

"Let me help," she offered. "You can lean on me—"

"*No.*" He tried pushing her away, but she didn't relent and stood her ground.

"Your Majesty, forgive me for saying this, but you're not in any condition to be walking alone. You need help. *My* help." Daiyu squared her shoulders and stared up at him levelly. The wind blew against their faces, making her already stiff face feel tauter. But this time, she tried to lean into that stoicism. "You may not like the idea of being helped, especially not by a *weak little thing* like me, but we both need to get out of here as fast as possible, so I suggest you take my help."

Muyang's lips flattened into a thin line, but he didn't disagree. He only nodded ever so slightly and turned his head away from her. A shiver ran down her spine at the small win and she pushed forward with him. He didn't lean on her too much, not at first, but after ten minutes of silently walking, he put some of his weight against her shoulder. His arm was slung over her, and she had to keep her arm around his waist to help him up. The smell of jasmine and blood intoxicated her senses, and she had to keep her face as far away as possible so as to not accidentally lean into him and breathe in his scent like it was a powerful drug. It was tempting, and she blushed over her lack of control.

Meanwhile, Muyang seemed unaware of her struggle. He seemed to be fighting for every breath he took. His forehead quickly dotted with sweat the more they traveled and his breathing became more ragged. It became too much for her to simply ignore.

"Are you poisoned, Your Majesty?"

"I hope not. Why?"

"You appear ..." She struggled with a polite way to say that his injuries didn't seem *that* severe, and yet he was completely winded. But any way she twisted it, it came across as rude and inconsiderate.

"Weak?" he finished with a snarl.

Daiyu shrank within herself, avoiding eye contact. "I didn't say that."

"But you're *thinking* it."

"No—"

Muyang scoffed. "Daiyu, you have no reason to lie to me."

She had all the reason to lie to him, *repeatedly*. Because he was a terrifying emperor, because he was all too powerful, because anything she said could be used against her, because her life wasn't her own when she was around him. But she bit her tongue and didn't divulge that.

Another strong gale blew against them, and Daiyu couldn't help but shiver as the cold seeped into her bones. Muyang shuddered beside her, and she somehow felt better that she wasn't the only one suffering. That he too was human enough to feel the discomfort of the frigid temperature.

Fifteen minutes must have passed before Muyang spoke again. And when he did, he didn't look at her, instead keeping his steely gaze forward. "I can't use much magic anymore and when I do, it takes a huge toll on me."

She blinked over at him. Had she heard right? Had he ... told her a secret? That sounded like private information that could have her *killed*. In fact, that sounded like something he would never, *ever* disclose to *anyone*.

"You said 'anymore.' Did something ... did something happen?" she asked quietly, her voice almost drowning away with the currents of wind.

"Everything changed when I took the throne."

She waited for him to elaborate, but he didn't. She had heard wild stories of his conquests on the battlefields during the rebellion where he took power. She had heard of him leaving behind scorched, unrecognizable corpses. Of his soldiers having to wade through the blood of his enemies after every victory. Of the dense air stinging with magic after he was done blighting his foes.

She had thought they were partial truths, but now she wasn't so sure. Were they all lies? Or did something happen during his usurpation of the throne that weakened him? She had too many questions, and she wasn't sure she wanted to bear the weight of the answers.

"Is it smart of you to tell me this?" Daiyu asked slowly. "I'm not going to be killed for knowing this, will I?"

He chuckled, low and soft, and the corners of his eyes crinkled with amusement. For a split second, she marveled at how beautiful he looked when he laughed. "After all the trouble I went through to save you, I don't think I'd want to waste it by murdering you here." There was a joking quality in his tone, but she jolted at how easily he spoke of her death. "I doubt you'd tell a soul. It wouldn't be wise for you, especially since you're to be my wife. It would do you better to want the best for me because if someone *did* depose me, then you know for a fact that your fate is to join me, do you not?"

Daiyu shivered but not from the cold and didn't meet his gaze after that. Truthfully, after an emperor was killed or overruled, it was common for all of his women to die with him. She doubted the rebels would want to keep her alive—other than for touting her around like a war trophy—if Muyang was killed by them. It wouldn't have been outlandish for his own trusted men to kill her if anything were to happen to him, as to save Muyang from the disrespect of having his woman ravished by another.

A sour and bitter taste coated her mouth. "I don't particularly like the idea of dying terribly, so I'll keep your secret safe with me."

"I expected as much."

"But we're not married, *yet*."

"True, but you're already mine." He said it with so much certainty that she could only stare at him. Did it come easily to him to take whatever he wanted? She shook her head. She would have to chalk it up to him being an emperor.

"You never did explain to me what you're doing out here,"

Muyang said, glancing down at her with cold, inky eyes that told her he wouldn't accept any excuses.

She almost tripped over a random tree root buried in the snow and had to right herself against a partially frozen tree. Thankfully, Muyang kept himself upright. She cleared her throat and tightened her hold on his waist. "Well ... I'm sure you noticed my absence."

"Not at all."

"Really?" She turned to him with wide eyes, and the corner of his mouth rose into a half-smirk. It took her a second to realize he was *joking*. She coughed, trying to hide her surprise and embarrassment. "W-well, I ... I decided to leave the fortress last night. And, well, things happened and I somehow ended up being chased by those ruffians. I believe they thought I was a part of your forces." She patted the dragon clasp of her cloak. "Anyhow, you really should deal with those rebels. There's a small army of them in the nearby village. Maybe thirty or forty men."

"I'll deal with them when the time comes, but I'm more interested in knowing why you left the safety of the fortress. Surely, it's not because you're a spy." His voice hardened at the last part, and there was an edge in his steely voice that made her blood run cold.

"I'm *not* a spy," Daiyu said. "I thought we already established that?"

"You're very suspicious. In many ways. Contrary to what you said, I don't think you're a *weak little thing*." Muyang's black eyes bored into hers and something fluttered in her chest, warming the pits of her stomach and turning her legs gel-like. "You're fierce and gentle, in such a way that I don't know how to handle you."

"You don't have to *handle* me in any way."

His lips twisted into a smile. "There it is, that little spark you keep trying to hide from me. I see it from time to time."

Daiyu's cheeks warmed and she didn't meet his gaze again.

His voice softened. "Did you leave because you no longer wished to be in my presence?"

She couldn't answer him and stared up with wide eyes. He

had hit the nail on the head, and she wasn't sure she was bold enough to admit it. But she didn't have to. He could probably read it all over her face. Instead of lashing out at her, he remained neutral, almost *too* calm.

"And how did you summon me whilst in that fray with those scum?"

Holding up her wrist so he could see her bracelet, she shrugged. "I'm not entirely sure, but I think I used this."

His eyes narrowed, and something flitted across his face— surprise, maybe? "And where did you get that?"

"I ..." She licked her lips. "I found it—"

"Don't lie to me." The sharpness of his tone made her flinch.

"It was given to me."

"By whom?"

She hesitated to answer. He had reacted terribly when she had used Yat-sen's magic and she doubted he would react better to knowing Feiyu was helping her. She also didn't want to get the high mage in trouble, not like she did with the poor prince. "One of the mages at the palace. I don't know who, but he gave it to me and said it could be useful."

"One of my mages approached you?" He almost stumbled when his foot caught against a slippery, icy, jagged edge of a rock, and he nearly took Daiyu with him. They both scrambled forward, holding on to each other for support.

"Are you o—"

"One of my mages approached you?" he repeated, standing straighter and pinning her with a displeased scowl. Even weakened, sweaty, and splattered with blood, he appeared as vicious as he had in the fortress hall when he was displaying his monstrous magic.

Daiyu nodded, not trusting herself to speak without giving away her lie.

"You'll have to point him out to me later," he said through gritted teeth. "I don't like the idea of my men acting without my permission, especially when it concerns *you*."

She didn't know how to take that—as a compliment, or not—so she said nothing.

~

THEIR NOT-SO-MERRY JAUNT CONTINUED IN SILENCE once more. When the sky darkened and the winds grew stronger, they took a break and huddled against a copse of dense trees, both of them shivering in the wintry temperature. Daiyu's teeth chattered and she hated that the weather up here in Geru, the northern part of the empire, was so frigid and unlike the rest of the country.

Daiyu's mouth was parched, her stomach was growling, and the bitter cold didn't help either. She hugged herself tightly and watched as Muyang sagged against one of the trees, his eyes closed and his expression more tranquil than hers could ever be.

"Why are you so calm?" She leaned against the cool, rough bark of the tree and brought her knees to her chest. Her butt and the back of her thighs were wet from the snow and she hated the combination of stiffness, dampness, and frozenness.

One dark, delicate eyebrow arched. "Do you expect me to be quivering in fear at such a minor inconvenience?"

"Well, you *are* quivering."

"In *fear*?" He scoffed, and she couldn't help the grin that stretched across her lips. "War is far worse than this could ever be. Besides, my magic will recoup itself in the morning and we can be on our way in no time."

Daiyu nodded slowly. "So you're not afraid because you have magic."

"If you're trying to say my lack of fear is because of my power, you're incorrect. I'm not afraid because I have faith in myself to survive. That's all."

She rested her head against the tree and felt the ridges across her scalp as she turned her head away from the biting breezes. How nice it must have been to believe in oneself so much, she thought with a frown. She wasn't sure if she had that same determination.

"It is often the smallest of creatures that have the highest drive for survival," he murmured as if reading her thoughts. He was sitting only a few inches away from her, their faces close together as they leaned against the same thick tree. His black gaze flicked to her lips, and she resisted the urge to blush as she ripped her attention away from him.

Daiyu placed her chin on her knees and curled into a tighter ball, her face flaming. "Are you suggesting you're a small animal? Perhaps I should call you *little* dragon, then."

Muyang's laugh startled her. He raked a hand through his dark hair, his body trembling with chuckles as he peered over at her. There was something otherworldly beautiful about him; like the stars themselves would shine brighter so long as he smiled. It was such a bizarre, poetic, magical feeling that Daiyu had to bury her face deeper against her knees to keep from staring at him like a lovestruck fool.

It was just his outer appearance. Nothing else about him was *good*. At least that's what she told herself, and a part of her believed it too.

"You shouldn't strain yourself too much. You're injured." Her nerves seemed to fire up all at once, and she toyed with the beaded bracelet to distract herself from her thoughts.

"I've been healing myself throughout the day, so you don't have to worry about me."

"I wasn't ... I wasn't *worried*."

"Hm." He tilted his head to the side, inching closer to her. "You've grown bolder lately."

"Excuse me?" She pushed a messy strand of hair behind her ear. Throughout the journey—perhaps when she climbed down from the fortress walls—she had lost all her hairpins, so her hair was loose and wild from the weather.

"You left the safety of my walls, you've insulted me several times, and now you lie through your teeth." He didn't say it with any ire, only mild amusement, but it still caused a ripple of anticipation to run through her body. "But I suspect this isn't the first time you've lied to me, or the first time you'll ever disobey me."

Daiyu picked at the dried blood crusted on her skirt, where the arrow had wounded her. She definitely didn't want to tell him that he was right on the mark, but she couldn't bring herself to refute him either. "I didn't disobey you," she mumbled.

"You aren't the type to listen often."

"Is that such a bad thing?"

Muyang lifted a shoulder, a light dusting of snow falling with the motion. "Perhaps not for the average man. But I am the emperor and everyone must obey me."

"Of course, Your Majesty," she murmured. She desperately needed that reminder. No matter how nice or charming he seemed right now, his true colors were that of an overbearing monarch who didn't take no for an answer.

An uncomfortable quietness washed over them. Daiyu bundled herself tighter within her cloak and snapped her teeth together to keep them from chattering too loudly, then stared off at the mounds of snow in the distance and the dark trees. Her stomach growled and she shoveled snow into her mouth with a rigid hand.

"Are you really part dragon?" she blurted out when she couldn't withstand the silence any longer.

Muyang pinned her with a neutral expression she couldn't read. "Why do you ask?"

"Aren't dragons"—she licked her lips, hating that she sounded so naïve and so much like the country bumpkin she was—"supposed to breathe fire and be warm all the time?"

"I'm not part dragon," he said slowly. "But ... I do have dragon's blood running through my veins."

Her eyes widened. "Really?"

"Yes." He stared off into the distance, his jaw stiffening as he seemed to think about something. "It's given me dragon-like properties for sure, but I was not born this way."

"What properties?"

"I appear youthful."

She blinked at him; she had expected an answer about his great strength, or the magical abilities he had, or something of that nature. Not about his appearance, but now that she looked at him, the pieces clicked together. Of course he couldn't be a twenty-something emperor with all that experience under his belt. "Then how old are you?"

"Not much older than you. Add a decade or so and you have my age."

"You're in your thirties?"

"Later thirties, but yes."

"That's ..." She couldn't hide her disappointment, but upon meeting his critical gaze, she shrugged. "You're not old either way. You're still in your youth ..."

"You sound dissatisfied." He raised both eyebrows, his shadowy eyes gleaming with amusement. "Well, forgive me for not being a three-hundred-year-old dragon, but alas, I am but a mortal man with magicked blood."

Daiyu laughed, and for the first time since they interacted with one another, she smiled over at him genuinely. They were too close to each other. His face was so close to her that she could touch their noses together with a simple push. And a part of her *wanted* to bridge the gap between them, even as something stronger within her resisted.

"I would have been more impressed if you were an immortal." She couldn't help the teasing quality in her voice, and it surprised her more than it should have—for her to feel so at ease around him in that moment. "I was hoping to marry an immortal thousand-year-old dragon, but I suppose—"

You will have to do, she finished in her head.

Whatever cheerful mood they had going between them seemed to fizzle out as Daiyu tucked her chin against her knees once more. Her mind traveled to the muddy thoughts she had earlier in the day and the choices she made to lead up to this moment.

She had been trying to escape him. She had been trying so, so hard to change this fate he had imposed on her. She didn't want to marry him. She didn't want to be his. And yet ...

"Your Majesty," Daiyu whispered, turning to him with wide eyes. Her heart was pounding loudly in her ribcage, her palms growing clammy and her stomach twisting with nausea. She had to make a decision, she realized, and it was now or never. "If ... or, more like, *when* we marry, what will happen to my family?"

Muyang didn't even blink. "They will be taken care of, if that's what you wish. Your family has been good to you, have they not?"

She nodded mutely.

"Then they will be looked after very well."

Feiyu had mentioned the same thing. And now, with her final worry seeming to abate, there was nothing holding her back anymore. This, she decided, was probably for the best. If she married Muyang, then her family would never have to worry about anything anymore. Whoever was threatening her family would back off once Muyang offered his protection. All of her worries about her family would disappear if she married him.

But there were so many sacrifices she would need to make—so many sacrifices that were necessary for any woman married to the emperor. She would have to be satisfied with being one of many. She would have to put up with his court, especially the other women in his court and in his favor. She would have to be content with the risk of being cast aside or disfavored by him in the future. She would have to deal with her children potentially being treated differently since she was a commoner.

There was so much of herself that she would have to give up, and she didn't *want* to.

But this was the only solution that would bring true peace and prosperity for her family. Her elderly parents wouldn't have to worry about food, or the rice fields, or their harvest. Her grandmother could finally relax after a long life of labor. Her siblings could have a chance at an education and marrying into a higher status. There would be no more danger upon them either.

And with the way Muyang was right now with her, she could imagine herself being content with him. She didn't love him, but it didn't really matter. She wouldn't marry him because of love—that was outside her scope.

"All right then," she whispered, a part of her wilting and another part of her coming to terms with her decision.

She had made up her mind.

She would marry Drakkon Muyang. Not for love, but for everything he offered—power, wealth, and status. And she promised herself in that moment if she ever felt like she had made a mistake, she would flee from him with everything she had, even if it killed her.

24

THE REST OF THEIR TRAVEL TO THE FORTRESS WASN'T
as arduous as Daiyu anticipated it would be. During the night,
Muyang had placed a magical shield over their bodies that kept
them warm, and by the morning, the weather had cleared up
enough that traveling was bearable. By the time they arrived at the
fortress in the evening, Daiyu was starving, but otherwise fine. She
scarfed down every bit of food given to her, and before she knew
it, it was nightfall once more.

Daiyu pulled the silk covers of her blanket over her body and
turned on the plush mattress in Muyang's room. Thankfully,
since arriving at the fortress, she hadn't come across her
betrothed, who was too busy getting back to work and, likely,
eradicating the rebel soldiers in the nearby village. She was more
than happy to be left alone, especially now that she had made up
her mind about marrying him. Although she was final with her
decision, there was a small part of her that didn't want to come to
terms with it.

But right now, with the loneliness of night, she wondered
what he was doing. She had been engaged once before, with her
childhood friend Heng, but everything about this betrothal was
completely different. For one, she didn't know Muyang like she

had known Heng. She had known everything about Heng and loved him dearly, but she didn't feel the same with Muyang. But … she also felt things with Muyang that she hadn't felt with Heng. She hadn't felt dark, guilty attraction. Her stomach didn't warm at the sight of Heng's face, nor did her body tingle with anticipation anytime he was near. Her chest hadn't felt tight any time he had been close to her. And she certainly had never thought about touching him or even kissing him.

She touched her mouth lightly, her face flushing with warmth. What was she *thinking*?

Daiyu yanked the covers over her flaming face and curled into a tight ball. She needed to focus on surviving in Muyang's court and it was better for her not to think of such … strange thoughts. And it was even better that Muyang wasn't around for her thoughts to tarry.

DAYS PASSED WITHOUT INCIDENT. DAIYU DIDN'T RUN into Muyang even once during her stay at the fortress. She had thought that maybe she would run away when she came in contact with him—for fear of how she would act around him now that she knew she would marry him—but she couldn't even execute her plan since she didn't see the man anywhere. It got to the point that she tried searching him out from time to time. She would walk the halls of the fortress, peek into the dining hall, and even wander the courtyards. But alas, the emperor was nowhere to be seen.

Daiyu fastened her mulberry-colored cloak tighter around her body and folded her sheep-skin gloved hands together on her lap. Her butterfly hairpins were studded with amethysts and every time she turned her head, the jangle from the dangling charms at the end of them startled her. She hoped she appeared like a proper noble lady, but she had no clue if she was actually succeeding. All she knew was that she was actually putting in an effort in her appearance, and Muyang wasn't even around. It made her wonder why she even cared, but at this point, it was just to spite him.

Soldiers sparred in the open courtyard, their breaths streaming white and their clothed bodies dampening with sweat. She had grown accustomed to the sound of steel clashing against steel, and even now, with the cacophony of drawn weapons and men grunting, she remained unperturbed. Daiyu drummed her fingers over her knees and watched the flurry of movements in mild boredom. It was still better than being cooped up in her room, though.

"Lady Daiyu?"

She turned her head and squinted against the harshness of the sun as Atreus came to stand a few feet away from the bench she sat on. His burned-honey-colored hair was brushed neatly back, and there was a sheen of sweat glistening on his tan face and neck.

"Oh. Atreus." She smiled at him and partially covered her eyes against the sunlight glare. "I didn't realize you were sparring here."

He shifted away from the brightness and motioned to the spot beside her. "May I?"

"Certainly."

He sat down on the cool stone bench and leaned against the backrest with a soft sigh. The ends of his damp hair curled against his neck, and Daiyu glanced over at the cross-collared, black and red military uniform he wore. "You look more in your element now that you're not associated with bandits," she commented half-jokingly.

The corner of his mouth rose and he rubbed the nape of his neck. "Ah, yes. I don't think I make a very good bandit. I apologize if I appeared vagrant and crude."

"Not at all." She turned to watch the sparring soldiers once more. Their weapons glimmered in the harsh light as they moved strategically. "You were only doing your job, and you did a splendid job at that too, if I may add. I might not be here if not for you."

"I'm sure you would have found a way to escape." He watched her from the corner of his eye. "Just like how you escaped this fortress. An impressive feat."

An unexpected laugh bubbled from her and an embarrassed flush climbed up her throat. "Oh, trust me, that wasn't impressive at all. I was running on pure determination, naivety, and blind luck."

"You managed to shock His Majesty, and not much surprises him these days," Atreus said with a hesitant smile. He laced his rough, calloused hands together, and the wind gently tousled his hair. "I wish you could have seen his face. Everyone in the room was terrified that he would kill us all for our negligence. Imagine our surprise when he *laughed*."

Daiyu tilted her head to watch him better. She hadn't heard this side of the story. She had assumed Muyang hadn't really cared whether she was in the fortress or not, or she had assumed he would be full of rage at the prospect of her fleeing from him. But laughing? She wasn't sure if his reaction had been from amusement or shock—or a mixture of both—but she found herself blushing, if only a tad bit, at the prospect of catching him off guard.

"He was probably just laughing at ways to end me."

Atreus gave her a puzzling look. "Why would you think that?"

"Hm?" She shook her head, her smile slowly fading. She had been half-joking when she had said that, but truthfully, no matter how charming of a man he was, or how wickedly beautiful he was, there was no denying that he was lethal. And that he wouldn't hesitate to cut off the short end of any stick that dragged him down. "Well, he's *Emperor* Drakkon Muyang. Of course that's what he would be thinking? You even said it yourself. You and everyone in that room assumed he might punish you all for me escaping."

"Yes, but he wouldn't actually hurt you. You're the woman he chose as his bride."

She remembered the way he had held a dagger to her throat,

and she suddenly didn't feel as warm and fuzzy as she had minutes ago. "Don't tell me you believe that he wouldn't hesitate to kill either of us if we disobeyed or displeased him?"

"I'm sure he'd at least *hesitate.*"

Daiyu couldn't help but burst into sardonic laughter. "Yes, yes, I'm sure that's what he'll do. Right before he—"

"I'm joking," Atreus said with a soft chuckle of his own. "I'm quite aware of His Majesty's personality. Though I doubt he would actually kill us if we displeased him. Unless, of course, we committed treason."

Daiyu wanted to laugh along with him, this time more cheerfully, but she found she couldn't. Not when an image of Prince Yat-sen flashed in her mind. She curled her hands over the edge of the bench and peered down at her pointed silk slippers. Tiny bluish-purple lotuses were embroidered on the sides of the shoes, distracting her momentarily.

"Atreus," she said quietly, her heart racing with sudden anxiety and guilt. "What happened to Yat-sen? I haven't seen him since ..."

The statement hung in the air for a few moments and Daiyu wasn't keen on finishing it. Yat-sen had been punished because of her, and she feared the worst for the youth. Knowing what she did about Muyang, there was no way he would spare the boy.

"Since the incident," Atreus finished with a nod. "Prince Yat-sen was sent back to the palace. He's not dead, if that's what you're asking."

"But ... he's not going to be executed for this, right?"

For a brief moment—so quickly that she almost thought she imagined it—something lit up on his face, like he knew something she didn't. But it passed so quickly that she couldn't decipher it or linger on it. He shook his head, his expression seeming to be made of stone. "His Majesty wouldn't execute him for that."

"Oh?" Daiyu sighed, but she couldn't shake her unease. Lacing her fingers together tightly, almost like she was making a prayer, she whispered, "But how can you be so sure? I really don't see the season why he would keep him alive, if I'm being honest. Prince Yat-sen was supposed to be ..."

"He was merely a useless prince before His Majesty took the throne, and he continues to be a useless prince."

She didn't miss the sharpness in his tone.

Sure, Yat-sen hadn't been the crown prince, or even next in line for the throne—in fact, he was said to be the disfavored son of the late emperor Yan—but that was *before* all the other princes were murdered by Muyang. Now, he was the rightful heir to a dying dynasty, and she saw no reason for Muyang to keep him alive. Wouldn't it have made more sense to cut off all ties to the past? To what could have been?

"His Majesty has graciously allowed Prince Yat-sen, Prince Daewon, Princess Liqin, and Princess Biyu to live. I personally don't know why he allowed them to breathe when they are remnants of a failed empire, but there is still kindness in his heart that won't allow him to kill mere children." Atreus stared straight ahead at two soldiers dueling one another with spears, their cloaks streaking behind them with every quick jut and lunge. His unnaturally green eyes flicked in her direction. "But the more they disappoint him, the more they will learn of his wrath."

Daiyu turned to watch the training men, her lips pressed together tightly. She would need to learn how to navigate life in the royal palace and how to keep her head low so as not to fall under that same wrath. Muyang might have favored her for now, but who knew when that favor would run out? She didn't want to live a miserable life. And she would have to learn of ways to escape if it came down to it.

A gentle wind jangled the tiny chimes on Daiyu's hairpins and she shivered. "I suppose I have much to learn."

"About?"

"Court life."

Their conversation came to an abrupt halt when a commotion in the center of the courtyard drew their attention. Soldiers began to crowd around a particular duo of fighters. From where she sat, she couldn't make out the fighters, but the cheers and claps made it out to be entertaining.

"I wonder what's happening there." She pushed herself to her feet and stretched her arms just in time to catch Atreus giving her a strange look. "What?"

"What are you doing?"

"Investigating. Aren't you curious?" She didn't wait for him to answer as she moved toward the circle. The soldiers made room for her when she gently pushed her way through. It didn't take long before she was in the front lines.

Two young men circled each other. One appeared like a normal soldier, with his uniform and his obviously Huo features, but the other soldier completely took her by surprise. With a shock of long, scarlet hair that shone in the sunlight like gleaming blood, which was held together by a single leather tie, and eyes so brightly blue they appeared demon-like, he stood out from the rest of the men.

He wore a wide grin on his face, even as he sported a small cut on his neck that was profusely bleeding and staining the collar of his mustard-colored tunic. Unlike the soldier he was facing, who fought with a long sword, he wielded two short daggers.

"Who is that?" Daiyu whispered, watching in awe as he moved with such speed against his opponent. He was unnaturally lithe and moved like flowing water—beautiful to watch, but deadly at the same time.

She hadn't realized Atreus had come to stand next to her until he spoke. "My brother."

"Your *brother*?" She whipped her head in his direction to find him smiling wryly at the foreign young man. Although Atreus and the other man—who, upon closer inspection, couldn't have been older than eighteen—both looked different than her own people, she could see that they were clearly from two different regions. This man was pale, red-haired, and blue-eyed, while Atreus was painted in shades of dark gold.

"We do not share any blood, but we grew up together under His Majesty."

"He is a member of ... the *Peccata*?" The word rolled off her tongue strangely and she wondered if she was saying it correctly—the name of the group of special soldiers under Muyang.

"Yes. Nikator." The corner of Atreus's mouth curved as the red-haired youth skillfully jumped from a lethal jab—causing a wave of *oohs* and *aahs* and cheers from the crowd. "He was supposed to come to the fortress in a few days, but he perhaps finished his assignment earlier than expected."

Daiyu watched as Nikator carried out a string of kicks and punches against the soldier, all of them meeting their target. The rest of the fight lasted less than a minute, and Nikator had the soldier pinned to the ground with a dagger hanging inches away from the man's heart. The whole time, his grin didn't disappear.

Daiyu clapped when the foreign youth extended his hand to the fallen soldier and helped him to his feet. Atreus rolled his eyes when Nikator flipped his daggers in the air, spun them against his knuckles, and strapped them to his waist in one fluid, flashy move.

"Impressive as usual," a velvety smooth, familiar voice called. All the hairs on Daiyu's arm rose up in anticipation and she swiveled to the side to see Muyang standing a few feet away from her at the lip of the circle. She had been so entranced in the fight that she hadn't noticed him slink by. And judging by the gasps from the soldiers—all of whom quickly lowered themselves in a bow in waves surrounding him—neither did anyone else.

Nikator's face lit up and he lowered himself briefly in a quick bow, jumped to his feet, and stopped in front of him. "Your Majesty! How long were you standing there? Did you see the whole thing?"

"Most of it." Muyang rested a hand on the younger man's shoulder and Daiyu could have sworn she noticed a hint of a smile on his lips. "You've improved."

"Naturally." His smirk grew, and his teeth glimmered pearl white in the sunlight.

Daiyu's heart thumped in her chest wildly as the two exchanged a few more words. She barely heard any of it, her brain stuttering for a good response. Was Muyang ... *ignoring* her? What other explanation was there if he had, seemingly, gone out of his way to avoid her, and then sprang up here without even speaking to her? Her mood soured instantly, even as her curiosity for the other member of the *Peccata* rose.

Her messy, bitter feelings were made all the more tangled by the fact that Muyang appeared stunning in his dark leathers, the maroon-colored cross-collared tunic he wore beneath the scaly armor, and the glimmering silver hair crown that pulled his inky hair away from his face. He was nothing like the jaded and lonely emperor she hoped he would be in her absence.

Just as she was thinking those things, another voice piped in, "You both look like jealous lovers."

She blinked over at Bohai, who was beside Muyang, and whom she hadn't noticed at all. His light brown hair was slicked back and he had an amused smirk on his lips that she didn't appreciate. It took her a second to realize he was talking to her and Atreus.

Muyang glanced over at them, as did Nikator. Daiyu's face instantly flushed with warmth and she sputtered, "E-excuse me?"

Atreus glowered at Bohai. "Don't joke with us like that, Bohai—"

"*Commander* Yao Bohai," Nikator chimed in with a snicker.

Bohai waved to the other soldiers, which they all seemed to understand since they all scattered across the courtyard and continued with their training. He ruffled Atreus's hair, much to the youth's chagrin. Almost immediately, Daiyu could feel the shift in the air between the group—they all seemed comfortable with one another.

Atreus swatted Bohai's hand away. "Forgive me, *Commander*." He said the last part with a sarcastic scoff and Daiyu could only stare at him in shock.

Nikator rocked on the back of his heels and slipped his

thumbs into the pockets of his tunic, his expression ever-so-cheery. "Been a while, Atreus. I figured you were still stuck being a worm-brained bandit, so I didn't bother sending you a letter or notice."

"I was *pretending* to be a bandit," Atreus said with a scowl. "*Pretending*."

"I didn't stutter, did I?"

"You—"

Bohai clapped the two young men on their backs, breaking their conversation. "You both can bicker and banter all you want later, but first, you should introduce yourself to Lady Daiyu, don't you think, Nikator?"

Daiyu looked between Nikator, Atreus, Bohai, and then spared a quick peek at Muyang, whose gaze was glued onto her. She fought the embarrassment warming her face and turned toward the red-haired youth. "It's a pleasure to meet you," she said, all too aware of Muyang's eyes traveling down the length of her dress.

"The pleasure is all mine." Nikator placed a hand on his chest and lowered his head in a sign of respect. There was a charming twinkle in his sapphire eyes that went along with his mischievous, lighthearted grin. "My name is Nikator. I see you've been acquainted with my brother Atreus, so I assume you've heard great things about me?"

Atreus rolled his eyes yet again and Daiyu released a sheepish laugh. "I'm sorry, but I haven't heard much—"

"What!" He shot Atreus a playful, mock-hurt expression. "*Atreus*. I'm wounded to think that you didn't indulge Lady Daiyu in my greatness—"

"I spared her the boredom."

"Well, I certainly have heard many great things about you," Nikator said to Daiyu with another teasing smile, one that made him appear all the more chipper. "It's the reason I rushed over here after hearing wind of your troubles."

Daiyu blinked back at him. What troubles was he talking

about? There were a million things he could have been referring to—her family problems with the burned rice fields, her running away from Muyang, being kidnapped a few weeks ago.

Muyang didn't offer any explanation as he watched her with an unreadable, calm look that gave away nothing of what he was thinking. In the morning light, his black eyes appeared even more like two pits of midnight.

Upon seeing her expression, Nikator raised an eyebrow. "You haven't heard? I'm supposed to escort you back to the royal palace."

"*What*?" She turned sharply to Muyang. She hadn't heard anything about this. Was that why he was avoiding her? Because he didn't want to tell her that he was going to ship her back to the palace, where she had even less freedom than she did here? At least in this fortress, she could walk and go as she pleased. The palace was no such place.

"Ah, was *I* supposed to tell her?" Bohai rested a gentle, gloved hand against his chest and quirked his bronze brows. "I hadn't received any orders, so I just assumed you told her, Your Majesty."

"I planned to tell you later tonight," Muyang said smoothly, unperturbed while Daiyu could only sputter in front of him like a blubbering fool. His dark eyes cut over to her and she couldn't stop the burning in her chest at how unbothered he appeared. Like it was so easy to toss her aside in the palace. Like she was an inconvenience. Like it was so easy to forget to tell her something as important as where she would be staying.

"I'm flattered you even thought to tell me," she gritted out through clenched teeth and shifted her attention to the others in the courtyard.

An awkwardness hung in the air for a few moments, interrupted only by Bohai's cough. "Well, how about you two spar with each other since it's been so long?" he said.

"I would never dream of sparring with His Majesty," Daiyu retorted, crossing her arms over her chest. It would have been a funny sight to watch—her and Muyang dueling one another when it was obvious who would be the victor. She almost snorted at how ridiculous it seemed.

"Ah. No, I meant Nikator and Atreus. Not ..." Bohai burst into a fit of laughter, coughed to conceal it, but couldn't wipe his grin off. Daiyu's face warmed with mortification and even Atreus's lips twitched in an almost-smile. "Not you and His Majesty."

She clamped her mouth shut, the heat clawing up her throat. Muyang's soft mouth curved at the corners and she wanted to sink into the ground at that very moment. Thankfully, Nikator and Atreus began a short conversation and moved farther into the courtyard to begin their fight. Bohai trailed farther away as well, giving Muyang and Daiyu privacy as he corrected other soldiers on their form.

Even though they were amidst the crowded courtyard, it seemed like there were only the two of them. Daiyu was hyper aware of Muyang's presence, just a foot away from her, and everything in her surroundings seemed to blur into nothingness. She didn't want to meet his gaze so she stared at a particular barren tree in the courtyard, at the swaying of its branches with every mild gust. She could feel Muyang's eyes on her, boring into the side of her face. But she didn't want to be the first to speak—not when she had this stinging in her chest.

"Daiyu, you appear to be displeased about something." He inched closer to her, and the intoxicating, warm smell of jasmine and orange blossoms made her swallow.

"I haven't the faintest idea of what you mean." Still, she didn't look at him. A dark feathered bird landed on one of the branches of the tree and she examined its tiny, toothpick-like legs as if it was the most interesting thing in the world. Far more intriguing than the emperor by her side.

"Liar."

"That is a big accusation to make, Your Majesty."

"Are you displeased that we can't spar together?" There was a teasing quality in his voice that made her blush, further exacerbated when he continued, "We can spar once we're married. I plan to do it very often."

"I am *not* upset about that." Daiyu still didn't look at him, but this time out of embarrassment more than spite.

"Then?"

"Nothing, Your Majesty."

"Nothing?"

"Yes, *nothing*."

He touched her chin ever so gently—so lightly that she almost felt like she had dreamed it—and she lurched back in surprise, her wide eyes flying over to him. But his hands were clasped behind his back, out of reach, and a tendril of smoke disappeared right before her eyes. She would have thought it was the wind itself, but the air smelled different and she could have sworn she had seen a shadow.

Daiyu narrowed her eyes at him. "Did you ... did you just use your magic?"

"You're finally looking at me now." Muyang smiled as if he had won, and yet it only infuriated her further.

She huffed loudly and turned away from him. "Are you really a *two-step forward, one-step backward* kind of guy? And don't tell me you have no idea what I'm talking about because I know you do. What's this about me being sent back to the royal palace?" This time, she pinned him with a dark glower that she wouldn't have been confident giving him over a week ago—but times were different now. They would wed each other, and she had seen an inkling of vulnerability in him earlier. This was one of the liberties she could take now, or at least she was testing it. "You didn't even ask me if I wanted to go back to the palace."

"I didn't," he agreed, nodding slowly and watching her with those unreadable, shuttered eyes that gave way to no soul. "But since when did I need to tell you anything?"

"Ah, yes, you're the emperor. You can say and do whatever you please, Your Majesty," she said carefully, keeping her tone sharp but without too much edge, "but I would appreciate if you divulged information when it concerns me. I would have appreciated to give some input about where I go. I'm not an item to be shipped to and fro without opinion."

"Some would argue a woman is just that."

Her throat tightened and she searched his face for a telltale sign that he viewed her as that—an item—but she found nothing. "Is that ... what you think, Your Majesty?"

"I don't."

Her lower lip trembled, but she wasn't sure if it was from anger, relief, or hurt. "Then I would have liked to be a part of the decision about what happens to me."

"I can't have you here, Daiyu. There is no discussion to be had." His dark eyes flicked down to her and for a split second, she spotted a hint of sympathy, but it was gone faster than it had come. "You aren't safe here. This is a battleground and this place can easily be overrun with enemies. You could be kidnapped again, or make a reckless decision to flee and thrust yourself in even more danger. I can't have that happen to you."

"I won't try to run again—"

"It's too dangerous here for you, and I'd rather have you somewhere safe."

"Like the palace? Where I was poisoned? Where I was kidnapped?" She raised an incredulous brow. The other soldiers surrounding them glanced in their direction from time to time, and she lowered her tone. "I'm not safe there either."

Muyang frowned, and she could see she had struck a nerve. "The palace is safer than here. I'll have more protection for you at the palace, where Nikator and Vita will watch over you. Trust me when I say that they are some of my best warriors." As if to prove a point, he motioned to Nikator and Atreus, who were fighting on equal footing. They exchanged blow after blow, their weapons glinting in the sunlight dangerously as they swiped here and there. "You'll be protected this time."

Daiyu didn't like it one bit. She didn't want to be thrown aside and forced into the palace once more. She had no allies there

—except for perhaps Feiyu—and there was nothing for her to do there but look over her shoulder. There was someone after her. She was certain of that. She had been poisoned, kidnapped, and her family's rice fields burned—someone was hoping for her downfall and actively attempting it. If she went back to Muyang's court, there was no telling what would happen to her.

"I don't like this at all," she said with a loud sigh. "It wouldn't kill you to include me in your decision on what to do with me."

He chuckled, low and soft, and it sent shivers down her spine. He leaned closer to her, and his warm breath tickled her ear. "It wouldn't kill you to listen either, little fiend."

"I told you not to call me that."

"But you seem to like it." His gaze traveled down her throat, which she was sure was bright red, and then to her flaming cheeks. "You look like a pouting, vermillion dragon. What else shall I call you other than a beautiful fiend?"

"I am *not* a monster," she whispered. "And my face is red because you infuriate me."

That only broadened his wicked grin. "Do you not like the idea of being far from me? Is that perhaps why you're pouting so much? You can't deal with the distance between us? Well, worry not, my dear, for when I return from battle, I will wed you and you will have all of me and we'll have all the time in the world to explore what it means to be married."

He was teasing her, she knew it, but her stomach coiled together and she forgot whatever retort she was going to make. She dipped her chin, hating that she was still a blushing, red fool. "I have no qualms with distance, Your Majesty."

"Are you sure about that?"

"Oh, positive." She cleared her throat and stared at him through lowered lashes, keeping her tone as neutral as possible. "We haven't seen each other in days and I've been doing just fine, and even though I've been alone in my bedroom—ah, *your* bedroom—I've quite enjoyed the quietness that comes with being alone. There's a specific, calming quality to it."

"You seem to enjoy being in my bedroom."

"Alone," Daiyu added, "I enjoy being in there *alone*, Your Majesty."

"So you've been fine without me all these days?" She couldn't read the inflection in his voice, but it was calm enough not to warrant an apology, so she nodded. Muyang only smiled thinly, and she was sure she'd annoyed him with that answer. Surely, he thought she would be pining after him like a lovestruck fool.

"I'll be fine at the royal palace without you," she found herself saying, even though it was the opposite of what she wanted. She wanted to spite him, that was all, and yet she felt like she had walked straight into a trap set by him.

Muyang smirked. "Ah, so we've come to an agreement."

"I ... I suppose we have." She had cornered herself. Frowning deeply, Daiyu shook her head and the bells of her hair jewelry tolled softly. "I don't like the idea of going back to the palace, but it seems as though you've made up your mind. And who am I to change it?"

"There are very few people who can influence my mind to change it," Muyang said with a sweeping glance at the training soldiers, to Nikator and Atreus wrestling on the ground with plumes of dust rising between them, and then down to her. There was something alarmingly cold and distant about his expression, and it made her straighten. "And, as you are right now, Daiyu, you are not one of those people."

A chill ran down her flesh in waves and she flinched away from him. She hadn't expected the harshness, and she felt all the more foolish for thinking that things between them were different —that she could voice her opinion and be heard. But this was the crushing reality—he was still Drakkon Muyang, feared emperor of Huo, and she was nothing more than a simple woman he had picked up. He was not her ally.

"Yes, Your Majesty," she murmured, voice tight. "I understand."

25

Daiyu was a foolish, foolish *fool*.

It was the conclusion she had come to as she hastily folded the dozen or so dresses she had received from Muyang—or more specifically, one of his servants. She shoved the silk clothes into the wooden trunk with dragons carved along the edges of it. Even though she was in Muyang's room, she hadn't seen or heard from him since yesterday, when he had told her she was leaving for the palace. And this morning, when a servant had abruptly woken her up, ushering her to hastily get ready for her departure, she realized just how naïve she had been.

Had she actually thought Muyang would change his mind? A small part of her had foolishly thought he would. Maybe he would think about that moment they had shared together in the woods, amidst danger, where they had opened up to one another just the briefest moment. But whatever rainbow-like dream Daiyu had was shattered that morning.

Just because she had accepted her fate to marry Drakkon Muyang didn't magically make him the perfect suitor. He was still crude, unapologetic, and terrifying—and she was just one of his many women. He might have "favored" her right now, but that wouldn't last forever, and it certainly wouldn't be enough to keep her alive in his court. And that was her number one priority right now—surviving and making sure her family was well taken care of. She wasn't marrying Muyang because she *liked* him, and this was the reality check she needed.

Slamming the lid of the trunk shut, she spun around to call for a servant, only to find Atreus standing at the threshold of the room. She bit back a startled yelp. "Oh, Atreus!" She laughed unexpectedly. "You scared me half to death."

"Apologies, Lady Daiyu." He lowered his head with a sheepish grin. "I knocked, but you were so lost in thought and I didn't know how to intercede without startling you. It appears I've failed either way." He motioned a tan hand toward the chest sitting on her bed. "May I?"

Daiyu nodded, moving aside as he came to take her small box of belongings—fancy things that she was somehow now in possession of, like the luxurious dresses she had just folded, metallic and jade hairpins with trinkets hanging on the ends, and pretty fur-lined shoes and cloaks meant for travel through the wintry landscape.

"I'm sorry to have you leave so soon." He hoisted the trunk easily off the bed and walked to the doorway as if the box weighed nothing. "You'll be in good hands, though. Nikator will offer more entertaining company than I ever could."

"No, you're entertaining enough," she said with a small smile as they entered the hallway. Although the youth had been a stoic companion during their travel after the kidnapping incident, it had been reassuring to have someone by her side. "Truthfully, I'd be more comfortable if you came along since I actually know you."

"I'm flattered. But you'll become accustomed to Nikator; he has a way of making the people around him comfortable." He frowned as if realizing he was complimenting his brother, who he seemed to have a playful rivalry with. "But don't tell him I said that. He's also the type to let those things get to his head."

Daiyu laughed and was reminded of her own brothers Ran

and Qianfan. Soon, her smile faded as she wondered how they were doing. It had been so many months since she had last seen or spoken to her family, and it was rare for her to be away from them for so long. Were they eating well? Were they still bickering about whose clothes belonged to who? Were they sleeping enough?

The biting wind jolted her out of her thoughts when they stepped inside the chilling courtyard just outside the fortress gates. Daiyu tightened her fur-lined cloak around her body as Atreus loaded her trunk into the back of the closed carriage. Half a dozen soldiers surrounded the horse-drawn cart with their own horses. Nikator poked his head out of the carriage window and waved down at her.

"Morning!" he called out. "Did you get everything you needed?"

"It seems like I'm the last one to arrive," she said, eyeing the soldiers clad in leather and armor, the dragon emblem emblazoned on their breastplates. She searched the crowd for Muyang but couldn't find him. Disappointment filled the pits of her stomach and she tried not to show it.

Nikator swung open the door to the carriage and hopped out smoothly. His red hair appeared even brighter in the morning light, and his blue eyes shone like a sparkling sea. He clapped Atreus on the back. "I wish we could have spent more time together, but I'll be heading off before you."

"Send Vita my greetings."

"Sure, sure." The two embraced, and Atreus eventually slugged the other in the abdomen playfully. While they quipped with one another, Daiyu turned to stare back at the looming fortress. It had been her home for the past few weeks and she found she was somewhat sad to leave it behind, but even worse was the fact that there was no one—other than Atreus—to see her off.

Her mood soured and she examined the windows of the fortress, hoping to see some movement, some sign that Muyang was watching her leave. But she spotted nothing of that sort.

"Lady Daiyu?"

Turning back to Nikator and Atreus, she could only strain a smile. "I'm ready."

～

TRAVELING WITH NIKATOR WAS UNEXPECTEDLY MORE entertaining than it had been with Atreus—just like the youth had warned. The red-haired young man would point out different pieces of landscape and tell her random stories of a crazed fight it reminded him of, or he would talk about stories he had heard during his travels, or anything to fill the silence between them. By the fifth day, Daiyu was more comfortable around him. Enough to probe with her own questions.

"So"—she stretched her legs out in the spacious carriage floor and leaned back into the velvet cushions behind her—"how long have you known His Majesty?"

Nikator, who sat across from her and was humming to himself as he stared out the window, turned to her. "Hm. For as long as I can remember," he mused, drumming his fingers against his thigh. The scenery of snow and slush passed them in blurs of white. "Maybe twelve years? I'm *about* eighteen, not sure of the exact age, but I would say twelve or so years."

"How did you meet him? I noticed Atreus is, well, foreign, and he told me he's from Sanguis. I just find it hard to imagine His Majesty meeting two foreign boys at such a young age—"

"Oh, he didn't find us here in Huo." Nikator grinned and rubbed a strand of his bright hair between his fingers. "You really think he'd find a red-haired kid here?"

Daiyu canted her head. "Where else, then?"

"In Sanguis, of course."

"He traveled all the way there?" Maybe it was because she was from the countryside, but she had never met anyone who had traveled outside of the empire. It was mostly unheard of, especially since Huo didn't have good relations with either of its neighboring kingdoms—Sanguis or Kadios.

"All members of the *Peccata* are from Sanguis," he explained with a wave. "I'm originally from Lebel, though, and was sold into slavery at some point when my village was raided by slavers. Atreus's mother was a slave, so he naturally became one too. Minos as well, if I remember correctly. And as for Vita and Thera, I believe they were sold into it by their families to pay off debts. Or something along those lines. Remus, like me, was stolen during a raid. Or so we believe."

Daiyu didn't know what to say, so she only stared at him. She had heard that slavery was common in Sanguis and Kadios, but she had, once again, never had experience with it before. She had heard tales as a child that those who lived on the border of Huo had a higher chance of being attacked by raiders, but she had chalked that up to silly stories to scare children into behaving.

"Did His Majesty ... purchase you and the others?" Even saying the words aloud sent an uncomfortable prickle beneath her skin, and she cringed inwardly.

Nikator's eyes widened in shock and he shook his head profusely. "Oh, no. His Majesty freed us."

"Oh." The awkward, itchy feeling seemed to subside, but not entirely. She shifted in her seat and fidgeted with her sleeves, unable to look away from him. He didn't look like he was mistreated in any way, and she assumed he was well taken care of if he was a part of Muyang's special forces, but a part of her wondered if he was forced to be this way. Forced into this lifestyle of being a special warrior. Surely, Muyang hadn't freed him and the others out of the goodness of his heart? For all of them to end up like this?

"His Majesty freed us and helped raise us," he continued, resting his chin on his closed fist as he leaned toward the window. A glassy, faraway look entered his eyes. "It was fun up until four years ago. We used to travel all over the world. There was no place we hadn't visited—or at least it felt like that as a child. But now we've settled down here."

"What happened four years ago?" She laced her hands together. "Isn't that when His Majesty took the throne?" She would have thought he would be thrilled that Muyang achieved his goal of taking the throne, but the youth appeared jaded.

Nikator sighed loudly and his breath fogged the ends of the window. When he turned back to her, his smile was faint. "Many things have changed since His Majesty took the throne. The dynamic of all of our relationships is different now and we're no longer children running amuck in a faraway adventure."

She wanted to ask more, but something in the air told her not to push it. She folded her hands together and let the silence envelop them both. The carriage bumped along the path, jolting them both with every rock or uneven ground it rolled over. The only sound from outside was the clomping of horse hooves and the crush of snow from the wheels of the carriage.

After a moment, Daiyu quietly said, "I think ... someone is after me."

"What?"

"I think someone's after me," she said, louder this time.

Nikator blinked at her like he had heard wrong and then shifted his attention to the window, squinting through the glass panes as if to find someone lurking in the trees. "Here?"

"At the palace." She picked at something beneath her nail and tried to calm her nerves, all of which screamed at her to keep this to herself. He hadn't shown her any signs that she couldn't trust him, but with so many enemies around in the palace, she didn't know who to trust with information and who not to. But she was going off on a limb here that maybe he'd be okay to talk to about this. "I was poisoned a few weeks ago at the palace, so there's clearly someone out there who wants to kill me. Maybe they're jealous that the emperor chose me? I don't know. But it's just too much of a coincidence for me that I'm poisoned and then a few weeks later kidnapped from the palace. And, to make it worse, my family's rice paddies—our livelihood—are then burned down. I truly think someone is after me." She blurted the words out in one sentence, and even to her own ears, she sounded slightly deranged and fearful. "I know it sounds crazy to think that someone would be after me—I mean, I'm a *nobody*—but I really do think—"

"You don't sound crazy." A tiny wedge formed between his eyebrows. "That *is* a matter to be concerned about. Like you said, there are too many coincidences. If I had to give my input, I'd say it's probably a noble family that wants you dead because they wanted their daughter to be the first to be chosen by His Majesty. Or maybe it's a noblewoman who's jealous that you gained His Majesty's favor instead of her."

Hearing the words out loud made it seem all the more real, and Daiyu's stomach knotted itself together like tangled thorns. "I assumed that too, but why would they target my family?"

"Maybe so you pull out of the royal selection?"

She couldn't help herself—she snorted. "As if I have that kind of a choice."

"Don't worry too much about it," he said with an easy grin. "Vita and I will be there to protect you. Now that you've brought it up to my attention, I'll be extra vigilant to look out for any threats. So worry not."

Even though he said it so chipperly, Daiyu couldn't ease the anxiety clawing up her throat. Because as much as she liked Nikator and Atreus, they weren't loyal to *her*. They were loyal to Muyang, and once Muyang's circle of women grew, they wouldn't prioritize her safety—only the safety of whoever His Majesty favored at the time. Right now, that might have been her, but who would it be months from now?

She needed to figure this out herself, she decided as she stared out the window at the colorless scenery, her mind traveling to the palace. If she wanted to survive in the royal court, she needed to be just as vicious and cunning as its emperor.

26

GOING BACK TO THE PALACE WAS AS LACKLUSTER AS
the first time she had been cooped up inside her fancy, jade
towered room. The servants treated her as though she hadn't left
in the first place—coldly, stoically, and without emotion—and she
didn't recognize the guards patrolling her hallway, other than
Nikator, who would stay outside her door until Vita, her true
personal guard, arrived. And there was no telling when that
would be.

Daiyu was just another unimportant face in the palace.
Nobody came rushing to her or offered her sympathies for everything she had gone through—not that she expected it—but she
hadn't thought the court would be *this* cold toward her. It probably had to do with the fact that she wasn't the emperor's wife yet,
so she was seen as replaceable.

She certainly felt that way.

She fished out the one-jade bracelet Feiyu had given her and
placed it atop her tea table, sat on her couch, and called out,
"Feiyu! I know you can hear me."

Tapping her fingers against the armrest of the couch, she
waited. Out of everyone who she expected to visit her, Feiyu was

definitely one of them. And he was, sadly, the only one. Yet the masked mage hadn't made an appearance at all. Not yesterday when she first arrived, and certainly not today.

The air shifted and Daiyu heard his boots click against the polished floors. She turned just in time to find the green-robed mage a few feet away from her doorway, a red and black dragon mask covering his face. Upon seeing her, he gave a small bow.

"You've returned," he said without a hint of surprise.

"I'm sure you realized it yesterday."

"I did." He waltzed toward the couch and plopped himself on the one adjacent to hers. He unceremoniously, and impolitely, propped his feet on the table and sighed as he reclined into the many plush crane-embroidered pillows adorning the velvet couch. "Is it me or do you sound disappointed that I didn't visit you immediately? I thought you'd like to rest."

"I'm not disappointed. Not at all." She crinkled her nose at how close his feet were to the platter of assorted nuts acting as a centerpiece on the tea table. "I just figured you would visit at some point to see how I was doing. I *did* get kidnapped, you know. Right from under your nose."

He steepled his fingers together and bobbed his head. "Yes, I'm aware, and I *did* visit you earlier, remember?"

"In my dreams? That doesn't count."

Shrugging, he leaned forward and grabbed a handful of caramelized cashews, salted almonds, and candied pecans and lifted the edge of his mask. Daiyu inched closer to him, trying to peek at his face. But he was quick as he chomped down on the nuts and all she could make out were three scars on the side of his jaw. "I figured you were fine," he said between mouthfuls, "and I wasn't wrong."

"Yes, but you can *pretend* to be diplomatic."

Feiyu motioned toward the colorless bracelet. "I see that came in handy."

"It did." She plucked the empty piece of jewelry and shook it in the air for emphasis. "Why didn't you tell me it would summon His Majesty if I used it?"

He paused in his chewing and pinned her with an unreadable stare—one that was hard to make out anyway due to the shadows of the mask—and then stuffed another handful of sweet and salty nuts into his mouth. "Huh. So that's who you summoned?"

"You make it sound like I had a choice." She quirked an eyebrow and dropped the bracelet with a *clank* on the glass-top of the table.

"It basically only has enough magic to summon the one person you think can protect you. It's a very powerful magicked item that, unfortunately, does cause *some* damage to the summoned party."

"Damage? What do you mean by that?"

"Well, perhaps damage isn't the right word." He dusted off the salt and sugar clinging to his fingers. "More like ... it consumes the magic of the summoned party. You see, magic comes at a price. Someone has to use up their energy for the summon, and part of it is stored in the bracelet, and the other part comes from the summoned party. Make sense?"

"Oh." Daiyu did remember Muyang being winded after he had finished fighting off the group of rebel soldiers, but she thought it had to do with his own magic being low, like he had mentioned. Perhaps that was the case, but maybe it also had to do with the bracelet? In that case ... "So you're telling me that I caused His Majesty's magic to be drained?"

"Yes. I'm surprised he didn't blight you on the spot." There was a joking, teasing quality to his voice, but she barely paid it any heed.

Her face flushed with unexpected warmth. Why hadn't Muyang told her any of that? "Oh."

"I'm a bit disappointed you didn't think *I* was the best candidate for your rescue, but I'm glad to see you're healthy and well."

She rolled her eyes, unable to help herself. "I was panicking and I didn't realize what was happening. And anyway, how did you know I needed rescuing?"

"The bracelet would only work if you were in a life-and-death situation."

"Ah."

"And seeing as how it's drained"—he shrugged—"I would say you were in need of rescuing."

Daiyu reached forward, plucked a caramel-coated pecan from the platter, and nibbled on one end of it whilst keeping a careful eye on Feiyu. She didn't appreciate how mysterious the mage had been about the properties of the magicked bracelet, and all of this seemed a bit too convenient for her liking. Did he know she would have summoned Muyang in the first place?

She didn't want to ask—not because she didn't want to know the answer, but she had to be careful around Feiyu. He was her only ally in this palace, and it wouldn't do good for him to realize she was casting suspicion on him.

"Anyway, have you learned anything about the person who poisoned me? Or who kidnapped me? Do you think the two incidents are related?"

Before he could answer, there was a steady knock on the door —in quick succession. "Everything all right in there?" Nikator called out, his tone level and nothing like the cheerful young man she had spent over two weeks traveling with. "I heard a male voice, so just wanted to check in to see if you're fine."

Daiyu froze, her mind reeling. She waved at Feiyu to leave and opened her mouth to lie and say there was no one in here with her, but Feiyu raised his hand and halted her mid-stride.

"It's just me, Nikator," he called out, fixing his mask in place. "You can come in if you want."

There was a pause. "Feiyu?"

"The one and only."

Daiyu raised an incredulous eyebrow at Feiyu—was it really wise to let Nikator inside? Wasn't it bad if Muyang heard wind that Feiyu was interacting with her? But the mage didn't seem to mind and the door swung open. Nikator strode inside and closed the door behind himself, his expression cautious as he stared at them both.

"Nik, so good to see you." Feiyu motioned to the couches. "Have a seat."

"What are you doing here?" Nikator gingerly took a seat beside the mage and looked between Daiyu and Feiyu. "How do you know each other?"

"We became acquainted a few months ago." Daiyu popped the rest of the sweet pecan in her mouth and chewed before motioning the platter to Nikator. "Have some, please."

Nikator picked at the salt-coated nuts and collected a few in the palm of his hand, all the while staring at the dragon-masked mage, who was leaning back on the couch with his hands folded across his abdomen casually. "I just find your pairing very strange and unexpected."

"There's been stranger allies," Daiyu said in what she hoped was a jovial tone, but came out slightly strained. She cleared her throat when Nikator gave her another strange look. It was true that it might have been weird that she was acquainted with Feiyu, and that he was likely her only friend in the palace, but surely it couldn't be *that* strange? "He's the head mage of the royal palace, so of course we were going to cross paths at some point."

"I ... suppose." Nikator chewed and swallowed. "But Feiyu rarely, if ever, shows his face anywhere."

"Do you mean that literally or metaphorically?" Daiyu eyed the dragon-mask Feiyu currently donned.

The mage chuckled, and his whole chest shook from the small movement. "I think he means it in both senses. No one has seen my face in years, and I intend to keep it that way. But yes, in a way, I do keep to myself. I don't like involving myself in the politics and drama of royal court life, so I avoid it as much as I can. So long as I do everything His Majesty wants, I hardly see why it matters where I am." He waved a dismissive hand. "Anyhow, let's talk about something other than me, shall we? Nik, I wanted to get your input on a few things, since this also pertains to you."

Nikator bobbed his head. "Sure, what is it?"

"We were just discussing Lady Daiyu's safety—or lack thereof." Feiyu wove his fingers together and nodded his masked chin in Daiyu's direction. "Maybe you can explain the rest?"

She frowned at the mage. There wasn't much to talk about since she just broached the subject. "Well, I had just asked you whether you had any information about who poisoned me and if it's related to the kidnapping a few weeks ago." She then turned to Nikator. "I was poisoned early on in my stay here and Feiyu was actually the one who saved me."

"I, regretfully, haven't been able to find out much of what happened," Feiyu answered. "I was actually going to suggest that you ask around yourself. There are some suspicious people in the palace who might know something. Or might be involved."

"Who?" Daiyu asked quietly, not liking the turn of the conversation. She didn't want to personally be snooping around in other people's business, but if that's what it took to keep herself safe, she would do just that. "And I'm assuming it's something you can't do? Even though you're a powerful mage?"

"Unfortunately, with the emperor's recent expedition to the north for war, I've been stretched very, very thinly here. So as much as I would love to help you get to the bottom of this, I haven't had the time." His voice lowered an octave and he sounded genuinely concerned for her, but then he clapped his hands together and said cheerily, "So I think it's best if you got to the bottom of it since you have so much time. I'll provide assistance from time to time, but I'm a bit too busy to help out."

"I should have expected as much," she grumbled. "But all right, I can't expect you to do everything, anyway. Do you have any leads on who might know a thing or two about what happened?"

"You *could* ask the princesses."

Nikator stilled and one of the nuts slipped from his hand and disappeared underneath the couch. Daiyu hesitated as well, gaze flicking to where the almond had skittered off to, and then to the painted mask Feiyu wore. "The princesses," she said slowly. "Who are currently locked away here? What do they know?"

"I'm not sure if they know anything." He lifted his shoulders. "But it's worth a try, isn't it? They're allowed afternoon walks in the garden once a week on Tuesdays. You can try to catch them during that time to see if they know anything. I wouldn't be surprised if they were plotting against His Majesty and everyone related to him—including you."

"We can go this week," Nikator offered, lounging back in his seat with a thoughtful frown. His sapphire blue eyes narrowed and he seemed lost in thought for a moment. "The two princesses are a bit suspicious, but do you really think they know something? It wouldn't benefit them to have Lady Daiyu killed, would it?"

"I'm not sure, but it would be unwise to rule them out simply because we don't know." Feiyu drummed his fingers on the armrest. "You can also ask a noble lady or two if they know anything or have heard anything? Make a list of people of who might be jealous of you."

"I don't know any—" The words died on Daiyu's tongue just as she was saying them. "Wait, I do know *one* noble lady. Have either of you heard of Lady Jia? I don't remember her family name—"

Feiyu tilted his head. "General Liang Fang's wife? Li Jia?"

"I ... would assume so?" The first time she had met Jia, she had been with General Liang Fang, and the second time she had mentioned that her husband had a meeting with Muyang. It should have been clear to Daiyu who her husband was, but she hadn't connected the dots. And quite frankly, she had been too concerned about escaping to care too much during that time. It was embarrassing to think that she had met the wife of a *general* but hadn't even realized it. "Is there any way I can arrange a meeting with her? Like for tea or something small."

Nikator nodded. "I can arrange it. I know her pretty well since I'm well acquainted with General Fang."

"Perfect." Daiyu clasped her hands together. At least this way, she'd be able to find more information and hopefully, more allies. And it gave her something to do while Muyang was away. Or at least, that's what she told herself. It wasn't like she cared whether Muyang came back early or not—her priority was on surviving his court. She only needed to marry him to secure her family's futures. That was it.

"Do you think someone might still be after my family?" She blurted the words without thinking too carefully about what she was saying, but once they were out, she couldn't hold back the flood of nightmarish anxiety that came with those thoughts. "I mean, His Majesty won't be able to protect them until we're married, right? His protection won't really be sufficient enough until—"

"His Majesty has already sent word to your family that you were chosen as his bride," Feiyu interrupted, his hand hovering over the platter of nuts, but then resting back on his lap. "But I'll be sure to put a spell in the area that will inform me if anything goes awry. Your family should be fine, though. I doubt anyone would actively try to kill them—especially not with magic, which can be traced depending on the type."

"Why are you so sure?"

"Because I'm the head mage at this palace, and I know more than most people."

"But then why can't you trace who burned our rice fields?"

"Well, that's a bit more complicated, since fire magic is so basic. But any spells that will kill someone does leave a trace, and I'd be able to track that. And, of course, if someone did try to murder your whole family, with or without magic, that would be highly suspicious and His Majesty would definitely open an investigation. I don't think any noble family would want to be under the emperor's ire. They probably just wanted to scare you enough to get you to back away from all of this."

"I hope you're right." She squeezed her hands together until her fingers blanched pale. If something happened to her family, she wouldn't be able to forgive herself for such a miscalculation because at the end of the day, she had two choices she could have made: run with her family and start a new life, or marry Muyang for a better life for her family. She prayed she was making the right decision.

27

"Daiyu! How have you been? It's truly been too long." Jia's bubbly, upbeat voice was a stark contrast to Daiyu's darker, more sinister and suspicious thoughts as she embraced the noble lady in her sitting area at her home. Jia smelled like an amalgamation of floral scents, none of which Daiyu could pinpoint, while her sitting room reeked of aloe and clove incense. When she pulled back from the embrace, her brown eyes were alight with true concern.

"I was so worried when I heard you were taken from the palace," she said, ushering her over to the array of couches splayed across the expensive crane-embroidered rug. Hot tea was already waiting for them at the tea table, and there was another woman sitting on the wooden framed couch. "This here is Lady Eu-Meh. Lady Eu-Meh, this is Yin Daiyu, the one His Majesty chose during the royal selection."

Lady Eu-Meh smiled, though it didn't reach her eyes. "A pleasure to finally meet the infamous farm girl! We were all so worried when we heard what happened to you. I'm sure it must have been absolutely *terrifying*."

Daiyu's own smile was fake as she sat down next to the young woman. When Nikator had arranged for her to meet Jia at her home, she had thought she would be alone with the cheerful lady, but maybe it was better this way—more women meant more gossip, and the more likelihood that someone knew something.

Jia eased herself into the seat across from them and picked up her porcelain, butterfly painted teacup from the table, her dark brows pulling together in worry. "I'm so sorry you had to go through that. How horrifying." The red painted lotus between her brows creased. "How did you manage to escape?"

"How did His Majesty react? Does he know?" Lady Eu-Meh interrupted.

Daiyu picked up her own teacup, her fingers warming instantly. "It's a long story, but I'm well."

Lady Eu-Meh leaned forward expectantly. "But does he know?"

"Does he know what?" Daiyu looked between Lady Eu-Meh and Jia, both of whom were staring at her as if waiting for something. It took her a second to realize what they were inquiring about: did Muyang know she was here after what had happened?

Of course they would be curious to see if he would even want her after she was abused by a rough group of men. Her face flushed with embarrassment and she hated the way they were searching her expression for answers.

"His Majesty is the one who sent me back here," she finally managed to sputter, bringing the warm tea to her mouth. She nearly scalded her tongue, but she didn't notice or care. "He took care of me while I was in the fortress and, quite frankly, I'd rather not talk about my experience."

"Oh, oh." Jia's polite grin was back in place, although her cheeks reddened as if she realized how rude they were being.

"*But.*" Daiyu lowered her teacup on her lap, her insides knotting together as she looked between the two women. She wanted nothing more than to leave this place and not talk to either of them, but she needed to probe the issue and figure out more, and since they were already on the topic, it was probably wise to remain there for a bit longer. "I do wonder why *I* was kidnapped. I'm not married to the emperor yet and so what worth is there in abducting me?"

"Maybe someone is jealous?" Jia raised her brows and sipped her tea. "You never know. It did cause a bit of a stir when you were chosen. Lots of jealous people out there."

"Oh, yes, I'm sure that might play into it." Lady Eu-Meh bobbed her head, her tone dropping an octave. "And there were so many noble families who were offended that the emperor chose a commoner over their daughters. I'm sure that played a part into it."

"So you both think it might have been a noble family?" Daiyu asked, trying to keep her tone as innocent and flippant as possible.

"Oh, heavens, you didn't hear that from me." Lady Eu-Meh laughed and reclined into her seat. "But I do agree that it's a bit suspicious why you were abducted when you don't mean anything to the emperor. Wouldn't it have made sense to do that *after* you were married to him? Or *after* he had taken you to his bed?"

"Huh, I didn't really think about that." Jia frowned. "I thought the rebels just wanted to insult His Majesty by stealing his bride. I don't think ... Well, at least that's what I think. Fang didn't mention anything else to me either."

"I said it was suspicious, but I highly doubt a noble family would do such a thing," Lady Eu-Meh said with a dismissive wave, the gold bands around her wrist jangling with the movement. "It makes more sense that the rebels did that to offend His Majesty. Although many noble families were slighted at the fact that he chose a farm girl, I don't think that means someone would want to abduct her. Especially since we know His Majesty will choose many others. I mean, have you heard the rumors of how many women have visited his bedchambers? Why go through so much trouble for one small girl?" She smiled thinly at Daiyu, leaned forward, and patted her on the hand. "I mean that with all the love in the world, Daiyu. You have nothing to fear!"

Daiyu returned her smile with an uneasy one, her mind spinning at this new piece of information. Muyang took many women into his bedchambers? She hadn't heard that one before, but she shouldn't have been too surprised—nobles likely knew more and gossiped more, since they were more entwined with his court. But still, she couldn't deny the sharp pang in her chest that made it hard to breathe.

"Ah, so he's been with multiple women?" She slurped the herbal tea and barely tasted the citrus undertones or the sharp mint. "I thought I was the first he chose as his bride."

"Oh, you are," Jia began.

"But he's been with several. Just"—Lady Eu-Meh lifted her shoulders—"unofficially."

Her pointed grin seemed to dig the point deeper into Daiyu, as if to say: *you're not that special, girl.*

Daiyu knew that. She was always going to be one of many when it concerned the emperor, but she didn't expect it to sting this much. And it bothered her how much she was actually troubled by the fact that she *wasn't* special and that he had been with many women before her. She was replaceable—he had told her that much—so why was she so hurt by the obvious truth? Even after he married her, he would marry many others. She *knew* that.

"Oh, remember that one girl he was with a few months ago? What was her name?" Lady Eu-Meh tapped her chin thoughtfully, her full lips twisting into a frown. There was something cruel about the glint in her eyes that Daiyu didn't like—as if she was ready to pull the rug from beneath someone's feet. "The one from the Wu family, was it? We all thought His Majesty would choose her, didn't we? But what ended up happening to her?"

Jia blinked back, her gaze flicking between the two women. She fidgeted with her teacup. "Oh. Right, I forgot about her."

"Wasn't she sent away a few weeks before the current royal selection?"

"I don't remember, but she was hastily married off once the emperor"—Jia shrugged sheepishly and stared down at her tea— "was done with her, I suppose, for lack of a better phrase."

Lady Eu-Meh bobbed her head, the heavy gold hairpieces intertwined in her hair bobbling. "Yes, yes. I didn't have the chance to attend the wedding since it was on such short notice and I was visiting family down south, but I was shocked when I returned to find out she was already married off."

Daiyu drank her tea quickly. Her chest felt tight, like someone had pulled a bowstring too taut. Like her ribs were being jammed together, squeezing her innards and making it harder to breathe. *Of course* Muyang had been involved with other women. She had assumed as much when she saw his wickedly beautiful face— someone like that wouldn't be alone for long. And even she had her own romance before—with Heng. But for some reason, there was a prickle in her throat that made swallowing hard. That made breathing feel like she had sandpaper rubbing between her lungs.

She didn't like the idea of Muyang having multiple lovers and discarding them like they didn't matter because ultimately, that was who she would become, wouldn't she? One of the many women who would be gossiped about, just like this.

"I bet His Majesty will choose you to light the first lantern in the Autumn Festival," Jia said with an enthusiastic smile. She sipped her tea quietly. "Don't you think, Lady Eu-Meh? I can't remember who did it last year ... was it Lord Sun's daughter?"

Daiyu had heard about the lantern lighting during the Autumn Festival, where the emperor's most favored woman, or a very important woman in society or in court, was chosen to light and launch the first lantern. It was usually an honor reserved for someone of high class and many women sought out to be the one to do it. Daiyu had no idea if Muyang would choose her and she hadn't honestly given it much thought.

"Oh, *maybe*?" Lady Eu-Meh shrugged. "It's quite possible. He did choose you for the royal selection, so maybe he'll do it again for the lantern lighting? But then again, I would think he would choose the daughter of his trusted allies first over you ... But I really don't know what His Majesty is thinking."

"I'm excited about the festival," Jia said. "And if it means anything, I think he'll choose you. It only makes sense."

"Right ..." Daiyu could only smile and nod.

"It's such an honor to do it."

There was a pregnant pause and they all fell silent for a moment too long.

"Anyway, it was so *very* cunning of you to send all the women away from the Lotus wing," Lady Eu-Meh said with another slick grin. This time, she winked at her as if they were conspiratorially sharing a secret. "I didn't think you would have it in you to ask such a thing from His Majesty, and even more so for him to oblige!"

"Many women were upset by that," Jia said with an enthusiastic nod. "I was pretty shocked too."

Daiyu tightened her hold on her empty teacup. "Ah, well, I figured it would be—"

"Good to cut off the competition?" Lady Eu-Meh winked again and chuckled. "I completely agree. I wonder how many enemies you made from that move?"

Clearing her throat, Daiyu smiled again, her cheeks stretching uncomfortably. "I feel as though I would make enemies regardless of whether I sent the women away or not."

"That's true. Many people probably feel threatened that you've *enchanted* the emperor," Jia said with a warm smile. "You're the first he's chosen, so I'm sure that means something!"

If that was supposed to make her feel better—it didn't. Instead, it only made her feel like she was inching closer to her expiration date. Muyang would realize soon enough that she wasn't any different than other women. There was nothing spectacular about her. She wasn't charming in any fascinating way. She didn't have experience in the bedroom, nor with romance in general. She didn't have much of anything that stood out. And the sooner her charm vanished, she would be cast aside like Lady

Wu, or the plethora of other women who had ultimately disappointed him.

I'm only doing this for my family. Her hold on the teacup fastened even more, to the point she was afraid she would crack the fragile porcelain object. Love was never a part of this equation, but even as she told herself that, it was becoming harder to breathe. Harder to think.

"I wonder if it would be wise to tell His Majesty that I think someone might be after me?" She tried to rein back into the original reason she was even here with these women. She tried to smile, but she wasn't even sure if she was doing it right. Not with the way they both were looking at her—like she was a pitiful fool. "I suspect a jealous noblewoman might be—"

"Oh, *heavens.*" Lady Eu-Meh burst into shrill laughter, covering her mouth with her jeweled hand. Her eyes crinkled with laughter and she thumped the armrest of the couch as if Daiyu had cracked the funniest joke in the world.

A tingling flush crept up Daiyu's face and ears. Every nerve in her body warred with the instinct to either run or spit back with fire. She replayed her words, wondering what she had said that was so funny, and resisted the urge to snap at the woman.

"Forgive me." Lady Eu-Meh's chest continued to shake and she wiped the corner of her eyes. "I just—" Another chuckle. "I just can't believe you think His Majesty is supposed to help you with this? What is he supposed to do? Make you feel better? Pat your head and say it'll be okay?" She giggled again and shook her head. "Oh, heavens. Dear girl, I can see that you're truly not from here."

She licked her lips, feeling their judgmental eyes on her. At least Jia had the decency to look embarrassed on her behalf.

"If all the emperors throughout history had to deal with the courtly affairs of their women, this empire would have burst into flames long, *long* ago." Lady Eu-Meh smiled thinly at her, and Daiyu's toes curled inward. "His Majesty doesn't have time for that and he certainly wouldn't care about what you're going through unless it involves bedding him. If you truly do believe you're being targeted—which, once again, all women involved with royalty have to go through with one another—then it's best to deal with it yourself. Has no one taught you anything about court politics and your place in them?" She reached into the folds of her sleeves and yanked out a silk fan. She whipped it open, and the sprawling design of a red-scaled dragon appeared in the center as she fanned herself. "Goodness, you've given me quite the laugh, Yin Daiyu."

If the ground could open up and swallow Daiyu whole, she would have preferred that than to have to continue sitting here, pretending to be jolly with these two women. She placed her teacup onto the tea table and couldn't muster up a smile, not with her face feeling like it was made of fire.

She felt so small in that moment. Wearing fancy dresses, shiny jewelry, and silk shoes didn't make her one of them. She would never be like a glittering, beautiful noble lady with poise and knowledge about courtly affairs. She was just ... Daiyu. Daughter of a humble farmer. Whose only skills were in gardening, harvesting rice, scrubbing pots, and sewing patches into her clothes.

Daiyu traced the drying, red smudge her lips had left on the rim of the teacup, her thoughts traveling to escape routes. For a moment, she wanted to flee from it all—from these two women, from His Majesty, from the empire ... But then she reminded herself why she had chosen to plunge into the uncomfortably cold, thorny palace. She couldn't let these women and their gossip get to her, and she needed to get used to being spoken down to like this. Like she didn't matter, like she was too stupid to understand what they were saying.

Placing her teacup on the table, she fixed a pleasant, albeit naïve, smile in her place as she looked at the two women. "Since we're on the topic of courtly affairs, I'd love to hear about the latest scandal with ... what was her name, Lady Wu?"

If she was going to survive in this unfamiliar place, she needed to learn everything she could. And gossip seemed to be the easiest place to start with, especially with these courtly, noble ladies, who turned out to be more like a den of vipers than anything *noble*.

Lady Eu-Meh flicked her fan shut, her calculating, laughter-filled eyes glittering with mischief. "What would you like to know?"

28

By the time Daiyu returned to the palace, her head was so stuffed with pointless, scathing gossip that she had to rest on her couch to process it all. The only useful information she learned was that once noblewomen began gossiping, their lips became loose enough to spill about *everything*. Even something as small as what so-and-so ate for lunch, and where, and how terrible it was. And despite everything she had learned, nothing stood out as to who could be behind Daiyu's multiple life-and-death situations. It could very well be every single noble lady who was connected to Muyang—and there were *many* women, apparently.

"Are you feeling unwell?"

Daiyu lifted her arm from over her eyes and peeked at Nikator, who stood by her doorway, appearing unsure of what to do. She had almost forgotten the youth had accompanied her back here.

"My head feels like it's going to burst." She rubbed her temples and sat upright so she was in a more appropriate sitting position—another thing she had learned about noble ladies was how important it was to carry herself. Considering how Nikator was one of Muyang's trusted warriors, it probably was wise to act in a respectable manner.

"Too much gossip for one day?" Nikator grinned.

She groaned and resisted the urge to flip back down on the couch. "You have no idea. I didn't think it was possible to talk *so much* about nothing."

"I didn't think lady Jia was into much gossip," he mused, shifting on his feet and crossing his lean arms over his chest. "She's always been a chatterbox, as opposed to her husband, General Liang Fang, but she's not one to gossip incessantly. But maybe I read her wrong."

"No, it was mostly Lady Eu-Meh who gossiped."

"That sounds more in line with her personality." Nikator eyed her carefully and frowned. "Anyway, are you still up for going into the gardens later this afternoon to see the princesses? You don't look like you want to entertain any more chitchat. We can always wait until next week."

She was already shaking her head before he finished. There was no way she was going to push her meeting with the princesses aside, not when she hadn't learned anything fruitful this morning. She was more determined than ever to find a culprit or two to focus on instead of the looming threat and trouble this entire union would bring.

"I'll be fine after resting my eyes for a bit," she said, smoothing down her navy blue skirts. "Do you think you'll still be able to escort me?"

"Of course." He raised a dark red eyebrow. "What kind of guard would I be if I'm only conditional?"

"Well, you technically *are* conditional, aren't you? Until Vita comes to the palace, I mean."

"I think the term temporary is more suitable."

An awkward silence filled the void between them as Daiyu's mind traveled to other topics—particularly what it meant to be Muyang's wife. She frowned and spread her hands over her thighs to flatten the creases that had formed when she was crumpled on the couch like a curled noodle. She hadn't realized how clammy her hands were until that moment.

"Um, Nikator?" She smoothed down a particular crease, avoiding eye contact as she zeroed in on it. "You've been with His Majesty for a long while, right? So you've likely learned bits and pieces of his personal life, right?"

There was a pause and a shift. "Yes."

She raised her gaze to meet his. He was now staring at her strangely, like he had his guard up. He probably thought she was going to ask something incredibly threatening. Like Muyang's weaknesses or his darkest secrets. He stood expectantly, his broad shoulders stiff and his bright blue eyes narrowed in expectancy.

"So you know about his love life, yes?"

He blinked. "Um. Sort of."

"How does he treat his lovers?"

If that was the question he was expecting, he surely didn't act like he knew it was coming. Nikator rubbed the nape of his neck. "I'm not really sure. His Majesty keeps his personal life personal. I've never met any of the women he was involved with ... until you."

She wasn't sure if she should be happy about that or not. She should have felt special upon hearing that, but it only made her anxiety gnaw at the pit of her stomach even more. Because there was nothing inherently different or special about her to make her stand out, so why was she treated differently than the other women? What was Muyang's aim with her? Why weren't the other women "good enough" for him to marry?

"Has he ever been in love?" she blurted out without thinking better.

Nikator pursed his lips together and seemed to think on it for a few minutes. Time ticked by slowly, and the more he seemed to ponder, the less sure Daiyu became of anything.

"I don't know," he finally answered with a shrug.

"Oh." Another red banner that screamed that something must have been wrong with him if he never loved before.

Nikator studied her carefully, and she could see the cogs in his brain grinding to a stuttering stop. "You don't ... look happy to hear that? I thought women swooned at the idea of being the first love."

"I'm really not sure what to think of"—she gestured toward the room, looking at nothing in particular before sighing and slumping over the couch—"any of this. I'm not used to this kind of life and I'm not sure if I'm suited for it either. I'm just trying to figure it all out, you know?"

He bobbed his head, but she could tell he didn't understand what she was saying. He must have lived such a difficult and different life than her—first as a slave, and now as a personal warrior to the emperor himself. He must have known what she was going through to some extent, but at the same time, he likely saw her troubles as trivial.

"Maybe you can figure it all out later." He lifted his shoulders and she could tell he was *trying* to be helpful, but it fell flat. The sheepish grin he shot her told her as much.

Daiyu picked up one of the embroidered, tasseled pillows and hugged it tightly as she leaned forward. All of this was so confusing. Marrying Muyang, the villainous emperor of all people. Finding the person trying to take her life. Managing courtly affairs. Even thinking about the future ... These were things she would have loved to talk to Lanfen about and bounce ideas so she knew she was doing the right thing. But she had no council here, no one whose words she could trust as being in her best interest.

"When do you think His Majesty will be back?" she asked.

"War takes time."

"*Sometimes.* But what would you say?"

"When did His Majesty say he would be back?"

"He didn't—" She paused. He had mentioned it at some point, didn't he? "I think he said he'd be back by the Autumn Festival?"

"Then he'll be back by then."

"That's not help—" She sighed and shook her head. "Never mind, Nikator."

Daiyu rubbed her head where the hairpins and hair jewelry

were pulling her hair tightly back, the tension loosening with each circular massage. "Can you give me some privacy for about twenty or so minutes? I'd like to freshen up before we head out."

"Certainly." He gave a small bow and left the room swiftly, leaving her alone to her tumultuous thoughts.

～

DAIYU TRAIPSED THROUGH THE GARDEN FOR WHAT felt like hours but must've been thirty minutes *at most*. She peeked over trees and rose bushes, trying her hardest to catch a glimpse of the mysterious princesses, but despite it being their day to stroll through the gardens, she and Nikator hadn't come across them yet. She was even allowed to enter the parts of the garden that she wasn't allowed to before—all because Nikator was escorting her, and the guards seemed to want nothing to do with him—but her efforts seemed to be futile.

"Maybe they weren't allowed outside today?" Nikator pondered as Daiyu stepped toward a greenish-blue pond with red and white koi fish and silver scaled carps swimming beneath its softly rippling surface.

Daiyu crossed her arms over her chest and stared into her reflection. The muggy summer heat was a contrast to the weather she had become accustomed to in the wintry northern state of Geru.

"Maybe," she said at last, turning away from the pond. "But these gardens are huge. Are you sure we've looked everywhere?"

"Not *everywhere*." The wind tousled Nikator's scarlet hair and in the sunlight, his eyes appeared like sparkling blue gems. "These are the only parts of the gardens they're allowed in."

"And these are the south gardens, correct?"

"Yes."

They passed by statues of dragons and cranes surrounded by clusters of tall lavender shrubs and an old, moss-ridden statue of a half-crescent moon. Daiyu paused by the statues to inspect the small details on the crane's feathers and the shiny scales on the dragons, when something brushed against her ankle, startling her. She jerked to the side, only to find a slate-gray, short-haired cat rubbing against her feet with its tail held up high.

"Oh, my." Daiyu breathed a sigh of relief—*it was only a cat.* Kneeling down, she ran her hand over the cat's head, and it obliged, pushing its soft face and whiskers against her open palm. "You scared me there! I thought you were some sort of monster."

Nikator eyed the cat with a strange expression. "It has a ribbon around its neck."

Sure enough, a purple silk ribbon was tied around its neck, accentuating the sharp green of its feline eyes. Daiyu continued to pet the animal, a small smile tugging on her lips. "Back home, we have a few farm cats that keep the rodents at bay. None of them let me pet them, but that didn't stop me from *trying*." She tapped the hanging pouch on the cat's stomach. "I can tell that someone is taking care of you."

Nikator's frown deepened. "There's only one person who—"

"Jade, Jade! Where are you?"

The cat's ears perked at the distant, female voice, and Daiyu turned just in time to see a young woman barreling through the lavender bushes, leaves and flower petals sticking out from her long, wavy hair. She nearly stumbled at Nikator's feet, the braids framing her face swishing forward and the streaming, lilac-colored ribbons brushing against his leather boots. She raised her head while he stared down at her, both of them appearing dumb-founded.

The moment was broken when the cat meowed softly, and the woman turned to the cat, her eyes widening in obvious relief. "Jade!" she cried out, scrambling toward the cat.

Daiyu smiled at the woman's unexpected entrance. "Is this your cat?"

"Yes! She escaped from my arms just seconds ago, and I was worried she'd get lost," she said, her voice soft and wobbly as she scooped the cat into her trembling arms. She cast a quick glance at

Nikator, swallowed, and lowered her head. "F-Forgive me if I'm interrupting—"

"Biyu! Biyu!"

"Princess!"

Seconds later, two guards with their hands closed tightly around their spears appeared from where the woman had come from. Another young woman trailed behind them, the front pieces of her hair tied in small buns on the sides of her head, while the rest of her billowing, thin hair fell down her back.

"Princess Biyu!" The guard, a salt-and-pepper bearded man, narrowed his eyes and huffed loudly in exasperation. "You can't run off like that. You know that—"

"I know." The woman hugged the cat closer to her body, her thin shoulders folding inward. "Sorry—"

"You're not allowed to go astray from the path," the other guard said sharply.

"Biyu—" The other woman's sour expression stilled when she took sight of Nikator, and all the color promptly drained from her face like she had seen a blood-sucking demon. She hastily averted her gaze.

The younger of the two guards stepped forward and grabbed the young woman, Biyu, by her bicep and yanked her forward roughly. "Come on, keep walking—"

"Let her go," Daiyu interrupted, a steely edge to her tone. "There's no need for you to be so violent with her."

"She's not supposed to be here," the man replied with curled lips. As if to emphasize his point, he pulled her even harder, making the young woman grimace. "It's best if you don't interfere—"

"I said, *let her go.*" Daiyu balled her fists together. She didn't like the way this man was pulling Biyu around like she was an item. Or that he was being so rough for no reason. "She said she would go with you—"

"Listen—" he began.

"That's enough." Nikator suddenly had a dagger in his hand,

a dragon body coiling around the hilt. He pointed the silver edge of the weapon toward the guard, who peered up at it in thinly veiled disdain. "Let the woman go."

The guard hesitated, looking between the dagger and then at Nikator before finally releasing her.

"She may be a prisoner," Nikator said, his own eyes narrowing at where the guard had been grabbing the woman, "but she's still a princess, and you're not allowed to touch royalty, unless you have a death wish. And if that's the case—" He waved the tip of the dagger near the man's throat, an angelically cruel smile twisting his lips. "I can most definitely oblige."

The guard licked his lips and stared down at the blade. "I didn't—I didn't mean to."

"This is actually perfect." Nikator jerked his chin toward the two women. "Both of you, come with me. We have business with you two."

Daiyu looked between the two women. So these two were the princesses? Just by their appearance alone, she could tell there was something different about them. Something regal. Something ... noble. They were both beautiful, with pale, creamy skin, inky hair, slim figures, and midnight-like black eyes. But that wasn't what made them appear ... ethereal almost. Daiyu could just tell right off the bat that there was something special about them. Magic, maybe? Or perhaps because she now knew they were the infamous princesses—one of the last of the MuRong dynasty.

The two guards exchanged troubled looks, and the older of the two finally cleared his throat and strained a smile. "Uh, we're supposed to be guarding them—"

"You can join us, but keep your distance," Nikator said with a noncommittal shrug. But he wasn't paying attention to the guard —no, he had his gaze locked on the princesses like they were prey. There was something about the way he was looking at them that made Daiyu shiver and realize that no matter how kind he was to her, he was still a warrior, and he viewed the princesses as a threat.

"We don't have time for any business," the other princess said quietly. "So if you don't mind—"

"No." Nikator jerked a thumb to the path he and Daiyu had been walking on just minutes ago. "Follow us."

Daiyu cringed at the rough manner of his speech. "It won't take long," she said with a hesitant smile. Neither of the two women appeared to be involved in anything sinister by the looks of it. And Biyu was practically shivering from being so close to the red-haired warrior. Daiyu didn't have it in her to interrogate them, but the one thing she had learned from the royal palace was that looks were deceiving.

Nikator led them down the winding paths of the gardens and Daiyu walked beside him, glancing every so often at the shuffling women following a few feet behind. The guards did as they were told and were a dozen feet behind them.

"Is this a good idea?" Daiyu whispered to him.

"Why wouldn't it be?" He lifted his brows at her.

She frowned, eyeing the terrified young women one more time. "They seem absolutely frightened of you."

"I was there when His Majesty killed their father and usurped the throne." He stared straight ahead and for a moment, he didn't look so young and innocent anymore. The polished veneer of a cheerful young man seemed to chip and unveil the groomed, cruel warrior who served the ruthless emperor. "I *might* have enacted a few scenes of violence in front of them. Not *at* them, but they may have witnessed it."

"Oh." She wasn't sure what to say to that. Guilt gnawed at the bottom of her stomach and she hated that she was making them go through something traumatic like this with a person they feared and hated. But … she needed answers, and they might have them. The softer side of her wanted to relent to the guilt and toss away the whole idea, but another part of her that was emboldened by the multiple death threats against her steeled her resolve.

29

All four of them—Princess Biyu, Princess Liqin, Nikator, and Daiyu—were seated around a circular wooden table with clouds and dragons engraved along the surface, and with carved snakes climbing up the legs. The chairs were similarly designed. Beside them, cherry blossom trees swayed with branches heavy with pink blossoms, their petals and sweet cherry scent carrying over to the somber mood hanging over the group.

Princess Biyu hugged her cat to her chest and petted her from time to time, while Princess Liqin picked at a loose, silver thread in her periwinkle-colored sleeve. Neither met Nikator's steely gaze as he bored holes into them. The guards were a dozen or so feet away, close enough to spring into action when necessary, but far away enough that they couldn't eavesdrop.

Daiyu traced the scales along the dragon carving closest to her and cleared her throat. "I'm terribly sorry for interrupting both of your time," she said with a broad smile that she hoped conveyed friendliness and openness. "My name is Yin Daiyu, and you both are ... Princess Biyu and Princess Liqin, correct?"

Biyu bobbed her head shyly, her wide-eyed gaze flicking between Daiyu and Nikator before she tucked her chin inward and stared at her cat intently. Liqin pasted a strained smile and pointedly ignored Nikator.

"A pleasure to meet you," Liqin said. "My sister and I have heard about you. Congratulations."

"Ah, thank you." Daiyu wasn't sure what the cheers was for—the fact that she had somehow been chosen by the emperor, would marry him, or was about to be the wife of the most powerful man in the empire? While at the same time straddling the anxiety, fear, and responsibilities that came with such a position?

She shifted on her seat and laced her hands together to keep from fidgeting. She needed to come across as a well-put-together lady, not someone who had no idea what she was doing. The more confident she appeared, the more likely these two would open up to her. Or so she hoped.

"I actually wanted to talk to you both about something related to the royal selection." She kept her voice level and watched the two of them carefully. "Ever since I was chosen, I've actually been targeted twice. Once by a poisoning, and the second time by a kidnapping. Both of these events *may* be linked. I was wondering if either of you know anything about them?"

Liqin's brows pulled together in worry. "Oh. I had heard about the kidnapping—which I'm so very sorry to hear about. But I didn't know someone also tried to poison you. That sounds awful. I'm glad to see that you're doing fine."

"Thank you." Daiyu glanced at Biyu, who simply watched her below long lashes. "I'm doing much better now, but I would appreciate any insight into who could have done such a thing."

"We don't know anything, unfortunately," Liqin continued. "We're rather cut off from society, actually, so we don't really know what goes on throughout the palace or the empire. It's been that way for a few years now ... But if we come across any information, we'd be happy to let you know. Right, Biyu?"

Biyu jumped in her seat, turning between Liqin and then Daiyu. She shrank in her seat. "Ah, yes. I'm sorry."

Was she being tense because she knew something or because Nikator was close by? Daiyu wasn't sure, and by the way Nikator was glaring at her, she was even less unsure. If she had to judge the situation on its own, she'd assume the princesses were telling the truth and had no part in this. After all, what did they gain from pushing her down the ladder? Only a noblewoman interested in the emperor would want to keep her from Muyang. And these two women were very clearly terrified of the emperor. But the way Biyu was acting *was* suspicious.

"Do you know of any noble lady who would want to hurt me?"

Liqin laughed softly but stiffened when Nikator shot her a look. "Pretty much every noble lady who's single?" She straightened in her seat, her smile twitching. "I'm ... really sorry that we're not very helpful."

Daiyu opened her mouth to speak, when something out of the corner of her eye grabbed her attention. It was a blur of color among the trees and when she turned her head, she caught sight of light blue clothes. Nikator sprang forward, grasped the edge of the table and shot something from his hand at the trees. Daiyu barely had time to blink—to breathe—before he lunged over the table and threw another blade at the assailant.

She scrambled back in her seat and one of the princesses screamed. The two guards swarmed them, shoving the princesses to the ground and holding their spears in front of them protectively. Everything happened so fast that all Daiyu could do was kneel behind one of the chairs, her wild gaze sweeping over the gardens.

What just happened?

Nikator grunted and rose up from a few feet away by a copse of cherry blossom trees. He frowned down at the light-blue-clad individual and cast a narrowed, suspicious scowl at the princesses. "Seems like we had some company."

"A spy?" Daiyu hoisted herself up on shaky legs with the help of the chair and inched closer to Nikator.

"No." Nikator leaned down and pulled something from the crumpled person on the ground. He raised it up for her to see—it was a short knife with a circular design with a bolt of lightning running through it on the hilt. "An assassin."

"A wha—" Daiyu's words died away on her lips when she came to stand beside Nikator. She grasped the rough tree bark for support when her legs wobbled further. The man was twisted into an unnatural position, a dagger buried in his forehead and slick blood coating his face in a vermillion mask. Her stomach twisted and she quickly looked away. It was the last thing she had expected—for the man to be dead and to come across the corpse so easily. "Well, Nikator, it appears like you're a good marksman," she somehow managed to say through the queasiness. "What, um, makes you think he's an assassin?"

"This." He handed her the knife that had been on the man. "This symbol belongs to Lei Sheng, one of the most infamous and largest known assassination group in the empire."

"Ah." She felt even more lightheaded with that new piece of information. She turned the knife over and ran a finger over the embossed design on the leathered hilt. Her reflection from the blade appeared calm, but she felt anything but that. "An assassin? Wonderful."

"If you ever had any doubts that someone was targeting you," Nikator said, frowning down at the corpse dressed like a servant, "then this should definitely resolve them."

So someone most definitely was after her, and by the looks of it, they weren't planning on stopping until she was dead.

Daiyu paced in her room for the hundredth time that week. Feiyu was casually sitting on her couch, ankles crossed and propped on her tea table, and an open scroll in his hands he was reading from. Nikator sat across from him, sharpening his daggers against one another. It was becoming more commonplace for the two of them to be in her room like this, doing their own thing while she lost herself in her thoughts.

"Feiyu, are you sure no one is after my family?" She spun around to face the mage, who wore a sapphire dragon mask today with snarling teeth at the mouth.

He didn't even bother looking up from the scroll. "I checked in on them earlier today. Nothing amiss."

"And the protection spell is still intact?"

"Like I said earlier, yes."

She chewed on her lower lip and continued pacing again. "Someone is after me."

"Yes, you mentioned that."

"You don't sound concerned." She pinned him with an accusatory glare, but he continued to read from the scroll and didn't bother meeting her gaze.

"Daiyu, I work for His Majesty, whose life is always in danger. I'm quite accustomed to threats and danger."

Nikator raised his head from sharpening his blades. "His Majesty will probably be able to investigate once he returns."

She wrung her hands together and continued to walk in circles around her room. She didn't like the idea of relying on Muyang to help her, especially when there was no guarantee that he would care. She was becoming more and more uncertain about this whole marriage in the first place—was all of this hassle worth it? Would she and her family forever be in danger so long as she was married to Muyang?

"You're safe here," Feiyu assured. "Nikator is a great guard and Vita will be here shortly, so you'll be even safer. If I had to make a bet on who's a better warrior, I'd put my money on Vita —" Feiyu raised his hand just in time as Nikator's dagger flung toward him and stopped it midair, inches away from his dragonoid mask. "Now that's not very nice, Nik."

"I knew you'd catch it." He snatched the dagger away and began sharpening it once more, his scowl ever present. "Vita is *not* better than me."

Daiyu sighed and flopped down on the couch beside Nikator. She had grown accustomed to the thorny banter between Feiyu and Nikator and the various attempts from both parties to attack the other—though, it seemed to be in jest, much to her horror the first time around.

"You both love to talk about random nothings, but when it comes to actually pressing matters, you have nothing to say." She gave them both a pointed stare and covered her eyes with her arm. "Someone is after me. Someone tried to assassinate me. Does that not matter to you both? Or are you so used to the people around you being attacked that this is nothing special?"

"I think the latter sums up our reaction." Feiyu's tone was cheery and she chucked an ornamental pillow his way, which he—as she had annoyingly expected—dodged with a short laugh.

"You're safe within these palace walls." Nikator eyed the fallen pillow. "Even in the gardens, I protected you, and when Vita comes over, you'll be even more protected."

"That's all well and dandy, Nikator, and I'm grateful you were there to help me, but just being within these palace walls isn't enough to protect me. Need I remind you that I was kidnapped during my stay here?"

Feiyu unraveled his scroll further, the crinkling of the parchment filling the sudden silence in the room. "About that, the guards that were guarding your room that night were interrogated, and they were actually drugged with magic before the attack happened. What that tells me is that this was definitely planned and whoever is after you has a mage on their side and is probably the same mage who burned your family's rice paddies."

"Do you think they're also the same person who employed that assassin?"

"Maybe?" Feiyu lifted his head from his reading. "Lei Sheng assassins are some of the best—if not the best—assassin groups out there, and to pay for their services, one must be wealthy. *Especially* if it's an assassination attempt that requires sneaking into the royal palace."

"So whoever is after me is probably a noble," Daiyu said with a long sigh. They had expected that much, since mages only worked under affluent patrons. She still guessed that whoever was after her was a bitter, jealous noblewoman—or her family—who had wanted to marry the emperor.

"*Probably.*" Nikator began sharpening his blades once more, the sound of the two blades smoothly grinding against one another filling the air. "But I really don't see what they would gain going after you."

"This is the world of politics," Daiyu grumbled, pushing herself onto her elbows. "There could be hundreds of women who want to kill me so they can be the *first* to marry the emperor."

"I don't see why it matters who the first is."

"Well, I don't know either, but I doubt it's someone from my hometown going through all this trouble to off me."

Feiyu chuckled softly. "Can you imagine that? Old farmer Chen is actually behind all of this."

Daiyu made a very unladylike snort. "That would be hilarious. And horrible. I actually like everyone back home."

"Now *that's* hilarious." Feiyu snickered.

"*Everyone?*" Nikator added.

"Yes, everyone." She rolled her eyes and sat upright. "Unlike the circles here, in smaller, rural villages, everyone is sort of friends with each other. You kind of have to be, since we all have to have each other's backs when things get rough. Like if there's a storm and you need to shelter somewhere. Or when you run out of eggs, who else do you go to? Or when you have too many carrots in your garden, who else do you trade with? Life is *much* simpler back home."

"Do you prefer it there than here?" Nikator lifted one of his daggers and inspected the edge of it. It gleamed menacingly and even she could tell that it was deadly sharp. "I can see the appeal if you do."

"At times."

"Do you still want to go back home?"

"Sometimes," she murmured, her gaze flicking over to the window.

For a moment, they all remained silent. Feiyu undid and wrapped his scroll, and Nikator continued sharpening his blades, the *zing* of the blades joining the crinkling of aged paper. Daiyu breathed out deeply, hating the sudden spike of anxiety churning in her stomach, making her want to vomit.

"What—" Her voice cracked and she cleared her throat. She turned to the other two, who paused in what they were doing. "What ever happened to Prince Yat-sen? Atreus told me he was sent to the palace, but I haven't seen him anywhere. Is he in the same place the princesses are kept?"

"No. The princes are kept in a separate wing than the princesses." Nikator spun the now-sharpened daggers in the air, caught them, and slashed the air. Seemingly satisfied, he tucked them into their black-scaled sheaths. "Prince Yat-sen is currently locked away in the eastern tower as punishment for using magic."

Daiyu cringed at the imagery. She had heard the eastern side of the palace was where the royal mages frequented, so it was likely he was being held captive and watched by those same mages. It only made sense since he harbored powerful magic, she supposed, for him to be guarded by those who practiced even more potent magic than he did.

"It's my fault he's even there. I ... I had hoped His Majesty would show him more grace."

"His Majesty is strict with his rules," Feiyu said quietly.

"Yes, but Prince Yat-sen was only helping me and now he's ..." She balled her hands together. "How long will he be trapped there?"

"Until His Majesty says so." Nikator shrugged, not seeming concerned at all.

"That could be ... years, couldn't it?"

"I doubt it. Probably a few weeks."

"You think so?"

Nikator nodded. "Yes, but if you want my honest opinion, it doesn't really matter if he's in the eastern tower or his bedroom. Because either way, he's still a prisoner here."

That deflated what little hope she had left of the young prince and she sagged against the couch. It was all her fault that he was being punished and there was nothing she could do about it. Sure, she could try to sneak into the eastern tower to help him, but she was sure that would only make his case even worse. And besides, with the mages frequenting that place, she doubted she would make it far.

"Is there any way you can help?" she asked Feiyu.

He was already shaking his head as if he knew what she was going to ask. "Forgive me, but I'm not going to go against His Majesty's wishes. Although I might help you from time to time, and one can even say we're friends, please don't forget that I work directly under His Majesty."

She sighed, her shoulders dropping even further as she sank into the cushions. "All right, I understand."

"You're not going to do anything stupid, are you?" Feiyu asked, his tone sharpening.

"No. I think I'd just make it worse for him."

"Good."

"But—" Daiyu's tone lifted. "Do you think there's anything I *can* do to help him?"

"Ask His Majesty to forgive him, maybe?"

Nikator sniggered. "That could also backfire and make His Majesty keep him there *even* longer. In my opinion, you should just stay away from the prince. It'll be better for you both."

Daiyu scowled but couldn't deny that. Maybe it was better for her, like Nikator said, to keep from meddling, but it was hard to sit there and do nothing when she was the reason the prince was being punished so severely. But maybe that was what she needed to learn how to do—to be a member of this court and to mind her own business.

She didn't like the thought of that at all.

30

The months passed by and the weather cooled. During that time, Daiyu wasn't any closer to figuring out who was after her than she was on the first day. She did, however, meet Vita, whose stoniness was a stark contrast to Nikator's cheerfulness. She was a beautiful young lady with bluntly cut hair down to her chin, sharp moon-like gray eyes, and a tall frame. She hardly talked, and Daiyu found herself blathering to her in a one-sided conversation most days.

In the middle of the night, with the crisp, autumn air filtering in through the ornamental, slated windows above her framed bed, the soft sound of cheering and revelry woke Daiyu from her slumber. She pushed herself into a sitting position, only to find Vita, who slept on the couch in her room, was awake as well.

"Do you hear that?" Daiyu whispered, pushing the silk covers off her body and swinging her legs around.

"I do." Vita folded her blanket neatly and placed it beside the seat she had been lying on earlier that night. Rising to her feet, she moved toward the doorway connecting to the living chambers. "Would you like for me to find out what the commotion is?"

"Yes." Daiyu was already combing her fingers through her hair and heading toward her dresser. By the time she had pulled on a random dress—a deep purple with sapphire waves along the skirts and cranes embroidered on the sleeves—Vita popped back into the bedroom chambers, a rare smile on her face.

"His Majesty has returned."

A giddiness she hadn't expected bubbled and frothed in the pit of her stomach, warming her chest. Daiyu hurriedly pulled her hair into a low bun and slotted gold hairpins into place. "Well then, we shouldn't miss the festivities, right?"

Vita quickly dressed herself while Daiyu slipped on her leather shoes, her heart racing to a wild tune. She shouldn't have been excited, but it had been months since she had last seen the emperor, and she wasn't one to miss a party. At least that's what she told herself. Deep down, she had an inkling of an idea of why she was excited, but she didn't want to explore those feelings. Certainly not now.

They both headed out of the room and down the darkened hallways. The closer they drew to the main hall, the brighter and busier the corridors were, with servants bustling in and out with trays of food and drinks.

"Why would His Majesty come here in the middle of the night?" Daiyu smoothed down the errant strands of hair that had come out from her hairstyle and cursed herself for not taking more time to fix it before they left.

"They were probably close enough that he didn't want to wait until the morning, so he likely used magic to have everyone in his immediate party transported here. He's done that several times before."

The doors to the main hall were sprawled open and the boisterous sound of laughter, conversations, and music hummed through the lively air. Daiyu hadn't heard of the rebellion being squashed up north, but maybe they were successful in quelling the rebel forces for now? It was the only explanation.

Crossing the threshold, Daiyu was blown away by the amount of soldiers milling about the hall with drinks in hand, their cups clinking one another, and the array of warriors lounging about or dancing unashamedly. She hadn't expected such lightheartedness from the warriors, particularly because they were still clad in imposing dark leathers that made them out to be demonic-like, and yet they appeared so carefree in that moment. So unlike the monstrous, soulless soldiers she had thought they were.

At the end of the hall, Muyang was unceremoniously reclined in his black-gemmed and ruby-studded throne, a drink in his hand and his dark leathers and silks appearing all the more foreboding. His hair was pulled back by a glinting gold hair crown, showcasing his wickedly beautiful face.

Her breath caught in her throat at the sight of him. It had been weeks since she had last seen him, and seeing him here, bedecked in his dark glory, he looked just like a victorious, villainous emperor returning home—probably because that's exactly what he was.

It was only when Vita nudged her shoulder that she ripped her attention away from the emperor. Vita pointed at the far end of the hall and said, "I see the rest of the *Peccata* over there. Would you like to meet everyone?"

"Oh." Daiyu's mind reeled to remember all the members and what she had heard about them; so far, she had only met three: Nikator, Atreus, and Vita. She was drawing a blank as to what the names of the other three were. "Yes, I'd love to meet them."

Vita grabbed her hand and wove through the crowds toward her adopted siblings. Daiyu looked over her shoulder at where Muyang was seated, surrounded by his group of advisors and generals. He probably didn't even realize she was here, and as much as she wanted to go over and make her presence known, something held her back from doing just that. A shyness, perhaps? Or bitterness with how he had sent her away here without seeing her off? She wasn't sure what the warring emotions tugging at her chest meant.

"Remus is the youngest," Vita said, leading them through the thicket. "Thera and Minos are the oldest at nineteen. They like to pretend like they're in charge just because they're older, but everyone really just does their own thing."

Daiyu was just about to ask where the group was, but her attention was instantly drawn to a group of foreigners who stuck out like sore thumbs among the groups of soldiers. They were all dressed in similar uniforms—black leathers and black-scaled armor. The one who stood out the most was a silver-haired young man. He had two gray horns attached to his head, curling upward sharply, and his eyes were blood-red while the whites were pitch black. He had a cup in his hand, and even in the distance Daiyu could make out the long, black-tipped, claw-like nails he had.

Beside him were Atreus and Nikator, who didn't see her yet. And beside them were two other foreigners: a beautiful woman with sweeping, dark brown hair that fell down to her waist, and a handsome young man with dark blue eyes.

"Is that ..." Daiyu swallowed, her attention stuck on the horned individual. "Is that a *demon*?"

Vita slowed in her steps and cast her a strange look. "Did no one tell you? Remus is half-demon."

If Daiyu wasn't already shocked by the demon's appearance, she would have stopped and gawked at her like she had said something outlandish. *A demon*? A real-life demon served the emperor? She had only heard about demons in passing: about their brutality, their inhumanness, and their depravity. She had never thought she would see one in the flesh.

"How old is he?" she found herself asking the closer they drew to the group.

Vita raised her hand when Atreus spotted her and waved her over. "Fifteen."

"So young," she murmured.

She didn't have time to delve into more questions because they stopped by the group promptly. Thera, the young woman, threw her arms over Vita the second she spotted her.

"Vita! Oh, gosh, it's been so long since we last saw each other!" the woman squealed, squeezing her sister tightly.

Vita, for all her impassiveness, cracked a smile and hugged her back. "It's been too long."

Atreus lowered his head at Daiyu. "Lady Daiyu, it's good to see you doing well."

Everyone in the party turned their attention to her and she suddenly felt heat clawing up to her face at the unexpected spotlight. A small, polite smile pulled at the corner of her lips and she gave a nod. "Good to see you all," she said. "I've heard a great deal about you all. I'm happy to see that you're all healthy." Her answer sounded stiff and impersonal to her own ears, so she laughed nervously and added, "I'm sorry, I just don't know what to say. You all are so different than what I expected—in a good way! My name is Yin Daiyu, by the way. I almost forgot to mention myself. It's not like you all would know who I am without an introduction, I imagine?" An embarrassed flush spread over her face. She was well aware that she was rambling at this point. "A-Anyway—"

"We've heard a lot about you too!" Thera said with a broad grin, nodding enthusiastically to the others. "Right? You're His Majesty's bride! That's enough to garner the attention of the entire empire. I'd be surprised if there's someone here who doesn't know who you are."

Daiyu's shoulders relaxed. "Oh, really? I wouldn't have thought anyone would know who I am. I mean, I'm not very important—"

"You're too modest!" the blue-eyed young man said with a low chuckle. His eyes crinkled and dimples formed on his tanned cheeks. "My name is Minos, and I'm the leader of the *Peccata*."

Thera raised an eyebrow. "Who died and made you king?"

"As the oldest—" he began.

Nikator rolled his eyes. "I'd rather be governed by anyone else."

"Governed? I'm fairly certain His Majesty rules over us," Atreus said in a serious tone, just as Vita pulled closer to Daiyu and murmured, "See, I told you they think they're the leaders."

Daiyu laughed at the quibbles among the group, but her laughter subsided when she noticed that the demon boy was staring at her intently, his face void of expression. There was something unnerving about his gaze; maybe it was the red and black combination, but it seemed like he saw more than he let on. And that thought sent a shiver down her spine.

"Maybe you should go see His Majesty?" Thera said, jerking her chin toward the throne with a wink. "I'm sure he'll be happy to see you."

"Oh?" Daiyu clasped her hands together in front of herself to keep from fiddling with her fingers, suddenly not sure what to say or what expression to wear. "I'm not sure he'll care—"

"Nonsense!" Her smile was contagious as she leaned closer to her, and Daiyu could smell the powerful scent of roses on her. "He'll be thrilled to see you."

Maybe it was the push she needed because she found her gaze straying to the grand throne he sat upon. She licked her lips. "Well, it would be impolite not to greet him, I suppose ..."

"Oh, I think so too." Another nudge and wink.

"Well ... I suppose I'll send my greetings."

With a few more smiles and nods to the group, she departed from them and began making her way through the crowds. Her heart sped a million beats a minute and her hands trembled with anticipation. She had no idea what she was doing. What would she say to him? Why was she so nervous? It didn't really matter, she wanted to tell herself, whether she saw him now or later, because at the end of the day, they would marry and that would be that. She wasn't marrying because she was in love with him, so why was she so giddy to meet him all of a sudden? It wasn't like they were lovers who were separated by war and only now reunited.

She somehow avoided bumping into soldiers until she was in front of the dais the throne was on. Muyang didn't seem to notice her until she lowered herself into a bow.

"Your Majesty, congratulations on your return," she

murmured, staring down at his boots. "I'm happy to see that you've returned victorious."

Everyone else seemed to disappear from the room until it was only both of them. Her surroundings blurred into nothingness and she swallowed down the nervousness clogging her throat. When she finally raised her eyes to meet his, her chest tightened at the smoldering blackness of his gaze. A slow smile curved at the corner of his soft mouth, and all the weeks separated from one another seemed to disappear in that instant.

"My sweet, little *fiend*," he murmured, so softly that it was almost lost in the sea of voices all around them. Her heart skipped a beat and she inhaled sharply—that one word sent a shiver down her spine, tingling her every sense.

"Your Majesty, please don't call me that," she whispered, lowering her head to keep from staring at him. She could feel the warmth spreading up her throat to her cheeks.

"Come closer."

Daiyu hesitated, looking between him and the others surrounding them—everyone else was in their own world, speaking to one another or drinking or eating. No one was paying attention to them.

She stepped up the dais until she was two feet away from him. She laced her hands together and couldn't help but stare into his eyes that reminded her so much of a starless midnight sky. There was something otherworldly dark about him. So intoxicating that she wanted to inch closer to examine him. To *learn*.

"My little *rabbit*." He spoke the word calmly as he swirled the contents of his cup. He took a sip, closed his eyes, breathed in deeply, and then stared at her again. The shadows of the room played across the sharp planes of his face. "Have you forgotten that you can't stare into my gaze so boldly?"

She blinked, for a moment forgetting herself before she stared down at her feet. "I—Forgive me, Your Majesty."

"Did you miss me so much that you wish to imprint my image in your memory?" There was a teasing quality in the deep rumble of his voice that told her he wasn't trying to reprimand her. "Don't look away. Let me admire you."

Daiyu peered down at him, suddenly caught in his gaze. She couldn't look away even if she wanted to—and she didn't want to. He stared at her unabashedly, his dark eyes flicking over her face, studying her hair, and then following the curve of her neck and down her body. She fidgeted with the end of her sleeve. It seemed inappropriate for him to stare at her like this. Like he wanted to see every inch of her.

Muyang rose to his feet in one swell movement and he was suddenly inches away from her, a slow curving grin on his wicked face. He held his hand out to her. "Would you like to take a walk with me?"

She stared down at his smooth, pale hand, with calluses along the palms and small cuts running over his fingers. Tension coiled in her lower belly, and she wasn't sure if it was anxiety or thrilling anticipation that made her so giddy. Or the fact that he was requesting something of her when he could have easily ordered her to walk with him.

Slipping her hand in his, she nodded slowly.

They descended from the dais, his hand secured in hers. The crowds of soldiers, as boisterous and lively as they were, parted for them as they swept through the room. Daiyu could feel everyone's eyes on her and she didn't know what to think of all the bowing and nodding and respect aimed toward them—aimed at him, but it felt like they were also showing respect to *her*.

Muyang took her out of the throne room into one of the balconies attached to a random hall she had never been to before. The cool night air brushed against her skin and the sky was bedecked with a thousand glittering stars. Daiyu breathed in the crisp air and found herself drawn to the scenery below them. The capital sprawled in the distance, the houses and buildings forming shadowy spikes and forms in the night, so unlike their usual busyness. Here, in the quiet of midnight, everything seemed to remain still. Like someone had painted the night city with a heavy, inky brush and left it immortalized for all to gape and gawk at its beauty and massiveness.

"It's a beautiful view," Daiyu murmured, her hands curling over the railing as she leaned forward. The wind greeted her, carrying the familiar city smell of woodsmoke.

"It is."

She turned, only to find him staring at her. Her cheeks warmed and she quickly averted her gaze, choosing to stare at the crescent moon. "I meant the city."

"And I meant what I meant." He grasped a stray strand of hair that had come undone from her quick updo and rubbed the lock between his fingers. Daiyu could only watch, transfixed, before he released it. The wind carried it over her face, and before she could tuck it behind her ear, he took hold of it again. "You have a beauty like none I've seen before."

"I find that hard to believe." Daiyu couldn't help the soft chuckle that escaped from her.

Muyang tilted his head, one dark brow rising. "Why?"

"You're ..." She turned her head to stare ahead, and her hair slipped from his fingers, joining the rest of her unruly hairstyle. She resisted the urge to push her hair into place. "You're the emperor. You've likely seen thousands of beautiful women throughout this entire royal selection. I've been told I'm beautiful, from time to time, but I can never compare or compete with others who've spent years perfecting their appearance."

"I didn't think you had low self-confidence."

"I don't—" She laughed again, this time more awkwardly than before. Tightening her hold on the intricate metal railing, she fitted her fingers against the grooves of the serpent engraving curling over it. "I'm still not accustomed to life here."

"That doesn't mean you aren't beautiful." He inched closer to her, closing the distance between them. "I have seen many beautiful women, that's true, but none have stoked my interest like you have, Daiyu."

Until you find another who will. She didn't say the uneasy words aloud. There was no real reason for him to be interested in her like he was, and it was only a matter of time before he found another just as beautiful, just as quirky, and just as fiery. And then he would take her as his wife, and then another, and another. It was just the way romance with an emperor worked.

She steeled her heart, tamping down her prior giddiness at being so near him. There was only heartbreak involved in being in love with a man like him, and she planned to guard her heart until the bitter end. "Your Majesty, what is it that you see in me? Someone naïve who has never left her farm? Who wishes for freedom? Who is inexperienced? Do you enjoy the adventure of chasing a maiden whose heart you must win?"

A flash of surprise passed over his face and Muyang watched her with a strange expression—maybe he didn't expect her to speak so brazenly. "Daiyu—" he began.

"Your Majesty," she interrupted, staring at him levelly. "I'm not as innocent and naïve to love as you may think I am. I understand you might find it thrilling to chase down someone who resists you so much, but my heart is guarded. I have loved before, and all it caused me was heartbreak. I hope you understand what I'm trying to say."

His eyebrows drew together. "Why are you telling me this?"

She wasn't even sure. She was pushing him away, she could tell that much, but she couldn't pinpoint *why*. And why now, when he just returned to her? She should have been excited to be here with him, and she should have given herself into the moment, allowed him to show her the beautiful scenery and perhaps even flirt with her. But there was an uneasiness in her chest that wanted him far away from her—particularly from her heart.

She knew what it felt like to have her heart ripped from her chest. To have it broken into tiny shards that made it irreparable to put the pieces back together. And she knew that if she fell in love with Drakkon Muyang, her heart would forever bleed as he took on more and more women into his circle.

But she needed him, a small voice squeaked in the back of her mind. She needed him for stability and wealth for her family. For the prestige and status and safety he offered.

"Your Majesty, I just want you to know that ... that I can't give my heart to you. I feel that it would be disingenuous of me to marry you without you realizing that," she whispered, hoping for her words to disappear into the night. She couldn't meet his gaze as she spoke, her voice dropping. "I have loved another for many years and I lost him four years ago. My heart seems to be buried with him in his grave."

She could feel him boring holes into her with his eyes alone. "How did he die?"

"On the battlefield." She pursed her lips together. The dull aching that usually accompanied her when she thought of Heng was gone, and in its place, there was only brief sadness—like a passing wind that gently reminded her of what used to be. "He was an imperial soldier."

"Ah." Muyang's voice flattened. "So he faced my armies."

"He did."

"And died."

She nodded, finally looking over at him. He didn't appear furious, or frustrated, or irritated like she thought he would be.

"Is that why you hate me so much? Because I stole the love of your life from you?"

Her mouth dried up and she couldn't rip her gaze from his. The space between them seemed to stretch farther and farther, even though they were so near. So close to one another that she could have touched his cheek if she wanted to—and she had an inkling of an idea that he would have let her. Her lower lip trembled and she hated the tightness of her chest, the closing of her throat. As if her whole body was resisting her. "I don't ..." She could barely form the words. "I don't hate you and that's ..." *That's what makes this so much harder.*

It would have been so easy to hate him. So easy to see him as nothing more than a wicked, evil tyrant. But she knew, over these past few months with him, that he wasn't as cruel as she believed him to be. A villain in his own right, but not to her.

"Daiyu," he murmured, grazing her cheek with the back of his knuckle. A shiver ran down her spine, and he studied her face seriously, his brows drawn together and his voice velvety smooth. "I never expected to be your first love. I would never dream of having such a lofty position in your heart. I hate that I could never be there for you when you needed it. And as much as I would love to be the first man to take your heart, I knew that would never be the case. But I am an emperor. A king. A man who takes what he wants, and who will stop at nothing to grasp what he covets. Daiyu, I do intend to be the last one to take your heart, and I don't plan to let it go until the ends of time. Do you understand me?"

Her lips parted, but no words came out, her tongue too tangled to speak properly. There was a fluttering in the pit of her stomach that reminded her too much of a cage of butterflies. He was planning on stealing her heart, whether she wanted him to or not. His intention was clear and although she should have laughed at him and told him it was futile, she could do no such thing.

Her cheeks flushed with color and she stammered, "Y-You're mistaken if you think it will be easy. I have no plans to give myself to you, Your Majesty."

"I never expected it to be easy."

"I won't let you have my heart."

A wry smile lifted the corner of his mouth. "We'll see."

Daiyu turned her back to him and hugged her elbows close to her body. Even with the cover of night, she didn't want him to see her blush, or the way her lips wouldn't stop quivering. "I think it's best that we head back inside. I'm cold here and I don't want anyone to think you whisked me away in the middle of the celebration in order to have your way with me."

He barked a laughter that warmed her down to her core. "Is that what you're thinking about? Me having my way with you?"

"Of course not. I'm thinking of my own dignity here." She cleared her throat and shot him a sheepish frown. "I'm not keen on the idea of people presuming strange things about me. Like how I've somehow *enchanted* the emperor with my skills."

Muyang laughed again, this time softer. "Then we should hurry back."

WHEN THEY REACHED THE THRONE ROOM AGAIN, DAIYU excused herself from Muyang to nibble on the snacks and delicacies being served in the hall. She hung in the back of the room, eating a sticky, sweet, rice cake filled with sugary red bean paste, and tried to clear her muddy thoughts. She was still unsure if she was making the right decision here—marrying Muyang and casting her fate to be one of the many women who would remain by his side. Was it worth the risks? The threats that would come her way? The heartbreak?

She couldn't take Muyang's words seriously. A man who coveted a woman would say anything to have her, but once he had her in his grasp, all his whispered promises would turn to ash. She had seen it on more than one occasion with the girls back in her village.

She had to seal away all these flighty emotions she had for Muyang. She could feel herself drawing to him more and more, and the idea of falling for him opened a deep pit of despair and horror inside her. She couldn't fall for him. She simply couldn't.

Popping the sticky sweet delicacy in her mouth, she chewed and mulled over her thoughts, her gaze traveling throughout the room of warriors. A familiar face caught her attention at one end of the room. A thin woman who was filling a cup for one of the warriors. All at once, the color drained from Daiyu's face. That was the woman who had entered her room and served her tea all those weeks ago—the same tea that ended up being poisoned.

Daiyu swallowed down the last of her food and bolted

forward. She wove through the throngs of people, never averting her attention from the woman. When she was ten feet away, the woman finally noticed her, and her expression dropped.

"Hey—" Daiyu started, but the woman had already spun on her heels and was rushing to the door.

The woman deserted her pitcher of wine onto a side table and hurried out of the hall. Daiyu bunched her skirts in one hand and chased after her, bumping into people as she went. She murmured her apologies, too focused on the woman, and made her way out of the room. She looked left and right—and noticed the woman disappear around the corner. Daiyu followed, her strides shorter than the woman's. Adrenaline pumped through her veins when she caught sight of the woman at the end of the hallway. She pushed herself faster, her thighs burning.

"Hey, you!" Daiyu shouted, nearly barreling into a servant carrying a platter of sweet cakes into the throne room. "Excuse me—"

The woman turned down another corner of the corridor, but Daiyu was hot on her trail, not wanting to let her go for a second. They were in a deserted hallway, farther from the loudness of the throne room, but close enough to hear the thrumming of music and conversation.

Daiyu grabbed the woman's bicep and yanked her back. The woman careened back and slammed into the wall, crying in protest. She tried wriggling to Daiyu's left to escape, but she shoved her into the wall again. Pinning her hands onto the woman's shoulders, she glared at her.

"*You.*" Her breaths came raggedy and she tried to calm herself, even though she wanted to slap the woman for almost killing her. Her nails dug into the woman's shoulders. "You poisoned me!"

The woman trembled, the whites of her eyes showing. "I didn't do anything!"

"Liar!" Daiyu narrowed her eyes at the woman, tightening her hold on her. "You poisoned me that night. And you wouldn't be running from me if you didn't do anything."

"I didn't—"

"Stop lying!" she shouted. "I know you poisoned me, but I want to know *why* and *who* asked you to do it?"

The woman continued to quiver and cry. Fat tears rolled down her cheeks and she choked back a response. "I-I didn't mean to. I'm terribly—terribly sorry."

"You almost *killed* me." She continued glaring at the woman. "His Majesty can have you killed for that. You understand, don't you? That he will kill you if he finds out?"

She sobbed, her face scrunching together and fear making her legs wobble into one another. "I'm sorry! I'm sorry!"

"Who told you to poison me?"

"I can't say."

Daiyu jabbed her nails deeper into the woman's flesh and she flinched. "If you tell me now, I won't tell His Majesty what you did."

She hesitated, the fear clear as day on her face, and Daiyu only had to push her a little more to crack her open. She could tell by looking at her. She leaned forward, hating that she had to resort to these measures, but knowing very well that she needed to find answers.

"His Majesty will torture you for days on end, with his cruel magic that will strip the humanity from you. Day in and day out, you'll wish you were dead. I'm the first woman His Majesty has ever wanted to marry—don't you think he will go to the ends of this empire to eliminate anyone who dares harm me? You went against His Majesty's wishes when you tried to poison me. If you think that he'll let you go just because the person who employed you is powerful, you're mistaken. You and I both know what happens to traitors. So speak. *Who* poisoned me? Only I can save you from his ire."

A sob bubbled from the woman's mouth and she slid down the wall to the floor. Daiyu kneeled with her, her hands still gripping the woman's shoulders. "W-Wang Yanlin," the maidservant cried. "She told me to do it. I didn't want to do it, but she offered

a substantial amount of money, and I ... I'm ashamed to say I—"
She buried her face in her hands. "I'm so sorry! I didn't ... I don't
know why ... I'm just ..."

Wang Yanlin.

Daiyu released the woman and clambered to her feet slowly.
She didn't recognize the name, but it was a start. She stared down
at the weeping, fearful woman. A part of her felt for the woman,
but the bigger part of her was disgusted by what greed and wealth
could do to someone.

This was what it meant to be in His Majesty's court. To
poison. To threaten. To kill. And to be clever about it.

And now Daiyu was a part of it too.

31

DAIYU'S HEAD WAS THROBBING WITH ALL THE thinking and planning she had been doing the past week since she found out Wang Yanlin was out to kill her. She had never been a planner—that had always fallen on Lanfen—so conspiring against someone, or even thinking of ways to protect herself made her head want to explode.

She rubbed her temples and stared down at the ink scrawled on the parchment in front of her. Feiyu and her were in the royal library, in a section designated for mages and those of higher status, and it was completely empty. She had asked Feiyu to teach her how to read and write a little, but instead the mage brought her here, disappeared between the bookshelves, and only popped in and out occasionally.

"Feiyu, I can't read this." She unfurled the scroll to stare at the crude images of tigers and women and mountains. She had no idea what was going on. Was it a piece of poetry, a story, or a historical piece? She was none the wiser. "*Feiyu!*"

Feiyu popped around one of the bookshelves, a handful of aged scrolls stacked in his hands. His dragon mask today was yellow and black, with bigger slits for the eyes and curling fangs by the mouth area. "Hm?"

"I can't read this." She picked up the scroll and waved it in his direction. "I'm not sure if the woman is getting eaten by the tiger or seduced."

Feiyu clucked his tongue. "Those things are worth a fortune and you're waving it like a flag."

"Is it really?" She set the scroll down a bit more carefully this time, noticing that the edges of the parchment were flaking. She cringed and rested her hands on her lap. "Well, gee, I didn't know. Sorry."

"Oh, I don't really mind. Just that His Majesty might burst a blood vessel." He chuckled as if that was truly laughable, much to Daiyu's horror, and rounded the table until he was beside her. Planting a hand on the table and leaning forward to see the scroll, he bobbed his head. "Ah, yes. *This* story. It's a rubbish poem about a woman who fell in love with a vicious tiger, only to be killed by it in the end. Moral of the story? Don't fall for obvious dangers and use your mind."

"Well then." Daiyu promptly rolled up the scroll, no longer interested in reading about something that paralleled her own life. "I suppose another moral of the story is not to fall in love with a beast."

"That's another possibility." He dumped his findings onto the table and yanked back the chair across from her. Plopping down on it unceremoniously, he began flicking through the scrolls with unnatural speed. "Anyhow, are you any closer to finding out more about this Wang Yanlin?"

"No." She sighed and rested her head against her folded arms on the table. The room smelled like dust, incense, and old parchment—which had a hint of vanilla and wood scent. She was no closer to knowing anything about Wang Yanlin than she was the other day. All she knew was that, apparently, the Wang family was one of the biggest, most influential, and wealthy supporters of His Majesty. They also, apparently, thought Muyang would choose their daughter, Yanlin, as his first wife. Other than that tidbit, she knew nothing.

"Maybe you're not asking the right people." He unfurled another scroll, scanned the contents, rolled it up, and repeated the process with the next one. "Nikator and Vita aren't well-versed in the dramas and gossips of court life."

"I'm well aware of that." She had asked the two *Peccata* members if they knew anything, and other than providing her with information about the Wang family estates that were spread throughout the empire, the two knew nothing personally about Yanlin. They hadn't even met her before.

"Regardless, I think you're stressing yourself out for no reason. This Yanlin woman might be bold enough to plot your demise, but she definitely won't be the last. You should focus on fortifying your own defenses first instead of trying to attack her."

"But isn't it better to take her down and leave a message to all the other women who want to take my position?" Daiyu lifted her head to pin the mage with a grim look. "I might not know much about strategies, but isn't that one of them? Isn't that why generals spike the heads of their enemies around their fortresses and castles? To scare off the opposition?"

Feiyu lowered the scroll he was reading, and through the gaps of his mask, she could make out his eyes crinkling in what she thought was amusement. "You plan to make an example out of Wang Yanlin?"

"I'd like to, yes." She drummed her fingers against the polished, emerald-painted tabletop and chewed on her lower lip as she thought of ways to send a clear message to the woman. Her gaze glossed over to the ceiling-high bookshelves closed around them, and then to the sprawling, metal-latticed windows with dragon designs along the frames, and then finally to the green-robed mage studying her with inquisitive, black eyes. "If you have any ideas, I'd love to hear them."

"My methods involve magic, torture, and killing—all of which I'm certain you're incapable of doing. So if *you* have anything you'd like to share with me, I'm all ears."

Daiyu shouldn't have been surprised to hear that, but she

couldn't keep the shock from her voice. "You've *tortured* people before?"

"Killed them too."

She could have sworn he grinned when he said it.

"But what else can you expect from the high mage of the royal palace, hm?"

"I didn't expect you to be so ..." She struggled to find a word. "Brutal?"

"Anyhow, Daiyu, I'm dying to know the next step of your head-spiking plan." Feiyu plucked a scroll from his pile and unfolded it like the others.

"I don't have a plan *yet*." She stared off at the rows of stacked scrolls, all of them with different shaped rods holding the parchment together—some wooden, some rotting, and some metal.

"You'll be married in a week," Feiyu said. "And then a week after that is the Autumn Festival. Maybe you can make a statement then? You'll be newly married, glowing, and happy—and His Majesty will likely be the same. I'm sure you can make a show of how much you've got the emperor wrapped around your finger."

Daiyu scoffed, rolling her eyes even as a blush clawed up her throat. "Very funny, but I don't have anyone madly in love with me like that."

"Hm." Feiyu closed his eyes and she could make out a faint scar running vertically down his right eyelid and under the eye. His dark gaze flicked over to the window and his voice grew soft. "I wonder about that."

"I'll probably meet her at the wedding," she mused. "Along with her family. The Wang family has mages, right? So it's highly likely that they're the ones who burned down my family's rice paddies?"

"Practically every noble family has their own personal mages and the Wang family is no exception. So yes, it's wholly possible."

"All the more reason why I need to make an example out of her." She pursed her lips together and bit back the urge to release a string of curses upon Wang Yanlin and the entire Wang family. It was one thing to go after her life, but another to go after her family. There was no way she was going to sit here and do nothing now that she had a name. But she couldn't think of *what* to do. She didn't want to resort to Yanlin's methods—poison, kidnapping, and burning of someone's livelihood—but she couldn't think of anything that would send a clear message for others to back off.

"You could ask His Majesty for help—"

"Out of the question." She reclined in her seat. "The emperor doesn't concern himself in the matters of his women, according to a few noble ladies I talked to earlier. It'll only make me look weak, too, if I run to him anytime I'm in trouble. I need to figure this out myself."

"Good luck, then."

"You have such high faith in me," she grumbled. "Anyway, what are you looking into?"

"Oh, *this?*" He motioned to the scrolls haphazardly sprawled on the table. "Research."

Daiyu didn't prod into what research he was doing—frankly, she didn't really care what magical things the mage was looking into—and picked at the gold embroidered threads of her sleeve forming tiny lotuses. "Feiyu, why are you helping me?"

"We have a deal, remember?"

"I remember." She gave him a long, hard look. "But you haven't asked for anything back."

"In due time, Daiyu. In due time."

"You're not going to ask for something outrageous, are you? Like my firstborn? Or like, I have to become your slave for eternity?"

Feiyu laughed, loud and rich and full of cheer, and crossed his arms behind his neck casually. "What do you take me for? A mage from an old folktale?"

"I don't know—" The words died on her lips when his sleeve slipped down to his elbow, revealing a black tattoo of a serpent

coiled around the moon—the symbol of the MuRong dynasty—
etched into his lean forearm. Just as quickly as she saw it, he
dropped his arms back down to his sides.

An awkward silence stretched between them, with Feiyu
staring at her with unreadable eyes, and Daiyu gaping at him like
she had seen a ghost. She had seen the serpent and moon royal
tattoo, hadn't she? But then that meant ... Feiyu was somehow
related to the MuRongs? Was he one of the princes? One of the
far relatives no one knew about? Was he supposed to be dead? A
million ideas ran through her mind, but a singular thought
threaded them all together: Did Muyang know?

"Feiyu, why do you have that ... *mark*?" She leaned against the
table until she was closer to him and her voice was barely a whisper. "The remnants of the *you-know-what* family aren't allowed to
use magic. So how—"

"Daiyu." There was a warning in his tone, a tightness there
that she hadn't heard from him before. "Please don't ask."

"But—"

"*Daiyu.*"

She couldn't ignore the desperation in his strained voice, but
she sighed and fell back against her chair. "I won't ask," she said.
"But I hope you know that if you need my help in any way, I'd be
more than happy to provide it to you. I'm indebted to you, with
or without our deal."

He stared at her unblinkingly and gave a quick nod. "Right.
Anyway. Let's talk about something else, yes?" He pointed to the
bookshelves. "How about you pick a scroll or book that interests
you and we can begin your reading lesson?"

"Sure." Daiyu heaved herself to her feet and lingered at the
table with the mage for a moment, wanting to ask him more but
unable to form the words. Finally, she left to the shelves and began
perusing. Feiyu did the same, but more quietly than her.

She pulled out various scrolls—mostly because of the colorful
rods or fanciful ones—opened them, scanned the contents of inky
writing, and shoved them back where she found them. She

wanted to find something that wasn't so complicated, maybe with a lot of drawings to help her visualize what was happening in it. But mostly, she was letting her mind travel as she carelessly checked the scrolls and put them back in place.

The morning light filtered through the metal windows, casting dragon-like shadows against the shelves. Daiyu breathed in the scent of old parchment, her finger dragging over the old ledges. It was still bizarre to her that she was inside the royal palace, reading from scrolls that only royalty and royal personnel were allowed to see, and now she would somehow be a part of this all.

She paused in her search when she came across a particularly fancy scroll shoved at the very top shelf. The rods were painted a fresh, bright, vermillion color that instantly caught her eye. Climbing up to her tiptoes and grasping one of the ledges for support, she reached for the scroll in vain, her fingers barely brushing against the shelf it was on. She grunted, trying to pull herself taller to grab it.

Right when she thought it would be futile, a hand snuck up behind hers and plucked the scroll out. Daiyu turned her head just in time to meet Muyang's glittering black eyes. A gasp escaped her mouth and she fell back against his lean, muscular chest. His other hand went straight to her hip, securing her in place. A flush spread over her face, warming her down to her toes.

"Y-Your Majesty!" Her head craned back in his direction, her mouth parting slightly. When had he snuck up behind her? And furthermore ... a quick scan of her surroundings revealed Feiyu, and all signs of him, was nowhere to be seen. "What are you doing here?"

"I should be asking that of you." He took a step back to let her breathe and his body warmth left her in seconds. She noticed the way his hand lingered on her waist before he released her. Raising the scroll, he lifted his brows. "I didn't think you were interested in magical writings."

She almost leaned forward into his touch to feel the heat again but stopped herself short. She instead spun around so she was staring up at him and braced her hands behind herself onto the shelves. They were still only inches apart.

When Muyang tilted his head to the side and gave her a wry smile, Daiyu snapped out of her reverie of admiring him. She had almost forgotten he had even said anything.

"I can't read, actually," she said quickly, motioning to the library. "But I wanted to look at some pictures. That scroll caught my attention because it was painted in such a vibrant color. I was going to see if it had any illustrations inside or not."

"You're always surprising me."

"Because I want to look at illustrations?"

"No." His smile grew broader and there was a twinkle in his dark eyes that made her chest tighten. He inched closer as if sharing a secret and whispered, "The fact that you always sneak into places you shouldn't be."

"Oh." She could feel a blush staining her cheeks and she was reminded of how they first met in his bathing chambers. "I didn't realize this library was off-limits."

"It's my personal library."

Her eyes widened. "Oh. *Oh.*" She glanced over at where Feiyu had been and then at the rest of the vacant section of the library. "I'm sorry, I didn't realize—"

"You don't need to apologize." Muyang's eyes flicked down to her lips. "You'll be my wife soon, and everything that is mine will be yours."

They held each other's gaze for a slow, electrifying moment longer before Daiyu motioned to the scroll. "Not *everything*. But I would like to look at that scroll if you'll let me."

He handed her the scroll. "Let me help you read it."

"Why?"

"Why not?" He smiled that slow-smile of his again and her stomach flipped at the sight of it. At the soft purr when he murmured, "Is it wrong for me to want to assist my wife-to-be?"

She swallowed down the dryness of her throat. It was

suddenly too warm in the room, too stifling, too uncomfortable. Even though she wore the finest silks, her clothes felt too rough, too tight, and far too prickly in that very moment. Like she was in the wrong place at the wrong time, and yet it felt right to be there next to him. To have him peering down at her like she was something to be coveted.

Daiyu cleared her throat. "It's not wrong, per se. But I'd hate to trouble you over something so simple and trivial."

"All the more reason for me to help you." He waved a hand toward one of the tables.

She went to the table she had been sitting at with Feiyu and eased herself into the seat. Muyang sat across from her and even though she had just been with Feiyu minutes ago, this felt all too different than it had been with the high mage. He felt closer to her physically than Feiyu had been. The distance between them seemed to be smaller, the desk narrower, and even the air felt less abundant, like it was harder to breathe with him around.

She hated the instant effect he had on her. Hated how her skin tingled with goose bumps and how her body warmed with one glance. She was too aware of him, of how alone they were in this room, and how they would wed one another in a week.

Muyang pointed a slender finger at the scroll. "Are you going to open it?"

"Yes," she replied, still breathless. She fumbled with the flap of the scroll and unfurled it across the desk, letting one end of the rod roll to the edge of the table. To her disappointment, there weren't any illustrations, just inky, elegant strokes along the cream-colored parchment.

"This—" Muyang stared at the writing, his forehead creasing and a strange look flashing over his face. "You picked a particularly interesting scroll, little rabbit." He dragged a finger over to the scroll and tapped against one of the characters written there. "This is about soul splitting and curses."

"Curses?" She perked up at that.

"You like curses?"

"Well, *no*." She fiddled with her fingers on her lap. "But magic is just so fascinating to me. I had never experienced it before until I came to the palace, so it's all so very new to me. I'm curious to know, what are curses like? Is it a type of magic? Like in those old tales about people being cursed into becoming monsters?"

"Curses are a type of magic, yes. A type that consumes." Muyang flipped the scroll so it was facing him. "Soul splitting is a type of curse. It's where the magic user tears their soul apart, corrupts themselves, and becomes unstable."

"Why would anyone do that to themselves?"

He shrugged. "Various reasons, I suppose. To cast aside a part of themselves they dislike. To split their magic into different beings. Or maybe in a sick effort to save themselves."

Before she could ask more about curses and magic, he curled the scroll until it was closed and placed it on the center of the table. Leaning forward on his elbows, he murmured, "I take back what I said. I'd rather not talk about curses and magic, when I can speak to you on other matters."

"Other matters?"

"Like our upcoming wedding."

She hadn't given the wedding much thought—other than what she needed to do and how she would deal with Wang Yanlin —but that was only because she didn't *want* to think about what it meant to be married to Drakkon Muyang. What it meant to be a married woman. If she was making the right decision for herself, her future, and her family. All of it swamped her with anxiety and unrelenting pressure. It was better not to think about it, and yet ...

Now that he brought it up, her chest tightened in apprehension. She would be married soon. To the beautiful man sitting across from her.

She didn't know what to think or feel anymore.

"Are you looking forward to it?" he asked when she didn't say anything. "Is there anything in particular that you would like at the wedding? Any particular poets you like? Certain traditional dances you would like to see? Specific types of foods and drinks?"

Those were all the things she hadn't even thought about. Back home, weddings were a big deal in her village, but she was sure the emperor's wedding would be grander than anything she could come up with. She didn't even know where to begin. It was over-whelming to think about: décor, music, poetry, dances, food? She had thought it would all be taken care of by someone else.

Muyang touched her chin ever so softly, jerking her back to reality. He held her face for a fleeting moment, studying her with dark eyes that seemed so unreadable, and then released her gently. "Don't stress so much about it. If you'd rather not think about the preparations, that's fine. I just wanted your input on it, since I know for some women they like to be involved in the process."

"I—Thank you, Your Majesty." She tucked an errant strand of hair behind her ear and stared down at the polished tabletop. There was a warm, fluttering feeling in the pit of her belly at his consideration for her. "I'd rather have someone else prepare every-thing. I'm not too picky about the planning stage of everything, and I trust your people to do a good job at it. The only request I have is that my family be present and be taken care of during the entirety of their stay here."

"That's already been taken care of. Your family is currently en route to the capital and should be here shortly—hopefully just on time for the wedding. I was planning on having them stay here until the end of the festival. How does that sound?"

She couldn't help the giddy excitement that coursed through her veins at those words. Her family would be here, *finally*. It had been such a long, long time since she had last seen Mother, Father, Grandmother, Lanfen, and her twin brothers Ran and Qianfan. She could imagine her family being angry at her for leaving so abruptly, without taking their worries into consideration, and throwing herself headstrong into this situation. But she could also see the opposite: of them beaming with pride at the prospect of their daughter being married off to the emperor, of all people. At the new status they would gain because of her. At the wealth, prosperity, and stability they would now have in their lives.

Mother had often worried about Daiyu not marrying after Heng's death and had insisted multiple times to find a suitable husband. She had even brought suitors to their home, but Daiyu had refused each and every one of them. She was sure that her mother would now be happy that she would be wed soon.

"Thank you, Your—"

"*Muyang.*" He leaned closer until their faces were inches apart. The corner of his soft mouth rose ever so slightly. "When we're alone," he murmured, his words seeming to caress her in a way that made her shiver, "I want you to call me Muyang."

She swallowed. She could have easily backed away in her seat, broken this connection between them, but she didn't want to. She fought with the urge to press closer to him, to feel the warmth of his breath more firmly against her face—against her mouth.

"I can't," Daiyu whispered, eyes darting from his lips to his eyes and to his perfectly sculpted face. He was too close, too warm, too *real*. Too wickedly beautiful for her. "You're the emperor."

"Must I command you, my wife-to-be, to call me by my name?"

"I don't want you to command me for something so small. In fact—" She hesitated, not sure if what she was about to say was treasonous. But he nodded as if waiting and wanting to hear more, and she blurted, "I would rather you not command me for anything."

"You wish to be equals with me?" That sinister gleam was back in his eyes and for a moment, she thought he would close the distance between them and lock his lips with hers. But he didn't, only smiled that roguishly beautiful smile of his. "Some would say that's very daring of you. Others would call for your death at such a traitorous wish."

"And what would you say?"

"That when it is just you and me, Daiyu, you can be whatever and whomever you wish to be. If you wish to be my superior, my equal, or whatever else your heart desires, then I will comply." He studied her expression, the way her face lit up like he had burst a flame beneath her skin. "So say my name."

"Muyang." The name tasted so foreign to her tongue, but it felt *right*. Like she had finally bridged the last gap between them. Like there was nothing more holding her back from falling into his cruel arms. She wanted so badly for him to hold her, to *touch* her, and yet she held herself back.

Muyang's grin slid back in place. "You're so lovely when you say my name, sweet fiend."

"And you ..." She licked her lips, not sure if she was allowed to speak to him so causally, "And you are so infuriating when you call me that name."

"You still seem to hate the fiend nickname, I see."

"I doubt anyone would enjoy it."

"I enjoy it."

"Because it's not your nickname." A hesitant smile graced her lips. "Muyang."

"What nickname have you picked out for me? I hope I've graduated from *monster*."

She cringed at the insult she had hurled at him weeks ago. "I already apologized for that. Will you continue to hold it over my head, or will you get over it?"

"I don't recall hearing an apology."

"I'm sorry," Daiyu added with an eye roll. "And I have chosen your nickname, remember? You're to be called *little* dragon, since you prefer to add little to every moniker you give me. I shall do the same to you. Is that acceptable enough?"

Muyang frowned, but there was nothing malicious about it, nothing that told her he would throw her in the dungeons for offending him. She had crossed that boundary a long time ago, she realized when she took in his scowl.

"I don't know about acceptable, but I will tolerate it," he said with a long sigh. "I see you're enjoying the nickname already."

"Oh, I'm enjoying myself all right," she said with a soft laugh.

Daiyu opened her mouth to say more, but someone cleared

their throat, and her attention swiveled to one end of the room. Bohai stood between one of the bookshelves, an apologetic, polite smile on his face. All at once, the small moment between Daiyu and Muyang seemed to shatter, and she found herself retreating back in her seat. Hopefully, the commander-in-chief hadn't heard too much of their conversation.

Bohai nodded at Muyang. "Your Majesty, you're running late for a meeting."

"I'm not running late anywhere," he replied with a wave, his own smile fading and a look of irritation flashing over his face. "Last I checked, everyone waits for me."

"True, but as your advisor and longtime friend, I suggest we make it to your war council in time."

Muyang rose to his feet smoothly. "Then let's go." He eyed the scroll in the center of the table before turning to her sharply as if remembering something. "Where's Vita? I thought she was supposed to guard you at all times?"

Vita was supposed to be with her, but when Feiyu snatched her away, he had given the woman a break and told her to take an hour off until he dropped her back off to the room. Seeing as how Feiyu was nowhere to be seen, she had no idea if that was still the plan.

"She was taking a break," Daiyu said slowly and carefully. She didn't want Muyang to know that she was involved with Feiyu, but she also didn't want Vita to come across as someone who would shirk their duties for no reason. "I can walk back to my room—"

Muyang's brows pulled together quizzically. "Vita, taking a break? Who has enough authority to convince her to do that?"

The high mage had enough authority, apparently. But the high mage wasn't supposed to be interacting with Daiyu at all.

She wrung her hands together beneath the table, her fingers itching to fidget with something. "I, uh, don't really know for sure—"

"It was me," Bohai pitched in. "I thought she could use a break. We all know how serious she gets with her work."

Muyang studied the commander-in-chief for a brief moment but nodded nonetheless, seeming to believe him, while Daiyu also stared at Bohai, unsure if she had heard right. Her shoulders involuntarily sagged and she released a muted breath.

"Have a guard escort Daiyu back to her room," Muyang finally said. "And have Vita report back as soon as possible."

"Certainly, Your Majesty."

Her secret was safe for now, but she wondered why the commander thought to help her. Unless he too knew about Feiyu's involvement? Whatever the case, she was grateful.

32

Daiyu couldn't sleep the night before her wedding. How could she, after all, when she would be marrying the emperor? She lay in bed and stared up at the ceiling of her bed frame, her mind a jumbled, thorny mess and her nerves shooting through the roof. She felt like she was suspended in a strange, fairy-tale dream where all her problems faded once she was married. But maybe it was because that wasn't true at all that made her feel like she was floating in a daydream—on the contrary, her troubles would likely multiply tenfold once she was married.

She pulled the silk covers up to her chin and closed her sore, burning eyes. Her body was fatigued, but no matter how much she tried to sleep, she couldn't fall into a slumber.

And yet none of it felt real.

How was *she* going to marry the *emperor* of all people? How did any of this even happen? It was easy to forget reality when she was so caught up in escaping from Muyang, surviving the palace, and freeing her sister, but now that she was on the eve of the culmination of all her decisions up to this point, she couldn't believe it.

She was going to marry Drakkon Muyang. The evil, cruel

usurper whose reign was drenched in blood and whose very name caused people to shudder. The same man who no one was allowed to stare into his gaze for fear of being punished. The very man whose magical prowess leveled battlefields.

A soft knock on her door interrupted her thoughts and she jolted upright in bed. Vita poked her head through the doorway.

"Lady Daiyu? I thought I would wake you up, but if you'd like a few more minutes—" she began.

"No, no. I'm awake." Daiyu pushed the covers off her body and swung her legs around the bed. "I've been wanting to get out of bed for ages now."

Vita tilted her head to the side. "Then why didn't you?"

"What would I do here so early?" Daiyu threw open the shutters sealing her windows and breathed in the fresh sunlight and air streaming through the metal-latticed gaps. She rubbed her eyes with the back of her hand and walked over to one of the many dressers against one side of her room. "I wanted to start my day, but not *too* early, you know?"

"I suppose I understand." Vita was dressed in a long, flowy pale-blue dress with matching ribbons interlacing through her short, honey-colored hair.

"Really? You also get so nervous that you can't sleep?"

"Yes. Of course." She bobbed her head. "When I have an assignment I'm either excited or nervous about, I can't sleep. I think about how I'll carry it out, who I'll kill, when I'll do it. That sort of thing."

"Ah." Daiyu changed into a maroon dress and slipped on a pair of dark gold slippers. She had slowly become accustomed to the often daily, strange assignments of the *Peccata*. They lived in a different reality than she did; one where spying and disposing of enemies was normal. "But you haven't been doing any of that since you became my guard, right? Do you miss it?"

"This is a nice change of pace," she said with a slow nod.

"But it's a bit boring, isn't it?" Daiyu plopped down in front of her vanity and raked through her long hair with a wide-toothed comb. She caught a glimpse of herself in the mirror. Even though she hadn't slept, she was wide-eyed and alert, nothing about her features seeming to indicate her sleeplessness. It was probably the adrenaline giving her a boost of energy.

"It's ... *slow*." She shrugged. "Should I call for your maids for your hair? Your breakfast should be on its way shortly."

"Oh, sure."

"After breakfast, I think you'll be happy to hear that your family is here."

Daiyu paused in untangling her hair and swiveled on the bench so quickly she almost fell off it. "Here? As in, in the palace? *My* family?"

Vita smiled one of those rare smiles of hers and nodded. "Yes. They'll be helping you prepare for the wedding."

Without wasting any more time, Daiyu practically tossed the comb on her vanity table and waved at the door. "Well then, let's get me ready so I can go see them."

"Certainly, my lady."

DAIYU DIDN'T REMEMBER WHAT SHE SCARFED DOWN for breakfast. The only thing on her mind was seeing her family again. Even though Vita had said she could see them early in the morning after she had eaten and gotten ready, it wasn't until the afternoon that they were escorted into her room. Lanfen, Mother, and Grandmother greeted her like they hadn't seen her in years. After several moments of crying and hugging, they finally began helping Daiyu prepare for the wedding.

Mother brushed her hair with a comb, her fingers deftly working through Daiyu's hair. "His Majesty bought us a brand-new house not too far from the royal palace. You should see the place, Daiyu! It's absolutely *beautiful*. Stone arches, new, glossy roof tiles, and it even has a *garden*. A garden! Can you believe that? And I'm not talking about a vegetable garden like we have back home, but a real garden to *admire*," she gushed with a toothy grin, nodding to Grandmother. "Isn't that wild? I would have never thought our fortunes could turn around so quickly. We thought it was over once ..."

Her words hung in the air for a moment and she paused in brushing Daiyu's hair. Lanfen and Grandmother fell silent too as if they were also feeling the loss of the rice paddies. Even with all the luxuries Muyang could give them, Daiyu was sure there was a lingering sadness at the life they had built together and ultimately lost.

Daiyu clasped her hands together. "Since the rice paddies were destroyed?"

"Ah, well, yes." Mother began combing her hair again and through the reflection in the mirror, Daiyu could make out the sadness in her eyes. "It's wild to see that we've worked our whole lives and we've never been able to have something as nice as what His Majesty can offer us with a single wave of his hand. Our rice fields might be worthless, but it was our whole life."

"I understand." Daiyu turned around in her bench and took Mother's wrinkled, sun-leathered hands into her own. "But now you won't have to work so hard anymore. You can rest, finally, and everything will be taken care of. Isn't that wonderful?"

Mother studied her face for a moment, her soft-brown eyes softening. "Yes, my dear."

"When will you move into this new home of yours?"

"We're thinking a month after the festival," Lanfen added from her spot perched at the edge of Daiyu's bed.

"Why so late? I'm sure you can move in immediately—" she began.

Mother clucked her tongue. "Yes, yes, but we'd like to give a proper goodbye to our home. To our village. To ... everyone."

"Well, I hope you know you can move in whenever you want to," Daiyu said with a frown. Truthfully, the sooner they moved into their new home in the capital, the better it would be for them. They'd be more protected, more secure, and she'd be able to visit them whenever she wanted to. She'd also have the peace of mind knowing they were close enough for her to go to in case anything happened to them.

"Now that we have all this good fortune," Grandmother said, braiding her silver-laced hair with trembling fingers, "it would be good to give what we have left to some neighbors. Everyone has been so good to us, so we need to be good to them. We can't just up and leave without showing our faces again. It wouldn't be kind, Daiyu."

"I understand, but I'd feel more assured having you all near me."

"In due time, dear." She smiled, and her wizened face creased even further. "Have patience, my dear."

For the rest of the evening, she talked to them and it eased her mind, even as maidservants rushed in and out of the room with bundles of dresses and jewelry and pretty things to prepare her for the evening. When she was with her family, it was easy to forget that in a few short hours, she'd marry the wicked emperor. She'd marry *Muyang*.

She wasn't sure if her heart was ready for that, but she kept it guarded like she promised herself she would because there was no way she was going to let him break it. There was an uneasiness deep in the pits of her belly, telling her that something would inevitably go wrong. That there was no way things could be smooth sailing. That she was making a mistake.

She prayed that wasn't the case.

33

HER DRESS WAS PRETTIER THAN ANYTHING SHE'D EVER seen before. With its heavily embroidered gold beads along the sleeves, the skirt, and the belt, Daiyu could barely walk without feeling like she was carrying the weight of the empire on her body. Scarlet silk covered everything that wasn't doused in gleaming gold. Her hair was woven together into a high updo with a fancy gilded headdress to go with it and her makeup covered her face like she was a painted doll.

She should have felt beautiful when she entered the palace hall, with everyone gaping and gazing at her like she was a prize, but she felt out of place. Like a picturesque statue forcing itself to walk when its legs were too stiff. She didn't belong among these nobles. Or at least, she felt like she didn't.

They stared and sent their greetings when she was seated on the dais, but she couldn't ignore the fakeness of their smiles. The way they seemed to laugh behind their bejeweled fans. Or the way the women sized her up like she didn't belong.

And the women ... Oh, the *women.*

They were dressed just as fancy as she was, even though *she* was the bride. It was clear what they were trying to do. They wanted to steal Muyang right from under Daiyu's nose. *At her own wedding to him.*

It was bizarre. It was infuriating. And she hated them all for it.

"I thought you would look happy on your wedding day," Muyang murmured into her ear, his warm breath tickling her neck and sending a shiver down her spine. "If you grind your teeth any longer, I'm sure people will think I'm holding you against your will."

Daiyu barely glanced over at him but eased the iron-like grip she had of her own hands. She couldn't look at him the entire evening. Not with the dancing people performing dragon dances, or the hum of the music weaving through the intricate vermillion-and-gold décor of the grand hall, or with the throngs of people dressed in clothes worth more than a brick of gold. She was on a battlefield of her own with all these luxuries surrounding her, and the last thing she needed was the distraction Muyang offered.

Because he was a grand, grand distraction that took the cake.

Dressed in deep maroon robes laced with gold, with his inky, midnight hair pulled together by a dragon-carved gold crown, he appeared like a famed dragon emperor. There was something hauntingly beautiful and terrifying about the smile he wore. Like he was a demon-general that had been victorious in battle. And Daiyu couldn't meet his gaze, not when he took her very breath away.

Not when he was sitting inches away from her.

"*Daiyu.*" He grasped her hand and she inadvertently jolted at the small touch, her gaze flying over to meet his glittering, black eyes. "You're not acting like yourself."

Her throat was too tight, her hands curling together subconsciously, and her head was too heavy with the ornaments hanging into her hair. She couldn't see past the sea of unfamiliar faces regarding her like she was a sheep sent to slaughter. Even Muyang's words seemed to come out garbled, like she had a filter covering her eyes and ears that only honed in on the negativity geared her way.

"Daiyu?" He squeezed her hand.

"I'm well," she finally managed, searching through the crowds for Wang Yanlin, who—she was sure—would inevitably cause a scene. She could have been any of the fancily dressed women crowding the dais, the tables, and trying to catch the emperor's eye. She could have been waiting to sink her teeth into Daiyu when she wasn't looking.

Muyang intertwined his fingers in hers, forcing her to rip her attention away from the hordes of people. He watched her with a grim expression. "What's bothering you so much that you can't even look at me?"

"I thought I wasn't supposed to meet your gaze?"

"You are my wife today." His voice was smooth and he brought her hand up to his soft mouth, planting a kiss against the back of her hand. "You should look at no one but me."

"Your Majesty, what are you doing?" she whispered, feeling the stares being sent their way.

"*Muyang.*" He leaned closer as he murmured into her ear. As if they were sharing a lover's secret. As if they were the only two people in this crowded room. "Call me by my name."

"We're not alone."

"We could be."

"If you desire it, Your Majesty, then I will oblige," she said without thinking too hard about what she was saying. The response came automatically, just like the other phrases she had learned to say while at the palace. "But," she included, glancing over at him with a raised brow, "I would prefer to stay at my own wedding."

"Then we shall stay." He kept her hand on his lap, his voice dropping an octave lower. "But I will keep this hand in mine until it's time we leave."

She could feel the flush of warmth scaling up her neck. With the amount of powders and makeup she had caked onto her face, she doubted anyone else could tell. "Why?"

"So you don't flee at the first chance you get," Muyang said with a touch of amusement. "You look like you either want to run as far away as possible, or that you want to skewer a few people alive. If it's the latter, we can certainly change our plans for entertainment for the evening."

A soft laugh escaped from her lips. The first crack in her barrier. "I'm not thinking of destroying anyone, Your Majesty."

"*Muyang.*"

"Muyang," she added in a whisper.

Seeming satisfied with that answer, he turned to stare at the people enjoying their wedding. She could see the *Peccata* in the distance, congregating around one of the tables stacked with food. They ate and laughed amongst one another. A few tables away, she spotted Commander Yao Bohai, General Fang, and his wife Jia, and a few other familiar faces. Everyone seemed to be enjoying the drinks, the foods, the entertainments. In the center of the hall, dancers bedecked in colorful, vibrant costumes danced whilst telling the story of the victorious dragon empress who defeated the Kadians decades ago. Musicians filled the edges of the hall, their music filling the spaces harmoniously.

Muyang nodded his chin toward the people. "What do you think when you see all these people, Daiyu?"

She looked back at the scene in front of her. "I see people who are happy."

"Happiness is what you see?" His dark, inky brow rose. "I see people who will eat us alive if given the chance. I see people who will bury a dagger into our backs if we turn away from them. I see people who will greedily open their hands for whatever we give but would never do the same. I see people whose loyalties are so flimsy I can tear them with a single flick of my finger. These people, Daiyu, are now *your* subjects as well."

Coldness swept over her, even though the room was warm with body heat. Her fingers inadvertently curled within his hand, her throat closing. She noticed Atreus, Nikator, Vita, and the rest of the *Peccata* smiling at something the demon-child was saying. "But not all of them are disloyal."

"Certainly not all." His gaze seemed to follow hers, and she noted the way his midnight eyes seemed to soften for a split second. But there was a steely edge in his tone as he spoke next. "But people change. Times change. Power changes." He rubbed his thumb in slow circles against the palm of her hand. "You will learn much about being in the helm of power, Daiyu. What it means to have people bow down at your feet. To know what it feels like to be backstabbed. To feel the burn of betrayal from those who you thought were your closest allies. There is much you will learn by my side. I hope it isn't selfish of me to expose that all to you." He placed a gentle hand on her cheek, studying the blush that crept up her face. "If I were a better man, I would shield you from all of that, but I think that would be a disservice to you. As an empress, you will be stronger and more prepared."

Somehow, all the people seemed to blur away until it really was just the two of them—or at least, in Daiyu's perception, it seemed that way. She didn't notice the stares, or the music, or the loudness of everything else. He was clear and she was somehow caught in a moment of clarity.

"You ..." Her voice tapered off with astonishment, losing its strength. "You wish to make me your empress?"

"Yes." He brought her knuckles to his lips again, watching her the entire time. "I would like for you to be by my side for all of eternity. For as long as I rule. For as long as I take breath."

The empress role was usually left off to a woman of great noble birth, someone who was bred to rule the empire. Someone who had power to use. Someone who ... wasn't her.

And yet he wanted to make her the empress of the empire. *His* empress.

It was almost too much to take in. Her head felt like it was ready to burst. Like a thousand ribbons had been stuffed inside her, overwhelming her, and were about to explode in an entertaining array of colors. And through all the messiness of her feelings, she could pinpoint a singular thread of *happiness* that coursed through her. At the giddy excitement that both terrified her and thrilled her.

"I ... I don't know what to say," Daiyu finally whispered. "I would need to think about it, Your Majesty."

"Think on it a moment longer."

"I ... I will."

Muyang, true to his word, held her hand for the rest of the evening. Even when the food was laid out in front of them, and when the drinks were poured out, and when people came up to greet them, he didn't release her. He would rub circles against her knuckles, her palm, and the back of her hand slowly as if telling her he wasn't going anywhere. It had a calming effect on her, surprisingly, even though a few months ago she would have felt unnecessarily tethered to him. But now it felt intimate, gentle even.

At one point, in the back of the hall, she spotted Feiyu. He wore his dragon mask as usual, this time gold and red, clashing with his emerald and silver mage robes. He gave her a wave at one point, which Muyang didn't seem to notice, before he disappeared minutes later in a swathe of dark shadows.

"Lord Wang," Muyang said. "I'm glad to see you could make it here."

Daiyu's attention swiveled to the tall, slender man kneeling in front of them below the dais. Clad in expensive, bright-purple silk robes, with sharp eyes and an even sharper smile, Lord Wang appeared just as wealthy and irritating as she would have expected him to. A young woman kneeled beside him. With sweeping black hair that was pulled into an intricate updo with various gold dragon-engraved hairpins intertwining through it, and garbed in vermillion and gold silks, she was dressed just as luxuriously as Daiyu was. A sapphire-encrusted necklace dazzled against her chest, glimmering in different shades of blue every time the light shone on it.

That must have been Wang Yanlin. The woman who everyone thought Muyang would marry, and who had likely spent her whole life training to be a royal woman. And here she was, dressed like she was a bride herself.

A surge of unexpected rage and jealousy rushed through Daiyu's system and she clenched her hands together tightly.

"Congratulations on your union," Lord Wang said, oblivious to Daiyu's razor-like glare that was honed in their direction. "You both look splendid together."

"Congratulations, Your Majesty," the woman said in an overly saccharine voice. She batted her eyelashes up at him from where she was kneeling.

"What's your name?" Daiyu asked, unable to keep the edge out of her tone.

The woman's gaze cut over to her and she shot her a sweet smile. "Wang Yanlin."

"I hope you enjoy the rest of our wedding," she continued with forced politeness. "Lady Yanlin."

They both bowed once more and dispersed into the crowds once more. The entire time, however, Daiyu couldn't stop from glaring daggers at the cursed woman. She was the one who had burned her family's rice fields. Who had poisoned Daiyu and had her kidnapped. Now that she had a face and a name, she couldn't stop the swell of pure hatred that burned her chest.

Muyang seemed unbothered by their entrance and continued to greet the rest of the guests who congratulated them in the same manner. Daiyu tried to keep up with the polite act, but it was hard when every other woman her age, or younger, was dressed like Yanlin—with the intention of upstaging her. They all batted their lashes at Muyang, giggled, and smiled as if to gain his favor. She hated the way they acted. Absolutely *abhorred* it.

It was hard to keep a straight face when every other person was thinking about shoving her from where she sat. She could read it on their faces. The nobles wanted their daughters to be in her place. The daughters wanted to smite her where she sat. And the rest of everyone seemed to sneer down their noses at her, like she shouldn't have been there in the first place.

At her own wedding.

The only thing that staved Daiyu's anger was seeing Lanfen, Ran, Qianfan, and the rest of her family smiling cheerily and eating at one of the nearby tables. They were all dressed nicely, in clothes finer than they had ever owned, and they all seemed oblivious to the tensions and drama and gossiping around them. She could see their starstruck, awe-filled gazes at the sights they saw, at the dances and performances and music.

She wished nothing more than for them to continue to experience the luxuries of the palace and royal life without the negative bite of all the nobles. She was reminded once again why she was doing this, why she was putting herself in such an uncomfortable position.

"You don't seem to like the festivities of our wedding." Muyang rubbed her hand again, bringing her back to reality—back to him. "What troubles you? Is it the music, the dances? Or perhaps the stories being performed? What isn't to your liking?"

Daiyu turned her body toward him, willing herself to ignore the people in her peripheral. "The wedding is just as grand and beautiful as I thought it would be," she said, "and I have no problems with any of it. The décor is fabulous, the music is enchanting, the dances extraordinary. But ... it's the people that bother me the most."

"The people?" He canted his head. "What about them bothers you?"

"Can I be fully frank with you?"

"Certainly."

She didn't know what brought upon this level of truthfulness from her, especially since she had resigned herself to dealing with her problems herself and not involving him, but she couldn't hold back the thorniness she felt when she looked upon the nobles. Maybe it was because he held her hand so gently that she felt compelled to spill to him, but she quickly said, "I feel as though they don't think I belong here. I'm not one of them and they know it. I can feel it in the way they look at me."

Muyang was quiet for a moment, observing her with an unreadable expression.

"I probably sound silly," she said with a short laugh. Maybe it had been a mistake to say that to him, to reveal that she was already buckling under the pressure of everyone's gazes.

"No, I understand." He grasped her chin gently and turned her face so she was looking directly at him. "Do you think these people like me? A usurper? They used to look at me the same way. But then I killed each and every one of them who dared to disrespect me, and soon, they were all bowing their heads at me."

"But I'm not you."

"Soon, all these people will call you *Your Majesty*. They will bow down when you walk by. They will whisper pretty nonsenses into your ear. They will seek your approval, your favor. And you will have to know who to trust and who not to. In my experience, it's a good thing that you haven't been enamored by the glamour of this place, by the glamour these people inspire and strive toward." He grazed his knuckle against her chin ever so softly, the light touch sending a ripple of electricity through her flesh. "Remember this uncomfortable feeling. Remember their faces. Remember it all because they *will* fall at your feet eventually, and you will have to remember how they treated you *today*."

Daiyu found herself bobbing her head, her throat tight with unshed tears. She was afraid that if she spoke, her words would be strangled and she would weep. Not because the pressure was high, but because he understood. Because she wasn't crazy to be feeling this uncomfortable, thorny feeling.

"I hate that on this auspicious day, your attention is driven toward these people," Muyang continued, his gaze searching hers. "When it should be geared toward me and our union."

"I'm sorry—"

"Don't apologize." He pressed another kiss on the back of her hand, black eyes never straying from hers. "This is your first day of power, Daiyu."

That power wasn't because of her but only because she was

now married to him. When she looked back at the hall, the tightness of her body didn't ease in the slightest because she had no power of her own. Not here, in this den of vipers. Not among this court who would viciously tear her apart if Muyang wasn't holding her hand.

But she was now married to the cruel emperor, and she planned to use that to her advantage. She could become their nightmare, she realized. She could become worthy of being the wife of the wicked.

34

THE EVENING CONTINUED LIKE IT HAD BEFORE, WITH Daiyu feeling more and more uncomfortable as she realized she was drawing closer to the night of the wedding. It was only when the night progressed that she even allowed herself to think of what would happen next—and the thought filled her with another layer of dread and anxiety.

She had never been with a man before. Even with Heng, they had never done more than hold hands. And now she was expected to do so much more, for a man who had more experience than her. The thought alone sent her heart rate plummeting and a cold shiver took over her body.

"Let's retire for the evening," Muyang said at some point.

Daiyu wanted to throw up, but she nodded stiffly.

He rose from his seat, holding her hand as he did, and everyone in the room dropped down to bows as they walked through the hall. Daiyu could barely keep her head up, her mind swimming with what was to come. It wasn't until they entered the less dense hallways that she felt like she could breathe again.

"Are you well?" Muyang squeezed her hand and she could only stare up at him with wide eyes. "You look pale."

"Me? No, I'm fine," she managed to sputter.

"Really?"

"*Mhm.*" She couldn't reveal to him that she was terrified out of her mind. She hadn't allowed herself to think too much about the wedding night, forcing herself to gloss over the details and focus on other things—like on Wang Yanlin, the actual wedding itself, and what it meant to be married to the emperor—but now that she was walking to their wedding night room, she wished she had prepared herself mentally.

She knew what was supposed to happen: he was supposed to deflower her. But all the details surrounding it were hazy for her. She had heard her married friends from the village giggle about what happened between a man and a woman, and she knew the anatomy behind it, but that was as far as her modest mind had wanted to know. She never ventured to find out *more*.

But now she wished she had more knowledge. More to prepare herself with. More to make her ... not make a fool of herself.

After going up a few flights of stairs, they stopped at one of the doors in the hallway. Daiyu barely remembered the way there. She hadn't noticed the twists and turns they took or the servants who bowed at them from the corridors. It was only when Muyang tugged her hand that she realized they were at their destination.

"Daiyu? Are you sure you're well?"

"I'm fine," she whispered, touching the ornate, gilded dragon doors.

When she walked through the threshold of the room, her stomach twisted into a tighter ball of nerves. Jade-painted pillars with gold embossed designs along the columns were erected on the sides of the room, the hexagonal caisson ceilings had dragon carvings engraved in the center, and the gold-stamped gray-tiled floors gleamed beneath the orange glow from the hearth. It was all too luxurious to take in, but the most intimidating feature of all was the giant framed bed sitting in the center of it all.

Muyang pressed a gentle hand on the small of her back. He

leaned forward, his breath warming her ear. "Is the room not to your liking? I can have us moved to my bedchambers if you'd like."

"N-No, the room is fine," she squeaked, pulling away from him and entering the room with hurried steps. Her head felt heavy with the gold headdress, which seemed to pull her hair back too tightly against her scalp. Her steps were light, even as her belly seemed to be filled with a thousand butterflies. "It's as fancy and luxurious as I would expect from the royal palace. I have no complaints."

She didn't even know what she was saying, the words tumbling out of her in quick succession. Daiyu brushed a hand over the ruby-colored silk sheets and covers, her fingers trembling all the while. She laced them together and sat stiffly on the edge of the mattress, her smile feeling as strained and painted on as the rest of her makeup.

Muyang shut the door behind himself with a final click and glanced around the room as if he were seeing it for the first time as well. His fingers danced over the mahogany dresser, his leather boots clicking against the polished tiles menacingly. His dark gaze swept over to her and she nearly jumped where she sat—there was such a deep, deep darkness hidden within the black depths that made her feel all the more nervous.

"You're finally mine," he murmured, crossing his muscular arms over his chest and leaning back against the dresser. "I knew the moment I saw you that I must have you, and here you are, *mine*. Finally."

Daiyu bound her hands together tightly to keep the trembles at bay. "Your Majesty, I thought I was always yours?"

"*Muyang*. How many times must I tell you to call me by my name?"

"Forgive me," she murmured, unable to meet his eyes. "I'm unaccustomed to any of this."

"You had a fiancé at some point, did you not?"

"I did, but ..." Heng was different than Muyang in every way.

She wasn't nervous around Heng, she didn't feel like she had to tiptoe around him, and they never interacted with each other flirtatiously or intimately. The way she felt about Muyang was otherworldly; he was a completely different beast. Every gaze, every touch, every breath she took in his presence made her feel like it would be her last and left her aching for more. "But it's not the same."

She could feel him staring at her, but she didn't lift her head, not even when he crossed the distance between them. It was only when he stopped in front of her that she finally peered up at him.

"You will always be mine, Daiyu." He kneeled down until they were at eye level. Grasping her chin in his rough hand, he examined her keenly. Searching for something. "You are too beautiful, too free, too *much* to belong to such a villainous monster as me, but I promise to love and treasure you for as long as I breathe."

She released a ragged breath. "You're not a monster."

"You can only say that because you haven't seen what I've done." Muyang cupped her cheek with one hand. "What I'm capable of."

"I didn't marry a monster." Daiyu stared at him—*really* stared at him. At his dark eyes, framed by even darker lashes. At the angular planes of his face and jaw. At the smooth paleness of his impeccable skin. At his impossibly perfect features. And once more, like she had thought the first time she had met him, he was too beautiful for the wickedness he possessed. "You may be a villain to many people, Muyang, but to me, you're ... not that. Not anymore."

"What changed?"

"Nothing and everything."

They both stared at each other. Daiyu's heart throbbed in a way she had never experienced and every nerve in her body seemed to jolt with electricity. He leaned closer to her, his eyes flicking down to her lips. She didn't know what to do with her hands, or what to feel when his soft mouth brushed against her lips. Her whole body stiffened, her eyes squeezing shut as his lips moved against her frozen ones. He tasted sweet, like a summer's night, but with a touch of coldness that made her gasp.

She wanted to breathe in more of him, more of his jasmine scent and honeyed taste, but she was as rigid as stone, sitting on the bed and bracing her hands on the edge of the mattress like a lifeline. Muyang grasped her face in one hand, tilted her head slightly as he deepened the kiss, and placed another hand on her hip. Warmth pooled in her belly, her skin tinged with heat everywhere he touched her, and yet she couldn't move.

Finally, after a few seconds, she broke off the kiss by turning her face away. She was a patchwork of warmth and blushing skin, her head feeling heavy and heady, and her heart hammering like never before. She couldn't breathe, couldn't think, couldn't do anything but lock up.

"Daiyu?" Muyang's voice was low and dangerous, but his expression was anything but that. "What's wrong?"

"I'm not ready for this," she blurted out without thinking. She clamped her mouth shut, feeling as though the floor was opening up beneath her feet and would swallow her whole. "I don't know what to do and I can't—I can't—"

Tears burned the back of her eyes and she blinked them away rapidly, hating the way her voice trembled.

"I'm sorry, just give me a few minutes and I'll be fine. I just ... I just feel so overwhelmed right now and so—" *So useless.* It was her duty to please her husband and yet she couldn't do that. She didn't even know what to do and now that her nerves were getting the better of her, she feared she would never be able to move from this spot.

Muyang watched her with furrowed brows. If he was displeased, he didn't show it. In fact, if she didn't know any better, she would say he was actually *concerned* about her. Him, the cruel and evil emperor, concerned about his wife? It should have been laughable, especially considering he had been likely waiting for this moment. It was his right to take her. And yet she was resisting.

She hated the way her body seized up. The way she couldn't think beyond how much she was already failing at being a wife.

"Daiyu, *shhh*." He gently took her face in his hands and brushed her tears with his thumbs. She hadn't even realized she was crying until she looked at him in that moment, his image blurring. "Why are you crying so much?"

"Because I know what I'm supposed to do, but I just ..." She pressed her quivering lips together. "I'm sorry. I'll be fine—"

"Daiyu, you don't have to do this. I hope you know that?" Muyang searched her face, his midnight-like eyes softening. "I would *never* force myself upon you. Do you hear me? I would never want you to force yourself to be with me either. You don't have to be so scared. I would never hurt you and I would never want you to do anything you're not comfortable with."

"B-But it's my duty—"

"It's *not* your duty."

"But ..." She blinked away the tears clinging to her lashes. "But it is?"

"Not like this. *Never* like this." He wiped the last of her tears and scanned her face again. She couldn't tell what he was thinking, not with his shuttered expression or the calmness of his voice, but she was sure he wasn't frustrated with her. "We'll go at your pace," he said, surprising her further.

"*My* pace? What does that even mean?"

"It means that *you* are in charge, Daiyu." He held on to one of the many pieces of jewelry intertwined in her hair and pulled at it softly. It came out without much resistance and, one by one, he began unraveling her hairstyle. Her face warmed and she was reminded of their time together months ago by the garden pond, where he had similarly pulled her hairpins out of place.

When the last of the ornaments were taken out and placed on the top of the nightstand, Daiyu tucked a lock of hair behind her ear and said, "What are you doing?"

"All of these look uncomfortable," he said with a small shrug, loosening his own hair crown and dropping it atop her jewelry. He took her hands in his and rubbed his thumbs over her knuckles, his expression softening. "Take as long as you need, Daiyu. And as slow as you need. I'm not going anywhere."

The lower pits of her belly warmed and she could only nod, her throat tightening unexpectedly. She hadn't thought he was capable of being so tender, so ... comforting.

Muyang brought her hands to his lips and kissed them softly, his gaze never straying from hers. "Tonight, you're the empress, Daiyu, and I'm nothing more than your husband. So do what you want with me. Kiss me. Embrace me. Love me. But don't hate me." Another gentle kiss against her knuckles. "If all you want to do is sleep in my arms, then so be it."

Her body trembled with another wave of nerves, but this time, it didn't scare her as much as the first. This time, she could feel the giddy excitement. The slow realization that she was in charge made her feel even more comfortable in her bones. Slowly, she could feel her body relaxing and her breathing calming.

Daiyu tentatively touched the side of his face, her fingers fitting so well against the planes of his jaw. "Don't be too sweet to me, or I might expect it every time you and I are together."

Muyang chuckled, the sound reverberating in his chest. "Expect it every time then, Daiyu, because I would never force myself upon you. And you *should* expect this type of behavior from your husband. Whenever we are together, I want every moment of longing, of passion, and of love to be mutual."

He was supposed to be cruel. She had expected it. Maybe even mentally prepared herself for it. And yet, all she found was a tenderness that stoked something from deep within herself.

It terrified her how easy he was making all of this. How easy it would have been to fall in love with him in that very moment. To drop into his arms and love him with every fiber of her being.

Muyang pushed himself to his feet, kicked off his boots and ceremonial clothes until he was clad in nothing but a simple black tunic and pants, and crawled into the spot on the bed beside her. Daiyu eased herself onto the bed, her heart racing. For a moment, neither of them did anything but stare at the ceiling. Daiyu could feel the exhaustion weighing her bones down on the soft mattress, but her flesh was tingly with anticipation. With a startling *longing*.

Daiyu abruptly sat up and peered down at him. He glanced over at her, dark eyes appearing like two beautiful chips of starless, midnight sky. He was too beautiful for her to ignore in that moment. Too handsome for her to ignore the embers that sparked and burned within herself. She had wanted to touch him for such a long time but had held back.

But now he was hers. And he had given her permission to take things as she wanted them. At her own pace.

So she touched the side of his face with hesitant fingers. Her skin tingled with electrical pulses, her body warming and firing at the sight of him. At the power she held in that moment.

"It's not fair for you to look like this," she blurted out. It took her a second to realize what she had said, and her cheeks bloomed with color while he grinned.

"To look like *what*?"

"You know what I mean."

"I'm not actually sure."

"You're too ..." Beautiful. A piece of art. A villain who embodied the idea of sweet poison. But she couldn't say those words out loud, not without laughing and thinking she was being too honest. Instead, she shook her head and smiled. "You know what I mean, Muyang. You've likely been told your whole life how you look."

The corner of Muyang's lips rose and her stomach clenched even tighter. "Isn't this the time for *me* to be telling *you* how beautiful you are? Not the other way around?"

"You told me that we can take things at my pace," she said with a light, playful tap to his forehead. Unlike him, she didn't have experience in these matters, so she had no idea what she was supposed to say or do, but she didn't want to say that out loud for fear of marring this moment between them. Instead, she took the reins again and inched closer to him. "You should surrender yourself better, Your Majesty."

"Surrender myself? To you?" His tone was playful.

"To your empress, yes." Before she could second-guess herself, or feel too embarrassed, she climbed atop of him and straddled her thighs against his waist. Her hands splayed against his chest and she quivered with an astonishing sense of nervousness, desire, and most surprising of all, *power*.

Muyang's gaze darkened with obvious need and he grasped a strand of her hair. "What do you want me to do with you, Your Highness?" he murmured, kissing the lock of her hair.

A thrill ran down her spine.

She felt like the most beautiful woman in the empire—*in the whole world*.

"For tonight, I want to feel like you've never loved anything more than you love me, and that you've never coveted something more than me." She cupped his face in her hands and leaned closer to him. "And I want you to beg for me, Your Majesty. I want you completely as you are."

"As you wish, my empress."

Their lips locked with one another and a pulse of electric desire ran through her body like a wildfire, coursing through her veins and lighting up every piece of her. She moved against him, her hands exploring his body, her nerves disappearing as their bodies collided with each other. She had never felt so empowered in her life. She was the most important person in that moment and he was so much more than just Drakkon Muyang—the usurper and villainous emperor.

He was her lover, her husband—but mostly, he was *hers*.

35

THE AUTUMN FESTIVAL IN THE CAPITAL WAS LIKE nothing Daiyu had experienced. The teeming streets were decorated with rich vermillion banners at every corner, with the royal dragon insignia plastered across them. Vendors selling sticky rice snacks, candied fruits, colorful masks, savory foods, and all types of festivities cluttered the roads packed with people from all types of backgrounds. The aromatic smells overpowered the usually pervasive woodsmoke, and the lights—*oh, the lights*. The city was alive by the evening, with bright lanterns strung together on every street, blazing firelight like she was in a different world altogether.

Daiyu watched—transfixed by the glittering lights—the sprawling, dazzling city below her. She leaned against the balcony railing, the crisp, cool air against her skin and the starlit midnight sky canopying above her. It was the second day of the festival and she already wished it would last all year long. At least then she could marvel at it forever and partake in the giddy delight everyone seemed to be stuck in.

"It's a shame my family left so soon after the wedding," Daiyu murmured, turning to Muyang, who was similarly leaning on the railing with his unreadable gaze set on the capital. Feiyu had warped her family back home the day after the wedding, since her parents wanted to celebrate the Autumn Festival at their village since it would be their last time living there. But now that she had witnessed the beauty and extravagance of this festival, she didn't want to go back to the now-dull festival that occurred in her hometown. "They're missing out," she continued with a sigh. "I told them it would be better to stay."

"They'll be able to witness next year's festival."

"I know, but that's a long time from now." Daiyu breathed in the smoky, fragrant smells permeating from the city. She had been at awe at the festivities yesterday and had walked through the streets, marveling at everything she saw—fire-breathing dancers, actors dressed in dragon costumes that looked far too realistic, and singers with rich sons—and even today, the second day, after all feasting and dancing, she was just as excited, albeit a bit exhausted.

"What a beautiful sight," she whispered at the twinkling lights.

"Indeed."

She turned to find him staring at her, a grin curling over his soft mouth. All at once, her face flushed with warmth and she was reminded again of his gentle touch. Heat pooled in the pit of her belly. "Don't look at me like that."

"Like what?"

"Like you want to devour me."

He chuckled faintly, leaning closer to her and wrapping an arm around her waist. He pulled her close to him and she gasped at the sudden motion. At the way her body reacted to him.

"Muyang, what are you doing?"

"Admiring my wife." He dragged a finger down her spine and she shuddered.

"Well, maybe you can admire me later." She turned to stare back at the capital, no longer able to focus on the glittering lights and the bustle through the streets. She leaned into his touch, her cheeks flaming. "Right now, I'd rather pay attention to the festival."

"Hmph." Muyang followed her gaze to the rest of the city. "It's the same as it always is."

"For *you*." Daiyu clucked her tongue. "Not everyone gets to witness this. I've never been to a festival as grand as this one."

"It happens every year."

"I suppose the glamour of it is lost on you," she said with a long sigh. "Probably because you've grown accustomed to all of this splendor. But I'm not like that. I hope to never become like that. I want to appreciate beauty at all times."

"You don't sound like you're talking about the festival."

"Well, no." She could feel her blush spreading, this time from embarrassment. "I mean in general. I don't want to ever become ungrateful, or get too used to all of this. I want to remember where I came from."

He was quiet for a moment as if mulling over her words. "Where you come from, huh?"

"Speaking of which ..." She peered up at him. "Where are *you* from, Muyang? You obviously had a life before you became the emperor. What were you doing? What was life like? Did you have a family?"

Muyang stiffened, the festive mood dampening in mere seconds, replaced by a storm that seemed to brew in his black eyes. He locked his jaw and stared straight ahead. "I'd rather ... not talk about it."

"Oh. I ... I'm sorry." She hated that she had ruined the moment. Whatever sparks were flying between them buzzed away. There was only coldness now. She touched his hand lightly, but he pulled away. "I didn't mean to pry."

"I don't have many fond memories of my past," he said carefully. "I don't ... really remember much."

"What do you mean?"

"*Nothing.*" He breathed out deeply. His emotions shuttered from his face and a mask seemed to slip back in place. Suddenly, he was calm again, unbothered, and closed off. And, it seemed, done with this conversation. "Daiyu, how about we talk about your life?"

"Um, there's not much to talk about." Tucking a strand of hair behind her ear, she watched him carefully; she hated that he was no longer as relaxed as he was earlier. She could sense the tenseness of his shoulders, the edge in his smooth voice. "I grew up on a rice farm. My father and his father, and his father before him, for many decades, grew rice. So of course, that's what we did too. Life was pretty ... simple."

"What were your days like?"

"I'm not sure you'd be interested in my boring life," she said with another laugh. She tightened her grip on the balcony railing and traced the embossed grooves along the metal. "Seriously, nothing interesting ever happened."

"I want to know." He placed his hand atop of hers. His fingers were warm, a stark contrast to the cool night air. "There's nothing boring about you, Daiyu. So tell me about your life. Your family. Your ... everything."

She began to tell him about her daily life on the farm, about the mundane tasks she did every day. Soon, before she knew it, she was telling him everything. About Lanfen, her brothers, her parents, her neighbors, all the farm animals they had, and everything about their small village. She told him about the flower fields she loved to frequent. About the friends she grew up with, the changing of seasons, the fond memories she had. She kept talking, and talking, and talking until she was sure he would grow bored.

But he didn't. He simply watched her and nodded, asking questions from time to time.

"Well, I'm sure I can talk forever at this point," she said with a nervous laugh. "But maybe we can do something else now? I'd hate for the night to pass and we realize we've done nothing but discuss my boring eating habits back at the farm."

Muyang smiled gently and her heart fluttered in her chest. "You're not boring me, Daiyu. I hope you understand that."

"*Yet.*"

"I don't think you could ever bore me." He wove his fingers into hers, intertwining them. Bringing her knuckles to his mouth, he planted a soft kiss against the grooves of her hand. "But since you insist on doing *something*, would you like to take a walk with me? Through the festival?"

Daiyu bobbed her head quickly—*excitedly.* "Yes, I'd love to."

He chuckled softly. "I'm telling you, you'll grow accustomed to it eventually, and then it'll lose its shine. But right now, when you're so full of enthusiasm and thrill, I'd like to relish this moment, since it might not come again."

"And *I'm* telling you, that won't happen." She turned to the glittering capital once more. "I never want to grow bored of this view. I want to enjoy it every time I see it. No matter how many times I see it."

She could feel him staring at her again, and her blush continued to deepen.

The night carried his voice away and she almost didn't hear it when he murmured, "Me too."

36

Daiyu smoothed down her sapphire and plum-colored skirts, feeling all the stranger to be at the helm of the festival like this. She was at the roof of the palace, where a plethora of nobles milled about the heavily decorated rooftop venue with drinks and food and merriment all around them. At the center of the event was the large, scarlet lantern that was meant to be lit by the emperor's chosen person—for this year, Daiyu.

She had never felt so out of place than she did in that moment. Nothing felt real. She was the wife of the emperor, she was somehow a part of his court now, and she was most definitely not making a mistake—or so she hoped. A few months ago, she had been on her family's farm, harvesting from their garden, picking flowers to decorate along their windowsills, and helping milk her elderly neighbor's goats every morning. And now, she was somehow important enough to light the first lantern to kick off the rest of the lanterns that would be lit and flown throughout the empire.

And even though she should have felt like the most powerful woman in the room, she couldn't. Not when everyone else formed their own little circles, talking to one another and laugh-

ing, while she sat alone on the dais with Muyang to her right and
no one else to converse with. She felt like an accessory more than a
powerful empress.

It was just the beginning, she told herself.

But eventually, even Muyang intermingled with the crowd to
speak to some of the nobles. Likely imperative political things,
but it left her utterly alone and even more out of place.

"Lady Daiyu!"

She turned just in time to see Jia bowing politely a few feet
below the dais, an ever-cheery grin on her face.

"Lady Jia, a pleasure to see you," Daiyu said with forced
enthusiasm. She still wasn't used to all the people coming up to
her and greeting her, all of them appearing either suspiciously
excited to see her or obviously uninterested in her. She wasn't sure
which category Jia fell into—gossipy curiosity, genuine delight, or
a mixture of the two.

"You look beautiful. That dress really brings out your colors,"
Jia said with a wide-toothed grin. She gestured to the rest of the
event. "Would you like to walk around with me? It'll be a little
while until the lantern is lit, and you look like you could use a
little adventure around here."

"Oh? What do you mean?" Nonetheless, Daiyu descended
from the dais and allowed Jia to link their arms together as they
strolled along the rooftop venue. From the distance, she could
make out the scintillating and brightly lit capital all around them.
She could imagine all the common folk and city dwellers waiting
and watching the sky for the first lantern to emerge from the royal
palace, signaling them to release theirs. A lightheaded excitement
rushed over her at the thought of it.

"You looked like you want to explore," Jia answered with a
shrug.

It was a more polite way of saying she looked lonely, Daiyu
realized with a flush of embarrassment.

They passed by groups of noble women dressed in colorful

silks with their bejeweled hand fans covering half their faces as they giggled over their conversations. Daiyu could feel their stares boring holes into every inch of her body. Every titter and chuckle seemed to pierce her and she wondered if they were talking about her. Staring at her. Laughing at what they saw.

"Have you made any friends since coming back to the palace?"

Daiyu almost didn't hear the question past her own roaring thoughts. "Err, no," she said with an uncertain smile. "Other than when I went to see you and Lady Eu-Meh, I haven't met anyone else, unfortunately."

"Oh, really?" Jia steered them toward a table of sticky rice cakes and honeyed sweets. She took one of the small plates and plopped the sugary desserts into her mouth in one go. "I would have been bored out of my mind being in the palace with no social events or meetings to go to. Have you thought of inviting over nobles from within His Majesty's circle?"

Truthfully, Daiyu didn't even know that was an option. "I'm sure I can figure that out once I'm officially ..." The sentence hung in the air for a second. Until she was what? The empress? She was already married to Muyang, so how long would it take for her to be his empress?

"A part of this court?" Jia finished for her between licking her fingers. "You're already married to him, so I think that means you can do whatever you want!"

Daiyu chuckled, taking a small plate of a sticky rice cake. "This is all so very new to me, so I'm still figuring it all out."

"I think it'll be great for you to break out of your shell and meet lots of noblewomen. Everyone is so curious about you, the woman who charmed the emperor." She winked. "If you ever need any tips on who to invite and what to do, don't hesitate to ask me! I'd love to show you the ropes."

"That's very kind of you." Daiyu wasn't sure whether to feel grateful or suspicious. Although Jia came across as a cheerful and kind person, she couldn't shake off the feeling that maybe it was all a ruse to get Daiyu comfortable so she could gossip about her behind her back. And one thing Daiyu had learned over the years was that she couldn't blindly trust the first person who lent her a helping hand.

She eyed the rest of the nobles, whose voices mingled together with the hum of the music. Among the crowd, she spotted Wang Yanlin, who was dressed just as extravagantly as she had been on Daiyu's wedding day. With startling vermillion silk and gold, and swathes of rich purple, she looked dazzling and more like the empress than Daiyu did. A surge of bitter rage filled her and she pursed her lips together at the woman.

Jia followed her gaze and made a small noise in the back of her throat. "Ah. Wang Yanlin, huh? She sure likes to be the center of attention."

"Hm?" Daiyu's fake smile was back in place, this time a bit more strained than usual.

Jia jerked her chin in Yanlin's direction before chewing on another rice cake. "You probably feel uncomfortable around her. I've heard her talking all about you during her tea parties. It's obvious what she's trying to do."

"And what's that?" She didn't want to come off as fishing for answers, but she was desperate for more information on the viper-like woman, especially since she was proving to be a thorn in her side.

"Oh, you know." Jia clucked her tongue. "She wants to become His Majesty's concubine. Or his second wife. She's vying for the empress position. I did some digging, you know, after you visited me a few weeks ago. Apparently, she's been wanting to become the empress for years now. She really did think she'd marry him before anyone else. But then, well, you showed up."

Daiyu barely tasted the sweets as she chewed and swallowed. She couldn't rip her gaze away from Yanlin, who was batting her lashes and speaking to Commander Yao Bohai. Was she purpose-fully trying to get close to Muyang's inner circle? Bohai was probably one of his closest men—his right-hand man—so that was very much possible.

"Her dreams and ego were crushed, but I'm sure that's not going to stop her," Jia said with a sigh. "What do you plan to do with her? With how her personality is, I doubt she'd want to befriend you and become sister-wives."

"I'm still figuring it out," she said vaguely.

"I'm sure it's only a matter of time," Jia said with another sigh.

Until Muyang marries her too.

The unsaid words sent a razor-sharp stab through her heart and she gripped the small ceramic plate so tightly she was sure it was about to crack. She had accepted the reality that Muyang would marry plenty of women after her, but the thought alone sent a nauseating wave of weakness over her.

She knew the reality. She knew it, had accepted it. But—

She abhorred the mere thought of it.

Her blood raged at the thought. At the images her brain formed of Muyang in bed with other women. At the future where he would have dozens of women flocking him, all of them carrying his children. And she especially hated the idea of Yanlin by his side.

Daiyu breathed out shakily, hating the fire that coursed through her veins and made her limbs tremble. Her stomach clenched together and she reminded herself of what she had promised herself—that she wouldn't fall for Muyang. That she wouldn't love him. For this exact reason. To protect herself from when he would take other women.

And as much as she wanted to follow that line of thinking, an uncontrollable fury and fear filled her at the thought of it.

She scanned the crowds for Muyang and breathed a sigh of relief when she spotted him, bedecked in his dark robes and gleaming gold hair crown, speaking to Atreus and General Fang. His expression was as shuttered as usual, and there was nothing about him that told her his eyes were straying to the fawning women that always seemed to be inching closer to him. Even without the fact that he was the emperor, he stood out among the crowd. Power and menacing magic seemed to radiate from him, and he appeared like a darkly clad general rather than the emperor.

Daiyu's heart nearly skipped a beat. She could remember all the ways his hands had traveled over her body and how she had felt so safe and secure in his strong, lean arms. She was reminded of their passion together, of how important he made her feel. So unlike all these other people who stared at her like she didn't belong.

Setting aside her now-empty plate on one of the side tables, Daiyu excused herself and wove through the crowds toward him. She needed to talk to him again, to feel reassurance that he was hers, and that she was his, and that all these worries buzzing around her head were just that—worries. Nothing more, nothing less.

Muyang spotted her almost immediately. His black eyes seemed to light up with something that appeared too feral, too animated, and all too much like the man she had been with last night. She could already feel a blush starting to claw up her throat as she stepped closer.

He pulled himself away from his circle and approached her just as she did him. Before she could even utter a word, he placed a hand on her hip and leaned closer, his lips brushing against the top of her ear.

"You look utterly ravishing," he murmured, sending a ripple of electric desire through her flesh.

Daiyu cleared her throat. "And you look utterly bored."

"Do I? It must be because you're not by my side."

"Funny you say that, considering *you're* the one who left *my* side." She smiled up at him, the chaos in her heart seeming to calm down at his nearness. It was only when she was around him that she stopped feeling all the terrible, terrible things that came with being the first wife of the emperor. She didn't have to think about the future too much when he was standing in front of her, showing her he cared for her.

Muyang grasped her hand, turned it around, and kissed the palm of it gently. The temperature dropped and she shivered at the suddenly brusque autumn air. "Forgive me for leaving you," he said quietly, his voice carrying a tone of mischief. "Maybe I should make it up for you later tonight?"

"Perhaps." Daiyu lifted her shoulders, aware that some of the nobles were shooting glances their way. She wondered if it was strange for them to see their usually callous and unbothered emperor kissing her hands so naturally, or showing small gestures of affection.

She certainly found it strange and would have found it stranger months ago, when all she had thought of Muyang was that of a coldhearted, horrible murderer.

"Lady Daiyu." Atreus came to stand by Muyang and tipped his head down in her direction in the way of a polite greeting. He was clad in his usual black and red uniform, his hand resting casually on the hilt of his sword. "I hope you're enjoying the festival."

"More or less," she said with a small laugh.

"More or less?" Muyang raised an eyebrow. "I thought you were enjoying yourself."

"Well, I certainly am, but I didn't realize how exhausting it could all be. There were just so many events we need to attend, so many feasts, so many people to greet ... I suppose it's not as easy as just enjoying ourselves, if you know what I mean?"

"Already tired of the political side of things, hm?"

"Maybe a little," she joked. Truthfully, she didn't like the social aspect of being Muyang's wife, especially since she was still figuring out royal etiquette and what to say around the nobles. She hoped that with time, she'd become better at interacting with people and that one day, she might not feel like such an outcast.

"Is Vita taking a break?" Atreus asked, sending a sweeping glance at their surroundings. "I don't see her around."

"When Daiyu is with me, Vita doesn't need to be here," Muyang answered sharply as if it was obvious.

"Ah, of course, Your Majesty. I didn't mean to insinuate—" Atreus started, straightening.

"I have enough power to protect what's mine."

"Certainly."

Daiyu clasped her hands together. "I think it's good for Vita to have a break anyway. She should be able to enjoy this festival just like everyone else."

"We don't usually partake in the festivities much," Atreus said with a shrug. He stared off at the lights in the capital that looked like a cluster of burning stars. "Festivals are prefect times for insurgencies."

Muyang placed a hand on the younger man's shoulder. "No need to scare her. There will likely be no insurgencies tonight, Daiyu. Not while my men work."

Daiyu looked between the two of them, then at the nobles milling about the rooftop, and lastly at the glitzing capital sprawling in the horizon. Was it possible that the rebel forces had infiltrated the city and were making plans as they spoke? Or that there were enemies within the palace right now? The thought made her uneasy and she was suddenly reminded of this aspect of royal life that she had surrendered herself to when she had married Muyang—the uncertainty. The possibility of Muyang's dynasty collapsing and her life being changed to collateral damage.

A shiver rattled her spine and sent goose bumps down her flesh. There had even been that attack in the gardens a few weeks ago when she had been having tea with the princesses. She had chalked that up to being Yanlin's work, but what if it was actually the rebel cause? Did they really think she was useful enough to be used against Muyang? A new sense of fear took hold of her and she had to remind herself that she was safe here with Muyang, with the *Peccata* watching her, and with Feiyu acting as the head mage.

She snapped back to reality when Muyang touched her lower back. "I'll be right back. I have to make the announcement soon."

"Oh! Sure." She waved him back while he made his way through the parting crowds. Another layer of anxiousness brewed in the pit of her stomach—this time completely different. It was almost time for her to light the lantern. Her hands suddenly grew clammy and she rehearsed her steps in her head: take one step at a time, one foot over the other, make it to the lantern, smile, light the lantern, and send it off to the night sky.

That was it.

And above all, *don't trip.*

This was going to be her first real step in becoming the empress. For getting acknowledgment from everyone that she was Muyang's favored woman. That she was his, period. It should have been enough that she was married to him, but considering how his reputation was so drenched in blood, it was no wonder that people thought she was replaceable. But at least this was one thing she could do to help her position. To make her seem more like the wife of the emperor.

"Are you all right?" Atreus asked. "You look a little pale."

"I'm fine." She plastered a smile on her face and tried to tamp down the clawing nerves rattling her being. She couldn't make a fool of herself today. Not when practically the entire empire— well, the capital, to be exact—was waiting with bated breath. She could imagine herself making a mistake and rumors spreading from these very nobles to their servants, and those rumors tumbling down to the servants in the palace, and from the servants to the common folk, and the common folk to the farmers —until the entire empire knew she had made a mistake.

She wrung her sweaty hands together and resisted the urge to wipe her palms across her skirt—the last thing she wanted was for someone to notice any stains on her. Though she was sure she was sweating buckets at this point, despite the chill of the night.

A hushed silence fell over the crowd when Muyang reached the giant lantern. It bobbed in the wind, secured by a rope

MAHAM FATEMI

anchored to the floor. It was just a few inches shorter than Muyang, which was impressive in and of itself.

"Good evening, my loyal court," Muyang announced, and everyone quieted even further, an excited buzz in the air. "As we enjoy ourselves during the last evening of this glorious Autumn Festival, let us remember that this is the beginning of a new era. Come next year, all the rebels will have been defeated. All of those who oppose the Drakkon dynasty will be ashes at our feet. Here's to many more prosperous years."

People nodded and hummed their approval while Muyang scanned the room, his black eyes narrowed as if waiting for someone to say otherwise. Daiyu shifted from one foot to another. Was she supposed to go up to him now? Or was she supposed to wait for him to call out for her? She turned to Atreus to ask him just that, but he was too focused on Muyang. She tapped her foot on the floor. Should she just go?

Finally, Muyang held his hand out. "It's time."

Daiyu took a step forward, but Atreus grabbed her bicep before she could take another step forward. Confusion marred her as she turned to the young man. "What?"

Atreus raised his eyebrows and whispered, "What are you doing?"

"What?" She couldn't hide the annoyance from her voice. She turned to Muyang with what she hoped was an apologetic smile, but whatever words she had planned remained stuck in her throat.

Time slowed as Muyang had his hand held out. Except, it wasn't Daiyu he was waiting for. In fact, he wasn't even looking in her direction. The crowd parted for Wang Yanlin, who strolled forward with her head held high, a pleasant smile lighting her face, and all the grace of a woman who was born to be there.

Daiyu felt like someone had punched her in the gut. All the air seemed to vanish from her lungs as Yanlin nestled her tiny hand in Muyang's. She looked over at the waves of people until her sharp gaze settled on Daiyu. She seemed to lock onto her and Daiyu realized with growing nausea that this was part of her plan all along. Victory seemed to gleam in her rich, brown eyes. Another viper-like smile lifted her thin lips.

Daiyu could feel the glances sent her way. Her body trembled, but not from the cold. She wanted to throw up, she wanted to pass out, she wanted to fall to the floor. Her knees were weak, her stomach empty. The sea of faces seemed to blur together into a singular laughing face.

She blinked, not sure what was happening.

Muyang had chosen ... *Yanlin* to light the lantern.

Not her.

But that couldn't be, she told herself, swaying on her feet. She was married to Muyang. She was his wife. He had told her that she was his, and that he was hers. He had shown her such love and adoration. And yet he had chosen *her*—Yanlin.

More people seemed to turn to her, and she realized with a sinking feeling that she was gaping at the two of them, all the color draining from her face. She probably looked absolutely horrified. She was sure they would gossip about it to everyone. But in that moment, she didn't care.

A giggle came from her left and she turned sharply to find a group of noblewomen snickering at her from behind their hand fans. They all leaned in closer together and began whispering, all the while sniggering and chuckling in her direction.

Daiyu's stomach clenched tighter and she turned back to the spectacle.

Muyang passed Yanlin a candle, a strong fire burning on the wick. Yanlin said something to him, but they were too far for Daiyu to make out what was being said. All she could do was watch in stunned horror as Yanlin lit the lantern, Muyang cut the rope, and the lantern buoyed in the air.

An eruption of cheers filled the rooftop as the lantern went up and up into the night sky. And soon, in the distance, she could make out the thousands of other smaller lanterns lighting up the horizon.

Daiyu's whole world seemed to be tipping on its axis.

He chose Yanlin.

She felt downright sick to her stomach. Her legs were jelly, her mouth too dry to even swallow.

He chose Yanlin.

Everyone continued to cheer and the more she looked around herself, the more she didn't recognize any of the people. They seemed to be staring at her, laughing at her, and yet she couldn't decipher who any of these people were. All she knew was that she was the outcast. The laughingstock of the party.

The naïve, naïve farm girl who had thought the wicked emperor loved her.

"Lady Daiyu?" Atreus touched her arm. He had probably been calling out to her, but she couldn't hear what he was saying. His mouth was moving, but she couldn't figure out the words. It was like a filter had been placed around her ears, making her deaf to everything but the laughter.

At the center of the rooftop, Muyang watched the lantern with a satisfied look, and Yanlin appeared even happier, her beautiful face alight with emotions. They looked ... good together, Daiyu realized, her queasiness growing. Like they belonged to one another. Like they were meant to be standing there, both of them uncaring about the sea of people who watched them. So unlike her, who was unused to this all.

Muyang's sweeping glance halted on her and the small smile on his soft mouth faded at the sight of her.

"I-I need to go," she whispered, unable to control the writhing betrayal wrangling her heart.

She spun around and headed toward the exit, not caring that she pushed past a few drunk nobles in the process. Her head was spinning and pounding, her hands quivering and her face feeling too hot.

This can't be happening.

She shoved her way out of the rooftop and into the stairwell. The palace guards were saying something to her, but she didn't hear them. She kept pushing her way down the stairs. She stumbled a few times, her clammy hands grasping onto the handrail.

Why had he chosen Yanlin? Was it because she was a noble? Did he think Daiyu couldn't have done the same? Or was he secretly like the rest of the nobles, all of whom were waiting for Daiyu to fail? Or ...

She inhaled sharply when she emerged into one of the hallways. The servants moved away from her, their own expressions stricken when they met her gaze. She probably looked just as crazy and frazzled as she felt.

Did Muyang marry her only to satiate his lust for her? His desire to have a poor, naïve woman by his side? Was Yanlin the one he was actually planning on making his empress? She was better than Daiyu in every way—she was exquisitely beautiful, she came from a wealthy, influential family, she had years of education, and she had been bred for this position. She was the perfect woman for the emperor.

Muyang had said he wanted to make Daiyu the empress, but she could see now that he was *lying*.

He had said all those pretty nothings to her so that she could love him.

So that she could happily spend the night with him.

So that ... she could fall in love easily.

"*Daiyu!*"

A million razored edges tore through her flesh at the sound of his frantic voice. She didn't turn around, only hurried her own steps. Tears—of betrayal, of rage, of heartbreak—burned the backs of her eyes.

"*Liar,*" she whispered, her voice coming out strangled.

"Daiyu!"

She hated him in that very moment. Hated that she was so, so stupid to fall for his tricks. That she had let him make a fool of herself up there. They were all laughing at her, laughing at how stupid the farm girl was to think that she had the evil emperor wrapped around her finger. She should have known her place in this palace. She shouldn't have expected to be more than a bed warmer.

Daiyu had known this was a possibility—that she would be tossed aside for someone better. But she hadn't realized how much it would sting. How painful it would be. How much she wanted to throw herself to the floor and scream at the heavens for how horrible she felt. She hadn't expected her heart to break into thousands of shards that continued to stab at her chest with every breath.

"Daiyu!" Muyang grabbed her by the arm. "What—"

She ripped her arm away from his grasp and spun around to face him. If she weren't shaking so much from rage, she would have even laughed at the shocked expression on his wickedly beautiful face. "Don't touch me!" she nearly shouted, the hallways appearing to shrink. "Don't you *dare* touch me."

He blinked. "Daiyu, what's wrong?"

"What's wrong?" This time, she did laugh, low and sharp. "You don't know? You *really* don't know?"

"Daiyu—"

"You made a fool of me today, Muyang!" Her fingers flexed and she had the urge to run her nails across his pretty face. To watch him bleed, and even then, he would only feel a fraction of the pain he had inflicted on her. "How could you do this to me? You humiliated me in front of the entire empire!"

"I didn't humiliate you." He sounded genuinely surprised, and that lit up her fury even more. Made her want to burn him on the spot like the burning lanterns. "I had already promised Lord Wang months ago—"

"Don't tell me that the lantern lighting isn't a big deal out here!" Daiyu screamed, not caring that the servants were hanging around in the background. She didn't care if the whole empire heard her shout and cry. It didn't matter, anyway, since they would all know by tomorrow. "I already have to prove myself as more than just a simple, stupid farm girl, and now you've made it infinitely harder for me to be anything more than ... more than just that! Everyone is already laughing at the fact that you chose me! That you even married me! You should have just—" A strangled sob escaped from her throat. She didn't even know what she was saying anymore. Her mind was too frazzled, too hurt, to think of anything. "*Oh.* I hate you. I hate you so much!"

"Daiyu—"

"You *humiliated* me!" Daiyu shook her head at him, hating the tears that blurred her vision. Hating that she was even standing here, yelling at him. "If you were going to make her your favored woman, why didn't you marry her instead of dragging me into your court? Into your palace? Why did you put me in this position? So you could laugh at me like the rest of everyone?"

"I didn't realize this was so important to you—"

"You didn't *realize?*" Her hands trembled and she clenched them into fists. She was nothing more than a simple commoner to him, she realized with mounting horror. She was never supposed to be anything more than that. She was the stupid one for thinking that she could be his wife. His empress. "You ... You lied to me."

Muyang reached out as if to touch her, but she slapped his hand away.

"Stay away from me!" Her voice grew shrill and she backed away from him. "Don't you dare touch me!"

"Daiyu—"

"You humiliated me!" She felt like she was screaming at a brick wall. The words didn't seem to sink into him and he kept staring at her like he was waiting for her to implode. And maybe that's exactly what she was doing. "You want her, don't you? You're planning on marrying that bitch, aren't you?"

"What are you—"

"Don't play dumb," she hissed through the burning tears. "You're going to marry Wang Yanlin, aren't you? You're going to make her your empress and I'll be pushed down the lines of concubines until I'm forgotten. Do you think I'm truly that stupid that I don't realize how court life works? I was so, so very stupid to think I had a chance at happiness with you. That I had a chance to become something more than just a—"

"Daiyu, I'm not—"

"You're not *listening* to me!" She jabbed a finger into his chest. "You're not listening, Muyang! I know what you're planning on doing. Don't you see? I get it now. I get it! You never intended to make me anything more than just your bed warmer. You were planning on marrying her all along, weren't you? I knew that, I knew it!"

And yet she hadn't expected it to hurt so bad. She hadn't expected the sharp pain that made her want to scream, and scream, and scream.

Of course he was going to be with other women. She had expected it. Everyone knew it was going to happen.

But she couldn't accept it. Now that it was becoming a reality, she *couldn't*.

"You—" Whatever words she was going to say died on her lips when she spotted Yanlin marching down the hallway toward them, a glowing, venomous grin on her face. Daiyu saw red, red, and *red*. Her nostrils flared and all the rage seemed to build up in that moment. She wanted to strangle the woman. How dare she?

She had poisoned Daiyu. Had kidnapped her. Burned her family's rice paddies. Tried to assassinate her. And now she had humiliated her in front of the entire empire.

All the while, she *grinned*.

"You can't speak to His Majesty that way," Yanlin said in a singsong voice, her smile growing wider as she took in Daiyu's appearance. "You should know that already. He can have you thrown in the dungeons for that, or even executed."

She stopped until she was in front of them both. She bowed to Muyang, who stood rigid with an expressionless look on his face, and then she turned to Daiyu. "You really should stop making such a scene—"

Daiyu slapped her.

Yanlin's head whipped to the side, her painted lips forming a perfect O.

Her hand stung, but she couldn't even relish the satisfaction of smacking the evil woman. Not when her emotions were all over the place. Not when she wanted to strangle her pretty little neck. "You *bitch*," Daiyu seethed, "you've been planning this all along, haven't you? To show the entire empire how important you are and to secure your own position within the emperor's court. Well, there you have it! You've won!" She shoved the sputtering woman against Muyang, who barely caught her by the shoulders. "You both deserve one another! You're both nobles who know how this world works!"

She whirled on her feet, grabbed her skirts, and sprinted down the hallway. She didn't want to give them the satisfaction of watching her burst into tears. She was already having a meltdown, she knew, and she was already making a bigger fool of herself. Everyone would be talking about her tomorrow. About how the emperor's new wife was left stranded during the lantern lighting and how the beautiful Wang Yanlin would marry the emperor soon.

"Daiyu!" Muyang called out for her, but she ignored him, continuing to run down the hall.

She yanked open one of the doors to an empty room and slammed it shut behind her. She locked it immediately, even as Muyang rattled against the doorknob and pounded his fists against it. She fell to the floor, her sobs breaking through her chest. She heaved in large gulps of air, hating how horrible she felt. Hating that she was even here in the first place. Hating that he could hear her strangled sobs.

"Feiyu! Please, I *need* you."

In seconds, his boots appeared in front of her. She sobbed softly, her body wracking with pain. He didn't say anything and it wasn't until he kneeled and touched her shoulder gently that she raised her head to meet his dark, dark gaze. He was wearing a sapphire dragon mask today, matching her own dress.

The door rattled with every punch Muyang threw at it, but for whatever reason, it didn't cave in. Not even when she sensed the heaviness of his magic behind her. It practically seeped through the cracks, but there seemed to be a barrier barring him and his magic from entering.

"Feiyu, please," she whispered, her voice broken, "please take me away from here."

He silently brushed a tear away, their surroundings already blurring away.

"As you wish."

37

DAIYU COULDN'T STOP CRYING UNCONTROLLABLY. THE torrent of tears just wouldn't stop, even when they were warped outside, the night chilling her down to her bones. It lashed against her and ripped her hair from its intricate updo that had taken the servants forever to do. Feiyu didn't say a word the whole time; he only stood there a few feet from her, watching her.

"You probably think I'm a fool." Daiyu fell to her knees, her face buried in her hands, and her tears streaming down her cheeks and puddling onto her palms. "A stupid, stupid fool."

The wind howled above her again, drying her cheeks and stinging her eyes. Feiyu didn't move, his long, midnight hair streaming behind him with every powerful gust.

"Daiyu, what happened?" he asked quietly, his voice almost lost to the night.

Her throat tightened. The humiliation she had felt just moments ago reared its head again, making her want to fall into fits of tears once more. She could still see the throngs of people staring at her, laughing as she stood there, awestruck and completely blindsided when Muyang had chosen Yanlin to light the lantern. She could imagine the whispers and gossips that would come to light by the morning. Her stomach clenched together again.

She squeezed her eyes shut as if that was enough to eliminate the images from her mind. As if it was enough to make her forget Yanlin's cruel smile when she placed her hand in Muyang's.

"He embarrassed me in front of everyone." Her voice cracked and she raised her chin to stare at Feiyu. The trees swayed all around him, their limber, long branches appearing like black tendrils in the night. She could make out the lights of the capital far, far in the distance. "He chose her, Wang Yanlin, to light the lantern for the Autumn Festival. It should have been *me*. And now everyone believes *she's* the rightful empress."

"Daiyu ..."

"I hate them all!" She grasped the ends of her hairpins and tore them from her hair. She tossed them on the ground at his feet and continued ripping the rest of the jewelry from her hair. Her chest heaved with every strangled sob. "I was never going to fit in with the rest of everyone! I was never going to be a proper empress! He told me that he would make me his empress, so why would he betray me like that? Why would he choose *her*, of all people?! Did he really care so little for me that he would humiliate me in such a manner? Do you know what the people looked like when they realized he chose Yanlin?" Daiyu angrily tossed the last of her gold hairpin. It bounced against the rocks and pebbles and disappeared into a thicket of weeds. "They laughed at me."

Her hair whipped around her face, some strands sticking against her damp cheeks. She wiped her face vigorously before sinking down to her knees again. When she was too tired of crying and screaming, she finally succumbed to the numbing cold. It dried her face and froze every ounce of rage within her until she was an empty shell of nothing.

Feiyu tilted his head and the dragon-mask looked even more frightening here, with the night canopying them and the rough, mountainous terrain. "Do you want to talk about it?"

Daiyu's lower lip trembled. "No."

"All right." He dropped down a foot away from her into a sitting position. "Then I'll just wait until you're ready to go back."

"I don't want to go back." She curled into a ball and tucked her chin against her knees. "I don't want to go there and have everyone laugh at me again. They think I'm nothing more than a farm girl. Someone who doesn't belong. I can tell they're all laughing at me every time they see me."

"Is that what they told you?"

"No, but I have eyes and ears and I'm not dumb." More tears threatened to spill and she blinked them away. "Do you know that even the servants don't treat me like a proper lady? They never talk to me, they look at me coldly, and they act as if everything I ask of them is a nuisance. Like ... like they're attending to someone who's supposed to be working with them."

"Ah, is that so?"

"Yes. It is." She frowned. "You must know what I'm talking about. I'm not crazy and it's not all in my head."

"I believe you. I know what it's like to not belong." His voice carried a soft, sad tune that she turned her head toward almost immediately. He was staring at the horizon. "I know what it's like to have people whisper behind your back. To have everyone think you're beneath them. To be abused. To be ... treated like you're less than."

"Feiyu ..." She thought back to the serpent and moon mark she had seen on his forearm, but she couldn't find the words to ask him what it meant. What it must have been like to grow up as a royal and to have everything ripped from him when Muyang took the throne.

So she instead followed his gaze. They were on the mountains, she realized a second later. The city lights were just as bright as they were when she was on the palace rooftop, but they twinkled in a way that reminded her of a dying star, slowly fading as some people retired for the night.

"Where are we?" she whispered.

"The mountains outside the capital. I like to come here when I want to clear my thoughts."

"Oh."

"It's quite beautiful when it's daylight." He glanced over at the shrubs and trees and boulders, all of which appeared like shadowy blobs in the darkness. "Especially in the early morning, you can hear the birds singing to one another and the gurgling of the nearby stream. The trees sway and creak, the leaves rustle, and the animals scurry ... it's beautiful and quiet, and it helps me think."

Daiyu watched him from the corner of her eye. "It's probably hard to think in silence at the palace. There's so much hustle and bustle there."

"Yes, and there are so many distractions."

"I like it here too."

She could have sworn he was smiling from behind his mask. "Yes ... I thought you would."

They were both quiet for a long time after that. The only sound between them was the *whoosh* of the wind and the wavering of the trees. Daiyu closed her eyes and wanted to disappear into the darkness of the night. To forget about all the pain and humiliation.

"I'll never be a proper empress," she finally said, refusing to meet his gaze. "I knew what it meant to be the wife of the emperor when I married him, but I thought I could handle it. I thought I could handle the idea of him being with multiple women. With him having dozens of kids with other women. With him gallivanting around with beautiful women who are so much better than me in every way. But the instant I saw him with Yanlin and when I realized he had chosen her to do the lantern lighting, it's like ... something snapped inside me. I don't want to be a second, third, or fourth choice. I don't even want to be the first choice if it means he'll have a dozen more after me. I want it to just be me and him, and I know that will never happen." Tears welled up in her eyes and rolled down her cheeks.

She didn't try to stop them. "I had no idea it would hurt this much."

She knew what it meant when she married him. She had thought she had grappled with the idea of it and accepted it, but she hadn't. And she felt more pathetic and miserable because of it.

"I don't want to be here anymore, Feiyu." Daiyu was suddenly tired—so very tired. "I want to go home. This is all too much for me."

"Daiyu ..."

"I'm not strong enough to be there." She rubbed her face with her arm. "I don't want to face him again. I don't want to see him with her or with someone else."

She could feel Feiyu staring at her, but she kept her eyes averted. She couldn't bear to see the disappointment she was sure was there. He probably thought she was so weak-hearted. So easily breakable and foolish. It wasn't like she had run into this marriage without knowing what it meant, and yet at the first sign of Muyang being interested in someone else, she cracked.

Daiyu breathed out shakily. "I want to go home. Do you think you can do that for me? Take me away from here?"

"Maybe you're not cut out for the royal life."

Even though it was something she had come to the conclusion to, hearing him say it out loud sent a painful pang through her heart. She swallowed down the bitterness clawing up her constricted throat.

"Maybe it's better for you to go back to your farm life," he said quietly. "Where life is easier."

She didn't trust herself to speak. Maybe she was cursed to never love anyone, or be loved by anyone. She should have realized it when Heng died on the battlefield. She wasn't meant to be with anyone. She was supposed to grow old alone.

"Will you take me back?"

"What will you do about the emperor?"

"I don't know." Her voice was barely above a whisper. "We'll just pack up our things and leave."

"Do you really want to do that?"

She pursed her lips together. There were so many things she wanted, but that didn't mean they were meant to be. All she knew was that she couldn't go back to the palace. She didn't want to see Muyang again. She didn't want to face Yanlin and the other nobles. She didn't want to repeat the humiliation she had felt tonight.

"Yes, I want to go home."

He stretched his hand out to her. "Then let's go."

Daiyu didn't hesitate to rest her fingers into his. His hand curled into hers and all at once, their mountainous surroundings distorted and twisted. In a split second, the chilling winds from the mountains disappeared, replaced by a gentle breeze. Daiyu gasped and blinked; they were suddenly in a field of flowers. She knew where they were immediately. She could have recognized it by the smell alone.

Even in the night, she could make out the tree Heng had carved their names into. She had played in these fields countless times as a child, but it was only now, when she was sitting here with Feiyu that she felt more in tune with her nostalgic childhood haven.

She was finally home.

Daiyu clambered to her feet, spinning around to take in the flower fields before she turned to Feiyu. "How did you know about this place?"

"You showed it to me once. Remember? In your dreams."

"Oh. Right." If she were in a better mood, she would have talked to him more, told him stories about how she used to play here with her siblings, or told him about Heng. But she was drained of all emotions. She was nothing more than a numb shell.

"Daiyu—" A startled gasp escaped from Feiyu and he fell down to one knee. He clutched the front of his chest, the mask nearly falling off his face in the process. Daiyu lurched forward, her hand flying to his shoulder to help steady him.

"What's wrong?"

"It's—" He breathed out shakily and gently eased her away. "Nothing. It's nothing."

"But, Feiyu, are you sure?"

His breathing was still shallow when he straightened. "I'm fine. Just ... go home, Daiyu."

She didn't want to leave him, not when he sounded like he was in so much pain, but there was a warning in his tone that frightened her. She backed away from him, torn between running back home and staying with her friend.

"Daiyu, I'm fine." Feiyu stepped away from her. "Go home. Please."

"I don't want to leave you—"

"You must." He waved her off and the lighthearted nature of his tone eased some of her discomfort. "I'm fine, Daiyu. I'm the head mage of the empire, remember? I was just surprised about something. Nothing more, nothing less. Now stop worrying and scurry back home."

Daiyu hesitated.

"I have to go back to the palace. If I'm gone for too long, people will grow suspicious. So go, Daiyu."

She finally nodded and began walking down the path that led to her home, albeit slowly. He watched her the entire time, and it wasn't until she was a dozen feet away from him that she whirled around to face him again.

"Thank you for being my friend in the palace, Feiyu." Her words pierced through the silence, carrying over to the swaying fields of flowers. "I wouldn't have survived without you. Thank you for everything."

He only nodded. And not for the first time, she wanted to tear that mask away to reveal his true emotions, to see what he was hiding from the world. She balled her hands together, her chest squeezing painfully. She would miss him, she realized. He was perhaps the only true friend she had made there.

"We had a bargain," she said. "You wanted something from

me in exchange for helping me, remember? Well, tell me what you want and I'll try to help."

"There's only one thing I've only ever wanted from you, Daiyu."

She waited for him to speak, but he didn't. He only watched her. The tall grass oscillated against his feet, the flowers and weeds joining in the dance and buoying with the gentle breeze. His mask looked black in the night.

Finally, he murmured, "I just want you to be happy. Do that for me, all right?"

She blinked.

Why did he sound so ... sad? So quiet? "Feiyu?"

"Goodbye, Daiyu."

She stepped forward, her hand stretching out like she could cross the distance between them in a split second, when his form rapidly changed in the blink of an eye. One second, he was a man, and the next, the mask flew off his face and scales erupted over his body. Powerful wind blew against her, ripping her hair behind her and sending her skirts billowing against her trembling legs. She stumbled back, mouth agape, as a giant white dragon stood a few feet away from her. He glimmered silver in the moonlight, his iridescent scales appearing like shimmering water.

He was ... beautiful. Like nothing she had seen before.

His eyes were two large pools of midnight, and he was staring at her.

"F-Feiyu?" she whispered.

The dragon stretched out his long neck and massive, leathery wings. He stepped closer to her, his face inches away from her. His hot breath steamed over her face and he continued to stare at her as if waiting for her to do something. Daiyu placed a hand against the side of his colossal face. The scales were smooth and slippery. He closed his eyes, a sigh seeming to escape from the gaps of his sharp, pearl-like teeth.

He backed away suddenly, his large wings flapping and sending her nearly flying backward. Without another sound, he soared up into the sky, his tail whipping behind him in a stream of silver light.

"Feiyu! *Feiyu!*" Daiyu's words seemed to fall on deaf ears as the dragon rose higher and higher, disappearing into the night sky.

Tears filled her eyes again.

"Goodbye, Feiyu."

38

When Daiyu stumbled home that night, nobody questioned why she was there or what had happened. They even seemed to believe her pathetic lie that she just came to visit. Nobody batted an eyelash at her red and swollen eyes, her unkept hair, or her messy dress. They didn't even say anything a week later, when she continued living home as if nothing had happened. She didn't have the gall to tell them what had actually happened and news of her embarrassment hadn't reached the village yet.

Even though she was home and back into the rhythm of things—milk the goats next door, take out the chickens' eggs from the broken coop, harvest vegetables from their garden for breakfast, visit the partially destroyed rice paddies in the afternoon—she was numb down to her core. This was what she had wanted all along. To be back home. To wear her scratchy, worn dresses. To slip into her dried-grass sandals and walk through the village. To eat dinner with her family.

But she felt empty. Like someone had scooped out everything that made her who she was and tossed it aside. She was just falling into the motion of things but not really thinking.

And it was made worse when, after eight days of being back on the farm, Muyang's men never came for her. She had thought Muyang would drag her back to the palace and punish her for fleeing from him again, but nothing happened.

She was already forgotten, it seemed.

On the eighth day, when she was kneeling on the ground in their home garden, with the barely repaired bamboo fence stretching above her, and her hands buried deep in the soil as she rummaged for beets, Lanfen finally spoke up.

"What happened?" her younger sister asked from beside her. She had her own grass-woven basket on the ground next to Daiyu's, but hers was filled with sweet potatoes instead of beets. "Everyone's worried about you, but you won't say anything."

"Nothing happened." She pulled out a cluster of beets with dried dirt clumped at the spindly roots.

"*Really?*" Lanfen stared at her in disbelief. "Then why are you home? Aren't you supposed to be in the palace?"

"I told you, I'm visiting—"

"Daiyu, tell me the truth."

"Lanfen—"

"I know you're lying. You've got everyone worried."

Daiyu placed the beets in the basket and busied her hands by digging through the dirt once more. Guilt formed in the pit of her stomach. She had married Muyang for her family's sake, and now she was forsaking them again, all because she had made a rash decision to leave. It was for the best, she had told herself, but at the same time ... all of their hopes of wealth and status would be dashed once she revealed the truth.

How was she going to tell them all that Muyang had humiliated her in front of the entire empire and instead of bearing with it, she had escaped back home and nobody had even come back to fetch her? How was she going to tell them that she was actually unimportant to Muyang? That she had naïvely thought she could handle being his wife?

Was it better to leave this village? For them to pack their bags and make a run for it? Even though Muyang's men hadn't come back for her?

"Daiyu?" Lanfen touched her hand, forcing her back to reality. Her sister's kind, soft-brown eyes seemed to plead with her as she scanned her face. "What happened? Really?"

Her throat tightened. "Nothing—"

"*Daiyu.*"

"Okay, *fine.*" She plopped another beet into the basket, this one smaller than the rest. Her voice wobbled and she wiped the dirt from her shaky hands. "On the last day of the festival, Muyang chose Wang Yanlin to light the lantern instead of me. You know what the lantern lighting symbolizes, don't you? Whoever lights the first lantern is the emperor's favored woman, or favored family, and it shows how important she is to the whole empire. Instead of choosing his new bride to do it, he chose the woman who ruined everything for me!"

Lanfen's brows pulled together. "Oh."

"Everyone was laughing at me." Her cheeks warmed as the memory of the noblewomen snickering behind their hand fans resurfaced. She wanted to duck her head into the coil, silty soil and forget about it all. "They don't think I'm meant to be the empress. And why should I be? What qualifications do I have? I don't know how to read, or write, or recite poetry. I wasn't born into a wealthy, influential family. I don't have any connections. I don't know any social etiquette. I'm just ... just Yin Daiyu."

"Oh, Daiyu, I'm so sorry." Unshed tears glistened in her eyes.

"Why are you crying?" Daiyu laughed softly, though her own eyes stung. "It's over now. I'm back here and ... and it seems like I'm forgotten anyway."

Lanfen quickly wiped her face. "So what happened afterward? Did the mage bring you here?"

"He did."

"And ... well, did you talk to His Majesty?"

"About what?"

Lanfen gave her a strange look. She lowered the lumpy sweet potato into her own basket. "Well, about what happened at the festival. Did you talk to him about it? What did he say?"

She tried to recall their conversation, but she could only remember her vivid rage and her screams. Nothing else computed in her mind. "We ... sort of talked."

"What do you mean by that?"

"I yelled, mostly."

"And?"

"And *what*?" Daiyu was beginning to grow frustrated. Didn't Lanfen understand the magnitude of the situation? Or how horrible Muyang was for choosing Yanlin instead of Daiyu to light the lantern?

Her sister crossed her arms over her chest and lifted a delicate brow. "Please don't tell me that you didn't even hear his side of the story? Did you even give him a chance to apologize? Or to ... I don't know, maybe understand the situation a little bit?"

"There's nothing more to talk about—"

"Daiyu! *Really*?"

"Lanfen, stop that!" Daiyu angrily wiped her dirt-stained hands against her skirts and pointed an accusatory finger her way. "I did everything I could in that palace. I would have never made a good empress, and you know it. Nobody wanted me there anyway, and there's no way I can handle being his wife in the first place. I don't want him to marry hundreds of women and for me to be forgotten within the folds of them all. I don't want to be stuck in the Lotus wing with the whole lot of them! You saw what it was like! You know how terrible they are."

She was being mean and she knew it, but her heart was aching and she didn't like how Lanfen didn't seem to understand what she was saying. She wanted to continue to wallow in her self-pity, not think about what she should have said or done.

"Daiyu, I know they're terrible people. The women at the

palace were mean to me too, and they were mean to all the women who were commoners like us, and I'm really grateful for you helping me get out of there—but that doesn't change the fact that you didn't ... you didn't discuss any of this with His Majesty. You just ... ran. Like you always do."

She flinched back like she had been slapped. "A-Are you serious?" Her voice wavered and cracked with mortification. A surge of anger filled her tone. "I married him for you, for all of you! And this ... this is how I'm treated when I want to go back home? When things don't work out in my marriage?"

Lanfen reeled back. "You did this for *us*?"

"Why else would I marry him?!"

"Daiyu ..." Horror leeched onto her sister's face, soon replaced with a furrowed, angry brow. "Are you kidding me right now? You seriously married him for *us*? I don't believe it for one second! You ... you couldn't have."

"Why else would I marry such a cold, twisted person like him? Hm?" Even as the words tumbled out of her mouth, hot and fiery and quick, she didn't completely believe them. "I wanted you all to be happy. For you to gain wealth, and status, and a good *life*."

"You were going to *sacrifice* yourself for us? Daiyu, do you have any idea what you're saying? You think that would make any of us happy?"

"Why else did you think I married him?" She gave her sister an incredulous look. "Did you think I *wanted* to be with him at first? He's the emperor! How could I say no? I had no choice and once I realized that it was perfect for everyone, I married him. I just didn't expect ... I just didn't—" The fight seemed to leave her. She hadn't expected it to hurt so much when her heart broke. When he had shattered it in a single moment.

"But you seemed so *happy*." Lanfen opened her mouth, then clamped it shut as if rethinking the words. "You ... you seemed so in *love*."

Her shoulders shook and scorching, stabbing pain entered her chest. Like her heart was cracking all over again. She hated the realization as it hit her with full force. The reality was that she had somehow fallen in love with the wicked emperor. She had found herself happy at the thought of being with him. She had enjoyed their long nights together. Had relished the feeling of sleeping in his arms. Of kissing him. Of hearing his velvety voice.

And she didn't want to share him.

She didn't want him to be with Yanlin, or anyone else.

She wanted to be the only one who was important to him. She wanted to be his only wife. His only lover. His and his alone.

"That's what makes this all so much harder." She cried softly, the tears streaming down her crumpled face and falling onto her lap. She ducked her head, hating how broken she sounded. Hating that she was in love with Muyang. "I can't go back there. Not when he ... when he doesn't even care for me. When I'm just one of the many other women."

"Then why did you run?"

"What?" She lifted her chin. She couldn't believe the callousness on her sister's face, or the hardness of her tone.

"You do this every time," her sister said, voice low and fierce. "You run at the first sign of trouble. You've been trying to protect yourself for so long since Heng's death that you run away whenever you can. You can't just ... flee whenever things get hard. You have to deal with your problems."

"What? Lanfen, you don't understand—"

"No, I understand." She reached forward and grabbed her shoulders, shaking her slightly. "I understand that it was difficult for you to see him choose another woman to light the lantern, I really do, but you need to talk to him about it. You need to hear his side of the story. You have to argue and fight for your marriage. You can't just give up! If you truly love him, then you'll *face* him. And if you decide you don't want to be with him anymore, then you *tell* him that. But don't just run away from it all."

"But I don't always—" The words dried up at her throat. It was true, she realized. Whenever she came across a tough situation, instead of dealing with it, she ran away. She was always running. Always looking for a way out.

She never stayed and fought. Never looked for another way.

But the thought of returning to the palace was too painful, too raw. She didn't know what to say to Muyang, what to tell him, what to feel when Yanlin would inevitably be by his side. It was made worse by the fact that he didn't even bother to bring her back to the palace. He had allowed her to run.

"Do you love him?"

She had never thought she would fall in love again after Heng. But she had somehow fallen harder for Muyang. Whereas her love with Heng had been sweet and simple and happy, her romance with Muyang was tumultuous, fast, chaotic, and full of passion. Full of longing. Full of *thrill*.

She loved the way his voice sounded. Loved the way he laughed. The way he captured everyone's attention with a single glance. She loved the way he made her feel—like she was something to *want*. That she was beautiful and worthy.

She wanted to learn so much more about him. About his past. About what shaped him to be the way he was. About ... everything.

She wanted so much out of this marriage.

"Yes, I love him," she whispered. "But it changes nothing. He'll still be with other people—"

"Did he say that?"

"What?" Daiyu shook her head. "No, but it's obvious he will. Why else would he choose Yanlin? And besides, he's the emperor—"

"What if he chose her to light the lantern just because of her father? You won't really know until you ask him, but it's not like he's chosen her as a wife or concubine yet. And has he told you that he'll take on more women? Emperor Zheng Feng Mian never took another wife, so it's possible—"

She was already shaking her head. "But his wife was the

dragon empress and the rightful heir to the throne. I don't compare—"

"It doesn't matter. As the emperor, it's his decision on whether he wants to marry multiple women or not. Have you asked him what he wants?"

Her shoulders sagged. "No."

Lanfen continued to stare at her. She sighed, loud and long, and wrapped an arm around Daiyu's shoulders, squeezing tightly. "I'm not here to tell you how to live your life, Daiyu. At the end of the day, I just want you to be happy. So do whatever you think is best for you."

"I ... thank you."

She laced her hands together on her lap and stared down at the wriggling bugs in the holes where the beets had been, and then at the piles of vegetables between them. Her heart felt too heavy to do anything.

She loved Muyang, but was she ready to go back to the palace and face him? To face the humiliation he had cast upon her? Wasn't it his job to run here and beg for forgiveness? Was it even appropriate for her to go back there now? A small part of her had wanted him to come rushing to the farm and beg for her to return to the palace—it was the only reason she hadn't made her family pack up and leave just yet.

Yes, she always fled from her problems, she realized that now, but her ego was bruised and battered. She couldn't just ... return, could she?

But she had never fought for anything seriously in her life. Even before Heng's death, she had just passively let everything happen. She had allowed him to go to war even though she hadn't wanted him to. She had allowed everything to go whichever direction without her input and had run away at every tiny disruption.

She couldn't run away from Muyang. She had to face him, she had to march back in the palace and demand his apology. Demand him to explain himself, and then make the decision of whether or not to stay with him. She had to *try* something.

"You know what ..." She turned to her sister sharply, steeling her resolve with every second. "You're right. I can't just leave things off like this. I'm going to go back."

Lanfen smiled. "I'll support whatever you decide to do."

She jumped to her feet. "I'll be back, Lanfen. Wait for me!"

She didn't wait for a response as she rushed back into the house, eager to return to the palace.

39

THE RIDE BACK TO THE PALACE WAS EXPECTEDLY faster than when she had made the first trip—back when she was rushing over to rescue Lanfen. The first time around, she had walked and it had taken over a week and a half. But this time, after hitching a ride with one of her neighbors who was headed in the same direction, it only took three days to reach the capital.

Clad in one of her pale-sunflower-colored summer dress and her woven sandals, it was no wonder none of the guards recognized her. They laughed when she told them she was the wife of the emperor, and even after telling them multiple times, they still didn't let her go through.

"Look, I'm telling the truth," she began for what felt like the millionth time. She placed a hand on her hip and narrowed her eyes at the guards, who peered down at her through the slats of their metal helmets with thinly veiled annoyance.

"It was funny the first few times," one of the guards said, narrowing his eyes, "but now it's just getting old. Scram, or we'll toss you in the dungeons."

"His Majesty won't be happy to hear that—"

"*Scram.*" He tightened his hold on his spear.

"But—" Whatever hope she had wavered as panic surged. If

she couldn't get back into the palace, what would she do? Would she be forced to go back home and forget this whole marriage altogether? Did Muyang really not want to see her at all? What if—

"Lady Daiyu?"

She recognized the familiar, curious voice and followed her gaze in his direction. Commander Yao Bohai was a few feet away down the road by the glimmering, jade-colored palace gates. Dressed from head to toe in his black, scaly armor, he appeared more intimidating than usual. He raised a delicate, light eyebrow at the sight of her.

"You're back? I didn't think you'd want to return."

"Err, well, I had some unfinished business." She tried to smile, but her nerves got the better of her and it came out as a grimace instead. She jerked a thumb at the guards, who had gone still at the door. "Do you think you can let me inside? I wish to speak to His Majesty."

"Ah, yes. Of course." He nodded to the guards. They all scrambled forward, yanking the door open quickly and ushering them inside.

She shot the guards one last nasty look before sauntering inside with the commander-in-chief. When the doors shut behind them, Bohai turned to her sharply, his voice dropping. "You came at the right time, I suppose. His Majesty is not doing so well. After you left ... well, things took a turn."

Her heart nearly stopped and her steps slowed. She didn't understand what he was saying at all. "What ... do you mean?"

Bohai waved her down the hall. "Come on, let's walk and talk."

She hurried after him, her strides slower than his large ones. "Commander Yao—" Her voice cracked with sudden terror. "What do you mean things *took a turn*? A turn for what?"

"There were enemies in the palace," he said quickly, his gaze flicking from one end of the hall to the other, and then back at her. "At the end of the evening, they attacked His Majesty.

Normally, Feiyu is able to protect His Majesty, but he was nowhere to be found in the palace. You left with him, didn't you? Because Muyang—I mean, His Majesty—told me he took you away. But anyway, Feiyu usually protects the palace since he harbors all the magic—you knew that, didn't you? Well, he wasn't around, and so when His Majesty was attacked, he couldn't ... he couldn't protect himself *that* well."

Daiyu couldn't wrap her mind around what he was saying, the words spilling out too hastily, but there were a few things that began sinking in right away. Muyang was attacked. Feiyu couldn't protect him because he was with her. Muyang didn't have much magic ever since four years ago. He wasn't able to protect himself—

She swallowed down the fear tightening around her neck. "But he's okay? Right? Muyang is all right?" Even to her own ears, she sounded small and absolutely petrified. "Commander Yao, please tell me he's all right—"

"He's ... hanging in there. But we can't find Feiyu anywhere." Bohai pursed his lips together, his steps hurrying along the polished tiles. The *click click click* of his boots barely registered to her reeling mind. "Feiyu has healing magic, but he's nowhere to be found. I don't know ... why he would disappear at a time like this."

She was supposed to return to the palace and confront Muyang about what happened at the festival. She was supposed to tell her side of things and listen to his explanation. She was supposed to tell him that she loved him.

This wasn't how today was supposed to go.

She couldn't believe it—Muyang was powerful, so very, very *powerful*. In her mind, he could never lose. And yet, and yet ...

Nausea rolled over her. "Is he ... is he *dying*?"

Bohai didn't say anything when they stopped by a heavy-set, ornamental, gilded door with ruby-painted dragons sprawled along the tall frame. Stoic guards stood on either side of the double doors, their faces expressionless and hard. They bowed their heads in their direction and one of them grasped the gilt handle and slid it open for them.

Daiyu dragged her feet to a halt, not wanting to enter the room. She turned her wide-eyed stare from Bohai to the door, and then back at him again. "Is he—" she couldn't finish the sentence, her lips wobbling.

"Go inside. *Please.*" Bohai motioned for her to enter.

"No." Her shoulders quivered. She didn't want to go inside. Not with this news hanging over her head. She wasn't prepared to see Muyang in a horrible state. Was he bloodied? Battered? Completely broken?

The tightness around Bohai's eyes softened. "He'll be happy to see you, Lady Daiyu."

She somehow pushed herself forward, one leg at a time, her breathing shallow as she passed through the threshold into what she presumed were his bedchambers. Inside, she noticed all the members of the *Peccata* scattered throughout the room. They sat on couches, the windowsill, and even on the floor by the hearth. None of them spoke, but they all turned to her sharply when the door clicked shut behind her and Bohai.

A quick scan revealed Muyang wasn't in the room. Atreus, who sat on the couch, his hands steepled together and a deep, worried scowl on his face, nodded his chin toward the set of sliding doors leading to another section of the chambers.

Daiyu took in the grave faces all around her. The backs of her hands grew clammy and she rubbed them on her thighs distractedly. Without another word, she headed to the doors. Her hands continued to tremor as she fitted them into the grooves of the handle.

She slid the door open, hurried inside, and slid it shut. It took a few seconds for her eyes to adjust to the darkness of the room. The only light source came from the windows, but they were covered with a thick, dark screen that obscured most of it. In the center of the room was a massive four-poster bed frame that could fit at least five people on it, and Muyang was on one side of it, his eyes shut closed. The curtains of the frame were pulled aside, revealing her seemingly comatose husband.

She inched closer, gasping at how pale he appeared. His dark hair pooled around him like inky splotches against the crisp, white sheets. With pale skin, darkness blooming under his eyes, and a shallowness to his breath that appeared like he wasn't breathing, Muyang looked like he was on death's doors. Thick bandages were wrapped around his chest, already seeping with a sharp scarlet.

Daiyu's knees grew weak and she stumbled to the side of the bed, her hands grasping the edge of the mattress as she sank to the floor. "Muyang?"

Ever so slowly, his black eyes peeled open. He stared at her glassily as if he wasn't really seeing her before a small, faint smile upturned his lips. "Daiyu? I thought I'd never see you again. I must be blessed to see your beautiful face one last time."

"W-What happened?" All the fight that she had bolstered within herself—in which she had rehearsed exactly what to say—crumbled and disappeared altogether. She could only stare at him in stunned silence. "Commander Yao Bohai told me you were attacked."

"I was ambushed." He closed his eyes, a sigh on his lips. "There were four of them. They came soon after you left with Feiyu."

Daiyu eyed the bloodied bandages around his midsection. She suddenly felt dizzy, her vision blotting with inky splotches and her limbs tingling. She clenched her hands together. This was all her fault. If she hadn't asked for Feiyu to whisk her away back home, then Muyang might not have gotten this injured. If she hadn't fled at the first sight of problems, then maybe ... maybe there would be a different outcome right now.

"It's better if you leave," Muyang said suddenly. He reached forward and grasped a tendril of her long hair. "You were too good for me anyway."

"What are you saying?"

"Go back home. Learn to love." He wrapped her hair around his fingers ever so gently, his gaze never straying from her. "I always hurt those who are near to my heart, and I hurt you badly, Daiyu. You should find happiness elsewhere. Away from this cursed place. Away from me."

"I-Is that what you want?" Daiyu flattened her quivering lips together. "Do you think that I would be happy leaving things as they are now? I wanted to run away from you and this place, but I have so much to say to you, and I'm not leaving without hearing a response from you."

He released her hair. "Why did you come back?"

Seeing the state he was in, it was easy to forget about everything that had led up to this moment—she could have easily forgiven him without talking about what had happened, for fear that she would never talk to him again. But she didn't want that. Her heart wouldn't be able to handle losing him in this way, so soon after he betrayed her, and she knew that if she let this matter go unresolved, she would be bitter forever.

"To hear your side of the story. I realize now that I left too early without hearing what you had to say. When I saw you with Yanlin, something snapped inside of me and I wanted to escape as fast as possible." She breathed out deeply. A part of her didn't want to know the answer, but she needed to know. "But I see things differently now. Muyang, why did you ask her to light the lantern instead of me?"

Muyang's hand lay limply on the bed, no longer trying to touch her or fiddle with her hair. He grimaced, turning his attention to the ceiling of the bed. "Her father asked me several months ago if I could have her do it. This was before I met you. I didn't think it was important; it's never been important to me, just a trivial social event that people gossip over—just like everything else in this palace, in this court. I know it holds weight for the women of the empire, but I didn't care if that woman wanted to boast or pride herself in doing it. For me, it was nothing more than a favor for an old friend."

Daiyu curled her hands together. She had expected an answer like this, but it sounded even more unsatisfying to her ears than she had thought it would. "And you couldn't have told him that you changed your mind?"

"I didn't think you would care. You ... don't seem to care for these courtly matters."

"Is that what you find entertaining about me? The fact that I don't know how court works?" She wanted to laugh, but her tone grew more heated, her cheeks burning. "That I'm just a stupid country bumpkin who wouldn't know any better if you take advantage of me or humiliate me or make a fool of me in front of everyone?"

He flinched, his midnight-like eyes widening. "No, that's not ... not what I intended."

"You could have told him that you changed your mind. That you no longer wanted her to do it because you secured yourself a wife, and you wanted to make your wife feel special rather than his daughter. You could have explained that to him," she continued hastily. "You didn't have to allow anything. You're Emperor Drakkon Muyang. You don't follow other people's orders."

"I know. I apologize, Daiyu." He closed his eyes again and he looked so vulnerable in that moment that her anger quickly dissolved. "I should have prioritized your feelings over slighting Lord Wang and his daughter. I realize now that it was a foolish mistake on my part to allow it in the first place."

"You need to talk to me more. You can't just do these things that pertain to me and not tell me. Do you know how embarrassing it was for me to be caught off guard in front of everyone when I realized you had chosen *her* to light the lantern?"

"I apologize."

"No, that's not *enough*." Her eyes burned once more but for a different reason. She relived the memory of the laughing women, the nobles eyeing her, and Yanlin's cruel grin. "You can apologize all you want, but it's not going to change that everyone views

Yanlin as the proper empress, while I'm just a farm girl. And now it's made even more clear that I'm not important to your court because *you* made it that way. *You* showed them that a noble's daughter is more important to you than your own *wife*."

Muyang reached for her hand. "She will *never* be my empress."

"I wish I could believe you, but you betrayed my trust."

"Daiyu, I have no plans of marrying her." He held her hand tighter. "Even before I was attacked, I had no plans to be with her. So don't think I'm only saying that now that I'm dying."

She wanted to believe him, but she didn't know what to think. She also realized how cruel it was for her to be asking this of him while he was bedridden and injured; it certainly could have waited until he was better. But she *needed* to know. She needed to be a bit selfish.

"You're not going to die," she murmured.

He rubbed her knuckles weakly with his thumb. "I never planned on marrying anyone after you. You're more than enough for me, Daiyu." Muyang tried to push himself into a sitting position, but Daiyu held him down in alarm.

"What are you—"

His face wracked with pain and the bandages grew redder. "Let me sit," he growled, eyes flashing. Daiyu freed his shoulders and he pulled himself together. He rested his back on the headboard and shifted on the mattress to make himself more comfortable. The whole time, his breathing was labored. "I won't be lying here like a dead man while my wife is speaking about the terrible ways I've hurt her."

"Muyang—"

He stared at her directly, his gaze more alert than before. "I'm sorry, Daiyu, for everything I've done to you. For prioritizing another man's daughter over you. I hadn't realized how humiliating it would be until now, and I truly do apologize for the hurt I've caused you." He breathed out deeply, like talking was taking a toll on him. "I never meant to hurt you, and I hope you understand that. I hope you won't hold it against me for too long. I ... I realize now that I can't easily make it up to you, but I want *you* to be my empress, Daiyu. Not anyone else."

Daiyu searched his face for signs that he was lying, that he was only saying these pretty words because he thought that it was what she wanted to hear, or because he thought he was dying. But she only found raw sincerity there and she wanted so badly to cling to it, to *believe* him.

"I wish I could make it up to you." Muyang rested his head against the backboard, his chest rising and falling with struggled breaths. "I wish I could make you believe what I'm saying. I really do, Daiyu. But ... I know my time is coming near. I knew it would happen eventually. Ever since I took this throne four years ago, I realized my reign would never amount to much."

Daiyu's mouth dried up. "What are you saying? You're not going to die—"

"This place is cursed. This palace, this court, this ... this *empire*." He breathed out deeply, painfully. Something dark swirled in his eyes, a kind of hatred that made her flinch back. "It will be better for me to die here and for someone else to take my place. I was never meant to be more than a murderer. I have accomplished what I wanted. I have revenged who I wanted, and it's time for me to rest now. Forever."

"Muyang!" Daiyu took his cold hand in hers and squeezed it tightly. She didn't understand what he was saying, but all she knew was that it terrified her. The thought of losing him, the thought of someone else taking this empire. "Why are you talking like that? You're not going to die! You're Emperor Drakkon Muyang. You're the most powerful man I know. There's no way you would die like this! We just—" A strangled sob escaped from her. "We just started our lives together. We have so much to learn about one another, so much to do, so many more years to spend with each other!"

Daiyu could have sworn there was pity on his beautiful face when he stared at her next. He reached forward with a tired, trembling hand and cupped her damp cheek. She could feel his tremors through his hand.

"I always knew I would be a curse to these lands. Ever since I was born," he murmured, searching her face with unblinking, glassy eyes. He wasn't here, in this room anymore, but in his memories, it seemed. Somewhere else because there was a darkness there that she had only seen glimpses of before, and now he was showing it to her full force. The tortured, angry soul that lingered behind his black, black eyes. "Remaining on the throne will tear this empire apart. I knew it would, but I had to do it. I had to spite all those people—"

"Muyang—"

He turned to her sharply as if brought back to the present. "Daiyu, you must leave this place. Go far away, take your family with you and disappear. Live a long life with another man. Find happiness. Once Yat-sen takes the throne, I don't know if he will be kind to you or if he will forsake you like I did his brothers."

"No, I'm not leaving you! Not ever again." She held the hand that was against her cheek, more tears streaming down her face. "I'm not leaving you here to die! We have to find Feiyu. We have to make him understand—"

Muyang pulled his hand back like her touch was electric. "No," he said quietly. "Not Feiyu. He knows the same as I do, that remaining on this throne will only throw this empire into more chaos. He realized that; that's why he left."

"The empire isn't in chaos—"

"There will always be unrest so long as I breathe and sit upon this cursed throne."

"But, but Feiyu is loyal—"

"He knows better than me what it means for me to remain alive."

Daiyu's hands shook. "What are you saying?"

"Find happiness," he said again, mimicking Feiyu's final words to her. "Daiyu, *please*. I have so many regrets to this day, but I've never regretted meeting you and falling in love with you.

You offered me a glimmer of happiness, as short as it may have been. All I want now is for you to move on and be happy."

She was more confused than ever. She had thought she would march up to Muyang, present to him all the problems he had caused her, wait for him to grovel and apologize, and then—hopefully—live happily with him.

This ... this wasn't how things were meant to unfold.

She hadn't planned on losing him forever. And she never expected for him to speak so morbidly, so vaguely.

"If Feiyu won't help you, I'm sure there are other mages who can heal." Daiyu leaned closer to him and grabbed his face in her hands. She couldn't find a glimmer of hope within him, only anger and resolve. She didn't understand him at all. Why was he so bent on dying here? Why was he so certain that he would die? That he was a curse upon this empire? "Muyang, there are others who can help you, but you have to let them—"

"Daiyu, you don't understand." He eased her hands off his face and she felt like he was rejecting her in that moment. "Even if these injuries are healed, my soul is dying. I will die soon. In a matter of days, perhaps."

"W-What?" Whatever hope had filled her disappeared that second and she sank back down on her knees on the floor. She blinked over at him, not comprehending what he was saying. What he meant. "I don't ... I don't know what you mean. Is this some sort of magical curse?"

"In a way."

"Muyang, but ... but there has to be something—"

"Daiyu, please leave from here." He suddenly looked exhausted. She could tell that this conversation was putting a strain on him. By the looks of it, he had already made up his mind about dying. About giving up.

"Make me understand." She grabbed the edge of the mattress and hauled herself up to her feet. It was maddening to see him like this, to see him so unlike himself, to see him resolve himself to his fate. "I don't understand what any of this means. Why are you so determined to die? Why won't you accept any help? And why is your soul *dying*?"

Muyang shook his head, choosing to lie back down instead. "I can't tell you, Daiyu. But know that this is for the best. For you and for this empire." He grunted, the little color on his face draining further. "I'd like to rest for a bit."

Daiyu felt like he had slapped her. He was clearly dismissing her, done with their conversation and not willing to listen to her pleas. He didn't even want to explain himself.

Her hands shook with fury and she wanted to shout at him. She wanted to cry and scream. She wanted to punch something. But mostly, she just wanted the dread and uncertainty and terror to go away. She wanted him to be okay. She wanted to start their lives together. She wanted to have him by her side. Especially now that she knew she was in love with him.

She opened her mouth to say just that—to tell him she loved him—but something held her back. She couldn't allow this to be one of the last times they talked to each other. She couldn't let him go like this.

"I'm going to drag Feiyu back here," Daiyu said instead, "and then you both are going to explain to me exactly what's going on. And then you'll have to stop this nonsense about dying because I'm not going to watch you die here."

Muyang didn't open his eyes again. Either he was ignoring her or he had passed out. It only steeled her resolve more and she batted away the remaining tears clinging to her lashes.

She gave him a moment to say something—to even tell her that there was no reason for her to do that—but he didn't.

"Just you wait," she said with finality.

Spinning on her heels, she marched out of the room. She wasn't sure if she was ready to fall apart at the seams, or if she wanted to get into a fight with someone to release all the pent-up tension inside her that had accumulated during this whole conversation.

When the door slid closed behind her, she turned to the rest of the *Peccata* and Bohai in the room. They all watched her with hopeful eyes. Did they think she was enough to save Muyang?

Daiyu blew out air, straightening her stiff shoulders. "Why is he talking like he's going to die very soon? Do any of you know anything about what's going on? And why can't we send in another mage to help?"

"We've tried," Bohai explained, glancing at the others in the room. "But the mages have agreed that something is wrong with his soul and that ... he's dying."

"Is it magic related?"

"We think so."

"And Feiyu isn't willing to help?"

"Not that we know of. He's disappeared."

Daiyu chewed on her lower lip and paced the room, choosing to steer clear from the *Peccata* members who were sitting close by the fireplace—she couldn't remember their names, but it was the young raven-haired man with blue eyes and the bubbly female with the dimpled smile. Minos? Thera? She didn't even remember or care in that moment.

"What do we even know about Feiyu? And why is he so closely tied with His Majesty?" she asked out loud, turning to the other members. They all seemed to be on friendly terms with the high mage—at least that was the impression she had gotten from Nikator and Vita. But why the mysteries? Why was Feiyu the only one who could help?

"We ... don't really know much about him," Nikator said slowly, fidgeting with the leather hilt of his dagger—it was a nervous trait of his that Daiyu had picked up on. "He showed up a few weeks after His Majesty took the throne. He's always worn a mask, so I have no idea what he looks like underneath it. But His Majesty trusts him and we all sort of followed suit."

"But who is he?" she pressed.

"I don't know," Vita said, shifting from her position on the couch.

"So no one really knows *anything* about him?" Daiyu asked.

Silence fell over the group.

There were so many things that didn't make sense—like who Feiyu was, how and why he was able to turn into a dragon, the MuRong royal tattoo on his arm, Muyang's supposed curse and the reason his soul was dying—but it was becoming increasingly clear that she needed to find the high mage and force him to explain himself.

She didn't know Feiyu very well either, she realized. Sure, he had somehow become her friend and sure, they had spent a good amount of time together in the palace, but she didn't know his past. She didn't know his real name. And she didn't know what he desired, what his goals were—anything, really.

"I'll ... I'll be right back," Daiyu finally said, heading toward the door.

Atreus rose from his seat. "Where are you going?"

"To find Feiyu."

"Let me help—"

"No, I have a feeling he won't cooperate if anyone else comes along." It was a gut feeling of hers. Something that had no teeth and likely was wrong, but she didn't want to risk it. The impression she had gotten from Feiyu was that he seemed to treat the *Peccata* like children, and she wasn't sure if he was willing to open up if they were present. At least ... at least that's what she suspected.

"Stay here and protect His Majesty," she said instead. "There might be more rebel forces lingering around in the palace, waiting to strike. Now is the most important time for us to stay vigilant."

They all nodded, and even Bohai was staring at her strangely.

Finally, he too bobbed his head.

"Yes, Your Majesty," he murmured.

It didn't even click to her the title he had used. It was only when she left the bedchambers and headed down the hallway, her head held high and her resolve steeling itself with every step, that she realized she was either one step closer to becoming a proper empress, or another step closer to becoming a widow.

40

Daiyu had a vague idea where Feiyu was located. He had given her the hint when he had whisked her away to the mountains on the last day of the festival, but her biggest problem, other than figuring out how not to break her neck while riding a horse, was finding his *exact* location. Because as it was, the mountains were, unsurprisingly, extremely vast.

She must have been clopping through every trail she could, listening to the sound of creek water or streams and crickets and birds—and whatever other magical sounds Feiyu had mentioned he enjoyed—when she finally dismounted her horse and began her trek on foot. It was possible, she guessed, that he was somewhere where the horse didn't want to go.

Through her jaunt, her mind traveled to everything that had conspired the past few days. Muyang choosing Yanlin, Feiyu's strange goodbye, Muyang's parting words about destroying the empire if he continued his reign, and his love toward Daiyu. The more she thought about it, the more confused she became. Why did Feiyu wear a mask at all times? Why was Muyang's soul dying? What did Feiyu have to do with it? Did Feiyu do this to Muyang?

All she knew with clarity was that she had to save the man she loved. She wasn't going to sit around and do nothing while

Muyang's soul slowly withered away. There were so many memories they needed to create. So many things they needed to discuss. So many ... firsts they needed to do.

"Feiyu!" she shouted with labored breaths, glancing right and left. She also wasn't sure what Feiyu looked like right now—was he in a human form, dragon form, or some other form he could shapeshift into? Nonetheless, she stared through the trees and rocky bumps for anything amiss, for any animal that was acting strange or any boulder that looked like it didn't belong. "Feiyu!"

Pushing aside a swaying branch in her way, Daiyu climbed the steep mountain path. Her thighs burned with exertion and her breath streamed out of her shallowly. Her ankles weren't used to all this hiking and her the soles of her feet were aching with every sharp rock, twig, and thorn she inadvertently stepped on. Her dried-grass sandals were barely hanging on by the time the sun began to dip into the horizon, painting the trees and boulders and terrain in orange-pink hues.

"Fei—" Her foot caught on a gnarled tree root and she flew forward. Daiyu raised her elbows instinctively to break her fall, but her knees slammed onto a pile of tiny rocks and pebbles first and she skidded down the unpaved trail. She screamed—her hand and knees and elbows scraping along the rough, rocky terrain.

She kept tumbling, the twigs and bramble catching on her hair and ripping it out of its low bun. Her fall was finally broken when she crashed into a large boulder surrounded by thorny bushes.

For a few seconds, she just lay there, breathing hard and staring up at the saffron-and-peach-tinged skyline. Her eyes filled with frustrated tears and she shakily pulled herself into a sitting position. The skin along her arms and knees was raw and shredded, and her dirt-coated dress was ripped in some sections.

A sob tore from her throat and she covered her face with her trembling, dusty hands. It wasn't until that moment, when she was twisted in thorny bushes and littered with dozens of cuts and bruises that the reality of the situation *really* hit her.

Her husband was dying.

Her friend had turned into a dragon and disappeared.

And she was no closer to finding him and saving Muyang than she was a few hours ago.

She had been so naïve to think she could easily find Feiyu just because he had shown her this place before and because he had always been accessible to her before—all she had to do was call his name in the palace and he would show up. She had taken that for granted: being able to see him whenever she wanted to.

And now, when she needed him the most, she had no clue where to even begin.

Daiyu picked at the spiky, knotted bushes stabbing her at every corner and did her best to untangle herself from it. Tears blurred her vision and she choked back her sobs. Muyang was dying. He was dying and there was a good chance there was nothing she could do about it. Here she was, stuck in the mountains, battered red and blue, instead of being with her bedridden husband.

Maybe she should have left this task for one of the *Peccata*. Maybe Atreus, or Nikator, or that young demon with red eyes. Maybe she should have waited by Muyang's side while everyone else worked to find Feiyu.

Releasing a wobbly breath, Daiyu continued up the path she had just slid down from. Her breaths came in shaky half-sobs, and the evening wind blew against her damp cheeks. It would have been easier to run back to the palace and tell everyone she had failed in finding Feiyu—nobody would have faulted her—but she kept pushing herself.

One leg in front of the other. One foot, then the other, then the other.

Her lungs were on fire. Her face grew numb with cold. Her feet throbbed painfully. But she kept pushing herself forward.

One breath, one staggered step at a time.

It didn't matter that she was a farm girl. It didn't matter that she wasn't a noble. It didn't matter that she would likely never truly fit into Muyang's court. If there was one thing she was certain about, it was that she wasn't going to give up on Muyang or Feiyu. And she didn't need to be someone important to be Muyang's wife, or Feiyu's friend, or someone who climbed this cursed mountain to find her dragon-turned friend.

Daiyu kept walking, even when the sun sank down the horizon, even when she couldn't see in front of her. She brushed her hands along the rocks, the boulders, the trees, and whatever she came across. It wasn't until she reached one of the flatter, higher levels of the mountainside that she halted to a stop. The wind tousled her unkept hair and she could taste the electrifying, heavy magic in the air.

She turned toward it and hurried her steps, her eyes adjusting to the dark blobs and shapes in the night. She kept climbing higher, and higher, and higher up the trail. Finally, when the magic was the strongest, and she could practically breathe in the fogginess of it, she came to a halt.

Curled up in a ball, a giant, moon-drenched dragon lay on the ground, his eyes closed and his heavy head resting on his arms. His scales shimmered silver in the light and her breath caught at the sight of them—at how beautiful he was, at how his wings seemed to reflect the moon.

"Feiyu!" Daiyu nearly tripped and stumbled toward him, her eyes misting with tears once again. There was no mistaking it. This was Feiyu, the dragon she had seen on the last day of the festival. She stopped a few feet away from him. "Feiyu!"

Slowly, he opened his black eyes and they landed on her instantly.

"Feiyu." Her hands trembled and she sank to the ground, more tears streaming down her face. "It's you, isn't it? Please, I need ..."

The words were stuck in her throat. She was always running over to him whenever she needed help. Whenever there was something she needed.

"Muyang needs you," she whispered, searching his dragon

face. He had to understand her. He had to listen. He had to *explain* himself.

His eyes closed once more.

"Feiyu? Feiyu!" Daiyu clambered to her sore, achy feet and hesitantly touched his face. His scales were smooth like marble and cold to the touch. "Please, wake up. I need to talk to you."

His eyes opened again and this time, she flinched back at the darkness she found in his gaze. He stared at her unblinkingly and then opened his mouth. His voice rumbled out of him unfamiliarly. "I am tired, Daiyu. Leave me to my fate here."

"What are you talking about? I've been looking everywhere for you." Her hands shook and she rubbed them against the back of her thighs. She didn't even know where to begin. What to start talking about. Not when there was so much she didn't understand. "Feiyu, what's happening? Why did you say goodbye to me like you did? Why ... are you a dragon?"

"Daiyu, I am tired," he repeated. "Go home. Live your life somewhere far, far away from here and the capital."

Something snapped within her at hearing those words—words that echoed hauntingly similar to Muyang's. "Why is everyone so hell-bent on sending me away?" She bunched her fists together just as a gust of wind howled above her head as if agreeing with her. "I came here to find you, Feiyu. I know what I'm doing. I didn't stumble here by accident. I need your help—I ... I know it sounds bad because I always seem to need your help, but it's not for me. Muyang *needs* you. He's—" Her voice thickened. "He's dying."

If he was surprised, he didn't show it. His eyes fluttered shut.

"Feiyu? Did you hear me?" She touched his head and tried to shake him, but he was too heavy, too grand. "Feiyu, Muyang is *dying*."

"I know."

Her eyebrows pulled together. "Aren't you going to do something?"

"No."

"Why?" Anger surged through her. "Aren't you loyal to him?"

"Muyang is a curse upon these lands," he said. "It's better for him to die. It's better for you and for this empire. Embrace it and run far away from here, for his enemies will look for you to parade around as a trophy. A relic of his abominable reign."

She couldn't believe his words, nor the way he delivered them so nonchalantly.

"Why are you saying that?" A steel edge entered her tone. "Muyang isn't a curse. You're supposed to help him. You're his high mage and he's your emperor. Commander Yao told me that his soul is dying and it's magic related; he said you could help! You're the only one I can turn to right now."

Another strong gale raged against them. This time chillier than before. It made her teeth rattle and her body ache.

"Feiyu, *please*." She inhaled sharply and continued quickly, "I'll do anything you want, but please, please save Muyang. I need him alive. You don't seem to understand the severity of the situation. He is *dying*, Feiyu. If you don't do something to help his soul, he will *die*. And I can't allow that to happen. No matter what, I won't let my husband die." Her throat closed up and she choked out, "I won't let the man I love die in front of me, so please, I'm begging you, please save Muyang. I'll do whatever you want. If you want to bind me into some sort of contract, I'll do it. Just ... just save him."

Feiyu watched her with midnight eyes that seemed to blend into the night itself. "Four years ago, he made his decision to take the throne and curse himself. He knew this day would come eventually. Leave him to his fate, Daiyu."

"I can't and I won't!" she shouted, her voice echoing through the mountains. She breathed out deeply and her hair whipped around violently in tune with the winds. "Feiyu, what is going on? Why are you allowing Muyang to suffer like this? What do you have over him? And what do you have against him?"

"There's nothing I can do."

"Why? Why is Muyang's soul dying?"

"He chose this."

"But *why*?"

He said nothing and her fury swelled once more, fueled by her inability to do anything. She clenched and unclenched her fists. She hated that she didn't know what was happening and she hated that both Feiyu and Muyang were keeping her in the dark.

"Feiyu! Look, you're a high mage. You know a lot when it comes to magic. If you're not willing to help Muyang yourself, then fine. But please, can you at least tell me what I can do to save him? I absolutely can't let him die. I won't ... I just won't." She blinked away the burning of her eyes. "Feiyu, *please*!"

"Daiyu, you know nothing about Muyang." He stared at her levelly, his head not rising from his resting position. "You know nothing about what makes him cursed. Why he should have never ruled and why he's currently suffering the consequences of his actions. You should hate him. You should rejoice now that you'll be free from him. You shouldn't be here, begging at my feet for me to save the very man who doomed you to live in the palace when you only wished to rescue your sister."

"I love him," she said quietly, her voice coming out strong despite the turmoil in her chest. "I don't want to lose him."

"You ran away from him mere days ago."

"I ... I see things differently now." She lowered her head, hating the tremor in her words and the weakness she was baring to him. "I don't want to run away anymore. I want to stand in the palace and face Muyang head-on. I made a mistake by running the first time. I want to stay and fight. I want to—"

"Who's to say he won't make another error and cast you aside? Will you run then too?"

"No—"

"What if he abandons you for another?"

"He won't do that."

"How can you be so sure? You know nothing about Muyang."

"I know enough to know that he wouldn't knowingly hurt

me. He wouldn't put me in that position—not again." Her voice faltered, but she remembered the confidence with which Muyang had spoken to her. How he had promised that he wouldn't hurt her. That he was so very sorry for breaking her heart. "And ... And if he does, I'll face him. I'll tackle that problem when—if—it arises. But I have a feeling that it won't happen because Muyang loves me."

"You're making assumptions about a man whose reputation is far worse than you can ever imagine."

She raised her chin. "I know who he is. I knew who Muyang was when I agreed to marry him."

Usurper. Murderer. Wicked.

He was Drakkon Muyang.

Feared across the lands for his vast power.

She didn't know everything there was to know about him, but that was why he needed to survive—so they could get to know one another more. So they could fall deeper and harder in love. So that they could live their lives together.

Feiyu watched her unblinkingly. The stars seemed to glimmer brighter, his scales appearing more silver as he lifted his head toward her. His breath streamed out of his mouth in white puffs. "Very well, Yin Daiyu. You seem to have put your bets on this man whom you know nothing about. I will put my bets on *you*, then. I can save Muyang, but I'll only do it for a price."

Her hopes rose and her breath cinched in her chest. "Yes, yes, *yes*. What's your price? Tell me and I'll be able to pay it—"

"My name."

She hesitated, unsure if she had heard right. But when he made no move to repeat himself, she murmured, "Your ... name?"

"Yes. That is my price." His gaze pierced her—dragonoid and dark. "Tell me my true name, and I will save your husband."

"But ..." Her mouth dried up. She didn't know his name. She didn't know *anything* about him. He must have been a MuRong, since he had the royal tattoo on his arm, but there had been dozens of MuRongs over the past decades. How was she going to guess which member of the previous royal family he was? She didn't even know all the princes' names.

"You have to give me a hint, or, or *something*. I can't guess your name without knowing anything—"

"I will share my memories with you, and by the end of it, you will tell me my name." He leaned closer to her, air steaming from his nostrils and warming her face. She instinctively touched the side of his jaw, her fingers gliding over the smooth scales. "If you're unable to tell me my name, I will kill your husband myself."

She opened her mouth to say something—to tell him that he was being cruel—but her vision shifted right before she could. Suddenly, she wasn't in the mountains anymore. She was elsewhere. Daiyu blinked, her mouth dropping open at the bustling, familiar hallway.

She was in the royal palace.

41

DAIYU SPUN AROUND TO STARE AT THE ORNATELY decorated halls, with its polished tile floors and the metal latticed windows and the servants running back and forth. But something about it was *wrong*. It took her a second to realize what it was—the banners throughout the palace had the MuRong insignia of the moon and the serpent plastered on them, instead of the dragon symbol she was so used to seeing. And instead of hues of red and black—the Drakkon colors—the palace had subtle shades of vibrant green and silver—the MuRong colors.

"Excuse me—" Daiyu tried to grab the forearm of a passing woman, but her hand slipped right through the woman as if she wasn't there. She gasped, taking a step back. Her hands, feet, her *whole body*, shimmered like she was a spirit.

Was she ... in Feiyu's memory?

She tried to step forward to investigate further, but she found that she couldn't walk more than two feet around herself. It was as if there was an invisible barrier barring her from exploring. She was a bystander, she realized, and there must have been something she was supposed to see.

She watched the hallways for anything amiss. For any clue to piece together who Feiyu was. But there were only servants milling about. Nothing was abnormal—

A little boy with shoulder-length hair walked down the hallway holding a serving tray with four silver-veined teacups balanced atop it. His face was a blob of darkness. As if someone had painted over the memory, overriding it with a shadowy rendition of itself.

That ... must have been Feiyu?

Right? It was *his* memories, after all.

A maidservant stayed close behind him. She opened her mouth and said a name, but no matter how much Daiyu strained her ears or tried to read the woman's lips, she was unable to.

"You'll have to go to His Royal Highness's room next," the woman said, her voice ringing out clearly now.

The boy's shoulders stiffened. "But ... I don't like—"

"*Shh.*" The woman's tone sharpened and she looked around herself in the hallway, but nobody else was paying attention to them. All the servants were focused on their own tasks. "The prince requested *you* to bring him his afternoon tea."

"But, Mother, he—"

"I know." The woman's face tightened with emotions Daiyu could read very well. It was an expression she had witnessed many times on her own mother's face whenever her siblings or herself were about to dive headfirst into trouble. The same expression Mother had worn when Daiyu announced she would go into the palace and rescue Lanfen herself.

The scenery began to shift again and Daiyu was whisked away into another memory. This time, the boy with the shadowy face was in a closed room with his mother holding his hand and a larger man poking his forearm with a sharpened bone. The boy screamed and cried, trying to yank his arm away, but his mother held him firmly, even though she looked like she wanted to cry just as much as he did.

"Please, make it stop! Mother, make him *stop!*"

His mother's lips trembled. She was still dressed like a maidservant, her hair pulled back simply with a silver ribbon, and her faded green and white robes appearing too simple. "I know, my sweet boy, but you must bear with the pain."

"No, *no!*" He thrust his head one way, then the other. "I'm not a prince! I'm *not* a prince!"

The man with the bone continued to whittle into the young boy's flesh, tapping in ink and magic and tattooing the royal symbol into his forearm. The boy's pained screams continued to echo against the walls.

"Listen—" The man formed words, likely the boy's name, but once again, Daiyu was unable to hear it, nor was she able to decipher his lips. "His Majesty has claimed you as his. Neither of us can refute it. I understand it's painful, but it's either this or your mother is flogged. Which would you rather have?"

"It's not her fault—"

"I understand she didn't do anything, but she's *your* mother, and if *you* misbehave, *she* will be punished for it." He pointed the sharpened, bloodied end of the bone to the woman and gave the boy a stern look. "So what will it be? Will you make this more difficult than it has to be?"

The boy sniffed and his body went slack. He seemed to have accepted his fate. "No."

"Good." The man went back to piercing his skin and the boy cried silently. The woman holding him eased her iron-like grip on her son, but the tenseness of her shoulders didn't go away. She wiped the little boy's face with trembling hands.

"How much longer?" she whispered.

"Another hour."

The boy made a choking sound. "B-But—"

The man gave him another stern look and the boy shrank back.

"It's not fair," he said after a moment, his breaths coming in short inhales as he sniffled and held his cries in. "I'm not a prince—"

"You are," his mother said firmly. "And your father has finally accepted you. Don't anger him by saying otherwise. You've heard the rumors your whole life, haven't you? This should be a joyous occasion."

"And besides," the tattooist said, "if you didn't have MuRong blood, this magicked ink would have killed you. So you *are* a prince, Your Highness."

The memory was changing again and Daiyu was once again carried away to a different section of the palace. The little boy was older now, maybe twelve, and he was on the ground in the palace, his body curled up into a ball as an older teenager kicked him in the stomach. The young man laughed, kicking him harder and harder, while a group of well-dressed youth watched with amusement.

"You think you're on the same level as me?" The young man laughed, high and grating, and kicked the shadow-faced boy with a grunt. "You. Are. *Nothing.*"

Daiyu stepped forward, ready to stop the violence, but she was hit with an invisible shield again. She could only cringe as the young man—who wore a gold hair crown and whose rich red robes told her he was royalty—continued to beat the younger boy.

The memory was evolving again, the grass disappearing and changing into polished wood, and the sky warping into walls. She was in a small room. The shadow-faced boy was a bit older, she would guess, by the deepness of his voice.

"Mother! Wh-What are you *doing*?" He was standing by the doorway of the room, his body quaking in barely suppressed rage or horror—Daiyu wasn't sure.

His mother was lying in bed, a blanket covering her naked body, and a similarly clad man beside her. She yelped something and pulled the sheets to cover her body. Clothes and a guard's uniform were strewn on the floor haphazardly.

"G-Get out!" his mother whisper-shouted, pulling herself into a sitting position. She tried to protect her modesty, but it was clear what had happened. "You should knock before you enter a room. You know—"

"*You* get out," he roared at the guard and then turned to his mother. "What are you *thinking*?"

The guard sheepishly jumped to his feet and began dressing. The shadowed boy turned around as the two adults quickly pulled their clothes on, grumbles on their tongues.

"You know what will happen once *he* finds out, don't you?" the boy said, his voice tight and panicked. Daiyu didn't need to see his expression to know he was terrified out of his mind.

"We don't plan on staying here that long, kid," the guard said with a low chuckle. "Or should I call you Your Highness?"

"*Get out,*" the young man snapped.

"We're going to leave this place," the woman said, smoothing down her skirts. "He won't be able to find us—"

"You don't know that—"

"That's enough," she said firmly. "I understand you're worried and confused, but I'm an adult and I can make my own decisions. I also want to fall in love and have a relationship, but your father will never allow it since I've had his child. He may think that I belong to him, but I *don't.*"

"But, Mother—" His voice became more strained—more frightened.

"We'll find a way to make it work. Sooner or later, we'll leave this place."

Daiyu shivered at the parallels in her own situation. How she had been taken by the emperor as well, but how things were vastly different between her and Muyang, and this woman and the emperor of this time period.

All at once, the background began to warp again. Daiyu was beginning to become accustomed to the discombobulating feeling of the whole world changing in the blink of an eye, and the dizzying effect it had on her for the first few seconds. But nothing could have prepared her for the next sight.

She inhaled sharply and fell backward. In the center of the room, the shadow-faced boy's mother was tied to a wooden post. Daiyu recognized the throne room almost immediately, but she could barely focus on that. Not when the woman was beaten and bloodied to a pulp, her hair missing in chunks as if someone had ripped it out, and her threadbare clothes barely hanging onto her thin frame. The room was crowded, the people speaking to one another casually while they sipped their drinks as if unaware of the battered woman in the center of the room.

The shadow-boy screamed and cried, held back by two guards who held a spear to his throat. But he was unaffected by the pain, not even when they stabbed his leg or kicked him down. On a dais at the end of the room, an emperor with silver streaks in his midnight hair sat on a throne, his entire body bedecked in glimmering gold and silver.

"Let me go! Let me go!" the young man screamed. "Mother! *Mother!*"

Daiyu covered her mouth at the brutality. At the twisted, awkward positions the woman's limbs were bent in. At the blood splattering the floor around her. At the broken teeth by her feet. At the way the nobles chuckled and conversed so indifferently.

Her heart ached for the woman and again for the young man, whose cries fell on deaf ears.

Below the emperor, a young man was lounged on a velvet seat, watching the scene with an amused grin on his face. Daiyu recognized him as the man who had beaten the shadowy-faced boy in one of the earlier memories. He must have been a prince, judging by the way he was dressed and the arrogant attitude.

"She did this to herself." The prince snickered, loud enough for everyone to hear. "*Whore.*"

"You—You—" The shadow-boy began shouting, but one of the guards slammed him to the floor, pinning his face down so he couldn't speak coherently.

"Yan, don't bother speaking to him," the emperor said in a gravelly voice. He peered down at the young man with narrowed eyes. "He's scum just as much as his mother, but he is still your brother."

Prince Yan only sniggered. "Yes, Father."

Daiyu turned away from the violence, her stomach twisting painfully. She had no idea why she was witnessing this, why Feiyu wanted to show her this gruesome, heartbreaking scene. But she had another clue to go off on—this cruel prince was Yan, who would later become Emperor Yan. He was Yat-sen's father and the previous emperor in current times, she realized. But then who was the shadow-boy? She couldn't remember anything about any younger brothers Emperor Yan had. They were all dead by the time he took the throne anyway.

The setting shifted again and Daiyu was more than happy for the change. She waited, with bated breath, for another piece of the puzzle to fall into place. But instead of finding a memory that was more pleasant than the previous one, her heart sank as another horrific scene took over.

This time, she was in a small cellar. The young shadow-faced boy was chained to the wall, his tunic ripped off to reveal a crisscross of scars along his pale body. Prince Yan stood a few feet away from him, a whip in his hand. He laughed and tortured the young man. Daiyu could barely watch, and it was only when the prince uncorked a small vial or red blood that Daiyu could look again.

The prince waved the glass vial in front of the youth's face. "Do you know what this is? It's dragon's blood. Said to be the most painful way to torture a man. Your blood will boil from within you. Your organs will melt, your skin will peel, and you will feel *unimaginable* pain until you die days later."

"I'll kill you one day," the shadow-faced youth whispered weakly.

"No, no, you won't." Yan took ahold of the young man's jaw and tried wrestling his mouth open. They both struggled, the chains smacking into the walls as the shadowed youth tried to wriggle away. But he was tied up, beaten and bloodied, and he was no match against the other prince, who smashed the vial into the youth's mouth. The shards cut into his mouth and tongue and cheeks, the thick blood coating his tongue.

"There!" Yan breathed out deeply as his half-brother writhed against the wall, trying to spit the blood and pieces of glass from his mouth. "Now I'll finally be rid of you, you cursed *rat*. Do you know how much of an eyesore you've been all these years? How incredibly embarrassing it is to see such a disgusting lowlife like you reach the same position as me? You are *not* a prince. You will never be anything more than a lowlife."

Once again, everything began to change. Daiyu was blinded by a bright light and she blinked back at the new memory. Except, it *wasn't* a memory. She was back where they had last been. Her hand was still placed on Feiyu's dragon face and she was in the clearing in the mountains, the sun bearing down on her. Birds tweeted in the background, insects chirred, and there was an early morning dew still clinging to the grass.

Daiyu backed away, her legs weak. "Wh-What?"

That couldn't be it. There were still so many memories she had to go through, so many more clues she had to figure out.

But Feiyu was staring at her now as if expecting her to have an answer.

"There ... There must be *more*," she said quickly. This couldn't be it. She had to see more. She couldn't guess anything by what she had seen. "Feiyu—"

"What is my name, Yin Daiyu?"

42

SHE OPENED HER MOUTH AND CLAMPED IT SHUT. WAS she supposed to guess based on those snippets of memories? He had lived a terrible, terrible life—she could see that. But it wasn't enough for her to know *who* he was. She didn't know the names of Emperor Yan's siblings. She didn't know anything other than that Feiyu was an abused prince.

She cursed herself for not knowing the names of the royal family and she partly wished she could rush back to the palace and ask Prince Yat-sen or the princesses the names of all their uncles. But she didn't have that kind of time and she doubted Feiyu would allow that—after all, this was a test, wasn't it?

"Let me ... think," Daiyu said after a moment, choosing to sit on a smooth, unfaceted rock. She drummed her fingers over her thighs to keep them busy. She should have been more shocked at the fact that it was morning—and that she had spent the whole night flicking through Feiyu's memories—but the adrenaline rushing through her veins and the pressure of answering correctly kept her from thinking too much about the morning. Or the magic. Or the fact that Muyang was likely in critical condition at this point. Or that everyone must have been worried about where she had been all night.

Daiyu tried clearing her thoughts of everything except what Feiyu had shown her. What did she know about Feiyu *before* these memories?

He wore a mask to protect his identity—apparently, because he didn't want anyone to know who he was, which now made sense. He was the high mage of the royal palace and worked closely with Muyang. He used a fake name to hide his identity even more. He had a few scars she had spotted through the eye slits of his mask and when he had lifted his mask to eat. And ... that was about it.

What did she know about Feiyu *after* seeing his memories?

He was severely abused by his brother Yan. He was the child of the emperor and a maidservant. He watched his mother brutally be tortured and executed. He had ingested the blood of a dragon and somehow survived.

She tried wrapping her mind around more. There must have been a reason Feiyu had shown her these memories, but how did they tie in with his identity? How was she supposed to figure out who he was with these glimpses of his life?

She was missing something, she was sure.

Did Muyang know that Feiyu was a MuRong? She couldn't see any reason why he would keep Feiyu around if he knew the truth, so he must have *not* known. Feiyu must have worn a mask around at all times in order to hide his identity from Muyang. Because he likely knew that Muyang would lock him up similar to how Yat-sen and the princesses were locked up. Or maybe Muyang would execute Feiyu since he was much more of a threat than Yat-sen and the princesses.

Or maybe ...

Daiyu kept going in circles. She tried wrapping her mind around Feiyu and Muyang and the rest of the royal family, but she couldn't figure out what any of it meant.

Tears of frustration pricked the corners of her eyes and she blinked them away. She stared down at her hands. None of this was making any sense to her. She didn't know how any of this tied together.

Why was Muyang's soul dying? Why was he a curse to this empire? What did this mean for Feiyu? How were they tied together?

"Take as long as you need," Feiyu rumbled, his black eyes boring into her like he knew she wouldn't be able to answer correctly. "But Muyang will die in a matter of hours, and then his cursed reign will finally be over."

"N-No! He can't—" Her lower lip wobbled and her throat closed up as the realization hit her. Muyang was going to die. He was going to die in a few hours. She didn't have time to waste here, thinking and thinking and unable to come up with an answer. She needed to figure this out, she needed to find Feiyu's real name, and she needed to do it *quickly*.

All the pressure seemed to land on her shoulders, making her tremble and fold in within herself. She curled over her knees and rested her head on her lap.

Think. She needed to *think*.

Muyang took the throne four years ago. During that time, was Feiyu locked away in the dungeons somewhere, or had he escaped at some point? Muyang had killed Emperor Yan in order to take the throne, so did that make Feiyu indebted to Muyang? Was that why he stuck around in the palace and worked under Muyang? Or did Muyang free him from Yan once he took over?

But then, why was Feiyu saying that Muyang's reign was *cursed*? Shouldn't he be happy that Muyang took over, since that meant Yan was killed and his family was mostly wiped out? Or ... did Feiyu want to take the throne? Was that why he thought Muyang's rule was cursed?

She was becoming more confused as the minutes ticked by. How was she going to figure this out? The more she thought about it, the more tangled everything became. The more she couldn't make sense of what was up and what was down.

"Feiyu ... after your brother forced you to take dragon's

blood, what did you do?" Daiyu lifted her head to pin him with a stare.

He didn't move, only continued to stare at her. "I was in excruciating pain for days. Like my brother had mentioned, my blood felt like it was boiling within myself, my organs felt like they were melting, and my flesh was on fire for days. During this time, I must have lost consciousness at some point and Yan assumed I was dead, so he tossed me aside somewhere. I woke up in a shallow dug grave not far from here." His gaze flicked over at the mountains in the distance, their spikes prodding up to the clouded skies. "Once I realized I was free, I left the capital and didn't return for many years."

She chewed on that for a few minutes, trying to make sense of it all. But when she looked over at him to ask more questions, to prod more into his past, a sudden shame took over. His eyes were so black, so unfeeling, and yet there was something terribly sad within them. Here she was, trying to strip down his memories to figure out his name, and she hadn't had the decency to even think about things from his perspective. How terrible must it have been to live in the royal palace? To go through so much abuse and torture?

She was a terrible friend for glossing it over for her own selfish purposes. Of course she wanted to save Muyang, but she hadn't had the decency to even think about how Feiyu felt during this. How traumatic it must have been for him.

"I'm so sorry, Feiyu," she finally said, unable to look at him as guilt and shame bloomed in her chest. "You've lived such a hard life. I'm sorry you had to go through all of that."

"It was a long time ago," he murmured, closing those midnight-like eyes.

"Did you realize immediately that you could turn into a dragon? Is that normal after ingesting dragon blood?"

"I don't know about normal, but I knew I was different than before when I awoke. My blood changed—it became magicked."

"That's ..." *Fascinating*. But she couldn't say that. It would be insensitive and inappropriate, especially since it wasn't his choice to go through that kind of torture and to be forever changed. "Muyang also told me his blood is magicked—"

Everything came to a pause as she uttered those words and something clicked in her mind.

Wait, wait, *wait.*

"Muyang told me ..." Daiyu's eyebrows came together and she looked over at Feiyu with renewed interest. With different eyes.

There was no way.

"Feiyu ..." She curled her hands over her knees. He didn't change in the slightest and she couldn't read his emotions at all. "In the library, I spoke to Muyang about curses and he told me that curses can ... can split your soul and corrupt them. Is Muyang ... Did Muyang curse *himself?*"

Feiyu didn't say anything, only continued to stare at her.

"Oh my—" Her mouth dropped open as she stared at him. All the pieces began aligning together. Everything was becoming clearer. "I ... I know your name."

Four years ago, Muyang took the throne. Four years ago, his magic changed and he couldn't use it much anymore. Four years ago, his personality changed—he became *darker.*

And it made so much sense. So much sense that it was crazy. Convoluted, even.

"You're ... You're MuRong Muyang," she whispered, gasping once the words were out. It didn't sound real. It couldn't be real, but it was the only conclusion she came to. "Muyang ... corrupted his soul by splitting it in half. *You're* the other half."

All at once, Feiyu's eyes widened and something sparked within them. A light shone from his body and he morphed, the shimmering scales appearing brighter as his body uncoiled itself from its sleeping position. The long limbs and dragon wings disappeared, replaced by flesh and blood. The scales sank into his scarred skin, disappearing in a split second as clothes magically appeared over his body. In seconds, he was back in his human form, dressed in his usual silver and green mage robes.

The only difference was that he wore no mask. Muyang's face stared back at her. Wickedly beautiful, with his usual dark eyes, and his soft mouth, he was ... her Muyang. But at the same time, he *wasn't*.

A faint scar ran down his eyebrow to his eyelid and under the eye. He had another set of three scars running vertically on his jaw. And there was something in his gaze that appeared so much sadder than her Muyang.

Her knees weakened and if she weren't already sitting, she would have fallen to the ground in disbelief. He was Muyang, and it made sense, but it didn't at the same time.

"How ... and why would you do this to yourself?" she found herself asking. Her heart was thumping loudly in her chest, the blood rushing to her ears. Why would Muyang split his soul in half?

Feiyu smiled, ever so gently. "When I took the throne four years ago, I thought I would lose my mind. I had discarded my MuRong blood for so long, but I needed to kill my brother and get my revenge. But once I did, and I took his throne, I couldn't bear to be in the palace anymore. I couldn't bear to be in the same halls my mother and I had lived. I couldn't bear the sight of the throne room, where so much of my own torture had taken place."

"So you ... split your soul?"

"Yes." His voice softened, but there was a spark of anger in his eyes that made her want to cringe back. "I split my soul and sealed my memories within *this* body." He tapped himself on the chest. "The other Muyang lost many of his childhood memories, many of the darkest moments of our life that made it unbearable to stay in the palace. Instead, *I* bore them. I also took most of the magic, though that was mostly by accident. We had planned on making our magic equal. I also took most of the scars." He touched his scarred eyelid. "These scars tell stories of torture my brother inflicted, and the other half wouldn't have known where they came from. So it only made sense ..."

Daiyu's head began to spin. "But you knew it would corrupt your soul to split it in half—"

"Yes. We both realized it would mean we would die in a few short years." He looked down at the ground. "The people around us realized Muyang had changed, but they didn't know why. The *Peccata* ... the children I raised, were confused when Muyang didn't know them like he used to, since I took some of those memories. And the others within Muyang's council, some of whom he knew before taking the throne, were also confused about why he acted differently. More unhinged, as is the case when one becomes incomplete. It was an unfortunate side effect, watching the people I care for be confused and hurt when Muyang treated them differently since he didn't remember them like I did."

Daiyu remembered back in the carriage with Nikator when he had sadly explained to her that things had changed once Muyang took the throne. This was what he had meant, but he couldn't have known that this was the reason why.

"I should have never taken the throne. I didn't have good intentions anyway. I only wanted revenge, but once I had my brother's throne, I couldn't leave it to just anyone. I had to rule." His long, inky hair whipped around himself with the wind. "I had to spite all the people who had made my life hell in the palace. I had to kill them all and get my revenge, and I could only do that as the emperor. But I knew it would be short-lived ... this rule of mine. I didn't want anyone to find out who I truly was. That I belonged on the throne. That I was—*am*—a MuRong."

"So you took on a new name."

"Drakkon." Feiyu nodded. "A moniker I received during my time in Sanguis."

Daiyu could only stare at him. She didn't know what to think of any of this, but she knew with certainty that Muyang was a tortured soul who had done what he had to in order to satiate his revenge. But now that he had it, he must have felt so ... empty? Angry? *Confused*?

As if reading her mind, he continued, "Muyang might not have remembered all the people who have wronged him, *us*, but that's why I stayed in the palace. To make sure that we got our revenge properly. But we never planned on staying on the throne for long. Eventually, our souls would die. And now ... that time is near."

"Feiyu—" She stopped herself, unsure if she could even call him that. "You can't ... you can't just—"

"When Muyang took you as a bride, it *angered* me." Something dark broiled in his black eyes, so scorching that Daiyu inched away from him. His scarred, calloused hands curled together and he clenched his jaw tightly. "He committed the same crime our father had done to our mother. He forced you to ... to be *his*, when he had no business doing such a thing. Daiyu, you must know that if we were in our right state of mind, we would have never forced you to become ours. We wouldn't have ..." He squeezed his eyes shut. "I never wanted to become the same monster my father was."

"You're not a monster," Daiyu said, rushing over to him. She took his face in her hands; it felt so natural to touch him like this, to stare into those eyes, like she had done hundreds of times before. "Even the other half of you ... he never forced himself upon me. You have to understand that the relationship between your father and mother is completely different than what I have with Muyang. He would never hurt me like your father hurt your mother, and he would never keep me around if he knew it would hurt me. You would never hurt me. You aren't a monster, Muyang. Not this version of you, and not the other."

He searched her face as if not believing her. "After knowing all of this, you still want to save him? To save *me*?"

"Yes. A million times yes."

"He's a cruel monster, and I am no better."

"You aren't a monster."

"I am. I should have never taken the throne. I should have never involved you in our mess—"

"Muyang." She held his face tighter, wishing he could see what she saw—a sad soul who couldn't find peace, who wanted to find it, and whose other half had searched for it. "I love you, *all* of you. What happened to you was truly terrible and you did what you could to cope with yourself, even if it meant mutilating your own soul. You were in so much pain. You only did what you could think of to help yourself. I can't fault you for doing that."

Behind all that rage, grief and pain shone on his face. He had likely never properly grieved over his mother, or the torture he endured, or everything he had lost whilst being in the royal palace. It must have been so painful, so traumatic, to walk through the same halls that he had been tortured in. To stare at the same walls that had housed his abuse. And to pretend like it didn't bother him at all.

"Muyang, what happens now?" Daiyu asked quietly.

He stood very still, the leaves rustling behind him and the grass swaying against his shins. "Now ... we go to the palace and reunite with the other half of my soul. But, Daiyu, are you sure you want to do this? We won't be the same."

"I want you alive, Muyang. I don't care if—"

"You didn't fall in love with the Muyang I was four years ago." The look in his eyes hardened, like he was expecting her to run. "I am much more of a monster when I have all of my memories."

"You aren't a monster."

"I have so much more anger toward the world."

"Then how are you standing here in front of me without lashing out at me?" she questioned. "Your part of the soul was burdened with the heaviest of your trauma and you can still find ways to smile and laugh and joke with me. You're still able to find kindness in your heart. The other half of you—whom I love very much—doesn't have that. He's much more ..." She struggled to find the words.

"Uncaring?" He smiled softly. "He doesn't remember all the memories of our mother and the lessons she instilled in us. He's much more confused than me."

"He cares ... but it's not the same." She loved Muyang, she really did, but he and Feiyu seemed to be two completely different people. The Muyang she knew was cruel, indifferent, and cold. Feiyu, on the other hand, was playful and kind. She couldn't imagine the two of them being the same person. But she loved Muyang, and she cared for Feiyu as a friend.

"Once we reunite, all of our memories will join together."

"You both are still the same person. Just ... different."

"And what if you don't like the difference?"

The corner of Daiyu's mouth twitched into a grin. "You think I would abandon you just because you're different? It's like you said earlier. I don't know much about Muyang—about you. We have our whole lives in front of us to fall deeper in love and get to know each other."

Once the words were out, she suddenly felt embarrassed to be standing in front of him as she was—unkempt hair, bruised and scraped knees, and covered in sweat and grime. He was her husband, but at the same time, he wasn't. He didn't have memories of their intimacy, of their love, of their stolen kisses. What if this version of Muyang didn't love her? Would that affect the other half?

He tilted his head to the side. "You ... think that I won't love you?"

"E-excuse me?" Could he read her mind?

"Daiyu, I'm—" A flash of pain crossed his face and he clutched the front of his chest, falling down to one knee in one swell movement. He gasped sharply.

Daiyu dropped down in front of him, her hands flying to his shoulders to help him from keeling over. "What's wrong?"

"My body—" He coughed, and blood splattered over her shoulder. His dark eyes flicked over to hers, wide and panicked and pained, but the emotions shuttered in a split second—like he didn't want her to see any of it. "I'm dying, Daiyu. We won't make it on time—"

427

All the blood drained from her face and she tightened her hold on his shoulders. "*No*. I'm not losing you."

"I don't have much—"

"Let's rush to the palace, then!" She tried hauling him up to his feet, but he was too weakened, too fatigued to even stand. She hadn't noticed earlier, since she was preoccupied with everything else, but he was pale—*too pale*. "Come on, Muyang! Pull yourself together!"

"I can't." He wheezed, squeezing his eyes shut. "I'm able to hold myself up only because I have more magic, but the other part of my soul is too weak." His head lolled forward, falling over her shoulder. "We will both die soon—"

"Is there anything I can do?" She took his face in her hands and tried to make him stare at her, but his eyes were already rolling behind his head. "Muyang!"

"There's ... nothing—"

"There has to be something! You're a high mage! Take my magic, take my energy, take something—*everything*! Just don't die!" Tears misted over her eyes, blurring her vision. She quickly blinked them away. She couldn't lose him, not when she was so close to saving him. "Muyang, *please*. You have to hang in there."

"Daiyu ..." He exhaled, blinking up at her. "You're too sweet for me. I could never burden you more than I already have."

"*Muyang!*" She slipped her hand into his and nearly crushed it. "Please, take my magic. Take what you need. *Please*."

"Daiyu—"

"Do it, *now*." Her voice hardened with panic, with the thought of losing him forever. She didn't want to go back and forth and argue with him about what he needed to do in order to save his life. Yat-sen had told her that everyone had magic within themselves, so it only made sense that she did too. Magic was essentially energy, wasn't it? So maybe he could take what he needed and buy them some time?

Something in her expression probably told him she wasn't

playing any games with his life because he nodded slowly and hesitantly tightened their hands together. "Just ... a little."

Almost immediately, she could feel her energy drain. She gasped, the pulling sensation feeling as though someone was leeching her blood from her body. All at once, a deep fatigue rattled her bones and chilled her flesh. She gritted her teeth together to keep them from chattering.

"Muyang, we need to make it back to the palace," she said, her words slurring together. "You need to save yourself. Let's teleport—"

"Can't. It requires too much energy—too much magic."

"Then—

"Hold on to me."

Before she could ask what he meant, his body began to shift. She barely suppressed a yelp of surprise when scales formed over his skin and his body lurched forward, transforming in mere seconds into a large, serpentine body. She held on to his neck tightly, watching with awe as his dragon body grew into its impressive size and height. His wings flared out behind him, the scales glimmering silvery white in the sunlight.

In seconds, he launched up into the air. This time, Daiyu screamed, hugging his neck tightly and pressing her thighs against the sides of his body. She dug her heels as hard as she could, but his scales were so hard and smooth that she could barely get a good grip on him. She couldn't even wrap her arms completely around him, and the spikes along his back and neck made it even harder to hold on without hurting herself.

"Muyang—" she shouted, but the wind rushed over her face, ripping through her hair and clothes and face with such speed that her words could barely keep up.

They zoomed through the sky and Daiyu's stomach plummeted at the sights below her—at the mountains that shrank, at the swells of the forest that seemed so tiny up here, and at the vastness of the empire along the horizon. It was a beautiful sight to behold, and yet the grand height terrified her. If she fell—

She shuddered, hugging the dragon tighter.

Feiyu—*Muyang*—would never allow that to happen.

They flew faster and higher, Muyang's powerful wings slicing the air. Daiyu held on, her mouth nearly dropping open as she looked down. They were passing over the capital now, on the outskirts. People on their farms and their open lands stared up at them in awe, pointing at the magnificent sight. Then they began to pass over the rest of the capital, the city just barely waking up. She could hear the screams of surprise even beyond the barrier of blustering winds. She watched as people poked their heads out from windows and looked up.

Muyang roared, loud and piercing as if to announce his arrival. A grin stretched up Daiyu's lips despite the direness of the situation. It was exhilarating being so high up, soaring up and up and watching the people down below. Watching the world wake up.

In mere minutes, the royal palace came into view. The sun gleamed against the polished, emerald-glazed roof tiles, the vermillion-lacquered balustrades, the raised pavilions, and the sprawling walled compound; the palace was even grander from above, appearing like a giant, beautified fortress.

They grew closer to it, but Feiyu didn't slow down. Closer, and closer, and *closer*.

"M-Muyang!" Daiyu held on tighter.

They were going to crash—

Right when she thought they would dive through one of the walls, he bucked his powerful wings and slid across the shingled roof. She screamed, holding on with all her might. Feiyu flapped his wings, threw his head back, and roared even louder. The whole world seemed to be watching them right now.

She could see the courtyard, the gardens, the city square—all of it full of people staring up at them with gaping, slack jaws. Daiyu's legs quivered, her gaze flicking from the royal palace to the rest of the capital.

He roared again, louder this time. Enough to shake the walls and the city. It took her a second to realize where they were—the rooftop where the lantern lighting ceremony had taken place. It was like he wanted the whole capital to view them.

"W-What are you doing?" she shouted at him.

Seconds ticked by and palace guards swarmed the rooftop venue. They trembled whilst holding their spears, like they weren't sure what to do. There was no way they could beat Feiyu, they seemed to realize that immediately.

"Don't attack!" Daiyu yelled.

"Y-your Majesty?" one of the guards said, bewildered. "G-Get down from there!"

"He won't attack you!" She scanned the crowds of soldiers for a familiar face, but she couldn't see anything beyond the gleaming steel helmets and spears. "Bring His Majesty here, now!"

Nobody moved. They just stared at Feiyu with bug eyes.

"Bring—" Her words cut off when she spotted Commander Yao Bohai pushing through the sea of soldiers, his face colored in surprise. Behind him, she spotted Muyang. Even from here, she could see that he was on death's doors. He could barely stand, his skin pallid and ghostly, and his cheeks gaunt. Her heart sank. It had only been a day and yet he had deteriorated so much.

"What are you doing?" Muyang stopped a dozen feet away from Feiyu, his shadowed, dark-circled eyes narrowing at the sight. The guards parted for him and even though he was so sickly, even though he probably wanted to keel over and pass out, he stood tall and proud and so like the man she had fallen in love with. He appeared fearless, even at the sight of the dragon.

"Muyang—" Daiyu's eyes filled with unshed tears. He was still alive, at least.

"Daiyu, get away from him." Muyang stared at Feiyu with such a look of disdain that she flinched back. His words whipped out of him like angry torrents. "Feiyu, what are you doing here? I thought you would never come back—"

"Neither of you is dying today." She wiped her eyes and

steeled her resolve. She peered down at him, watching the surprise on his face. "I told you I'd be back with Feiyu."

"Daiyu—" he began.

She could tell that he didn't want her there. That he would rather be in bed, dying alone. That he wished she had gone somewhere far away and lived a life without him. Well, she wasn't going to let him have that peace. He was stuck with her now, she thought with a faint grin.

"If you thought you could die peacefully, away from all your troubles, then you're wrong. You're going to have to continue being the emperor, Muyang. You shouldn't have chosen me as your bride if you thought I wouldn't try to save you."

He blinked over at her. "What are you saying?"

"You don't remember who you are, do you? Your *real* name?"

"*Daiyu.*" There was a warning in his tone that told her she was crossing into boundaries she had no business being in, but behind that veil of anger was *terror*. He didn't want to know who Feiyu truly was—what kind of past they both shared.

"Your real name *isn't* Drakkon Muyang," she said, her voice growing louder. "But you knew that, didn't you? You knew you discarded a part of your soul so that you could keep your sanity. You never wanted to find out what really happened to you—"

"Daiyu!" His eyes were wide now, so black and void-like. "I can't find out—"

"I'm not losing you! Not to yourself." She pleaded with him with her gaze alone, wishing he could just accept who he was. But she didn't want to tell him right away, she didn't want to force it onto him. "You have to save yourself, Muyang. *Please!*"

Feiyu shifted on his feet, lowering his head to better stare at Muyang. As if that was enough to make him realize who he was.

"What have you done?" Muyang whispered, backing away. "You convinced him to come back?"

"I can't let you kill yourself like this." She breathed out deeply. "You'll have to continue your reign. I know you're scared—"

"I'm *not* scared," he snarled, even though he couldn't rip his gaze away from Feiyu.

"You're lost and scared and confused!" Daiyu exhaled. The other guards exchanged glances, all of them appearing baffled. Nobody spoke to the emperor this way. Not even a woman riding a fearsome dragon. She knew that, but she didn't care what anyone thought at that moment. All she cared about was saving him. Saving the man she loved.

"Muyang, you have to accept this part of you," she said, quieter this time. "Please. Let's build a life together. Let's be happy. Let's have dozens of children. Let's *live*—together. *Please.*"

He hesitated and she could see the emotions warring on his face. The desire to give in, but the stubbornness not to find out who he was. What his past was about. She could see the resignation on his face. The fear.

"I love you, Muyang." The words came out before she could help herself. And it was so true, so true she wanted to shout it to the world. To let everyone know that she was deeply and madly in love with Drakkon Muyang.

His eyes widened.

She held her hand out to him. "Muyang, I want to be with you. Forever and ever, and I won't let your stubborn pride hold you back. You can't die here. Not when you have so much to do."

He stared at her hand and then back at her face—searching, *thinking.*

He was so beautiful, with the early morning sun shining down on him. With the vulnerability across his face.

He stumbled forward, his hand stretching out to meet hers.

"I love you, MuRong Muyang," she whispered just as their fingers touched.

A spark came to life and Muyang's eyes grew even wider. All at once, light shone from Feiyu and darkness whirled around Muyang. Daiyu bit back a scream as she was thrown forward, off Feiyu's back.

She crashed onto the floor, rolling as she went, the shock

rattling her bones. Shadows and lights writhed from both Feiyu and Muyang, warping together like a storm. The sky cracked with magic and darkened in seconds, the air growing thicker and volatile. Daiyu scooted backward, the winds howling all around. The two bodies began to fuse together—one part dragon and the other part human.

"W-What's happening?" Bohai shouted, coming to kneel beside her. He stared at the magic lashing out from Muyang.

"His souls are combining!" Daiyu said.

Understanding seemed to dawn on Bohai's face.

In seconds, the blustering magic stopped altogether, but shadows continued to form around Muyang's feet, swirling around him like banners of night. He slowly raised his head and turned to the crowd of terrified soldiers, his eyes appearing blacker than before. Finally, his gaze landed on Daiyu.

He didn't look weak and sick anymore. In fact, he looked more powerful than ever. The shadows continued to whip at the ground, at the sky, and over his body protectively. She had never seen such a cold expression on his face. Such madness and anger and fury that played over his black, black eyes.

She clambered up to her feet shakily. Her vision tunneled so that everything else disappeared until it was just him and her. Her mouth tasted ashy and dry.

Their gazes locked on one another.

She held her breath.

Now that his fractured soul was together again, did that mean ... he didn't love her anymore? Did he hold resentment toward her for bringing him together? Would he hate her now?

He must have read her mind, he must have seen the fear on her face because his gaze softened, the shadows waning and a faint smile curling at the corner of his soft mouth. "Daiyu, I could never hate you."

It was all she needed to run to him. She didn't care about anything else anymore. She launched herself into his arms. He stumbled backward, embracing her even as she smacked his chest with her hand. Even as the tears rolled down her face and she hugged him tighter and tighter.

"Y-You!" she cried, burying her face in his chest. "You frightened me so bad! I thought I would *lose* you!"

"Forgive me," he whispered, tucking his chin over her head.

"I thought you would *die!*" She wept against his chest, not caring that she likely appeared hideous—with her dusty and torn clothes, her windswept hair stuck with twigs and leaves, and grime and dirt clinging to her like a cloak. Even then, when she peeled back just enough to stare up at him, he was looking down at her like he had never seen someone so ... beautiful.

He pushed a strand of her hair out of her face. "Did you realize that I loved you in both souls?"

She sniffled, blinking away the tears that adhered to her lashes. "You did?"

"Yes, though it shouldn't come as a surprise. I will always love you, my dear, dear sweet *fiend.*" Muyang brushed his thumb over her eyes, swiping at the tears that rolled down her damp cheeks. "I would choose you again and again. Only if you'll have me."

She laughed. Now that the panic and fear of losing him were gone, she was incredibly exhausted. The rush of adrenaline was finally seeping away from her. But even amongst the sea of guards who were staring at them, she didn't care one bit that she didn't look like a proper empress.

"And I will always choose you, *little dragon.*"

A furrow formed between his brows and she chuckled, weaving her hand onto the back of his head. She rose up on her toes and pressed a gentle kiss against his lips. Her eyes fluttered shut. He pulled her closer to his body, his hands warm against her cold flesh. She breathed in the familiar scent of jasmine and spices.

When she pulled back, her throat closed up and more tears blurred her vision. "Promise me you'll never do anything like that again. Promise me you'll always live your life, and you'll never break your soul like that again. Promise me you'll never leave me, Muyang."

"I promise." He cupped her cheek with his calloused hand. The scars on his face were a new addition, but he was just as beautiful as he was before. "It's painful to remember everything. To know ... everything." Darkness washed over his face, and the shadows of his magic continued to writhe around them, growing stronger. "I have so much anger and hatred in my heart, and so much ... *rage*. But"—he stared at her and something softened within him—"I will remain strong. For you."

"Not just for me." She placed a hand over his heart. "For yourself, Muyang. You must find peace. Whether I'm here or not, you *will* find peace."

He stared at her again, and right when she thought he wouldn't agree, he nodded.

Daiyu fell back in his arms and it was only then that she could finally breathe easy.

43

Daiyu pulled back to tell him how much she loved him, but his body grew slack against her and she toppled to the floor in the next second. She blinked up at the sky, Muyang's heavy body pinning her in place. Gasps and startled cries filled the air as the guards rushed forward.

"M-Muyang?" She turned her face to find his head lolled against her shoulder, his eyes shut and his skin pallid. It must have been too much of a shock for his body, she thought, or maybe ... maybe she didn't make it in time? What if his souls rejected each other? What if—

A blind panic overtook her senses, and she inhaled sharply. She couldn't lose him. Not after everything they had been through. Not after being *so close* to saving him.

"Assist His Majesty!" Bohai shouted, dropping down on his knees in front of them.

The guards lifted him up and Daiyu was finally able to push herself into a sitting position. She couldn't tear her eyes away from Muyang's lifeless body. Tears filled her eyes. He couldn't be, could he?

"Muyang?" she called again. "No—"

"He'll be fine." Bohai held his hand out to her, his light-brown eyes softening. "You saved him, lady Daiyu."

"But how do you know?" She struggled up to her feet and reached out to Muyang, but her legs were leaden and everything began spinning. She stumbled forward and Bohai grasped her forearm lightly to steady her.

"You look exhausted. How about you rest?"

"Where are they taking him?" Daiyu didn't want to part from Muyang, not with all the uncertainties she felt at that moment. And definitely not after going through so much to see him. She didn't care that every bone and fiber in her body was resisting, that she also wanted to collapse to the floor and pass out from fatigue.

"To his bedchambers." Bohai nodded to the men and they continued carrying him away. He followed them and waved her forward. "Come now, you should stay with him too. We have a lot to talk about."

Daiyu trailed after them, too tired to complain or think too hard about anything. It wasn't until they took Muyang to his bed, laid him down, and she noticed his chest rising and falling, that she allowed herself to fall on the velvet couch and sag against the embroidered cushions. All the energy seemed to leave her in that instant, and she closed her heavy eyes. She hadn't realized how fatigued she had become from traveling up the mountain, traversing the rocky terrain, finding Feiyu and looking through his memories all night, and finally flying to the palace—until *this* moment. When everything was seemingly okay.

"So what happened?" Bohai eased himself onto the couch across from hers. He glanced over at Muyang's slumbering body and then back at her. "You said that his souls combined?"

"Yes." She explained everything to him, from Feiyu helping her at the palace, to how she knew where to find him, and every-thing in between. By the time she finished the story, Bohai was staring at her like he had never seen her before. Like he couldn't believe his ears.

He reclined in his seat, his eyebrows furrowed together. "I always had my suspicions that something was off about Muyang ever since he took the throne, but I never ... I never thought *that* was what happened. Feiyu and Muyang were the same person this whole time?"

"Yes," she murmured. "I'm sure it's quite shocking to you since you knew him—well, both of them—for so much longer than I did."

Now that Feiyu and Muyang's souls were stitched together again, didn't that mean everything she had told Feiyu—her gripes about Muyang, her desire to flee from him, and so much more— were also privy to Muyang now since they were the same person? Her cheeks warmed at the thought of that and she fiddled with one of the many tears in her dirtied skirts.

"I always found it strange that Feiyu showed up when he did, and that he seemed to know so much about everything. Muyang has never been a trusting person, so when he brought in a masked mage who he seemed to trust so easily, I found it ... troubling, to say the least." A pensive expression crossed Bohai's face for a moment and his voice lowered. "But Feiyu had a way about him that made everyone comfortable around him. Like we always *knew* him, and I suppose we did."

They were both quiet for a moment. Daiyu watched Muyang's sleeping form with a pang in her chest. How painful must it have been for Feiyu to be around the people he loved and be unable to say anything about who he was? And how confusing for Muyang must it have been to have gaps in his memories for the people he was supposed to love? She couldn't imagine going through the stress of being the emperor for four years without a solid support system. Without his memories intact. He probably felt like he was going crazy at some moments. At least that's how she would have felt.

A knock on the door interrupted their silence and Vita poked her head through the doorway the next second. Upon seeing

Daiyu, a look of relief passed over her face and she stepped inside tentatively.

"I heard His Majesty collapsed? Is everything well?"

"He's fine, for now. Just exhausted." Bohai waved her inside and soon, the entire room filled with the rest of the members of the *Peccata*, who seemed to have been waiting in the hallway the whole time. After Bohai retold everything Daiyu had just told him, they all crowded his bed and stared down at him like they were seeing him in a new light—and they sort of were.

They all began chattering at once.

"So Feiyu was Muyang this whole time?" Atreus asked, eyebrows raised.

Nikator frowned. "The *whole* time?"

"And he never told you?" Thera asked Bohai.

"Why would he tell him and not us?" one of them asked at the same time another said, "He should have told us."

Bohai raised his hands to quiet the group. "Alright, alright. I get that you're all confused and we can share all our thoughts with him later, but right now, Muyang needs his rest. And, by the looks of it, lady Daiyu needs to rest too. So how about we all take this elsewhere for now? Leave the couple alone."

Daiyu was more than appreciative when everyone filed out of the room and left them alone. When it was just her and Muyang, she sat on the edge of the bed and rested her hand against his. His fingers were cool to the touch and she brought her lips to his palm. Tears welled up in her eyes, stinging them as she blinked rapidly. She had so much to talk to him about, so much she needed to clarify with him, so much she wanted to discuss. And she was bone-weary. She finally felt every single cut and bruise littering her worn body. Every scrape she got when trying to save him. And she wanted nothing more than to curl up by his side and remain that way. To feel him close, to know that he was going to be fine.

Because what if he *wouldn't* be fine? What if his souls would war each other? What if the souls were incompatible after being separated all these years? What if he didn't love her as much anymore? What if—

Before her mind could be swamped with the worst-case-scenarios, Daiyu coiled up on the bed beside him, her face inches away from Muyang's. She placed a gentle hand against his cheek and breathed in the scent of him—of jasmine, of orange blossom, of spices and outdoors. Her eyelids grew heavier, her exhaustion winning over.

DAIYU AWOKE TO THE FEELING OF SOMEONE BRUSHING her hair gently. So gently that it almost felt like a soft, summer wind tousling her hair. She didn't even know what she had been dreaming of, but she was sure it was something to do with summer—with laying in a bed of flowers and breathing in the scent of jasmine.

She slowly opened her eyes to find the blackest of nights staring back at her. It took her a second to realize she was staring into Muyang's gaze, and she gasped sharply, her body jerking upright.

"Muyang!" She hadn't even realized she was tucked into his impressively tall frame until that moment. Her face warmed with sudden embarrassment—she shouldn't have felt so awkward around him, but knowing that he differed from before, that he had both Muyang and Feiyu inside him, made everything with him feel strangely new.

The corner of Muyang's mouth curved and all thoughts of him being different fled in that moment. He looked just like her Muyang. The same villainous smirk, the same dark, brooding eyes, and the same mischievousness that told her he was other-worldly wicked.

"You were drooling all over my arm," he said with a hint of teasing in his voice.

Daiyu could feel the heat creeping up her neck and ears. "No, I wasn't."

"You were."

"W-Well—" She cleared her throat and smoothed down her hair with shaking hands, only to discover she *still* had twigs stuck in her hair. More embarrassment filled her as she plucked out the bramble, twigs, and thorns that had gotten stuck there at some point. "Why didn't you tell me I looked like such a mess?" she grumbled.

"You don't look messy at all. Only ..." His gaze skated over her face, her head, and the rest of her body. She relaxed at the softness in his sharp, midnight-like eyes. "Adorable."

"*Adorable*?" She laughed, covering her mouth. "That doesn't sound like a word that belongs in your vocabulary."

"It's a testament of your bravery and determination to save me, from me, and to find me." He reached forward and tugged out a thin, wiry twig from her hair. He twisted it between his fingers, staring at her the whole time. "What different way can I describe it other than absolutely adorable?"

"For starters, Muyang, *adorable* doesn't suit you at all. Not even coming out of your mouth." Daiyu relaxed against the backboard of the bed and peered down at him with lowered lashes. It was easy to fall into a rhythm of banter with him, and she almost felt naïve for thinking that things would be different.

The corner of Muyang's lips rose to a smile that sent shivers down her spine. "You only want filthy things coming out of my mouth, then?"

"I—I never said *that*."

"Oh, you didn't have to." He propped himself up on one elbow, reached for the back of her neck, and pulled her into a kiss. She didn't have time to prepare for it, not with their bodies flush against one another, and certainly not with his soft mouth pressing against hers. Her eyes fluttered shut, the familiar warmth pooling in the pit of her stomach and warming her chest. She moved her lips against his, gasping slightly as his tongue flicked into her mouth gently. She splayed her hands against his chest.

Their closeness—their sweet kiss—bridged a gap that had broken within her from anxiety from the idea of never having him again, of never seeing him again, and never touching him again. When he pulled away, she breathed in deeply, her gaze fervent and a deep desire blooming within her. She wanted every piece of him. Forever, and ever.

Muyang dragged a finger over her jaw. "You are the most beautiful woman I have ever laid my eyes on, Yin Daiyu. You've captured my whole heart from the moment I saw you. I'm fortunate to have met you for the first time on two separate occasions. The first when you tried sneaking into the palace and pretended to play coy and secondly when you burst into my bathing chambers and, once again, pretended to play the part of a blushing maiden."

"I am a blushing maiden."

"You *were* a blushing maiden."

"Nonetheless, I wasn't acting."

"Oh, but you *were*." Muyang brushed his thumb over her lips slowly, his gaze flicking between her mouth and her eyes. "Because I know you are fiercer than any woman I have met, and you are so much more than a timid creature who will let me have my way."

She inched closer to him and kissed him again, this time deeper and longer than the last. Her heart felt so full in that moment—being so near him, being able to kiss him like this, and being so deeply in love.

It wasn't until hours later, where they both were laid on the bed, the blanket covering their bare bodies and the night air breezing through the open windows that Daiyu traced the dragon tattoo on his forearm, and then serpent and moon tattoo mirroring his other forearm. She could practically feel the magic thrumming beneath his flesh from both marks. Now combined, he seemed more powerful than before.

"Is it strange to see me like this?" Daiyu murmured, peering into his face. "Feiyu never saw me naked."

Muyang blinked back in surprise and then chuckled, clearly not expecting such a response. "I don't think *strange* is the word I would think of." He crossed his arms behind his head and stared up at the ceiling. A furrow formed between his brows. "I'm back to how I used to be, I suppose. No more confusion, no more wondering why I can't remember many things. It is a bit ... *strange*, I suppose, to have memories that occurred concurrently from one body to the other, but it also feels so much more natural to be in this form."

"Have you thought about what you will do now that you have your souls combined again?"

"I will continue to reign." He turned his attention back to her. "I know I said that I am a curse upon these lands and that it's better for me to die than to rule, but now that I'm back, with both my memories intact, I see no reason to wither away and give my throne to another. It's true that I don't deserve this empire, and that maybe it would be better for someone else to rule, but I am selfish, Daiyu. I will continue to reign until our children are able to take over where I left. And maybe then, because our children will have your kindness and resilience, we will finally have an emperor worthy of this cursed throne. But for now, I will rule and I will protect those important to me—notably *you*—and I will carve a path for the both of us in this twisted, dark dynasty."

Daiyu nodded. Truthfully, she had expected as much. She didn't think Muyang was the type of person who would give up his throne, his empire, or his reign—not while he was sound in mind. But she hadn't realized he was thinking of a future for the both of them and their future children. Her chest tightened at the thought of that, and she knew in that moment that she too needed to have strength and cunning in order to survive in this vicious court. Not just for herself, but for her children and their futures.

Because Drakkon Muyang—*MuRong Muyang*—had many, *many* enemies.

"We'll be fine," she murmured, snuggling back into his arms. He embraced her loosely, and she tucked her chin against his collarbone and pressed a kiss on his jaw. "Whatever happens in the future, know that I will always love you, Muyang, and I will always be on your side. Through thick and thin, through war and peace, through happiness and grief—I will stand by you."

"Are you declaring your love or your loyalty to me?" There was a teasing quality in his voice that made her roll her eyes.

"Both."

He kissed the top of her head. For the rest of the night, she rested in his lean arms. The two dynasty tattoos etched into his flesh were a reminder of who he was and what he was capable of, but she never felt so safe as she did in that moment.

44

A WEEK PASSED AFTER MUYANG'S SOULS JOINED together, and all of Daiyu's fears—that he wouldn't love her as much, that he would be more maddened, more unhinged—didn't come to light. In fact, he was more affectionate than he was before —stealing kisses between meetings and catching her in the middle of the hallway—but there was an undeniable darkness about him that was stronger than it used to be. There were moments when she would catch him staring off in the distance, his magic thickening the air in what must have been fury, before he calmed himself.

Daiyu smoothed down her brilliant vermillion-and-gold-embroidered dress. Her hands trembled and she exhaled deeply. Her head felt heavy with the various ornaments intertwined and dangling between her hair. She was even more dolled up than she had been during her wedding, which was saying something.

Muyang slipped his warm hand into hers and gave it a squeeze. He was clad in darker robes than she was, creating a stark contrast between the two of them. It was probably on purpose that he had chosen dark maroon and emerald silks, choosing to let her shine today.

"You appear nervous," he murmured, his voice chilling and velvety.

They were both outside the grand balcony overlooking the capital square and she could hear the bustle and buzz from behind the heavy doors. Today was the day she was crowned as the empress and even though she should have been excited—should have been ecstatic—she couldn't help the nausea, the fear, and the panic from overwhelming her.

She was going to be crowned the empress of the *entire* empire.

That was a heavy responsibility and she was still grappling with the idea that she was married to the most powerful man in the empire, and now she had to accept that she was going to rule by his side for as long as they both breathed? It was daunting. She had never, ever thought that she would rule the empire. *Ever.*

She was just a simple farm girl—

Who just so happened to marry the fearsome, wicked emperor. Who just so happened to steal his heart. Who also just so happened to save his soul.

"Everyone already knows you as the striking empress who tamed and rode a dragon throughout the capital. That hasn't happened in decades, Daiyu," he said, grazing his knuckles over her jaw. "Not since the Dragon Empress. You're more than capable of taking that position."

"I'm not—" She exhaled, not quite sure how to feel about that. "Since you're actually a MuRong, doesn't that mean the Dragon Empress was your ... grandmother?"

"She was, but I never met her." He dragged another finger along her throat, this time stopping at her chin and pulling her face up to stare at him. "Daiyu, today is about *you*. Don't compare yourself to any other empress throughout history. You are just as worthy to have the same title. You will grow to become your own kind of empress—someone powerful, and beautiful, and kind."

"How can you believe in me so much?" she whispered, searching his face. Her heart felt like it was beating a million beats a second, fluttering like a mad dragon in flight. "You don't know if I'll be any good—"

"I know it in my heart. I believe in you."

She released another shuddered breath and turned toward the doors. Just behind those doors, the people were waiting for her to be crowned as the empress. All she had to do was muster up the courage to enter the balcony, to smile at the seas of people—*her* people.

Among the crowds, she knew her family was there, waiting with bated breath. The *Peccata*, the soldiers, all of Muyang's men —they would all be present. All she had to do was go through the doors, but something held her back. Her nerves, most likely. But something else—something that told her maybe this wasn't a good idea. That maybe it was better, easier, to go back to her room and forget about the whole ordeal.

But she didn't want to run. Not anymore. Never again.

Daiyu breathed out deeply, squeezing Muyang's hands again. "Tell me this gets easier with time," she whispered, gaze darting from the door and then back at him.

"I have no advice for you. I quite enjoy the sight of people bowing down to me," he said with a hint of playfulness. "It's an exhilarating, powerful feeling to know that you are ... in charge." He lifted his shoulders and flashed a wicked grin at her. "You will grow accustomed to it. Trust me."

She nodded.

"Whenever you're ready."

She breathed in and out again. Tremors ran down her body and even though she wanted to turn around and flee, she gave him a small nod toward the door. She was ready.

Muyang wasted no time blasting the heavy doors open with a wave of his shadows. The cheers and chatter were deafening as they stepped through the threshold. Light nearly blinded her before her vision righted itself to the seas of faces—thousands of them—all staring at the two of them. Daiyu tightened her hold on the crook of Muyang's arm. They swept toward the railing of the balcony, the noise so loud she could feel it vibrating through her chest.

She had never seen so many people gathered in one place. The air felt heavy, the shouts and hurrahs growing louder. Daiyu could only watch, stunned, as the people waved to her, pushing one another to get a better look. Old faces, young faces, scarred faces, tanned faces—people from all walks of the empire were there.

Daiyu swallowed down the nervousness clawing up her throat.

Muyang looked down at her, his dark eyes capturing hers. "Don't be nervous. I'm here."

"I know."

"Are you ready?"

"I am."

He raised his hand and a hush fell over the throngs of people. "My people, I present to you my lovely wife and empress, Yin Daiyu." Magic swirled at his fingertips and in seconds, a gold, dragon-shaped hairpin materialized in his hand. He slipped it into Daiyu's hair and the people began to cheer once more.

A rush of excitement coursed through her veins as she stood tall, staring at the faces of the people. She spotted her family in the front row; Mother and Father were crying, her brothers were pushing each other to see her better, and Lanfen and Grandmother watched on with wide grins on their faces. Her heart swelled with warmth. At the pride gleaming on her family's faces. At the sudden thrill she felt as everyone applauded her.

She wanted to laugh, she wanted to cry, she wanted to beam at the world.

She turned to Muyang, her mouth curled into a wide smile. She was with the man she loved more than anything, and that counted for more than this new position as the empress. She knew that as a fact.

"Muyang—" she began, but something shoved into her just as the words escaped her mouth. She fell forward, her hips smacking into the railing, and her body tipping over. She barely could hold back her scream.

The last thing she saw before she fell was Muyang's shocked expression—

And then she was falling. Spiraling and flailing, her arms waving from side to side, the scenery blurring all around her. People screamed, gasped, and shouted—but she couldn't decipher it all. It happened so fast, like a flash. One second, she was next to Muyang, and the next, she was plummeting.

Right when she was about to crash to the ground, shadows warped around her body. They engulfed her tightly, the magic wintry to the touch, and when she blinked, she was back on the balcony. She gasped, sitting upright and looking around herself.

Muyang dropped down to his knees in front of her, eyes glossing over her body quickly. "Are you hurt?"

"I—no. No, I'm ... not." Her words came out breathlessly and she looked to her right and then her left. She had fallen, but Muyang seemed to have caught her just in time and whisked her back here. Her stomach twisted, her body trembling with the sudden change.

After scanning her over once more, Muyang rose to his feet and stared into the crowd. He raised his hand and shadows erupted from his fingertips. He flicked his wrist and a man flew up in the air, his body coiled tightly with Muyang's magicked black whips. The man struggled, the hood of his emerald robes falling to reveal an unfamiliar face.

"*You.*" Muyang snarled the words like he was still in his dragon form. The shadowy ropes around the man tightened, squeezing him until he grew redder and redder. "You dared try to assassinate my wife? In *front* of me?"

Daiyu pushed herself to her feet, her hands and feet shaking. "Who do you work for?"

The mage gritted his teeth together but said nothing.

"*Who?*"

Daiyu breathed out deeply. Now that the shock was wearing

off, she could see things more clearly. Like the startled, worried, and excited faces in the crowd, or smell the fear thickening in the air. Everyone likely thought this would either become a gruesome spectacle, or something entertaining for them to see.

She refused to have her big day marred by such an event. And besides, she already had an idea of who was behind all of this. She scanned the crowds, and sure enough, in the front row all the way to the left, Wang Yanlin stood, a hand fan pinched between her delicate fingers. When their eyes met, a grin twisted her cruel mouth.

What a fool, Daiyu thought.

She was still pining after Muyang.

Still trying to take Daiyu's position from her.

Little did she know that Daiyu wasn't going to run away again.

But she wasn't going to give the Wang family the satisfaction of ruffling her feathers, of ruining her crowning day. Wang Yanlin was only the first of many, many other women who would try to steal Muyang from her, who thought they could steal her title as empress.

"Muyang." Daiyu touched his lean arm and inched closer to him so only he could hear. "It's her. You and I both know it."

Muyang searched the crowd and Daiyu watched as the color drained from Yanlin's face when his gaze fell on her. Something about Muyang darkened, but Daiyu leaned in closer again, her words whispering over to him.

"We'll deal with her later. I won't give her the satisfaction of ruining my day."

"Are you sure? We can make an example of her," he murmured. "Like you wanted."

"I don't want people to think of me as a cruel, wicked empress." She winked at him. "Let them think of me as the sunshine to your night. We'll deal with her after this, when no one else is watching, and you will punish her for what she did."

Muyang watched her for a moment, and she wasn't sure if

pride glimmered in his eyes or if there was a hint of fear—but she giggled nonetheless.

"You laugh in the face of death?" he murmured. "You were almost *assassinated*."

"But I wasn't." She nodded toward the man still suspended in the air. "Deal with him later. Warp him to the dungeons or somewhere he can't escape from. I wish to finish this ceremony with a smile."

With a flick of his fingers, Muyang's shadows engulfed the screaming man and he vanished without a trace. People gasped, likely never seeing magic before. Daiyu had been like that once, she lamented, smiling at the awed expressions on everyone's faces. These were her people, and they were more similar to her than the nobles who watched on with wicked, bloodthirsty grins—they loved this kind of distraction, watching others be ripped apart for entertainment's sake.

"We will deal with Yanlin later," he agreed.

"Yes," she murmured, watching the suddenly flustered noble-woman in the crowd. But she didn't want to put her focus on the bitter woman. She didn't want to mar this day with thoughts of revenge or pettiness. She wanted to begin her reign more favorably. More ... like herself.

So she instead focused on the people all around them. On the commoners, the farmers, the people who were just like her. The people who she would now rule over. Many of them would probably come to love her, many would probably loathe her and want everything stripped from her. But she wasn't going to rule alone; she had a powerful man by her side. One who would never let anyone hurt her.

"Everyone," Muyang called out, waving another hand toward Daiyu. "Bow down to your empress."

Scores of people fell down to their knees. Daiyu slipped her hand in Muyang's. Her gaze went from the seas of people dropping down in waves, to her husband. To his beautiful, scarred face. To the darkness in his midnight-like eyes. To the great power pulsating beneath his flesh.

"I don't know if I can get used to this," she murmured.

"The people bowing down? You'll be fine."

"No, I mean *this*." She held their clasped hands together, a grin curving up her lips. "To being married to *you*."

He chuckled. "You chose this when you saved my soul."

"I did."

"Are you starting to have regrets?"

She placed her hand on his chest and pushed herself to her tiptoes. He leaned down, making it easier for her to brush her lips against his. She didn't care that this was highly inappropriate. Or that people were watching. Or that this should have been a private moment between them.

After everything they had gone through, she deserved this small victory. And it was another thing that would get people talking about something other than the assassination attempt— the fact that she was claiming him as hers.

"*Never*," she whispered. "If I had to do it all over again, I would do it for you, my love."

He kissed her back, and they both turned to watch their people. She squeezed his hand tightly.

She would be the sun to his moon, the morning to his night, the empress to his empire.

There would probably be many people who would try to tear their world apart, take Muyang's throne, and destroy their happiness. As long as the rebel cause was alive and well, they would be targeted. But as long as they had each other, she knew they could weather any storm.

He was the beautiful, wicked, and bloodthirsty emperor, and she was his empress, the light that would hold him together through the darkest parts of the night. And she knew their love would triumph and reign. For she believed in him, but mostly, in herself.

ABOUT THE AUTHOR

Maham Fatemi is an avid reader and writer of fantasy romance, epic fantasy, and dark fantasy. When she isn't weaving tales of brooding anti-heroes and magical worlds, she can be found drinking an unhealthy number of oat-milk lattes, obsessing over her five cats, or curled up in bed with a good book. Maham lives in the Chicagoland area with her husband and two children. For information on new releases and to purchase signed copies of her books, visit her website at mahamfatemi.com